GIGAPOLIS

S. CHRISTOPHER

Gigapolis
by S. Christopher

Copyright © 2009, S. Christopher

First Edition: October 2009

Published by Onyx Neon Press
http://www.onyxneon.com/

Editor: Shane Warden
Interior and cover design: S. Christopher & Shane Warden
Logo design: Devin Muldoon
Editorial assistance: Nathan Gray, Gabriela Sanchez, Miranda Opell,
Esther Chung.

This book was typeset on Ubuntu using Perl,
Pod::PsuedoPod::LaTeX, and LaTeX. Many thanks to the free
software developers who make these and other projects possible.

ISBN-13: 978-0-9779201-3-6
ISBN-10: 0-9779201-3-5

Then

Eratosthenes ran.

Across blasted plains, where desert hues painted by weak suns faded from oranges and reds to a palette of grays and dirty whites, he ran. He ran from crushing teeth and flashing eyes. From huddled shadows that lash out to rend and tear, he ran.

His beard grew long. His hair tangled. Sweat puddled beneath his arms and dribbled down his back, drying his clothing into stiff wrinkles. Blisters bubbled and burst on his heels. Still he ran.

Eratosthenes ran beyond the line where day becomes night and night succumbs to day. The desert grew larger with each step. He grew smaller. His breath came in sharp slices. He pushed further. He stumbled. His aching knees and raw hands puckered with blood; blood speckled his brittle and chapped skin.

Wind whipped sand and debris into a cutting frenzy. He squinted through the haze. Behind him a ragged tattoo of footprints cut through the wasteland. Purple mountains squatted at the horizon. There he collapsed.

Some time later, he awoke, drool and sand sticky on his face. The rhythm of his heart disturbed the preternatural quiet. The wind was silent. Something was coming.

Eratosthenes willed himself up to a crouch. He teetered there as his pulse steadied, willing his pinprick of vision to expand outward. He shook off sand and grit and ran his fingers through his hair, wincing as he tangles caught at them. He adjusted his robes, snapping them first one way and then another until they shone clean with an inner light. He blinked away the cataracts that threatened his sight. He rocked himself up to a standing position and stood for a moment, dazed with the effort of regaining himself.

Eratosthenes ran.

Nothing followed him. His motions alone broke the silence of this place. Nothing wheeled overhead. No large gray speckled birds rode quiet thermals far above the lives and demises of lesser creatures.

Memory overwhelmed him and he gasped in its deluge, even as he forced himself to look into a devouring maw of gnashing metal teeth and rush and decay. Light flashed. Thin smoke and blood tainted the air with harsh miasma. Colors puddled and pooled and faded into a muddy gray river that swept away everything he'd ever known.

Eratosthenes fought the desire to run still further, to lock himself away in the unknown, untouched purple mountains, to dare decaying metal teeth to find him even at the edge of the world. Behind him, shifting sands scoured away his footprints.

The past bore no trace of his presence.

Eratosthenes ran from the future.

Now

John-Paul fumed, fourth in a line of foot-tapping, watch-checking, and muted phone conversations. Of the four tellers at four open windows, one counted money and two giggled in whispered camaraderie, stealing glances at the final teller, who straddled an awkward line between death and sleep.

John-Paul tapped his foot and checked his watch. "You lazy bum," he told himself, "you promised you'd have plenty of time to get your check and pay for classes before registration closes at 4:45." The second hand on his watch taunted him as it completed another revolution.

A single main wall bisected the bank lobby with classic, pre-unification sensibility. Wainscoting showed off its dark ribs. Precisely spaced brass lamps splashed small ovals of yellowing light on the wall; penumbras enhanced the ceiling's complex texture. Armless stuffed chairs chuffed in twos and threes between the lights,

3

promising far more comfort than they could deliver. A huge sky-light provided actual illumination, recessed a man's height above the fake ceiling. Spidery shadows scuttled across the floor as the sun moved through the sky; the skylight had eight–no, twelve–metal fingers holding the glass in place.

Promotional posters advertised free checking, small business loans, and a fantastic rate on mortgages. John-Paul had a sick vision of himself scouring the posters for any hints of hidden meaning or at least obvious font kerning problems while waiting for a personal banker to return from lunch somewhere across the river Styx which separated the bank's ostensible customers from its tellers.

The lobby's single clock, embedded in cherry paneling above and just between the centermost cashier windows, had a tiny analog dial but no second hand. It jerked from 11:22 to 11:23. John-Paul pulled his arms together in a tight fold across his chest.

His backpack sagged as one strap slipped off of his shoulder. His mother's voice gently chastened him to wear it properly and to stand up straight. Homesickness swayed him on his feet. He imagined that he could enter Mark David's head to see through his eyes, but nothing happened. He chided himself for believing that one day their special twin powers would activate such that they could work together against injustice, evil, and the adult conspiracy that kept the passion and energy of youth from accomplishing great things.

The simple, bored incompetence in front of him ruined his appetite for grand conspiracies.

A shiver and a whisper passed through the room–a congregation of ghosts and wandering spirits–and he saw it again as if for the first time. Everyone else remained frozen in place, awaiting some mystical spring thaw. He idly fingered the phone in his back pocket, but Mom would be fixing lunch and Mark David at physical therapy. He tapped his foot to a strange staccato rhythm. Tap. Tap tap tap. Tap tap. Tappity tap tap.

The floor buckled. Shards of the skylight rained down seconds before a horrible thunder clap shook the block. John-Paul pulled the hem of his trench coat to cover his head, cape-like, as broken glass sliced the air on its way to the floor. A second explosion robbed him of his footing; more glass tinkled and sparkled.

The somnambulist teller's eyes snapped open. She screamed and pointed out the front windows.

The other people in the bank gawked from windows and doors, but John-Paul stared up at the broken skylight. A patch of clear sky beckoned as the wild blue tugged at him. His feet voiced a desire to leave the ground. He tasted the wild freedom of impending flight until the cashier's shrieks became hysterical babbling.

A crowd gathered outside, shocked, in a semi-circle around a twisted bubble of metal and fiberglass. A diagonal smear split the intersection. Chunks of asphalt lay sprayed at its edges, exposing pipes and cables. The traffic lights at the corners bent in toward the rubble. A steep scar of shorn bricks decorated the side of the bank. A murmuring rippled through the air, one word repeated in overlaps: Protector.

In the center of the rubble, the remains of a door and its framing scraped and groaned with twisted metal protestations. Something inside banged fists or feet or tentacles, denting the outer layer. Finally it gave way; the door flipped end over end to land in a No Parking zone between two cars on the other side of the street.

A thick white glove emerged, a fist, smeared with ash and dirt. Wisps of smoke rose from the opening, thin streaks which became the thick graveyard fog of a well-funded rock and roll show. The fist relaxed into a hand and groped for a handhold. It half-pushed and half-pulled until an arm, an elbow, and a shoulder emerged.

The Protector pulled himself out of the debris and crouched beside a few tons of unidentifiable remains. He noticed the crowd.

"Oh dear," he murmured.

His cape was torn. Great gashes rendered his stylish logo unrecognizable. His boots smoldered: puffs of dark smoke slithered up his legs. A bruise formed over his left eye, threatening to swell and cloud his vision, and he ached all over. Every joint protested his upright state. Every muscle warned that unless he found a hot bath and perhaps a double-dose of anti-inflammatory, he wouldn't walk tomorrow.

He focused his will on staying upright and avoiding reverse peristalsis.

Another shock wave pulled the traffic poles inward. They groaned and bent and fell. The Protector threw out one hand and croaked "Get back!" to the spectators. They Obeyed, a single mindless mass, shuffling several simultaneous steps backwards.

John-Paul chuckled at the unintentional poetry of the crowd's gasps and applause. He remained at the bank doors, even as the other customers retreated.

The Protector scanned the scene again, eyes wary. He squeezed his eyes closed, then jumped lightly away from his craft, imagining a gentle descent. Instead, the pavement grabbed him out of the air. He bounced and threw out his left foot wildly to regain his balance, but the abused asphalt cracked and gave way. He slipped and landed face-first on the pavement.

"Oh, dear!" he mumbled again. Darkness rose up to claim him. He heard metal strain and give way and pop. He heard screaming and the sizzle of electricity from now-freed wires. Sparks rained down as the red tunnel in his vision constricted and that was all he knew.

Screams like deflating balloon animals escaped the crowd as the enormous metal poles knelt in obeisance toward the prone figure. Ozone crackled in the air. Rustproof paint wrinkled and blistered. A stampede began; waves of onlookers crashed in complex tides of chaotic retreat, describing complex Brownian motions of high-energy particles desperately escaping to regions of lesser energy. Abused metal screamed until, with frustrated sighs, the great bolts relaxed their grip on deeply rooted concrete. The intersection collapsed into itself.

Dust and small pebbles shot outward to cake adjoining buildings in gray grit. The stack of rubble broke its silence with a soft sigh and a gentle whoosh, gentle in contrast to the shrieks of the retreating crowd. A water pipe in the abused street gave way, first with a hissing sprinkle and then a groaning gush after its fittings tore themselves apart. Dust and water mixed in the air to throw muddy spatters on the whole scene, on prostrate and kneeling onlookers wringing their hands as well as the unrecognizable mess of the accident and the balconies of luxury apartments several floors above the detritus.

Everyone else inside the bank had covered his face or cowered on the floor to shield her eyes. The noisy teller had run out of words. She thumped a grief tantrum on the floor, one hand pressed over her mouth and eyes wild. John-Paul scanned the debris for a flash of red or a moving white glove, but a breeze threw fat bullets of smeared spray against the glass door panes. Everything was already a dirty brown-gray.

Behind him something *wrong* twisted at the edge of perception. He shielded his eyes as he turned. A man-sized hole tore itself in the bank's drive-up teller wall. A puff of dried gypsum filled the gap for a second, then shards of brick clattered on the ground. One boot stepped through, and another, followed by a leg, knee, thigh, and finally a smirking man in a purplish-gray jumpsuit and a purple belt.

Sound assaulted his ears. First came the protests of studs and masonry and the building's steel frame. Then the man with the belt chuckled. Everything else ceased.

A phone burped. "Silence!" bellowed the man, throwing his hand wide. The door handles behind John-Paul stretched impossibly thin, then tied itself in a neat bow. He dove forward two steps. All eyes turned toward the intruder and the hole behind him and a whisper rang out from behind the teller desk. *The Twisted Man.*

Twist punched the wall next to his entrance. The building shook with an earthquake's low after shocks. "Silence, I said. My badness, do I need to spell this out for you? Hush. Do not speak. Do not whisper, murmur, wonder, hiss, retort, snort, chuckle, or cry." He paused. "Back up. You may cry or sniffle or sob quietly to yourself, for this bank is now mine. Though I suppose you could cry before then, but now you have a better reason."

He punched the wall twice again for good measure. The remains of the skylight's frame tore away. It landed in the middle of the lobby. Tiny shards of dirty glass skittered into the corners of the room. Muddy rain peppered the floor.

Twist kicked a chair. It skittered out of the way, crashing into and overturning a desk full of papers, paper clips, and an aging computer. Pamphlets fluttered through the air, like a family of legal-sized four-color butterflies migrating south for the winter. He stabbed at them with bored fingers as they landed. "I suppose," he started again, "you're wondering why I chose this bank. That's a good question. I would have asked that question of myself. I'd be happy to tell you." He jumped atop the teller counter. "While you're *opening* the *vault*." A series of mighty foot stomps punctuated that sentence. The desk's fake paneling cracked, and a finishing nail worked its way loose. It descended in a slow arc and bounced twice in tired, end-over-tip parabolas.

John-Paul smelled strawberries. An itch filled his muscles with the desire for a really good morning stretch before getting out of bed.

No one else had moved. The teller had gathered sufficient courage to turn her eyes toward Twist as far as they could go without moving her head. The kneeling man sat stunned several inches from a sharp piece of skylight frame that had dented and scuffed the tile next to his thigh. John-Paul eased out of his crouch to stand.

"Well?" bellowed Twist. He kicked another monitor toward the teller. She cringed and whimpered. It dented the wall behind her, sending plastic splinters in all directions even as it trailed stripped wires. "Open the vault! This is the banking district. They call it the banking district because there are so very many lovely banks here. Do you know how many banks there are within walking distance? At an average walking speed of four miles per hour, minus one mile per hour for crosswalks, and at an average time per bank of twelve minutes, there are *oh so very many* banks."

The bank manager–a pudgy woman with short blonde curls–poked her head out from under her arms. "Um...we don't...that is to say, I'm sorry sir but...we don't actually, not in this branch...it's just... we don't have a vault!" A single bead of sweat escaped her hairline. It joined its muddy comrades pooling on the floor.

Twist leaped over the counter, triggering another spray of paperwork, to land in front of the woman. "Why does it keep doing that?" he snapped, pawing at and crumpling papers with both hands. He hoisted the woman by the lapel of her blazer. Her feet dangled, and one shoe fell off. It careened off of the counter and landed near the ruined monitor. She gasped and stared at his hands.

She wore a black pantsuit over a maroon shirt that revealed just enough cleavage to indicate that today was casual Friday. Twist stared into her eyes, but a stray sunbeam sparkled off of a metallic gold "10-10-10" broach. His grimace twisted. "What's this? You don't have a vault, but you *do* have a Protector ribbon? What do you have to protect if you don't have a vault? Hmm? Tell me! What! Do! You! Have! To! Protect!" He raised a finger. The pin tore itself away from her jacket and the ribbon untied itself in mid air before hurtling toward John-Paul. He thought he heard thunder.

He shifted his weight slightly, and the pin embedded itself harmlessly in the well-worn wooden wainscotting by the front door.

Twist turned and leapt off of the counter, still carrying the woman. Her remaining shoe dangled two inches off of the ground. He reached for and tore away a cash tray. "Do you think I came here for money? I could have money if I wanted money!" He waved the tray in front of her face, then threw it at the kneeling man. The underside of the tray hit him in the forehead. He fell backwards, drooling. Coin rolls bounced and rolled and tens of thousands of dollars clouded the air.

Twist dropped the woman. She landed lopsided on her heels, then sat down hard and scrabbled, crab-like, away. "Why is it doing that? STOP THAT! Ugh!" He pounded his fists on the counter again. A stapler bounced off the floor by his feet. His roundhouse kick sent it flying out the hole he'd come through.

John-Paul's phone burped again. It was Mark David's ring. He slapped his pocket to find the silence button, but it was too late. "I thought I told you to be quiet! Are you mocking me? You're not going to like what happens if you're mocking me!" Twist punched through another monitor and hurled it one-handed at John-Paul's head. He sidestepped; it missed, shattering one glass door. Trailing wires grazed his face as he turned his head away. "I think you get the picture," screamed Twist. He stalked toward the manager.

This time, the light played off of a key dangling from a curly plastic stretch bracelet on her wrist. It was unspectacular, neither out of place unlocking the front door of a house in the suburbs or a stand-alone garage in a gentrified downtown neighborhood. Something on it caught his eye, and he waggled his eyebrows at it. "You don't have a vault, but you do have something locked up here? Keys are for locks. Don't you!"

She looked at the other tellers, but he snapped his fingers in her face. "Don't wait for an explanation, answer the question! What do you have locked up here!"

She stammered. "We *don't* have a vault, but we *do* have a small safe."

"Aaaaaaaahhh!" he screamed. John-Paul's ears popped. "Do you think I'm so literal that I have to have an elephant-sized door with a huge spinny wheel and little poofs of pressurized air escaping and an enormous wall full of tiny heavy drawers? NO! I just want what you have locked up and hidden here. It's picturesque language." He leered. "I'm so glad we worked *that* out. March." He pointed vaguely elsewhere and tucked his thumbs into his purple belt, rocking on his heels. "Next you'll tell me you don't have a safe, because obviously if I'm here, it's no longer safe."

"I can't," she sniffled. "It takes two keys, and my assistant isn't...."

Twist raised his hand. "You should think very carefully about how you are going to finish that sentence. *Very* carefully."

She squeezed her eyes shut. Another fat tear escaped.

John-Paul felt an immense wrongness wrinkle near him. His vision blurred around the edges; objects smeared as he moved his eyes. A golden glow filled his senses. Salty sweat and sour fear hung in the stale air just as the tang of copper-tainted water sprayed in the street. Dust clouds billowed with tiny puffs as more of the wall collapsed. Individual muscles and tendons in Twist's arm tensed as he prepared a vicious backhand that would probably send the manager sprawling head-first into a crumpled heap under the drive-up window, breaking her neck instantly if she were lucky.

Surprise blinked his eyes as John-Paul saw himself move.

"Excuse me." He jumped from his position by the door across the lobby, landing on the other side of the teller desk. "Is that a jumpsuit? With a belt? A purple belt? Really?"

Twist had started to turn as soon as he heard John-Paul's sneaker leave a dent in the tile by the door, but John-Paul ducked under the retargeted backhand, and came up inside to pin Twist against the wall by both shoulders. "Are you mocking me? Are you *mocking* me! I warned you before, and now I am NOT happy!" He squirmed to face the manager. "Hold on a minute sweetie. We are *not* finished yet, but I'll get back to you after the beep. BEEP!" He brought up his knee and brought down his head. John-Paul had to relax his grip and dance away to avoid both.

Twist spit. "Good work, kid. Now you've made me angry." He threw a punch where John-Paul's head had been a moment earlier. "This is going to hurt you." He aimed a precise straight-leg midsection kick, John-Paul flipped his trench coat to deflect and tangle Twist's foot before wrenching him to the ground. "More than it's going to hurt–WHY DON'T YOU STAND STILL FOR A MINUTE AND LET ME POUND YOU!" Twist flipped up to his feet and raised his fists.

A golden glow trapped the scene in amber, revealing where Twist would aim. John-Paul willed himself not to be there for the first, second, and third punches. He gathered his strength again to feel the floor wrinkle under his feet. He jumped, just as Twist's final, weaker punch missed. The velocity swung the other man wide, and they few together through the hole in the wall where the wall still crumbled away from its exposed metal bones. John-Paul felt his left arm leave about a sixteenth of a pound of flesh on a brick as they landed heavily in the parking lot in a surprised tangle.

They bounced once, then stopped in a spray of fresh bark chips and dirt clumps. A tiny thunderclap struck, and John-Paul shook his head to clear the tinnitus. He scrambled to identify his own arms and legs.

Twist gasped, sucking in air, and his left hand grabbed at his solar plexus. The other hand felt its way toward John-Paul's belt and pulled him back to the ground.

"Leggo!" He freed his left arm. "Let go of me," he threatened– and fell into Twist's eyes. Deep pools of green flecked with purple spread wide, flicking back and forth, refusing to rest or focus. Wide white rings surrounded each iris. Tears gathered in the inner corners by his nose.

Something snapped. John-Paul pivoted from his right hip to land solidly on his back. His head narrowly missed a wicked-looking brush hunkered in a berm between cars. The underside of his thigh slapped the concrete railing, jarring his teeth. The thought of the imminent bruise and an awkward week of limping demanded his attention.

Twist finally sucked air between his teeth in throaty, wet gasps. Then he giggled and gagged on a chuckle, and giggled again.

John-Paul lay on his back for a second. "Where am I?" he began. He had been in a bank, and now he decided that he was underneath a sky of patchy clouds smelling of copper and rain. Someone cackled nearby. His ribs felt raw. He wiggled his fingers and his toes. Crooked fingers grabbed his collar and yanked him halfway off the ground.

"Oh that was stupid, boy. Very stupid of you." Twist slammed him into the ground. Wet bark scattered, leaving a bare spot of sun-baked mud. "I was having *so* much fun in there, and you had to play hero. Do you know what happens to heroes? Do you know why there are heroes? FOR ME TO SMASH!" The mud cracked under repeated impacts.

John-Paul's eyes snapped back to his assailant. Twist's unfocus had given way to preternatural concentration. His mouth was a raw slash of determination as his one-handed rhythm of rage pounded John-Paul into the ground.

John-Paul forced his left leg to bend beneath him and timed the rhythm to push himself off of the ground just as Twist pulled again. They flipped through the air. Twist lost his balance and landed on his backside, while John-Paul wobbled and skidded on his feet. Golden sparkles danced away at the edge of sight. He shook his head and threw his arms to the side, flexing his fingers. Something sharp popped in his back. He felt inches taller as he stood over the crumpled figure.

"Smash this."

He hoisted Twist in the air by the collar, then punched him once, twice, and three times with his left hand. Each blow stole madness from his eyes. John-Paul let go, and the other man slumped back against a car to slide slowly to the ground. His head lolled to the right. His body shuddered between his shoulders and his knees, sending tiny, uncontrolled jerks to his fingers and toes.

John-Paul ran a hand through his hair, dislodging clumps of dirt and tiny pebbles. He winced at the bruise in the making behind his right ear. He brushed more dirt off of his trench coat and jeans. A brief bright flash of light caught his attention, and he crouched and half-turned, raising cautious fists. A large camera lens several feet away tracked him as the flash went off again.

"Um," he said.

"One more picture?" asked the camera. "C'mon Big P, I have in mind a front page shot above the fold." A lithe hand spun a dial on the lens. The shutter clicked staccato.

"Um," he said again, glancing between the camera and the drooling Twist.

The camera dropped to reveal a pixie-like face with big green eyes and a button nose. She had chin-length walnut hair, with two longer bangs on either side. One earring was a silver dolphin and the other a silver gecko. "Heh," he said.

The camera girl's tiny, amused smile disappeared into pursed lips. "Wait, who are you? You're not the Protector. That's Twisted Man, and that damage over there sure *looks* familiar, but. . . ."

John-Paul looked back at the bank and its new egress. His muscles dissolved into tired water and he staggered. Camera girl took two quick steps and ducked under his arm.

"Careful," she said. "This guy may look crazy but he's strong. At least that's what they say. You're crazy yourself to take him on, but you really did a number on him. C'mon, let's sit you down." She eased him onto the curb.

He found his voice. "Are you a reporter?"

She swung her camera to her right hip and sat. "J-school student actually, but I have an internship at the paper this year. How'd you know?"

"No one else uses that many clichés before introducing herself."

Her blush highlighted freckles on her nose that he hadn't noticed before. She offered her hand. "I'm Pandora. Pandora d'Avril." She blushed again as she saw his eyes drink in a streak of mud across the palm, and she quickly rubbed it away with her left hand.

"John-Paul Harrison." An electric glow descended at their touch. He stared at her hand to savor the lingering, then looked up at her eyes to see her tilting her head and staring at him.

"How'd you do that?" She nodded toward the wall and then the unmoving Twist. "I've seen pictures of other guys who went up against supers like him, and most of them couldn't stand up afterwards. You have a nasty bump on your head right there, and you were wobbly walking, but you're all in one piece."

"What kind of a name is Pandora?" Her expression told him everything he'd forgotten about not saying what he was thinking. "Oh. Sorry. I mean, I've only been officially in town for two days, and there's some serious bizarre here I don't remember from visiting when I was younger."

She giggled. "Tourists never see the real deal unless they have someone to show them around. I haven't been here long myself, but I know enough not to pass for a gawking farmboy."

Her smile and her laugh and her question stopped bouncing around in his skull long enough to tickle neurons to send electric impulses to other neurons and endocrine glands. His memory flashed briefly back to the third punch he landed on Twist and a squishy cracking sound. Looking again at the man in the jumpsuit with the purple belt, he didn't see a cackling and menacing villain, just a wiry figure folded messily into a heap, blowing saliva bubbles.

John-Paul jumped up and pointed, forcing his left knee to bend in the correct direction. "I just maimed that guy!" Blood drained from his face with a cold fury.

Pandora snorted. "I've seen pictures of him in the morgue, toe-tagged and short sheeted. He's as indestructible as the Protector." She fiddled with her camera. "But wait, if you're not the Protector, then he's around here somewhere and I have to get there before someone else gets the sco...." She caught John-Paul's smirk. "I mean, takes better pictures than I do. Which no one else does. At least none of the other interns."

A buzzing prompted him to grab the girl and throw his trench coat wide to shield them. A tremendous boom shook the ground and rattled his eardrums. Shards of broken building and hot metal rained. She smelled of vanilla and cherries. A soft pop echoed between the buildings, followed by a soft sigh.

His unshakeable confidence surprised him. "Don't worry about him anymore. We have bigger problems."

She extricated herself and toed a large piece of brick out of the way. Her stare dropped twenty degrees as she fixed her fists to her hips. "What do you mean?"

He shrugged. "It seemed like a good thing to say, you know, like 'We're safe, but for how long?' or 'That's the end of that chapter!'"

She sucked her bottom lip. "Bizarre. Why don't we...." A thin wail pierced her words and she trailed off, eyes swiveling and head following to track a white and blue police cruiser squealing to a stop yards away. "So much for *that* idea."

Two uniformed officers disembarked. The driver was thin and

blonde with rough eyes and what might someday be a mustache given six months of proper disciplined fertilization and watering treatments. The passenger was solid with black hair and a posture which signified that nonsense had to straighten up and swallow its back talk or face being shipped off to the kind of military school that produced officers with the kind of posture that signified the circular nature of his presence. They beamed and swaggered up to John-Paul.

"Heya Big P," said the driver. "Heard about the bumpy ride, but you always bounce back, doncha?" He slapped John-Paul with an awkward whap that fizzled halfway through with the gradual dawning horror of unexpected and undesired familiarity. "You guys sure did a number on the bank this time."

The passenger nodded toward Twist. "Chasing Twist again, Harvey. No surprise there's little collateral damage. Is this guy seriously off his meds again, Protector? You slap him less silly?"

John-Paul swallowed. "Um..." he cleared his throat. "I just...."

They laughed. "No need to explain, big guy. Always with the snappy comebacks. I *love* your work. I bet you get that all the time, though. That's why I joined the force, you know?" Harvey knelt and shone a penlight in Twist's eyes.

"You're gushing." The larger officer's nametag read "Brown". "Any concussion?"

"Out cold. Sheesh, Big P. There's not even a mark on this guy. I don't know how you did it, but you pounded the ... er, snot out of him and I don't see a scratch. Last time you cracked a couple of ribs, not that I particularly mind. Rough job, but he knew the risks when he signed up for it. I remember when he planned to pinch off both ends of the Crosstown Bridge and dump it in the river during that bicycle protest rally, and...."

"C'mon Harvey, just ask for his autograph already." Brown pulled two notebooks from his shirt pocket and thumb-flicked the cap off of a pen. As John-Paul completely failed to take the bundle, Brown let out a low whistle at Pandora. He leaned in. "Man, I wish

I had your job, rescuing cuties like this. How does Clownfish not get jealous?"

She stared back, eyes narrowing at the failed stage whisper. John-Paul watched three-dimensional puzzle pieces rotate and slide together in a frictionless dance. Her pupils tore a hole in the air around him. He felt like a bug helpless under a magnifying glass, forced to give up his secrets and doomed to slot forever into a tidy, two-cubby taxonomy. He shrugged and returned to the relative comfort of scribbling platitudes in unreadable scrawls.

Brown beamed. "You're the best, man. Seriously. It's a pleasure to clean up after you. I don't know what we'd do with out you, and...aw, man. Now I'm gushing. Listen, give us a couple of minutes to tape off the scene here, and then we just have a couple of questions to ask and then maybe your little friend there could snap a couple of shots, you know, if that's okay, and we'll be off. It'll only take five minutes, big guy. What do you say?"

Harvey let Twist's head drop back to his chest. A puddle of drool had already soaked through the jumpsuit. "Three minutes. We're old pros at this, even if we've never worked one of your cases before."

Pandora stepped between John-Paul and the police. "I'm outta film, and he's not finished rescuing me. Why doesn't he come down by the station later and catch up when he's off the clock? What's your station number?"

Suspicion jumped onto their faces, but disappointment crowded it out. "Aw," said Brown.

"Oh," said Harvey.

"It's 348," Brown offered. "On the corner of Cass Street and...."

"He'll be there." Pandora waved her hand. "You boys are doing great work, but we really must be off."

They stood to offer their hands. "Serious pleasure, man." Brown had a sturdy handshake, with more warmth and passion than John-Paul expected. Harvey offered a vigorous pump. John-Paul mumbled something gracious and stole back his hand. The tilt of Pandora's head and subtle shift of weight at her hips warned him to follow her right now, or else the next heavy object she could lift would get his attention like a blow to the head. He sped after her, pausing only to offer a nervous fingertip wave as the police called after him.

"Remember, 348!"

"Good to meet ya, Big P! We'll catch up later, okay?"

He jogged to catch up. "Do you have any idea what they...."

"None," she snapped. "I don't want to talk about it."

"But you were taking pictures of me earlier, and you seemed...."

She spun, aiming her index finger at a spot in his forehead just between and an inch above his eyes. "You are talking. You should not be talking. Stop talking. Now." Something soft and metal flashed in her expression.

He pushed her hand away. Her fingers were soft and warm. "Fine. I'm not going to ask about something that's so *obviously* painful, but in the past eight minutes something crashed into the building I was in, landed in the street, and exploded. Some sort of robber, I suppose, broke into the building I was in and threatened the cashier who ignored me in line for half an hour. I beat him up, then gave the police autographs instead of a statement before they arrested me for assault and, who knows, manslaughter, and now I'm following a cute girl where? I don't even know. Also I'm bleeding." A thin red snake slithered down his hand through his coat and dripped on the tip of his shoe.

Pandora closed her eyes and counted to ten through a long sigh. "Okay. John-Paul. That's you, right? If you ever repeat this, I will beat you with my shoe, but I don't know what's going on either, and something I can't explain tells me that if you stick around, someone will figure out that you're not the Protector and something bad is going to happen. You won't like it. I won't like it. We are going to my apartment until the noise dies down. You can wash up there, and I'm going to look at these pictures and figure out what's going on, and that's going to be that. You can let go of my hand now."

He stared, then released her. Pandora stomped off at a pace no less determined before, but her shoulders slumped into a more relaxed position. She chewed the inside of her lip to keep from smiling. "I'm over here," she pointed.

A yellow scooter sat in the shade of a tree, chained to a parking meter. John-Paul followed Pandora across the empty street. She opened a small compartment on the back and removed two helmets before stowing her camera gear. "Put this on."

"Why do you have two helmets?"

"I'm not answering why questions today. Are you coming?"

By the time he had the helmet on and fastened, she was on the scooter and had started the engine. He stared. "Uh, where do you want me?"

She stood and patted the seat. "I'm gonna have to sit on your lap. Don't get any ideas. Also don't bleed on me."

"Bleed...?"

She pointed to his left hand. "This shirt's dry-clean only, so drip into the wind. Can you ride one-handed? I'll take it easy."

John-Paul scanned the empty street. He climbed aboard and Pandora plopped down on his lap. "Oof," he said.

She kicked away from the curb and accelerated, and his right arm tightened reflexively around her waist. He tried to ignore how she felt beneath his arm. She threw her head back against his helmet. "Ouch," he said.

"My eyes are up here," she yelled. "Yours should be too."

He shifted his weight. She corrected with a swerve. Then they were off, his right arm holding her, her eyes fixed on the road, and his left arm out to the side, shooting ruby drips through the air to splatter into tiny gems on the pavement.

o o o

Pandora zipped into a narrow driveway between respectable brick buildings. The driveway widened downhill into an alley between a tan cinder block wall and an open garage beneath a building. She parked and hopped off and shook out her hair before he realized that they had arrived. By the time he removed his helmet, she had gathered her equipment and stood by a pair of fireproof doors. "Leave that on the handlebars," she said.

She waved a key fob at the wall. Thick bolts slid out of place and a metal screen unrolled over the garage's entrance. John-Paul tried to slide ahead to open the door, but she ducked inside two steps ahead.

The doors opened into a narrow stairwell painted in industrial grays. The air felt ten degrees cooler. Pandora's flip flops ricocheted slap-slaps up the stairs. On the second floor landing, he sidestepped a red wrench lying on the floor beside a pipe as thick as his thigh. A huge wheel the color of post-mold cheese rusted at waist height. Pandora pushed open an access door on the third floor.

Instead of rubber mats on rough-painted concrete floors, the hallway's modest carpet reminded him of the modernist movie theater that closed when he was fourteen. He tried to ignore the feeling of the floor springing beneath his steps, but failed, feeling a Moon Bounce between the rebar reinforcements of the building's floor. He managed to wrestle his eyes away from Pandora to pause before a window. A tree-lined street stretched straight for blocks. Purple mountains lurked in the distance. Brass poles and building numbers complemented the reds and rich earthy browns of the buildings across the street.

"Nice neighborhood," he said. She shrugged and waved her fob at a door labeled 308.

The room was sunny and spacious, monk-sparse of furniture. A glass far wall opened onto a narrow balcony. Sunlight streamed in above his head from wide windows over the door. To his left was a kitchen covered in ivory enamel held in place with blue trim. The long wall on the right was canary yellow, broken only by what he assumed was a coat closet and stairs covered in shaggy white carpet. Pandora threw her jacket over the side of a hulking tan couch previously out of sight against the kitchen's half-wall. She gestured.

"There's a bathroom beneath the stairs. It's not big, but you can wash up in there. I'll find you bandages."

He walked in. Something caught his eye on the wall opposite the stairs. A framed poster dominated the room where he would have put a television. Three separate panels expressed time and motion. A ruined city lay unlamented at the bottom of each; buildings twisted and creaked and offered exposed steel bones skyward in silent screams. The sky glowered and howled. Thick clouds swirled and shot lightning at each other.

A lone bird stretched mighty wings to fly right to left in the first panel. Blinding white plumage burned its image into his retinas even as the wind from its toil ruffled his hair. In the second panel, tendrils of smoke or cloud or darkness embraced the bird as lighting flashes illuminated distant hills of rubble.

There was no bird in the third panel.

"I hope you're not dripping. The floor is real hardwood." Pandora called from the top of the stairs.

John-Paul half turned, flushed. "Oh no, I was just... I think it's mostly stopped bleeding now."

"Eratosthenes," she said. "Some nickname a bunch of painters and poets and revolutionaries used to use back in the Reconstruction days. It was here when I moved in. I like it, I guess. Nice use of contrast of color and theme. They weren't very popular, but sometimes the truth isn't."

He scanned the poster again. "The Gathering Storm? Sounds pretentious."

A plastic bag full of bandages and antibiotics bounced off his head. "Art criticism can wait. Go clean up. Just throw your coat on the couch." She popped back around the corner. Unlike the hallway, her floors didn't creak.

The bathroom itself was long and narrow. The first switch he flipped bathed the walls in a dull red glow. The second switch added yellow. He sat on the toilet and examined his arm; it glowed golden under the lights. A thin scrape ran from mid-arm to his elbow, where it deepened to a clotted puncture. This was the source of the blood. He winced in anticipation, but it felt mild under his probing finger.

Instead of a mirror, a large series of empty shelves stuck out above the sink. He washed up and down his arm, dabbing at the edges of the scab, then toweled dry, trying not to stain a fluffy white towel.

He left the bathroom, dabbing at ointment seeping out from under the bandage. "Sorry about the towel," he started. Pandora sat on the couch with her legs folded under her and her right arm dangling off of her knee. He hadn't noticed the television behind a footrest. The volume was low. Captions scrolled across the screen.

A pile of debris smoldered and spit muddy steam in infrequent bursts. Police tape lined the square; officers clumped in twos and threes, nodding sagely or rubbing their short hair with their hat hands. The camera angle shifted from overhead to handheld and went shaky and fuzzy in a handheld unit. A ratty blue scrap of fabric the size of a baby-doll t-shirt flapped in the breeze.

Pandora stared at him. He offered, "Some bleach or peroxide should take it out. I can do it if you want. The towel, I mean. Okay. You're giving me a look. I don't speak looks."

"Don't you recognize that?"

"Some bomb exploded somewhere. It happens."

The scene changed again. An agitated Harvey waved his hands. The captions struggled to keep pace, then devolved into gibberish. Brown stood nearby, face ash-gray from mud–and something else.

"Do you recognize them? Yes?"

"The cops we just ran away from. So?"

She turned up the volume. "...just talked to him a few minutes ago! Look, he autographed my notebook!" Harvey waved a paper. The camera focused just long enough for John-Paul to recognize his own scribble.

The helicopter view swung around to the front of the bank. "So far, we have no further confirmation that anyone else saw the Protector leave the accident, but we remain hopeful. I'm getting an update that we have a camera inside the bank now, is that... is that right? No... we'll switch to that just as soon as we can get inside. We've had a report that we have some eyewitnesses in...."

Pandora muted the sound and threw the remote on the cushion. "Humor me. Who are you?"

Blood roared in his ears. "I was just in the bank to get a cashier's check. The ground shook, the skylight broke, and then that guy in the jumpsuit crashed through the wall. You saw everything else." He paused and stared back, then decided to find his shoes fascinating. "How about *you* tell me what you think is going on, and then... well, we'll figure that out."

She sighed, and he watched her count silently again. "Alright. Fine. Like I said, I was minding my own business, when work sent out a text to see if anyone was in the area. I was. I hadn't seen anything on the schedule, but I was lucky to have my gear with me, and figured I might be lucky enough to get an editor to bite on a few lucky shots. I made it to the bank just as you and Twist came flying out of there. I'd taken a handful of pictures before I realized that you weren't the Protector." She checked her hair for split ends. "They're saying on TV now that, um, they think he's still in the wreckage."

"Those cops sure thought he, or me, whoever... was up and walking around."

She shrugged and started her bangs. "You autographed their books. They're happy."

"I've never seen him. Do I really look like him?"

"I have no idea. Not really. Maybe you were just in the right place at the right time, and it's just a silly coincidence. What about the other guy?"

John-Paul slouched against the wall and stuffed his hands in his pockets. "I doubt he even noticed me until I made some noise." Something felt wrong. His wallet was gone. He patted his pockets, then forced the sick feeling in his stomach to recede as he turned his coat inside out in his search. Nothing. He checked his pants again. A cold feeling crept over his skin.

"What? What is it?" asked Pandora.

"My wallet...the last time I saw it was in the bank, when Twist saw me and when everything started to go weird. Weirder, anyway. Your city's weird." He pulled on his coat and ran to the window. Smoke smudged the afternoon sky like a greasy thumb print blurring a lens. He followed the road in his head briefly, fished in his pocket for a pen, then knelt by the couch and grabbed Pandora's hand.

"What?" she said.

"Call this number," he said as he scribbled in blue ink, "in...ten minutes. If I don't pick up, call again every couple of minutes after that. We'll continue this conversation then." He fixed her with his best determined gaze, trying to emulate the golden glow he'd seen on her as she guided him to the scooter.

Two steps later he stared at the balcony door. "This opens, right?" She nodded. Then he was outside. He leapt over the railing.

"That's three floors...!" she cried. When she reached the balcony, only a golden smear remained.

o o o

Mark David sat on his bed and leaned his head back into the room's corner. His legs *hurt*. Though he'd broken the left one more severely, the right was tired from bearing extra burdens. Even standing was exhausting, some days.

John-Paul had responded only briefly, tapering off in the first few days to infrequent texts. He was probably living it up in the big city. If there were justice in the world, he allowed himself to think, they'd be...no, that wasn't helpful. Pride jostled resentment, and all he could do was look forward to hearing about all of his brother's adventures and hoping that next semester he'd be able to join him in the university.

Besides, Jupiter had promised coming over later, and she'd make him reveal that he'd been, in her words, "wallowing in pity like a pig in its own filth."

Someone knocked on his door. "Honey?"

"Yes, mother?" He wiped his eyes with his palms and smoothed his clothes.

She pushed open the door. "I brought you a sandwich and some milk. How are you feeling, dear?"

"Thanks. . . I'm still sore. They pushed me pretty hard this morning."

"They said you're walking again." She sat and searched his eyes. A stray sunbeam illuminated half of her face. Silver had begun to supplant gold in her hair, and the worry lines in her forehead had grown deeper and more visible now than the laugh lines at the sides of her eyes.

"Can't stop me. The less I need this," and he nodded toward his wheelchair, "the better."

She sat, then hugged him hard enough that he squeaked. "Mom!" She kept holding him, then let go as if he'd caught fire. He thought he saw her eye go moist.

"I'm sorry. I'm just. . . well, I'm going to miss you, you know? John-Paul's already off having his adventures in the big city, and you'll be with him in a couple of months, and it'll just be me in this big house. Promise you'll come visit, right?"

Mark touched her hand. "I'll call every day."

She laughed away a sob. "Every week will be fine, right? You make sure your brother stays out of trouble? You're a good influence on him, you know."

"Now that's not fair! I've always been more popular than him. If anything, he's the one who should be keeping me out of trouble. You know what Dad always said. Girls can't resist a man with his own set of wheels."

This time, her laugh bubbled up with true delight. "When's Jupiter coming over?"

"Three, I think."

She stared at him again. Her smile started slow and sad, then lit up his room like always. "Alright. I'll let you rest then. Do you want one of your pills or anything?"

He shook his head. "It's not so bad. I'll be fine after a nap. Don't worry about me." His phone beebled. "Speaking of whom!"

"Jupiter?"

"Jayp. Texted me."

She wiped crumbs into her hand and stood. "Get your nap in. Tell him to call his mother. She worries, you know."

"It'll be okay, you know." He hoped she'd never catch him in the lie, that she'd never suspect that he worried about the day when every burden he took on would bend his back further and shatter his bones.

"I know." She closed the door behind her.

The message read "News on channel 47." The local news was channel 5, and at this hour was likely to be about a beet growing contest. Channel 47 was a rebroadcast over the mountains of the largest station in the city. On some nights the signal bounced off the ionosphere in particularly pleasing ways so that they could stay up late watching old monster movies. He rummaged through the mess on his beside table for the remote.

It came in fuzzy, but watchable. The current program was a montage of images of a large but otherwise indistinct man with blonde hair, gray eyes, and a blue cape. He stood on a dais with important looking officials. He posed heroically in a park. He ran out of a burning building covered in soot. He allowed several schoolchildren to climb him simultaneously. It was at once immensely heroic and unbelievably dull, obvious as prepackaged public relations sent to as many stations as possible in the hope that one would eventually run it. Mark fumbled with the dialer.

"Hey."

"Hey, Jayp. What am I watching here?"

"Ever heard of the Protector?"

"No idea. Is he some sort of mascot?"

"They treat him like a hero here."

"Did he save the mayor?"

26

"More than that."

Mark-David snickered. "Does he, what, fight bad guys and fly and patrol the city from his secret base of operations?"

"I don't know. Maybe. It's all very unspecific."

Mark shifted, and tugged at his shirt to smooth the fold that suddenly bothered him under his hip. "Is this some daytime television show that they've thrown up to get that lucrative teen demographic? I expected better than amateur hour here."

"Emdy, I can't explain it, but when you get here you'll see that everything makes a strange sort of sense. Hey, there it is. Look, now."

On the screen, the bland man traded punches with an equally large figure dressed all in green. The second man had dark hair and a jet-black Van Dyke beard. They stood in a large concrete circle surrounded by iron benches and short shrubs squatting in concrete planters. Sparks flew when fist connected to face. The camera shook and the heroic soundtrack nearly covered screams and shrieks–not from the two silent pugilists but from hidden spectators.

"Two guys in tights fighting. Nice effects, but isn't professional wrestling usually an indoor sport?"

"Everyone seems to think he's the real thing. The one in blue is the Protector and the one in green is the Defiler or something. You know as much as I do now, but apparently things like this are normal here."

"So are 24-hour takeout curry restaurants, a fact which I still find impressive from my gawrsh-shucks vantage point here in the middle of the sticks. Aren't you supposed to be registering for school, rather than bragging about how awesome the big city is compared to little ol' Nowheresville?"

John-Paul paused. "It's not... No, you're... Alright, fine. You're right. I'm sorry. I didn't mean that. It's just that it's so bizarre. This guy practically exploded in the street right next to the bank I'm in at the time, where this crazy arch nemesis villain immediately breaks in and tries to rob, and I end up beating him up when this really cute girl starts taking pictures of me, and then she takes me back to her place, and...."

"What?"

"Um. Yeah. So how was PT today?"

"Meh. Fine. Cute girl? So soon? Or should I ask what took you so long."

"She was trying to take pictures of the Protector!"

"Yeah. Him. And she settled for you?"

"Here's the weird part." Sincerity added an undertone of steel to his voice. "She thought I was him."

"Is she new in town too?"

"She's an intern at the paper, but no, thank you very much. She's not the only one. If you see two cops arguing with the reporter, they showed up just after she did. Just after the girl, I mean. They also thought I was the Protector."

"You look nothing alike."

"I know."

"This is difficult to believe."

"Awesome always is." John-Paul chuckled.

"Oh, *now* I'm convinced. You made up the part about the cute girl. It's okay, though. I'll live."

John-Paul snorted. "I *knew* you wouldn't believe that part."

"That's because I'm the handsome one."

"Sadly for me, you're also a better dancer." That line rarely failed to work to gather female attention and sympathy at dances.

"I'll make you a deal. Why don't I stick around here for a few months so you can drive her off with your own personality before I swoop in and steal her from you?"

"You're the best little brother a guy could want."

"That's younger, not little, and by two minutes."

"Still counts."

"Jayp, my legs are sore and I really need a nap. What did you want me to see here?"

"If they're still broadcasting from the scene, you should see the bank I was in and all of the debris, and you might just catch me. I had to sneak back in because I lost my wallet during the fight."

"In town for less than a week and already a big television star!"

"It only sounds creepy when *you* say it."

"Not creepy, but definitely sad. I always figured you'd get on that there teevee by painting your chest some team's colors and shivering in the bleachers during a snowstorm."

"You're holding out to be a senator or a judge. We'll see who makes it first."

There was a long silence as the montage cut to live footage of mud-colored firemen digging into a sloppy, wet pile of debris. Several men stood near the base of the pile, groaning as they levered away piles of rock and broken panels of plastic. Everyone crowded around an opening as one fireman knelt and reached inside. Then they turned away, one by one, wearing looks of unbearable sadness.

The kneeling man was the last to leave. As he stood, the camera zoomed in first on his face. He shook his head, then turned away with a hand covering his face. Finally the camera came to rest inside the cavern. When it adjusted to the light, a pale figure lay half-buried inside. Bland features lay indistinguishable in slack rest.

"No way," breathed Mark.

"What is it?"

"Are you watching this?"

"No, I'm walking back to Pandora's apartment. I was watching the monitor on the news van when I texted you."

"You have no idea... oh wow."

"What? What is it?"

"This Protector guy, he crashed into the street a little bit ago?"

"Maybe an hour, yeah. Why?"

"They say he's dead." A thud sounded. Another long silence passed. "John-Paul?"

"Sorry, I felt dizzy for a second and tripped. What was that last thing?"

"They say the Protector is dead."

"That's... I don't even know what to say."

"Me neither."

The silence ran deep and profound. Jupiter called these pauses "Unbelievable braggary telepathic twin powers," and punched the closest one in the arm for hijacking the conversation that way. Finally Mark sighed. "Jayp, I really have to go. I'm falling asleep here."

"Yeah... sorry, yeah. You take care of Mom, right? Don't get in trouble there."

"Sounds like I'm not the one who needs to worry."

John-Paul laughed. "You like the name Pandora too, hmm? I met her first, remember."

"Hah. Yeah, if that's the only trouble you get in, I'm proud of you."

"I'm proud of you too, bro. Catch you later."

"Yeah. Bye."

Mark flipped his phone shut and rubbed his eyes, trying to remember if he'd ever heard of the Protector before. Nothing came to mind, but John-Paul had seemed so *sure*, and there was no way he could have faked the television images after only a week in the city. Maybe after a month... no.

He stared at his sandwich. "This is seriously weird." The walls closed in on him and he felt four years old again, rag-doll tiny and sitting cross legged on his bed.

o o o

Clownfish picked imaginary fuzz from her temporary uniform. "Black. Slimming, but dull," she said to no one in particular. Pierre studied his fingernails. Claude tracked subtle motions in patterns of light and texture on the ceiling and walls.

Pandora glowered. "Why don't you just send him an invitation or offer him a ride?" she snapped. "If he's so fascinating to you, why are you using me as bait? How do you know he's even coming back here?"

"Shut *up*, kid!" Pierre grimaced at his nail and focused the 75-watt glare of his flinty face toward her. "When you turn big and strong like us, then you get to make the calls and call the shots and ask the big, deep, existential questions. Get it?"

Pandora struggled, but handcuffs prevented her from making the specific rude gesture she had in mind. It sufficed, though. Claude cackled as Clownfish's lighting-quick slap sent the rushing Pierre sprawling face-first.

Clownfish frowned as she tucked a stray curl back into place. "No damaging the bait. 'Bait.' That's clever. It's short, memorable, and poignant. You can tell she's in journalism. She has a way with words. Besides, I like her. She's pretty enough. A little mascara would bring out those big, exotic eyes." She leaned over the younger woman and tugged at her own lapel. "Promise me something, sweetie. Pick a better color than black. You have that lovely pale skin, and you'd fade into a ghost. What's worse, it shows all the dirt just as badly as white. Next time I'm coming back as an autumn."

"No wonder the magazine business is failing. Roving gangs of breaking and entering thugs who offer makeover advice must be a lot more expensive then trial subscriptions. If you're not here to give me a pedicure, would you mind very much being a mite more specific?"

Claude grunted. "Easy as pie. Pretty girl, single guy new in town, and you're snip-snapping pictures of him beating up Comic Relief Boy before you give him a ride and he stage-dives off of your balcony. He's coming back to get your number, or at least a great rejection story to lie to his grandkids about someday."

She rubbed her right hand behind her back, willing the remnants of the phone number to fade. The metallic taste of the ink still curled her tongue, but as far as she knew there was no particular evidence that pointed back to John-Paul.

"I'm curious," she started, "as you all seem to be in a well-intentioned expository mood. How exactly did you find us, again? Mind-control satellites? Public-minded citizens who just happen to have trained telescopes and binoculars on innocent people minding their own business within view?" A stray sunbeam flashed through the room, reflecting off of the windshield of a car driving by.

Clownfish studied her face. Both women had inscrutable expressions, Pandora mixing confidence with concern and Clownfish trying to keep amusement and confusion out of her eyes. "Why?" she managed.

"Professional curiosity. Small talk. Killing time. Pick one, I don't care. I'd be a bad hostess if I couldn't keep up a conversation. I'd offer you a drink, but I'm tied up at the moment."

Pierre groaned. "Why'd ya have to hit me so hard?" he mumbled.

"You talking to the ground? Gravity's worked that way as long as I can remember." Claude barked a laugh. His smile distorted a tattoo of three dots on his right cheekbone.

Clownfish paced to the window, then raised her leg to the ledge for a ballet stretch. "Quiet, let me think." Her left pant leg came untucked from the military style boot, revealing a dizzying flash of color. She scowled and knelt to fix the damage.

"Colorful. I have some leggings like that, or did, back when I was a teenager."

"Shh!" Before the fricative faded, her gloved hand covered Pandora's mouth. "We're undercover here. I don't know how you recognized us, but I'm not above erasing your memory, and you won't like it. I forgot my special magic ray gun. Understood?"

Pandora nodded, but chuckled when Clownfish stepped back. "Unless you're invisible too, you're on the building's video. Don't bother; offsite storage. Daddy's little girl isn't as na*iuml*ve as you might have believed."

"Smart girl," mused Claude. "Maybe we've underestimated her too. Maybe the kid's hanging out with her because...." A sharp look from Clownfish ended his speculation.

"Alright. No threats. We're all adults here. Play nicely and manage your own forgetting, and we can leave on friendly terms." She stared at the younger woman, searching for something. There was a long pause. "I said...."

"Fine!" Icicles hung from Pandora's interruption. "Whatever. I saw nothing. I see nothing. I conjugate every possible variant of the infinitive 'to see' nothing. Happy?"

Clownfish scanned the room's corners. Pierre joined her. Claude sighed and chewed his thumbnail.

"You have an explosion," prompted Pandora, "and you have something rather more destructive than your normal fistfight, and you're the cleanup team sent to make sure every little detail stays quiet. When you finish criticizing my paint job, I'd like to understand my part in this matter."

Claude hopped off of his barstool. "We are in need of some fresh air." He collared Pierre; they slunk through the balcony doors. "We'll stay out of :sight," he offered over his shoulder.

Clownfish pulled over a chair and sat on it sideways. "That's complicated. It's a big city. Interesting things happen everywhere, but not *interesting* interesting. *Unexpected* interesting. It's rare, but when it happens, you pay attention."

"Dangerous interesting?"

The other woman grimaced. "The law and order or order and chaos terms aren't quite right. Think of it like predictability. You can probably feel it. The balance of power these days is precarious. The wrong push in this direction or the other at the wrong time and everything could collapse. No one wants that. Everyone wants stability. You look for people and situations that could threaten that stability, and you encourage them to work toward more productive ends."

"You sound like an economist." Clownfish's grimace shifted into a scowl. "People are perfectly predictable; you just follow them by aggregate flows of information and you can use that as a model of future behavior."

"That's a cold description."

"That's your description. The Protector blows up, and you're here instead looking for John...Doe because you think he'll give you leverage somehow. He is...or *has*, isn't that more right? He has something you think you can use."

Clownfish stood up abruptly. She pulled off her sunglasses and paced the kitchen area, shielding her eyes from the glare. They were dawn's wild blue flecked with green and gold. "That's not it at all. It's a lot more complicated than that. I...can't tell you what it is, or why it's important, but woman to woman, can you believe me? Please?"

"Uncuff me."

She did. Pandora rubbed her wrists. The cold metal had left deep marks in her wrists from her struggles, but there had been no loss of circulation. She stretched, then sat back down in the same chair. Clownfish continued her pacing.

"Thanks, I guess."

"For?"

"For letting me go. You didn't have my permission to do it in the first place, but you could have left me there."

There was a long silence, as if for the first time Clownfish pondered the fact that she *had* released Pandora. "You're not going to run off, are you?"

"No."

"Nor tell anyone what happened?"

"I'm not even sure what happened myself."

Again Clownfish watched reflections on the ceiling. "Good...."
Metal grated on metal as the balcony door slid open roughly. Claude
and Pierre entered, the latter visibly upset.

"What's she doing loose? Clownie, you know what Titian said,
he was very...."

Clownfish's two steps left a blue smear in the air. Pierre traveled
backwards through the air until she dangled him by his collar off
of the balcony. "First of all, no names. Second of all, no questions.
This is the part where you say 'Yes' and 'I am very, truly sorry.' very
quickly, or you scream something obscene and land very awkwardly
and hope you don't need the aid of a machine to breathe, or worse."

"'m sorry," he mumbled.

She removed one hand and turned away. He scrabbled for the
railing.

"I'm very, truly, amazingly sorry!" Pandora played back the
words to add spaces between them.

Clownfish threw him in a heap in the corner of the balcony. He
rubbed his chest through the black shirt. "I think you tore off some
hair."

"I already knew who you were," offered Pandora. "I knew when
I saw you on the CCTV."

"That's just great, kid." Claude snickered. "Let's break out a box
of cookies to celebrate. Drinks are on the house–milk, skim. One
ice cube. Dirty glass; I'm daring."

"Leave her alone. She's alright." Clownfish snapped her sunglasses back into place.

A shrill beeping shook the air, then ceased, leaving a deep relaxation in its wake with its cessation of interruption. "Proximity,"
mused Pierre.

"You stay put." Clownfish wagged a finger at Pandora and pulled
on her black leather gloves.

"Don't hurt him."

"Not sure that's possible anymore."

"He tore up his arm earlier. There's probably blood all over my bathroom. I'll get you some paper towels. You clean it, you keep the DNA samples. You're public servants, right? I'll get the mop. It'll help me forget." Her smile was wicked; her nose crinkled and she looked as likely to strike as laugh.

Clownfish palmed her forehead. "Would you just *stop*? Does everything have to be a discussion with you? We had this all carefully planned out until you showed up and started ruining things!"

"I can't tell whether you're half-serious or half-joking. I *live* here."

The other woman growled and gestured. Pierre and Claude took up flanking positions by the door and shot each other a puzzled look.

"That's the closet, you know," offered Pandora. She plopped down on the couch and pulled a magazine from a side table. "Not that I expect people like you to come through the front door. Do you think this dress would look good on me?"

"Thanks for the tip." Clownfish sighed and waited for the knock.

o o o

John-Paul took the stairs three at a time, daring gravity to take notice of him and reveling in its failure to do so. There were no pipes visible from this staircase. A thin layer of carpet covered poorly-painted concrete.

His hand turned the knob of the door to the third floor hallway, and a wave of humidity burst out as he pulled. Though the hallway was wide enough to walk four abreast, its poor lighting made him hunch and cling to the middle. Absorbed sunlight and heat rising from the other floors wicked drops of sweat out of his skin.

He jogged down the hall, feeling the hallway bounce with each footfall, and lifted a fist to rap knuckles on door 308. The instant his flesh touched the door, instinct threw him backwards and sideways. The heavy metal and wood frame scraped only the barest tip of his flesh as it exploded open. An angry woman glowered in the remains.

"Hello," he began. "I'm looking for Pan...." The fleshy lower part of her palm caught him under the chin. His mouth snapped closed as he flew backwards into the hallway. "Oof," he said. "She didn't say anything about a sister."

Clownfish spun to aim a clunky black boot at his chest, but he bent backwards and slapped her foot away. She swiveled further, losing her balance. She fell, but scissored her legs together and jumped to her feet. Pierre and Claude peered out around the door, which had slammed shut and now slammed open again. One hinge sagged.

"You leave me a souvenir like that, I don't forget you." Pandora rummaged in her fridge. "I *liked* that door. It kept out everything that wasn't my apartment."

Clownfish advanced again, and John-Paul swatted away three quick jabs and a vicious side slap. Clownfish yelped with frustration.

"Seriously, she'll vouch for me." He dodged a groin kick and sidestepped a knee sweep that left a scuff mark on the wall. "I even cleaned up the blood in her bathroom. I'm a great house guest." He ducked, then pulled up his coat sleeve to reveal his neatly-bandaged arm. "This was from her first aid kit. Am I even getting through to you?"

"This one talks too much too," said Pierre.

"Kids these days," agreed Claude. They leaned against the doorway.

Clownfish sprang forward in a shoulder-first tackle. "Oof," said John-Paul. "You've never done that before." They landed in a tangle of arms and legs. She won, pinning him to the ground.

"I always wanted to," she said.

Pandora whistled and knocked a jar of mayonnaise to the floor. It shattered, sending shards of plastic into the corners of the kitchen. Furry green and white goo splattered her cupboards. "That's funny," she said. "How long has this been in there? Jar went *brittle*."

Pierre and Claude turned at the noise, crouched into fighting stances.

"Where's that mop?" asked Pierre.

"Keep your shoes on," suggested Claude.

Clownfish pinned John-Paul's arms to the ground and stared down at him, hair framing her face like some fallen halo. "Why'd you do it? It's not fair."

"You already understand. Don't look for me. I don't want any piece of what's next."

She pushed away his arms, and cradled the back of his head with long fingers. Her lips were soft and warm. She drank his lips as a thirsty woman drowning in the sea might lap up sweet, pure rain.

John-Paul's face flushed, and when the world came back into view he saw her big eyes tremble and watched her bite the right side of her lower lip. "Wow," he said. His head swam, as if someone else had watched through his own eyes.

She rocked and knelt beside him, then stood, then, wiping her mouth with the back of her hand. "I'm...I'm so sorry."

He lay on the ground. Her eyes–visible behind her glasses–had a red tinge. "What was that all about?"

Then there was only a golden smear in the air where she had been.

Pierre poked his head out the doorway. "Clownie? Sorry, had a bit of a dustup in here too." He focused on John-Paul. "Where'd she go?"

He shook his head. "Ran off."

Pierre whistled. "That was fast. Could be a new record." He fumbled in his pocket for a moment, then tossed a small plastic card at John-Paul's feet. "Your reward."

The door closed, and he heard a brief, hurried conversation, then the grating of the balcony door, and finally a whoosh.

By the time he reached his feet, he heard locks slide into place in 308. "Pandora!" he said.

"Go away," she said.

"Let me in," he countered.

She undid two locks, then opened the door as far as the chain would allow. "You're trouble," she said.

"That wasn't my fault."

"Prove it."

"I came back, didn't I?"

"Therein proving my point."

"I wanna continue that conversation we started earlier. I'm sorry I ran off. It's just that. . . ."

"No," she said. "Let's not. It isn't."

"But I. . . ."

"No," she repeated. "No, not, nohow, nowhen, never. No thank you. No more. No, no no."

"Maybe later? Or we could talk about something else, that's fine too."

She paused. He drew little pink heart shapes in the air around her lips until her puzzled expression caught his attention. Finally she said, "You have lipstick right there."

"That wasn't my fault."

"Prove it."

"This conversation is dangerously close to self-parody."

She laughed. "*That* I can believe."

"Can I call you sometime?"

"I still have your number." Her eyes flicked toward her hand.

His hand snaked in between the door and the frame and the chain creaked as he shouldered it open. He pulled her left hand out into the dim light of the hallway. It was blank.

She waggled her right hand in front of the opening. "It was this one." Two smudges of blue ink were still visible.

"Oh," he said. "I see."

She found her shoes fascinating. "I know how to get in touch with you if I want to," she concluded, pulling her hand away and closing the door.

"Oh," he said again. He stood there for a moment. He raised his hand to knock again, feeling something witty work its way through his brain to his tongue, but it never arrived. He put down his hand and turned to walk away.

Claude watched him go, squinting until the figure turned the corner. "It's done," he said to no one in particular. "I don't know about the girl, but I think he's in. He's malleable. What a pleaser. Something bothers me about her."

Pierre shimmered into view. "Seems familiar, doesn't she? Much like our new fearless leader."

"History repeats itself. The kid too. Doesn't he remind you of– ?"

"Not now. Not here. We don't need to set her off. If she sees it too...."

"I wouldn't worry. Clownie's just rattled. Embarrassing, but it happens."

They nodded, then departed in opposite directions.

o o o

Fifth Street snaked up a hill rising from the bay. By the time John-Paul reached his destination, he had crossed the street four times to dodge sidewalk-blocking construction. Two blocks earlier, the slope had started in earnest as the street turned to parallel the water. Long, loping steps forced his torso almost parallel to the ground. His feet hurt. He paused to catch his breath, leaning against a light post amidst a crowd of tourists and workers on early lunch breaks.

The building itself was a nondescript sandstone slab which occupied the entire block. Some architectural deliberation made it appear as if a giant hand had chipped away everything that wasn't the building before dropping it into place. A brief staircase extended to the sidewalk, while a gateless, black iron fence separated the sidewalk from the immaculate grass surrounding the building. Smoky-glass windows peered out at ground level; the break between first floor and basement was at the street's level. Light escaped from a few upper-floor windows though nothing was visible inside. John-Paul looked around for other gawkers, but his was the only eddy in the stream of pedestrians.

The building's only decorations were the numbers 111 in wrought iron with brass highlights centered above two massive doors and the symbol of a waning moon carved into each door. He looked again at the plastic card; all it said was "111 Fifth Avenue, 11 am". Again he hoped he had the day right, but something about Wednesday just *seemed* to fit.

John-Paul sighed and walked around the north side of the building. The fence continued, but the building jogged in to accommodate the punctuation of a concrete pad holding immense green boxes with rounded corners and cryptic stenciled letters. They skulked an arm's length from the outside wall. Wrist-thick power lines crossed the street from the adjacent building. The dark and narrow street's one-way traffic was sparse. Behind him, the flow of pedestrians had thinned, revealing an impressive view. The clouds had begun to part out over the bay, turning the gray muck of the water into azure dappled with white and gold. Further out, the distance made even giant cargo ships tiny, visible even as far away as Freeman Island.

He jammed his left hand in his jacket pocket and fiddled with his phone. It burbled. 10:53. He resolved to search for another five minutes and then reconsider his options.

The east side of the building had a long parking strip, suitable for a bus or all but the longest single-trailer tractor rig, guarded by No Parking signs. The space stood concomitant with a gate heavier and less inviting. There was still no visible entrance. Instead, the curb inlet gave way to solid metal plates embedded in the ground at the building's foundation.

He walked down Sixth street to the south side of the building. Unlike the north side, there was ample parking here. The bay was barely visible over the top of a massive warehouse squatting as the westbound road curved south. The fence continued and the lawn remained unbroken except for two aging iron cannons atop cement pads. He paused to examine one. Its opening could have held both his fists together with room to spare. Heavy chains threaded through iron bars in the pads locked wheels half his height into place. The other cannon sat further back from the street, pointed kitty-corner toward a modernist office building. What appeared to be a crumpled fast-food bag slowly molded inside its barrel. Either someone had tremendously accurate aim, or there was a way in.

10:56. Something shimmered high to his right. He snapped his head that direction, but there was nothing. He scowled, but it happened again–and then he saw a hairline seam on the outside wall near the level of the second floor. He backed up, keeping his eyes in place, until he was perpendicular to the plane of the seam. It was a thumb's width wide at most, as if someone had closed the inner of a two-door pair on the outer door. All he could see inside was a flicker of warm light escaping from a modest glass and brass chandelier. The ceiling was high and arched so that the fixture was on the same level as heavy wood molding on the walls.

If it were a door at all, it appeared to be a normal section of outer wall. There were no visible bells or buttons or levers or knobs or knockers, nor push-bars or even a platform for entrance or egress. Yet it was clearly *an* entrance; he moved again and saw the tip of an easel with a welcome board and a long, low table with a milky blue vase sitting just in front of a truly ancient mirror with a heavy, carved frame.

"Psst," hissed a voice.

Claude crouched gargoyle-like on the southwest corner of the fence. Passing pedestrians ignored him.

"Heh," said John-Paul. "Good balance you have there."

"Shaddup." A coat hung from his frame like pounds of extra skin and his skinny elbows and knees poked through his slacks. "You're on time, boy. Early, even. I've been watching. Good thing, too. Now get on up here and let's get you to business."

The fence had a crossbar near the ground and near the top, some eight feet higher. Claude's feet formed a V between two of the spearhead spikes topping each vertical pole. John-Paul threw a careless foot on the lower crossbar and reached for the upper. Claude snickered.

"Maybe you're not so smart after all, are you? Punctual but dumb isn't a great combination. *Use the stairs, kid!*" He jerked his thumb over his shoulder toward the main entrance.

John-Paul scowled, then jogged around the east side once more. Now a gap in the fence greeted him. He couldn't see how it worked, but he ignored it and took the stairs two at a time. As he reached to pull the door open, Claude grabbed his arm. "Don't tell anyone I told you, but I'll give you a hint. Our entrance is back thataway." He nodded southward.

"I'm not in the mood for games." He tried to recall the encounter at Pandora's apartment, but his head went fuzzy. "Again?" Then John-Paul looked down to see Claude standing on empty air, level with the landing at the top of the stairs. "Oh. Nice trick. How does that help me?" He brushed away Claude's hand.

The other man stomped off. "Follow me or walk away, kid. Your choice now." He disappeared around the corner of the building, still a story off the ground.

John-Paul reached out a toe and tapped the spot where Claude had stood. It felt solid enough–even invisible, perhaps. He took a deep breath and put more weight on that foot, trailing his fingers against the building's wall in anticipation of a rapid scrabble for handholds, but solidity remained. If anything, the air felt firmer even than the cement of the landing, which wobbled in his imagination as he pushed off with his trailing foot.

He stood in the middle of the newly-revitalized business district of the city on a cushion of air at eleven in the morning on a Wednesday, surrounded by tourists and students and business-people. No one noticed. He continued around the corner, keeping his eyes on the sandy curves of the building's edge and its speckling of pigeon droppings.

Claude was gone when he reached the other side, as was the door seam. John-Paul stood where he thought it was, mentally retracing his steps between the cannons, but the wall was blank and feature-less... except for a sense of heat and light. He reached out for where the door fixture would have been if there were a door there and found nothing. He ran his hands up and down the likely spot, but all he felt was gritty stone.

He leaned back against the building and closed his eyes, then fell on his backside with a thump, knocking over the easel. A large printed sign bounced off of his head on the way down and he stared first at the wall, then the words on the sign: Code Gray, and finally his own open-mouthed reflection gaping back at him from a pair of patent leather shoes.

Charcoal pants draped lightly onto the shoes. A knife-sharp seam ran almost a yard up the length of a very tall man. He idly flicked a piece of white fuzz off of the underside of his sleeve. John-Paul watched it float idly to the ground by his own left hand. Claude's gravely chuckle pulled his gaze back to the very tall man, who filled up the hallway with his girth even more than his height.

"Better get up, kid. This is the big man himself, Titian, you see?"

John-Paul pushed himself up off of the floor and did his best to meet the large man's eyes. Something in the back of his neck creaked as stared upward. Two red eyes made tiny from rolls of fat stared back from a head the size of a toilet. The man was bald except for a top-knot which protruded about the height of a nor-mal man's fist, then hung loosely down the man's back in dozens of tiny braids. Even accounting for his enormous size, the man was unremarkable—until he smiled.

Brilliant teeth the size of John-Paul's thumbs gave a silvery glint.

"Mr. Harrison, I presume." It was not a question. John-Paul's hand disappeared into a wad of warm flesh the size of a catcher's mitt. It was surprisingly gentle and soft. "Shall we?" The man waved his other hand down the hallway.

Claude disengaged himself from the wall and stepped through an arched doorway. The room seemed larger on the inside than out, even after the high ceiling of the hallway. Even Titian seemed small inside the cavern.

The room might have been an entire floor of the building, but for a few small hallways and closets. There were no windows. Illumination came from the transparent ceiling. After squinty deliberation of the cold, silver light, John-Paul decided that it was merely a very high resolution projection of the actual weather conditions outside.

Despite the partly-clear sky and the room's size, he felt claustrophobic, as if the walls were barely sufficient to contain him. Thick, dark paneling lined the walls up to chest height, where half-columns rose to support white arches across the ceiling. One side of the room hosted a huge bar with bronze fixtures and leather stools. Private cubbies clustered on the other side, with raised seating around enormous round tables hidden behind thick curtains.

A modest fireplace flickered in the corner. Despite the relative warmth of the day outside, this room had a distinct chill. Orange flames licked at a stone structure that seemed more the bones of the building than an addition. Heavy wooden and leather chairs gathered in twos and threes, all turned individually toward each other while still partially facing the fire.

The nearest portion of the room was open and otherwise unoccupied. John-Paul turned again to Titian. The man also scanned the room, eyes flicking over all of the patrons and resting briefly in empty nooks and crevices. He drank in the room's negative spaces, ignoring the other occupants. They seemed unaware and unconcerned of his benign neglect.

A golden arm pushed aside a heavy gray curtain, and John-Paul recognized Clownfish sitting in the booth. She wore a black dress which pulled at all light in its vicinity, reflecting it back with a silvery tint. As she stood, a slit in the dress exposed a thigh as tan as her arm.

Titian motioned Claude to guard the entrance and propelled John-Paul toward the booth. Clownfish favored him a thin, sad smile and embraced Titian, stretching up on her toes despite four-inch heels, yet barely reaching the top of his shoulder. His right arm encircled her and his hand nearly covered her back.

They sat, Titian in the middle and Clownfish on the end. Somehow Titian stuffed himself into the gap between table and booth bench without spilling over onto the lacquered surface. John-Paul tried to navigate his way around the table to a point equidistant from the other two, but Titian's bulk overshadowed his actual size, and the younger man felt off-balance, as if trying to maintain orbit in a gravitationally complex closed system. Clownfish's bright blue fingernails sparkled as she pulled at the curtain. Smiling skulls in gold relief beamed out from the nails of her ring fingers.

Titian drummed fist-sized fingers on the table. His red eyes shifted between the other two, daring Clownfish to start the conversation. She leaned forward to rest the point of her chin in the palm of her hand and pursed her lips, silent and watching.

Titian rolled his eyes. The pupils vanished into his fat eyelids, giving the impression of a seizure. John-Paul wondered what would happen if the man ever sighed. "So," he began. "I understand you're new in town." It was less a statement than a question, yet spoken with no obvious desire to learn the answer.

"I've transferred for my junior year...."

"Wonderful. A good *education* is so *important*, I find. It's wonderful to find such industriousness in the youth of today. May I inquire as to your field of study, as well as perhaps your cumulative GPA?"

John-Paul tried to meet his eyes, then flinched and caught himself staring at Clownfish.

"Just get into it," she purred. His eyes snapped up. "He has this sincerity gig going on today, and he'll give you honest answers to all of the questions you never really meant to ask him. Take advantage of that while you can. It's rare and precious." She chewed her lip, and he reminded himself later to ask her what she meant.

The drumming paw stopped, then slapped the table. A metal clap rang back from the opposite side of the room a second later. John-Paul's eyes watered. The silence itself grew deeper until a gurgling chuckle burbled up and out of a meaty throat. "Ah, ha ha ha. I see. Shall we then dispense with these pleasantries and begin our delicate business negotiations?"

"Actually," shrugged John-Paul, "I had the impression that this was a meal."

"A guest might consider his host somewhat lacking if such disappointment were to occur, would he not?" Titian's left eyeball bulged and his pupil rolled downward to point at the tabletop. His bulk again seemed to expand and consume all of the air in the cubby.

Clownfish leaned back and toyed with the curtain again. "I mean it. If you're just messing with this kid to mess with him, I'm done. You either trust me or you don't, and if you don't, I can invent better places to be."

The eye returned to normal, then joined the other in a solemn restful blink. The large man brightened, and John-Paul felt tendrils of tension leach away. Titian seemed to shrink to a size still larger than normal but substantially less than his previous bulk. His left hand picked absently at a silver and red cuff-link. When he opened his eyes, they were brown and steady as he scanned his companions yet again.

"You know how difficult this is to believe," he began. "Steven, the Protector, and now Mr. Harrison. What an unstable matter."

"Yes," she agreed, idly fingering at the curtain, "but here we are."

"Yes, we three–youth, wisdom, and power. A triad untried."

She scowled, but leaned back in the booth and spread both hands on the table. John-Paul noticed a pale gap in the tan on her right ring finger. "Puns are a terrible tell." A quick smile tightened soft lines around her mouth.

"If I knew you had invited me here to watch you flirt or argue over me," said John-Paul, "I would have slept in."

He kept his face blank as they turned back toward him. Clownfish gave an air of almost infinite sadness, a personal wrenching. Titian matched the dull stare, but his eyes spoke of some gain unrealized.

"Brunch it shall be," he declared. "Are you pescetarian, my boy?" John-Paul shook his head. A waiter materialized with a bottle of champagne, an ice bucket, three flute glasses, and a tasteful arrangement of sunflowers. Titian gestured and whispered; only a ripple in the curtain betrayed the intrusion.

The champagne was sweet, but dry. John-Paul managed to hide a disastrous first sip with a wince instead of coughing and sputtering. Clownfish traced the lines of her glass with a long index finger. Titian drained his first drink and smiled a genuine smile.

"To business," he said, raising the empty glass. "Now Mr. Harrison, there seems to be some belief that you were present when the Protector, may he live well in our memories, had his unfortunate incident the other afternoon. Is that the case?"

"I didn't see it precisely, but I was in the vicinity. The Protector *died*?"

"Ahh. Hmm. I also understand that you were present when our resident clown prince decided to take advantage of the situation and liberate a small safe from the bank in which you found yourself during said unfortunate and regrettable situation?"

"The guy in the jumpsuit, yeah. I didn't catch what he wanted exactly, but he wanted something. What were you saying about the Protector?"

"There was a resulting altercation, was there not?"

John-Paul paused and squinted at the effort of memory. "Things get blurry from there. He said something and the next thing I remember, we were out in the parking lot and he was trying to strangle me. I'll call that an altercation." The word amused him on his lips.

"My sources seem to indicate that you managed to get the better of our oddly-dressed friend, to quite some degree."

"I didn't mean... it was self-defense.... He just sort of, well, crumpled."

Titian laughed again. This time there was no hint of cruelty. "According to officers Harvey and Brown, you quote 'really did a number on him'. I love their earthy turn of phrase, don't you?"

Clownfish reached out and yanked John-Paul's left arm up on the table. "Hey!" he started, as she rolled back his sleeve to expose the fresh bandage he'd applied after the morning's shower.

"How'd you get in?" She stared at him.

"I followed Claude."

"Around the building three times, or up the front stairs?"

"The stairs, why?"

She ripped away the bandage and a few stray hairs. "Ow," he began again, but stopped as he saw unbroken skin beneath. If anything, it looked healthier than it had been *before* the altercation. He pulled his arm away and examined it more closely. There was no sign of abrasion or scab. There would be no scar.

Titian fairly beamed. "On to the matter of the physical evidence, as I note with some bemusement that my colleague has so rapidly, if obliquely, recommended we discuss, may I take by your evident surprise that you expected to see a wound you received during the physical confrontation with our amusing friend? Mere hours later, there is no sign of the damage where there was a visible marking perhaps one or two hours ago. Is all of this to your understanding as well?"

John-Paul nodded. A question formed in his mind, but it slipped away as he tried to catch it.

"Chronologically speaking, I have one more question for you. Is it indeed the case that, when proceeding to the domicile of the fetching young lady whom you encountered at the conclusion of your fisticuffs, you found my attractive colleague here waiting for you with, shall I say, a small physical test of her own?"

John-Paul tried to meet Clownfish's eyes, but failed. She unhelpfully studied his face, fingers threaded on the table. His memory, however, was unhelpfully direct, even as he sensed an uncharacteristic warmth between them. He thought he could hear a faint humming, but she looked away as he looked at her lips. His heart thumped even less helpfully as he jerked his eyes back again.

"Yes," he said. "We have met." The memory twisted and skipped like film stuck in a projector. He could remember still images–photographs, really–and the thick, humid air in the hallway, but little more than still life impressions of what had seemed like a real event.

"Wonderful." Titian beamed. "Marvelous. Then I shall take all other descriptions of you and your actions exactly as delivered by this faithful eyewitness sitting here with us. How delightful." He chortled and wiped his face with a silky white kerchief that somehow appeared in his hand. For an instant, he looked nothing more than a fat, sweaty man in well-tailored clothes, but the glamour came upon him again. He opened his mouth, then snatched back a corner of the curtain with a red-veined hand to reveal an androgynous waiter clearing his throat politely.

The waiter bent from the waist at a perfect forty-five degree angle to whisper in Titian's ear. He shot up out of the bench onto his feet with a gait that belied his size. "I shall return forthwith...ah ha. Perhaps our food shall precede me!"

As the curtain closed again, Clownfish's hand snaked out and pulled John-Paul's shirt, bringing his head close to hers. His eyes closed reflexively. "Listen, kid. We have just a minute here. Whatever you do, whatever you say to Titian, tell him it's a very generous offer but you have to think about it. He'll give you a week, and that ought to be enough time to...." She trailed off, noticing that her other hand had worked its way around the back of his head to tangle in his hair.

"We can still leave, Sandie."

She released him and bolted upright, thumb rubbing the fourth finger of her right hand. Her tan paled.

"Enough time to...what?" he repeated.

She slid back down to a seated position, legs gone spaghetti-limp. Shock danced across her face. Long-practiced calm won.

"Seeing ghosts?"

She shook her head. "Enough time to figure things out?"

"I hate to sound like our fat friend, but that one particular adverb...uh, pronoun...could mean a lot of things."

Clownfish laughed. "More nasal. You almost had it though."

"Thanks. What things?"

"You're really better off not knowing." She stifled a yawn and gave a tremendous stretch.

"I see that our food has indeed *not* preceded my glorious return. How disappointing!" The curtain opened again and Titian snapped his fingers. The fleshy sound reverberated as sharp as a hand clap.

Two identical waiters appeared bearing a large silver tray. One slid it onto the table. The other whisked champagne flutes full of sparkling water beside the other glasses on the table. Lemon wedges gave them electric yellow glows. John-Paul sipped his and eyed a centerpiece with fruit piled several layers deep. He started to ask about meat when the first waiter plopped down a platter full of sausages and bacon and the other offered a plate full of hash browns.

"I myself prefer a more refined fare, but sometimes the simple pleasures of the familiar are the most profound." Titian waved a cloth napkin unfolded and tucked it into his shirt. Clownfish raised an eyebrow at John-Paul, hiding it behind a tall glass pitcher already starting to sweat.

"I agree."

"Then shall we suspend our discourses in favor of this lovely spread of nourishment?"

John-Paul opened his mouth to ask for silverware and a plate, but the waiter pair was already setting his place, tucking his napkin beneath his chin, and sliding a fork into place. He shrugged and forked a sausage.

The table was silent for a few minutes. Clownfish demolished several plates of fruit and a large bowl of cream-colored yogurt and granola. John-Paul picked out grapes and various berries between sausages, hash browns, and bacon. Titian ate everything.

As waiters cleared away the remains of the meal, Titian again filled the champagne glasses and raised his. "A toast: to new possibilities, old friends remembered, and new business successful and prosperous." Clownfish shifted with irritation.

John-Paul felt a warm glow somewhere between his third glass of champagne and the week's supply of calories he'd just ingested.

"What new business do you have in mind?" Again the words seemed to twist between his intentions and his lips, but everything still sounded sensible.

"Ah ha ha! Glad you asked, my boy. Either my intentions are much more transparent than I had imagined, or you are perceptive beyond the normal... but we have already established that you have exhibited certain abilities that put you in a certain peerage."

"Such as Clownfish here, or the Protector."

Titian shifted. "One might so say, but in the absence of a truly *objective* measure I might prefer to suggest that you possess a proclivity in that general direction, if you understand what I mean."

"Then the nature of this business is important." He cringed at how self-indulgent he sounded. Something about Titian summoned in him a false sincerity wrapped in a formality thick enough to hide nasty daggers.

"My boy, I know of no business more important, both to my interests and to the health of the city in general. Why, you have a gift, a gift found so rarely and employed so effectively that it would be almost a sin, I dare say, to neglect it. My business is very simple: ensuring that you have the time and resources to maximize your opportunities to exercise this gift for the good of our wonderful fellow citizens."

"To work for you, you mean."

"To work for the good of everyone. You have been a resident of our fair metropolis for a few days, and you have already foiled a bank robbery without suffering a scratch, at least as things have turned out. Now imagine the good you could do if you had the resources to know where to be, rather than stumbling blindly into the right situation at the right time. Perhaps we can give providence a nudge."

"I've already signed up for classes this semester. I'd really like to finish those."

"Of course, of course! Education is the only truly perfect investment, I've always said. There are plenty of opportunities that will fit between your classes and your studies. I think you'll find that it's possible to reward the best and brightest among us with generous acclaim and remuneration while still allowing them full and normal lives." He waved a sticky hand in Clownfish's direction. She scowled back, still running a bare foot up the outside of John-Paul's left leg. He squirmed.

Titian didn't notice. "I have taken the liberty of drafting a brief contract for your perusal and, I hope, your approval." He brandished a fat envelope. "The final page shows a conservative breakdown of our financial numbers. We prefer transparency even in prediction."

John-Paul slid his leg away from Clownfish's wandering toes. A distant look passed from her eyes and she jerked her napkin to her mouth. He risked an exploration with his own toes; the area around his feet was clear again.

The figures on the final page were indeed very generous, certainly more than enough to fund the family farm for the next few years. He managed to keep surprise out of his voice long enough to say, "That's a very generous offer. I'd like to think it over for a few days, if you don't mind?"

Titian clapped. "Of course, of course. There's no sense in rushing the inevitable, is there?"

"I'll let you know by next Monday. Is there a good way to contact you?"

Titian's grin was larger than John-Paul's head. "Return anytime, my boy. Just walk around the building twice and then up the staircase on the south side. Claude took you the short way, but I like to think the rest of us are civilized people. Oh, and I assume you're joining us on Friday?"

"What's Friday?"

Clownfish sputtered on her water and choked. Titian offered his kerchief but she waved it away as she turned to cough.

"What my dear beautiful friend meant to say, I believe, is that we shall lay the recently lamented Protector to rest with a tasteful memorial service. Some of us wanted to let him lie in state for a week first, to give the plebs a chance to pay respects and to say farewell to their fallen hero. Yet the specter of practicality always haunts and guides our actions, does it not?"

"He's…dead?" John-Paul forced the question, fighting the cotton in his mind and mouth. The effort left him drained.

Clownfish gulped the remainder of her water, then downed John-Paul's for good measure. Her tan had retreated from a pale green tint.

Titian blinked. "He is, unfortunately, no longer with us." "Still," he continued, "one must make the best of every opportunity, and as such I very much look forward to seeing you there. Claude will be in touch regarding the time of day and appropriate conveyance. I trust we shall see you there?"

"I…yes. Yes."

The large man grinned what John-Paul later decided was a poorly practiced smile intended to seem genuine and spontaneous. It reminded him instead of ancient fish caught occasionally by deep sea trawlers, pale from lack of sunlight and possessing too many rows of teeth. Then he pulled back the curtain and hopped lightly to his feet.

"Regrettably I cannot walk you out, but I leave you in the very capable hands of my lovely colleague as well as her, erm, erstwhile bodyguard, shall we say? Ah ha!"

Color returned to her face as her stare drilled holes in the back of Titian's skull.

John-Paul stood and shook Titian's hand. Again it engulfed his, but he noticed that it was soft and doughy, almost childlike. For the first time, he saw that the flat gold ring on the man's smallest finger was large enough to hold both of his thumbs with room to spare. The symbol was strange; it resembled nothing more than a figure eight cut in half vertically, then twisted so that the right half of the top and left half of the bottom were visible. Two tiny diamonds sparkled silver light from their positions inside each quarter of the eight.

Clownfish grabbed his upper arm at the thinnest spot, where the deltoid and bicep and triceps meet and marched him across the room. "Ow," he mumbled, half to himself.

Claude disentangled himself from the wall where he had almost become a decoration and slipped a short, sharp knife back into his pocket almost surreptitiously enough that John-Paul didn't notice. His mouth was open; his tongue clicked with a sharp intake of breath before the sour look on Clownfish's face made him pause.

"Hey...he was in a mood today, wasn't he? I'm sorry. You know, Sa...."

"Shut up," she hissed. "He set it for Friday, and you're the one making the plans for the kid. This time I'm done, I swear." She rolled her eyes up at the ceiling as they passed through the archway. John-Paul thought he heard an audible pop and he yanked his arm free and stopped. "What *is* it?" She folded her arms without turning around.

"Was that purple glow always there? I didn't see it when we came in."

"Purple?" asked Claude. Sandstone shrapnel tore into the side of his face before Clownfish could yank him to the ground, too. Blood splattered on John-Paul as he crouched on the floor. "Aw, no," moaned Claude as he slumped against the wall. "I *hate* when this happens."

"Stay sharp," Clownfish ordered. "I'm not burying two people this week."

He spit a thick wad of blood on the floor. "That gives me until midnight Sunday morning. Take this." He pressed the knife into John-Paul's hand with surprising firmness. It was nasty and sharp. "Hey. Look me in the eyes." They were brown and sad, with subtle golden flecks that made him think of nobility as well. Then Claude blinked a long, gentle blink and slumped.

"Oh no," moaned John-Paul. "I think he just...he just...."

"Don't worry about that now. He's been through worse. Titian'll just send someone through the barrier and drag him back in."

John-Paul remembered men (or women, he supposed) in padded

black shock uniforms. They wore personal shields on their left arms like ancient leather bucklers and carried arm-length rifles containing ferocious fires. They formed three rows, the kneeling front row activating powerful energy shields that overlapped and repelled bullets and beams and other projectiles, both particle and wave. The second row crouched and fired as they advanced in quick, short steps.

He looked down at his hands, strong and powerful and scarred with tiny white streaks numerous enough to form patterns but random enough that his grandchildren might one day find ships and ponies and bunnies and other forms of wonder as they sat on his lap listening to stories of bygone days, women loved, and battles won. Wasn't he holding a knife? Where had it gone?

Titian was there, and Clownfish–except that wasn't her name, and Billie, and Rondal, and Miranda, and Neveah, and Stewart, and James. Steven led them all and they loved him like a brilliant, strong, talented older brother. He floated down from the roof. Fire crackled beneath his feet, and somehow always sunbeams broke through the ceiling of the heavens to illuminate his path.

John-Paul had always expected flowers and grasses to spring up if Steven stood in place too long, reclaiming pavement and restoring nature's wild magic.

Troopers trembled. Ripples of doubt shook the line. The energy barrier dissolved in spots as soldiers gaped. The crackle and hum of overlapping shields was the only sound.

John-Paul drummed his fingers and glanced between his teammates. They were tense with energy and nervousness. James tossed a ball of energy between his hands, pushing and deforming it, then restoring the sphere. Neveah sneezed, twice, her long beaded braids flying with clicks and clacks as they jostled their way back into place.

Steven touched down and static electricity jumped from his clothes in brilliant, painful blue arcs. He smiled. He always loved showmanship. "You can do good," his words echoed, "and that's a good thing. But if you don't love what you do, if you don't put care into doing it well, doing it *right*, is it really worth doing at all?" The speech sounded hollow and rehearsed, and not for the first time John-Paul wondered if it were his words at all.

His smile was broad and genuine, not the lecherous grin of the fanatic or the well-practiced smile of the salesman trying to make you his friend before influencing you to do what he wanted all along, but a simple expression of peace and joy and the brotherhood of mankind.

Clownfish's hand closed on his. "I don't like this," she said. "It's all wrong. The Youth Corps should have been here." The roof buckled. Then the building imploded.

As John-Paul watched, two combat engineers with green arm-bands vacated the cover of brick pillars supporting a nearby office building. "They planted explosives!"

Titian appeared. Eyes jerked his way as he leaned way out over the edge of the roof and concentrated. The rumbling continued but the roller-coaster sick feeling in his stomach relented.

Dirt and pebbles showered Steven, bouncing off in improbable parabolas to form a perfect conical pile so precise in its fifty-five-degree slope that you could use it to tune architectural instruments. His smile faded as the power went out from him. He turned and watched the columns continue to crack, feeling Titian's strain and hearing subatomic agonies as electrons stayed in unstable orbits and nuclei tried to tear themselves apart and yet his heart still melted when he considered that every man or woman or child hidden bug-like in the exoskeletal armor had a wife or a husband, a mother and a father, and that the stories of their lives written individually would fill libraries of books, and it was only a horrible, terrible confluence of events that led them all here to this tangled knot of a thread in the fabric of space, and time, and intention and he sang a single pure note of the song that he'd always heard hiding in the background when he first smelled fresh air and stood barefoot in dewy green grass of the island just beyond the city's reach where he felt sunlight on his face and he sang them this single, pure note, so that they could join in the song too.

Smoke rose from a hole in his chest.

The shot echoed through the city. Then there was silence.

Steven dropped to his knees. "We had peace," he said. "Years of peace, uninterrupted. Why didn't–" His eyes flashed golden one final time, and the troops facing him threw their arms in front of their eyes. Flower petals floated gently to the ground from their guns. Their shields flickered and faded.

John-Paul saw something different this time. Superheated air rose from the barrel of one rifle. Its bearer stared in horror obvious even from the body language of a bug-like helmet and chitinous armor. He peeled off his helmet to stare more closely and there they were, the three dots tattooed on his right cheekbone in an inverted triangle.

Titian moaned and the building gained a basement by losing a parking garage; every other floor dropped a number. Clouds of dust billowed. Windows shattered and doors splintered, as if a hand had smashed the building from above. Displaced air and energy and emotion spread out *elsewhere*.

Troops flew into the air, limbs akimbo, tangling and knocking into each other. The fortunate ones landed roughly. Others splattered like freeway bugs.

Somehow, the shooter remained standing. He was field-stripping his gun, ignoring smoke rising from his gloves and the threat of blisters. He worked frantically, throwing away his helmet and tearing off his vest for better mobility. As he ejected the cartridge and went through manual diagnostics, he emitted a loud cry, a minor second above Steven's single, pure note. The ragged howl dropped him to his knees. He flung away pieces of the gun and beat the ground. "No," he sobbed, and he couldn't put a name to the grief.

Behind John-Paul, the woman who would be Clownfish hugged her knees and shook. Titian retched emptily behind an exhaust fan. Everyone else was unconscious or comatose from shock.

The ground was only 45 feet away now, so John-Paul vaulted over the rim of the roof. He was never any good at floating or making smoke and card-trick explosions. Concrete cracked like ice melting on a spring pond where he landed beside Steven.

The wound had cauterized immediately on entry and exit, and the scorch mark on the building would be visible when they excavated several months later. Steven jerked, then closed his mouth and swallowed. "Barry," he croaked. "Barry, you were always like a brother to me. I know I've said the same to everyone, but you were the kid brother I never knew. You know that, don't you?"

"Hush," said John-Paul. "I saw them drop a building on you before. This is *nothing.*"

"Ha." He coughed, reaching deeply into his lungs to find the air. "You don't understand, but you will. It's too big for me now. It always was, but he talked me into it. I *knew* better. He bested me. I let him. Now it's too late."

"Don't talk that way! No! Steven! You can't.... You can't."

He swallowed, and then peace came into his eyes. "Barry, we can win. We can win now. In a minute everyone's going to sleep, and some of us won't wake up and some of you will. You have to remember, okay? Remember this. Everything's going to change, but it's going to be the same too. You're going to have to remember what we were fighting for, because I can't promise you that anyone else will. I see it now."

"Steven...." He allowed himself the luxury of believing that he was growing stronger, that he'd climb to his feet and dust off his uniform, and that pink, healthy skin would burst free from lacerations and punctures and abrasions.

"Barry, promise that you'll remember. Remember, and keep fighting. Don't surrender, not to them and not to yourself. Promise me!"

"I promise. Steven, don't go! You can't! We need...."

The thunderclap threw him backwards, squeezing his eyes shut against the bolt of golden lightning.

Clownfish forced his head against the ground. "Head *down*, I said. You want to get yourself killed? Are you even listening?"

John-Paul flicked his right hand. White light leaped out, filling the hallway and rushing toward the false door. "I'm going. You watch after Claude here."

She grabbed his foot and yanked him to the ground. "You really are an idiot, aren't you? We don't know who's out there or what they're doing, and you're acting all indestructible. You know we're not. We've never been. Not even. . . ."

He snaked out a hand to deflect a bolt of purple energy. Sand spilled on the floor. She slapped him, and he felt his teeth rattle.

When his eyes rolled back around to the front of his skull he was back inside the great room. Aides ran back and forth. Clownfish wagged her finger in front of his face. "You don't ever, *ever* pull a stunt like that again, you hear me?" Something wild had snapped in her. Fury and excitement raised goosebumps on her bare arms, and she quivered. "I'm just about through saving you, and if this is how seriously you take it, I know a great way to prove that you're not bulletproof. We do this my way, and everyone stays safe."

She peeled at her dress. It stripped away to reveal a fitted uniform that changed colors as he looked at it. He grinned and shook his head. Then Claude caught his eye. His breath came in rough bursts, and what was left of the skin on his face grinned stupidly.

The building wobbled once more and John-Paul went down.

○ ○ ○

When John-Paul regained consciousness, the clock said 9:42 am. He groaned and rolled over. Then his phone burbled, chasing sticky strands of sleep out of his mind. "Argh," he repeated, hoping the other person didn't hear it. "Hello?"

"John-Paul. . . sweetie, are you safe?"

"Mom?"

"Oh, I'm so glad I reached you. I've been so worried. You wouldn't answer your phone! Did I wake you?"

"Yeah."

"Lazybones! It's almost 10 in the morning. Why aren't you awake?"

He swam through thick fog back to consciousness. His jaw hurt and something pounded in his head, but it wasn't the hangover haze of alcohol and dancing. "I don't think so. I've been pretty busy and haven't watched the news much. Is it about that Protector guy?"

"No. There was a *bombing* downtown yesterday. They announced it a couple of hours ago. At first they thought it was just a collapse of an old building under renovation, but now they're saying it was deliberate. A bomb, can you imagine? Tell me you're safe, honey. Tell me you're staying safe and won't go in any buildings they're going to bomb. I have to run, but promise me you'll be safe, honey. Stay safe, okay?"

He sat up in bed. Sleep was now the last thing on his mind.

o o o

Clownfish threw another outfit on the floor. More clothes piled behind her than remained in her closet. She'd reached the dusty, dark back corners of her wardrobe, where every blouse or skirt scrabbled long fingers through boxes packed once and forgotten as she moved from place to place and era to era.

She had absolutely *nothing* to wear.

This had happened before. She and Titian and not-quite-Claude gathered near dawn in a thin strip of park running along the northern finger of the bay. Seabirds wheeled. Tidal winds spread the scent of salt and near-fog inland through the western neighborhoods. She'd worn all black, then–a sensible black suit, modest heels, and a pillbox hat and veil, bought in the grip of a grim humor. No one laughed that morning.

Barry arrived late, pale and reeling, complaining of dizziness and vomiting. He fingered a scrap of Steven's costume as an eidetic totem: a scrap of brilliant blue fabric, singed and torn but dazzling. It reflected stray morning light from the pearl-gray clouds at odd angles.

Then they were four–three plus one–standing in silence around bare earth. Steven had brought them here individually in the beginning, to explain how easy access to ocean-bound shipping and the confluence of fresh water and fertile delta attracted the city's earliest settlers. He pointed north and south and east at landmarks visible only in memory as he described the founding of tiny villages which grew into townships and boroughs and, since then, to the post-unification city itself. He concluded, as always, by moving his feet to reveal a bronze disc, inscribed with geographical information: the starting point for every one of the city's navigational systems. This was the origin. Industry and business and suburbs and exurbs had their own centers and poles, but they all described complex, strange orbits around the city itself.

"Remember the beginning," he would say. "Without your center–the starting point–you cannot know where you are going."

She knelt in dewy grass to brush wind-blown silt from the marker. A cargo ship slipped by in the bay, a gray duller than the morning's clouds.

Barry crouched beside her. "Hey."

"This is everyone? This is what's left?" She covered the disc's coordinates with a pale hand. She didn't shake.

"Of Steven, or of everyone?"

"It's not fair. He didn't *do* anything. He never did."

"Everything ends sometime. Prepare for it as long as you like, but it's still knife-sharp. You always think you have more time, and you never realize you've wasted the little moments until you miss them."

"It didn't have to end."

Titian wore a light white suit he'd picked up on a trip to the tropics. He looked strange out of uniform, fanning a thin-brimmed hat. Even in the chill air sweat still pocked his forehead. He was always built like a fat man, even then when most of his bulk was muscle. "Joggers will be here soon. We only have a few minutes of privacy." He sighed and glared at the ship, but it continued its slow journey north.

At the grass's edge, a thin ribbon of pavement spit oily black pea-sized stones into the greenery. Claude stared up and down the path. "It's empty." No one questioned his presence, assuming that he belonged there just as much as they did, or perhaps that each of them belonged there as little as he did.

Barry put his head between his knees.

Clownfish wiped her hands in the grass, then shook off the dew and she stood. "You okay?"

He raised a hand to wait, then looked up. "Still dizzy. It feels like the world's spinning all around me now, like I'm the center of its rotation. . . like I'm the only one keeping it from careening off into space."

She laughed. "You sound like him, like he used to talk. Minus the poetry, of course." Formless, translucent blobs bobbed in her view and she adjusted her veil again.

She wanted to ask about the others—the absent, fortunate ones who'd managed to wake up with most of their mental facilities intact. Miranda had broken out of the hospital. Her most recent sighting was in an airport security line, staring at the ubiquitous monitoring cameras with an odd look in her eyes. The rest of the tape was blank.

Neveah simply refused to talk, bodily throwing both Barry and Titian out of her apartment without apparent malice or comment. A week later no one in her building remembered her.

In a month they could enter their building again, this time as representatives of secretive shell companies Titian had created to lease the other offices. Already the event blurred in their minds. Seven months later, when reconstruction began in earnest, it had become a shared myth: gods raining down on the earth to trick and expose the wicked. "The bombing," everyone nodded, the sage two-word denouement of their glorious revolution.

This was their legacy. Clownfish discarded a sleek suit and sighed at the memory of size zero. This was their bloody, useless legacy. These were the wages of their choices. She offered the ceiling a fair trade: let her never again bury a friend or colleague and she would never mouth the useless platitudes and slogans of those days.

Titian gathered them into a rough square around the disc to offer words of memorial. Barry mumbled about Steven's current whereabouts, hoping that he was in peace. Clownfish sobbed the word "goodbye". Claude refused to speak.

The sun burned at the edges of the fog, but her past grew murkier. They melted away, the three plus one, to drink or work or sleep away shock and pain and anger. The weeks after blurred in subconscious sensory experiences: work, sleep, lethargy, waving to neighbors whose names she vaguely remembered as she drove in and out of the perfectly suburban driveway of her new house with the pastel-perfect crocuses.

Sometimes she missed the raw emotion of the city with its own animal logic and the noises and the sounds and the smells of several million people packed into a narrow strip of real estate jammed between mountains and water. She moved back a few months later, eschewing the planned desperation of her too-perfect neighborhood for glorious chaos and her old friends. Fate and necessity and a new sense of the old mission joined them together again as they sat among rubble piles in their ruined basement.

She threw the suit on the pile.

The air was perfect with poison. She gasped at a sudden desire to slip beneath the water's calm surface until her lungs stopped burning, to sink–to float–near the bottom of rough waters until the ripples of her presence stilled. The ache shook her as tangibly as the desire for sleep, or food, or the brush of a loved one's hand.

The last item in her closet was a perfectly preserved dry cleaning bag spotted with cobwebs. Despite the intervening years, she knew the contents would fit. She hated it for its perfection of form and its subtle appropriateness. Its dark weave was as black as the day she bought it, two funerals ago.

○ ○ ○

John-Paul crouched. He was *certain* something had happened here, but there was no sign of the scuffle, no scratch or tear or break in the wall's smooth blandness. Likewise the door seemed intact. It hung straight, with no frame damage or chipped paint. He complimented himself on his amateur forensics skills while berating himself for not knocking already.

The flowers had already drooped in the hallway's urban hothouse. He fanned them through the air, hoping wind would revive them, as he pushed away the sentences he'd rehearsed despite his own best intentions, willing them not to bubble out like the proclamations of a crazed street prophet.

He knocked. She answered. She looked fantastic in a knee-length navy dress. He blinked. "Wow. Wow."

"Right. Well?"

"Um, hi." He thrust the bouquet at her. Reflexes took over: she reached both hands to receive them, holding the door with her hip, and smelled deeply. "These are *beautiful*!"

He beamed.

"Why are you here?"

He bit his tongue, lest it take off on the rehearsed conversational paths, dragging him bruised behind. "I figured we're going to the same place. It doesn't feel like the sort of event anyone should go to alone."

That pulled her nose out of the bouquet. "Do you have any idea what happened the last time you came around here?"

"No, Pandora. I don't. I don't even know why I came back that day. I can't come up with a reason that makes any sense besides that it felt right. If I'm wrong, I'm sorry, and if you want me to go, I will. Look me in the eye and tell that's what you want. I'll go." His intestines shivered as he tried not to ask himself why he should be so honest to someone he'd talked to for all of an hour, who'd slammed the door on him the last time they met, and who hadn't called. He flashed a smile he hoped looked more sincere than rehearsed.

"I like your flowers anyway. I'm going to put them in water." She closed the door. He counted to ten, then twenty, and promised he'd stop counting before the hidden cameras caught him in an awkward lie. He counted to ten again, then leaned back on the windowsill and closed his eyes. Mark David had talked him into buying one nice suit with their graduation money. His girlfriend at the time taught him how to shop for shoes that wouldn't cut off circulation after thirty seconds of standing. He thanked her for that, at least.

"You look pretty good yourself," she said. His eyes snapped open. A black shawl covered her shoulders. Her camera bag dangled at her side. It almost complemented her shoes.

"I didn't hear the door open."

"I came up the back way to watch you. You obviously think this is important. First question, you tell me. What's going on?"

"I wanted to ask you the same question. I grew up in Goshen, right? We visited the city maybe once, twice a year. I've never heard of the Protector before this week, but everyone seems to take him for granted. I've lived here officially a week and even I'm starting to have trouble remembering a time when there wasn't a Protector, and he apparently died two days after I arrived."

"Good."

John-Paul raised his eyebrows.

"I was afraid you were going to ask me if this was a date. That's a much more dangerous question."

"Dangerous? Dangerous... how?"

"Is there a good answer?"

"Number one, you spoiled the question by asking it. Number two, you changed the subject."

She chewed her lower lip. "I did, didn't I? I'm sorry. Let me put on my serious hat." She pantomimed a sidestep into a dressing room where she crowned herself with an invisible tiara, patting the curl of her hair into place with the practiced economy of royalty.

John-Paul rubbed his eyes. "Is it impossible for you to be serious? Just give me a straight answer to something." Her big eyes drilled into his soul. His face heated.

"I...can't," she said. "I can't tell you why. I just...can't discuss it. I want to but the ideas just slip out of my mind. It's like when you're absolutely sure there's someone following you, and you keep turning around, but there's nothing there."

He nodded. "That's right. No, wait. That's not right. That doesn't make any sense. What are you telling me?"

She shrugged. "I don't know?"

"Don't be coy. Please."

Her right hand had balled into a white-knuckled fist; she shook with effort. "I just don't remember." A tear escaped. "I want to, but I *don't*." She pushed her hand against her lips and sniffled.

John-Paul offered a tentative hand. "Hey," he said. "You have really soft shoulders." She half turned, sniffling again through a half smile, and caressed his hand. "They're waiting for us downstairs."

"Who?"

"I...don't know. Did I wake up on the stupid side of the bed this morning? My head feels, hazy, I guess, like I'm walking through a thick fog or someone sneaked in and stuffed cotton in my ears."

"Me too. It feels good to admit that." Pout lines in her forehead and around her lips melted.

He led her downstairs. Their fingertips brushed and sent tingles through his arms. Outside a black limousine purred. A blandly handsome chauffeur opened the door and offered Pandora his gloved hand. "Ooh," she called. "It's *shiny* in here."

They sat together in leather seats deep and spacious enough that they'd have to lean in to speak if they'd chosen the corners. Tinted windows polarized the light such that even the brightest days would barely raise the ambient inside temperature or bedazzle the occupants.

John-Paul's eye lit on the full eclipse of an enormous sunroof. "How did you know you were coming with me," he wondered. "Or is that too close to the awkward question?"

"Can't a girl dress up once in a while without risking interrogation?"

"Do you always answer a question with a question?"

"Don't you?"

He gasped in mock offense. "How could you tell?"

She laughed. "You win this one. Let's just say I had a feeling that if I showed up I'd be able to talk my way into a private ceremony."

He smiled. "Pretty girls can be convincing, but that doesn't explain it. Assignment from work? Hey, ouch!"

She shook out her hand, then blew on her knuckles. "Ouch, yourself ox-boy. You bale a lot of hay on that farm, huh? Or were you too poor to buy a tractor and too stubborn not to pull the plow by yourself?"

"Something like that."

"You may be a farmboy and you did just break my hand. but you saved me cab fare. We're even."

"It's a deal, if you promise to stop laughing. We *are* going to a funeral, you know." Something clicked in his head. "Hey, did you ever meet this guy?"

"No, never."

"Me neither, unless you count almost crashing into a building I was in as a formal introduction."

She shrugged. "I'd have held out for a handshake. Maybe an autograph, but you've already done that." She offered her hand and they shook. "*Now* we really can go to this thing together."

"Good point. You can let go of my hand now."

"Ooh, sorry."

"You're a terrible liar."

The limo glided to a stop and the silent chauffeur opened the door. Pandora punched John-Paul when he turned back to close the door, then choked back giggles. "Hey," he whispered. "Solemn occasion."

She snickered harder.

"Stop it," he hissed. "Game faces, remember?" He dropped his head and eyes and stuck out a pouty lower lip. "Oogly boogly!"

"You're drunk." She slapped him on the chest. He staggered. "Ooh," she said. "Pretty."

They stood halfway up a hill, beneath an arch of parallel aspen trees. Bricks formed a path which curved up to the crest. Beneath them lay a well-tended valley with a dazzling stone pavilion one end and a small pool fed by a bubbling creek at the other.

"Did you know this was here?"

"I had no idea. I've seen the trees from the road before but I didn't know there was such a nice park in the middle of downtown!"

Rows of white chairs dotted the grass in front of the pavilion. Most of them had occupants. "Ulp...looks like we're late." He snorted, and she doubled over with silent laughter. "Stop, ha ha.... stop it!" He forced himself to shoot her a stern look. She clamped both hands over her mouth, shaking from the effort. "Listen. Just breathe with me, okay?"

She nodded, squeezing her eyes tight.

"Deep breath in. Good. Now breathe out." She snickered. He clenched one fist in his pocket and bit his lip. "That's okay." A shiver danced the tarantella on his spine.

"Alright. Whew." She fanned herself. "Am I red or what?"

"Little bit."

"Shaddup, you're gonna make me...heh. Okay. It's under control. Heh."

He clenched his eyes shut and thought of baseball, wheat fields, and the bay roiling with wind and the wake of uncountable ships. The feeling passed. "Inappropriate," he mused.

"What?"

"I was hoping you'd tell me." Her eyes kept sliding away from his. "M'lady?" He straightened his jacket and offered his elbow.

"Okay, okay...please stop!" She tapped her left foot and rapped her fist on her thigh.

69

"You look like you just swallowed a lemon. Oh sheesh, sorry!" She stifled another laugh and waved him to be quiet. He leaned against a tree stump. "I'll just have a seat until you get it out of your system."

She threw back her head and screamed. Birds took to the air. Semi-domesticated urban forest creatures scurried for cover. John-Paul hid behind fanned hands as several heads snapped up in the clearing below.

Pandora pulled her shawl tight and hitched up her camera bag. "Much better."

"You're amazing. Did you know that?"

"Nice of you to recognize. A lady gets tired of waiting." She grabbed his arm and they strolled down the path.

A near-twin of their driver met them as they approached the chairs. He held a sign reading "Harrison/d'Avril" and lead them around the left side to the second row.

Clownfish scowled behind dark glasses. Pierre twisted and un-twisted a candy wrapper. "Uh," said John-Paul, gazing after the silent usher. "You, uh, remember Pandora right?"

"I love your shoes," Pandora said. "Where did you get them?"

Clownfish looked over the rims of her glasses, a tiny smile on her lip. "Oh, I have had these for *years*. I never have a good reason to wear them. Your shawl is darling, by the way...."

John-Paul stepped over the empty front row and sat in the seat in front of Pierre. "Hey...how's Claude?"

"Eh?"

"You're Pierre, and he's Claude? We met at Pandora's house, and then Claude took a nasty hit in the explosion the other day. Clownfish said he's in the hospital."

"Nobody told me you were there, kid."

A cold wind ruffled the grass and sliced through John-Paul's jacket. "I didn't see anything, except that he was pretty beat up." The temperature dropped further as a shadow fell on him.

"My dear boy, how considerate of you to warm my seat for me!" Titian beamed. He wore an enormous white suit with a light gray vest. A pocket watch dangled from a chain; he carried a walking stick black as coal with a tarnished silver knob.

Pierre leaned back in his chair and smiled at a group of mayoral aides clustered around a man in a long trench coat and a hat pulled low on his forehead. The women nudged each other and tittered and waved; the man slipped away into the back row with uncharacteristic authority.

"Oh, Titian. Good to see you again." John-Paul rose and offered a hand, trying not to wince as the fleshly embrace consumed his hand.

"Let us hope fervently to meet infrequently at such events, hmm?" The large man eased himself into the chair. "Such a shame, you know. We had pinned so many hopes and dreams on Barry, hadn't we?"

"Barry?"

"The Protector. He had a real name. He was more than a mere amalgamation of our best intentions. He was as real as you and I– and I have confidence, my boy, that you will join us in the inner circle. We all await your answer in the affirmative this coming Monday, correct?"

"Uh, yes... I'll have an answer for you then."

"Excellent. Now as pleasant as our small talk is, I do believe the service is starting." The knots of standing conversations untied and dissolved and filled the remaining seats. John-Paul slipped next to Pandora and tried to identify the various ranks and relationships of everyone else, but failed when he hit the second row on the other side and ran out of politicians whose faces had peppered the front page of the newspaper in the past three days.

The service lasted an hour and twelve minutes. He shifted in his chair and counted backwards and tried to invent plausible reasons for putting his arm around Pandora before finally getting bored and faking a yawn. She leaned in and whispered, "This is almost as dull as city council meetings."

"Why give the key to the city to a dead guy?"

She shrugged. "You don't have to worry about him stealing things."

He covered his snicker with a fake sneeze. Titian offered a lily-white satin hankie over his shoulder.

The speeches were predictable and dull until Clownfish ascended the makeshift steps under curious eyes.

"Hi. Um. Hi everyone.

"I don't know what to say. Thank you, I suppose, for coming to pay your respects. He would have appreciated it.

"We don't have it easy. We have respect and power. I can't imagine doing anything else, but it's no easy life. Imagine walking out your door in a cloud of recognition. Imagine losing your temper for just one moment and forever tainting your reputation. Imagine having every move you make criticized, how you accidentally dropped a building on someone who was trying to hurt other people. No matter how many people you save, someone always calculates the cost of collateral damage. No one weighs that against the potential costs of loss of life, or limb, or property, or security, or freedom. You can't. You have a fraction of a second in which to decide to act.

"I make no excuses. I ask no sympathy. This is neither the time nor the place for regrets. He had none. I know this. If you spent time around him, you know he was the best of us. He wasn't perfect, but we were all the better for having known him.

"He was never one for speeches. He'd never be caught dead...." She winced. "He'd never speak to a crowd when he could meet a person for a real conversation, but I can say something he always felt but never said. Thank you. Thank you all. Thank you for trusting us with your lives and your families and your safety. Our work is difficult, but we only do it for you. We couldn't do this without you, and it wouldn't be worth doing without you. That's how he felt. That's how we all feel. Thank you."

Polite applause accompanied her back to her seat. Pierre blew his nose and Titian nodded approval. Pandora reached over and squeezed John-Paul's hand. "What was that for? Not that I'm complaining."

"Just because."

The mayor announced that the city planned to rename a street in honor of the Protector and would erect a statue in the town square as soon as the city council could approve a design. Titian remarked over his shoulder. "I made a strong suggestion that it stand in front of our building or, barring that, an expansion of the waterfront park, but they refused to listen."

Clownfish studied the crowd. Something wistful played on her face.

The emcee asked everyone to stand for a moment of silence. It ended with the firing of an antique cannon. "Hey," whispered John-Paul. "Is that one from the. . . ?"

Pierre snorted. "Just a replica. Ask Claude about it sometime. Funny story."

The mood of the crowd lifted as the smoke and report faded. The funeral broke up into clumps of conversations.

"I trust you found your conveyance more than satisfactory?" Titian nodded at John-Paul and Pandora.

"Oh, yes. It was more than satisfactory. Thank you."

"My pleasure. I don't believe I have met your pretty young companion, though."

John-Paul flushed. "Oh. This is Pandora, Pandora d'Avril."

Titian took her hand and brushed his lips across her knuckles. "Charmed, I'm sure. Are you a photojournalist? Your handbag is of a size appropriate for nothing as much as photography accoutrements."

Then she blushed. "Oh, my. I completely forgot. Yes, and I need to get some photos. Would you all mind. . . ?" She dug in her bag, mumbling about overcast outdoor lighting and film speeds and apertures, waving the the other four into a straight line when one hand found itself free.

John-Paul watched Clownfish squeeze between the enormous Titian and a sullen Pierre. Even beside the large man, she loomed taller than he'd ever noticed.

Pandora snapped together a large lens and flash combination. "I only need a few shots, so look friendly and smile!"

Titian grabbed John-Paul's arm as Pandora pulled Clownfish aside for some solo photos. "You're making a fine choice, my boy. I know how difficult this will be for you, but this particular young lady is strong and smart and, perhaps most importantly, very tough."

"Huh?"

He winked. "Trust an old man, son." He twisted his head, listening. "Ah, I do believe our rides await!"

As John-Paul turned toward the path, a cloud dimmed the already-weak sunlight. The sound of boots shuffled into place. An enormous figure crested the eastern hill, a bald, bland humanoid, blank eyes staring ahead, raising its right hand parallel to its body.

It was the statue Progress from the town square. That statue was eight feet tall. This version was several times that size... and mobile.

Smaller figures in black armor and helmets marched in wary formation near the feet of the statue. "Hand over the body," purred an electronic voice. "We have you surrounded."

Clownfish narrowed here eyes. "Forget that." The air around her crackled.

"Wait–" said Titian.

"What?" asked John-Paul.

"Not these guys again." Pierre shook his head.

Clownfish's dress burned away in a swirl of colors. They shuffled and mixed together in rainbows and sworls of hues. Fire leapt from her eyes.

Titian scrambled and caught her arm. "There are hundreds of civilians. Think of them... this isn't the place."

She pushed him away and leaped. The statue's leaned forward, raised hand swatting her from the air. It continued and ground its palm into the ground. Titian fell backwards into Pierre and they rolled down the hill. The figure straightened to reveal a large crater. Troops rushed to its perimeter, postures wary and guns raised.

John-Paul shrugged out of his jacket and thrust it at Pandora. "Hold this for me."

"What? No... you're crazy."

He kept his eyes on the statue. "Trust me. I only own the one jacket. Get everyone else to safety. I'll distract it."

"Wait, stop!"

John-Paul ran. The iron monster swiveled to watch as he crashed through the line of troops bowling over several.

Pierre staggered back up the hill, panting. "Where'd he go? Oh." He followed Pandora's scowl. "Hey, give him one for me, kid!" Several heads jerked their direction, guns following, and he pushed in front of Pandora. "Looks like they like the hard way. Get everyone else out of here."

"Don't call me *kid*," John-Paul yelled. He threw his arms out sideways and thrust out his chest. A dark funnel formed and swirled and frothed in the sky above him. A blinding beam of golden light leapt from him to the clouds and back. Something came upon him.

Flame licked at his hands. The molten iron of his torso gleamed. His eyes were terrible, cold gems. The ground rippled beneath his feet and he took one slow step and another and then he was running. The stunned air behind him slapped together in sloppy, tiny sonic booms.

He thrust a fist in front of him, the point of a spear as he left the ground. The force of his yell cracked windows. Waterfalls of shattered glass poured onto the streets.

The golem moved in an eye-blink, but it was not fast enough. John-Paul hit it near the left shoulder joint. The creature spun backward as its arm tore away. It screamed wordlessly at the useless stump.

John-Paul skidded to a stop on a rooftop, kicking up a spray of pebbles and a surprised flock of pigeons. He shuddered. Flaming metal fragments sprayed from his hair and dripped from his fist. The golem swung its head and blinked blank eyes. It shuffled into position and leaned forward. Ruby energy sliced the air. John-Paul dove to his left as the smell of scorched tar and sublimating steel girders rose in clouds of steam and particles. Ducts vanished in a trail of silver goo.

The creature marched, nudging aside cars and streetlights. Past the machine, John-Paul glimpsed Clownfish pulling herself out of cracked ground, Titian and Pierre battling the men in black helmets, and Pandora overseeing fleeing mourners. Over his right shoulder, the bay stretched out to Freeman Island, and then the ocean.

The remaining hand opened to swat at him like a fly, but he rolled over the lip of the roof and jumped at a brick patio across the street. He overshot and mangled a fire escape as he landed. His breath escaped with a low groan. The building rebounded and resonated. "What have you done for me lately, earthquake mitigation codes?" he wondered, sucking in air. The whole structure groaned as bolts pulled away from the wall. His fingers scrabbled for handholds. They fell in a tangle.

He jumped free at the last second, landing in a pile of garbage bags. "Kitty litter!" he thought, but scrabbling in folded cardboard and discarded clothing. Nearby clanks focused his attention. He allowed himself a few short breaths, then jogged down the alley to put the building between himself and the creature.

An enormous head peered between the buildings, then blinked in confusion at the empty alley. It raised its palm to eye level, then shrugged. As its gaze swung upward to the rooftops, John-Paul yelled and brought both fists together somewhere between its eyes. The golem's head wrinkled; a seam on the right side burst, spewing clouds of steam and sparks. The monster reeled, then lost its balance. Its remaining arm clawed at an apartment building but undershot, tearing off the front wall. Furniture rained down to the ground in a mist of water from broken pipes.

John-Paul wrinkled his nose as he judged the distance to the bay. They were close to a park but far from the fountain, the square, and open spaces where people might gather. Something suggested an abandoned quarry, but he dismissed the idea; none were visible.

The golem worked itself to its feet with its remaining arm, knocking over a large elm tree. It rocked and flailed, then steadied itself. John-Paul jumped up and down and waved his arms. "Hey! Over here!" It lumbered after him, favoring its right leg.

He leaped across rooftops, landing lightly, only once cracking masonry with a careless footfall. He watched a stone gargoyle fall seven stories into a flowerbed, shaking the leaves of a purple azalea in full bloom. "Mom grows those," he thought. Behind him, the air sizzled as another eye beam charged. Heat from the twin beams singed his hair. He imagined the aglets on his shoelaces catching fire like misplaced candle wicks, then resolved to have himself checked for a concussion as soon as possible.

"Ahhhhhhhhhhhgh!" he shouted at nothing and no one. Lightning crackled around him and struck twin tines at the statue. A transformer exploded near its feet. It slapped hot oil and sparks away from its leg. Its features had grown more lifelike. He leaped to a rooftop three stories lower, as apartments gave way to one- and two-story buildings.

He stumbled and skidded to a stop. The northernmost tip of the bay park was a sandy finger across a four lane one-way street empty of cars. Gentle gray waters lapped at a stone wall interrupted occasionally by wood and concrete piers. He looked both ways, then ran across the street, chuckling at his instinct to watch for traffic while fleeing a hostile seven-story ambulatory statue.

A thin path of tan, hard dirt separated the park from unclaimed wildlands. Millions of feet preferred to cross the grass than to skirt the hardscrabble brush, dunes, and gravel piles leading to the stone wall. He took his stand there, daring the monstrous statue to meet him.

It came lumbering between a bank and a half-circle plaza of

restaurants and shops. It swung from its left torso with a violent jerk, as if throwing a punch with its missing arm and John-Paul grinned.

Something old and powerful swam through his muscles, clenching them. He felt the ground propel him upward. He landed feet-first on the side of the statue's head, willing his momentum to continue. The sound of another seam popping rewarded him as he flipped backwards and slid down the thing's chest. He gave another push, and rolled away as it slapped at his previous position. Its head rang, hollow and dull.

Its lips parted and the statue gasped, drawing its first breath. A moan—a low hum of sorrow and pain and rage—echoed across the bay. It raised its right foot, hip and leg seams screaming, and stomped.

He waited and concentrated and willed time to slow until the precise moment to jump up and kick, spinning from the pelvis to add a fraction of rotational velocity to the remaining friction of the sole of his abused shoe. The impact caught the bottom of the golem's foot and spun its leg. The statue crashed to the ground, inches away. The shockwave made his teeth ache and his head ring, but a hip joint burst with a screech. He rolled far to the side, hoping that it would fall and be still, but it moaned again.

"Come *on*," he screamed. It rocked back and forth, trying to convince its right leg to move. John-Paul dove for the thing's shin, then climbed its leg by punching handholds, one over the other, until he stood on its knee to look it in the eyes. He stood on its knee and looked it in the eyes. It blinked, and swung its right hand.

He flopped on his back and punched the hand as it whizzed by overhead. The arm seam tore away. Animate metal tumbled end around end, sparking and skipping and skidding and skipping to rest near a small white pavilion. "That's June from my calendar last year," he thought.

The statue's eyes cycled to red as it prepared another beam strike. John-Paul rushed up its leg again, atop a thigh parallel to the ground. The statue drew back its head, and he dove for the water, off of the knee, as the beam burned the air in his wake.

He landed hard and flat and tried to keep his lungs full of air as he skipped across the water. He lost velocity after four bounces, and sliced downward through the gentle waves. Steam rose above him, but the beam faded.

When his lungs burned, he pushed himself to the surface for a timid gasp. He sputtered and looked around. No noise–not even seabirds–interrupted his splashing. He kept his eyes on the horizontal debris as he frog-swam until his toes touched the sandy bottoms. Nothing happened.

The statue lay one-legged, face down, great cracks decorating its body. A pool of liquid metal cooled beneath it. Its head had smashed the stone wall; it stared unblinking into cold gray water. The remains of the severed leg had fallen over separately.

He shook sand and water out of his hair and wrung out his clothes. A wave of weariness sent him to his knees in a tuft of untouched grass. One last burst of energy stood him, righteous energy propelling him to condemn his foe to the perpetual grinding of sand and surf. He dragged the remains of the statue into the water, where unceasing waves licked at cracks and fissures, dragging it first to the bottom of the bay, then further to the endless sea by tide and wind.

He wanted it gone, the offensive reminder of a swath of debris and destruction he'd personally lead through the city, far from the untouched sanctuary of his apartment and hours away from his mother and twin brother. Then his vision shifted to Pandora and Clownfish and the others as he considered a park full of mourners a fine trade for a few buildings.

○ ○ ○

Titian slammed the report on his desk. His tidy inbox exploded into a blizzard of entropy. He leaned forward and massaged his temples, running his fingers through his hair. From every angle he considered, he could only reach the same inconclusive result as that blasted report.

No one had any idea what had happened, who was responsible, or why anyone could or would attack a secretive memorial service known only to the city's elite.

He snickered, hating the situation's grim humor. He'd run out of fingers and toes before he could stop counting potential leaks. The calculated risk of holding a service was tiny in comparison to the risk of denying that nothing had happened. People *saw* Barry's final act. A likely replacement for the Protector had appeared in the right place at the right time. Give them a chance to grieve, Titian had ordered. They'll forget again in a few days. He mocked himself out loud, "Long live the dead king," still half believing it to be true.

He pondered again the dark-haired girl. She seemed young and harmless, but unplaceably familiar. Every time he thought he had it, his mind slipped away, like marbles through greasy fingers. She'd appeared out of nowhere in the same fashion as the kid, as if there were a connection. Fontaine had received an invitation, of course, but he'd declined, calling it "the kind of sideshow distraction your organization specializes in". Had he relented and sent her as a spy?

Titian pressed a fat thumb to his desk just so and spoke in a low voice. "Have Pierre check Mr. Harrison's invitation and alert me to any connection to Ms. d'Avril."

Two sweeper teams had worked through the afternoon and into morning's small hours to remove all traces of the giant statue and the battalion. His most trustworthy staffers were still crunching plausible scenarios for another attack.

His left knee throbbed. He poured a glass of ice water and palmed another analgesic, feeling the pill catch in his throat before peristalsis could continue. "I'm getting too old for this," he said to no one in particular. "I never wanted to be a bureaucrat, never wanted to be a fighter, and never wanted to bury any of my friends." The report didn't answer. He flung it across the room. It fluttered, an angry moth.

The sudden violence resonated with a hot thread of anger still present from the previous day. He blinked, feeling salty-hot water well in his eyes as images washed over him.

Titian rolls to a stop at the bottom of the hill, fuming, only to dive out of the way. Pierre groans as he follows, landing in the same spot. The milling crowd turns at the sounds of crashes and curses. Titian climbs to his feet, brushing away crushed grass and feeling a rising anger. "Go on, get out of here!" he threatens. "Go! Move!"

Pierre, kneeling, shakes his head. He works his jaw, where he'd taken a fleshy elbow, and tries to convince his eyes to focus. Titian drags him to his feet and points at their retreat. "Are there any troops up there? Tell me!"

"No," he groans. "Just to the east."

"Good. We're cleanup this time."

"Titian. . . it's like before, isn't–"

"With hundreds of civilians to keep safe." He pants as he runs up the hill, pulling at shrubs and weeds for speed and balance. Pierre breezes past, and he resolves yet again to lose a couple of hundred pounds or learn how to control gravity.

Pandora tears downhill as he nears the crest. The mob below shouts and roils. He raises his hand to catch her attention, but she's gone before he can catch his breath to offer a suggestion or encouragement or a stupid question. Pierre, dancing, dodges bullets and lures half of the troopers away from the crater. Titian assumes Clownfish is still there, dazed, confused, and stuck. There's no sign of John-Paul or the statue, but the ground shakes and he wobbles. The creature appears behind a building, head rearing back in pain.

His knees creak. Filthy sweat pours down the back of his shirt, but he concentrates and launches himself. His silver blur bowls down several soldiers. Chitinous cracking explodes outward. Bodies shred through trees like shrapnel. He sticks the landing and pauses for breath. A tearing sensation raises the hair on his arms, stuck somewhere between emotional and physical. The shouting has increased but the shooting has decreased. Their distraction has begun.

"Freeze, fat boy!" Heavy distortion crackles the voice, which resonates as if it were inside his head. A safety disengages. A bolt clicks into place. He raises his hands, turning to see a short, thin attacker. He's far enough away to squeeze the trigger before Titian can clip him at the knees. Where did the incompetent PSF gunmen go? They used to stand within arm's reach. He feels tired and old and unwilling to bet that several inches of well-groomed fat will stop a bullet at this range.

"I'm unarmed." He winces at the gravel in his voice.

The figure nods and turns its head sideways. "Bravo one, this is Bravo niner, and I have target two immobil–"

Titian swims through the echo of the voice and brings his hands together. A thunder crack of sound launches the trooper and his gun in opposite directions.

His pockets hold nothing identifying. His pockets hold *nothing*. A piercing scream sets off the throbbing in Titian's bones. The ground buckles, and he clutches a tree for support as clods of dirt and small pebbles and a very surprised worm pelt him.

"This suit will never come clean," he thinks.

Larger objects bounce by: two soldiers, helmets shattering as they crash together, and a boulder. He ducks, scooping up sidearms and a loose rifle, and runs toward the blast.

Clownfish hovers. Oily reflections distort the scene through a rainbow of blue and yellow and orange; a bubble of power surrounds her. White light erupts from her breastbone. Groaning troops crawl away, but she aims terrible fists and earth erodes beneath them. They drop away into a muddy crater where her dress lies crumpled and filthy.

She turns to the south and gestures. Trees explode in puffs of toothpicks and pine needles. More black-clad troops crash together.

Titian feels muffled thumping in the earth; Pierre finishes off the rest.

Clownfish's pupils roll forward as the bubble floats to the lip of the crater. Titian shuts his eyes against the soapy pop and catches her as she stumbles. "Dizzy," she says, "but alright. Give me a minute. I think I caught all of them."

"What *was* that?" His thumb presses against her carotid artery. Her pulse is quick but strong and her pupils show coherence.

"I don't know. I was so angry when that thing hit back. I snapped, I guess."

He closes his eyes and scans outward. "Everyone's okay. We have an unconscious battalion of unknown assailants and an orderly mob of mundanes, but no friendly fatalities and very little collateral damage. We were lucky."

"Where's the kid?"

"I didn't see him. Can you sense him?"

Now she closes her eyes, then shakes her head. "I can't see that thing that hit me either. Never could. We can hope they're off somewhere without people around. Let me up now."

She adjusts her garments. He clicks, trying to turn on his communicator, but it's not on his collar. His pockets are empty too. Pierre jogs out of the southern tree line. His eyes are wide and weary.

"Was that you?" he gasps.

Clownfish nods.

"Where did that come fr–"

The ground heaves, and Titian spends all of his energy staying out of the crater. Something flashes red. Unconscious bodies float into the air, spin and orient themselves together. He blinks; they dissolve into after images smears as they converge on a point high and distant in the sky.

They gape in stunned silence. A driver, perfect in appearance and composure, appears before they regain their speech. Hard-fought instinct drives him now.

"I want two sweeper teams, one to search the entire park for anything left over, any evidence. The other one needs to clean up after Mr. Harrison and his adventures. I have the strong impression that he's left a trail of modest destruction. Please bring a car around."

The driver nods and disappears. Titian grumbles at his suit, and gives up, sitting on the muddy ground. He amuses himself by field-stripping and reassembling one of the confiscated sidearms.

"Pretty speech though," offers Pierre.

"I meant it. Even those people," she waves a weary hand idly in the direction of the pavilion and scattered chairs, "don't know everything we do for them, or why, and I'm still thankful. I can't imagine doing anything else... but enough small talk. What happened here?"

Titian shrugs. "It's not like the last time. It's different. Did you feel it too?" He tells himself he's getting too old for revolutions, that the next generation can very well do its own fighting and scheming, that the white hot iron of his zeal has cooled and strategy and ideals are very well more important than fisticuffs, but always the giant metal hand crushes his friend, and he curses that he is so easily manipulated.

She shakes her head. "I thought this was a fad long done. Reconstruction was *ages* ago. When was the last time you ran into a PSF?"

He has no answer. He sets the pistol aside and leans forward to massage his temples. He runs his fingers through his hair.

The door chimed and he tensed, raising his head from his arms and cursing the sudden sharp stabbing in the back of his neck. "Enter," he called. The weariness of his voice surprised him with its cotton-fuzz mumble.

An assistant crossed the floor briskly, bearing a report entitled "Preliminary Analysis of Headquarters Attack."

His memory swirled. He felt again the rough concrete of the roof ledge as he struggled to hold retaining walls together. His will snaked around groaning rebar, coaxing it to hold its shape; it whispered gently to hardened steel beams, promising them relief if they could stand a few moments longer. "Right. Right. Thank you."

The attendant nodded and spun a well-practiced half circle before marching out of the room.

Titian had expected no insight from the report. By the time they'd ruled out any possibility of an earthquake, tsunami, or other large-scale natural disaster, there was no evidence larger than a dust particle. He scowled at his original decision to erect the perception barrier, but couldn't bring himself to believe that a random passer-by might have seen anything useful.

That line of thinking was a dead end. Who knew what the building contained? No one inside at the time was likely to have set a bomb. The only people outside the building at the time were ignorant of its contents, equally loyal, or. . . well, dead.

A little voice nagged at him in an unknown language. Something forgotten waved its hands furiously. He fumbled with the bottle of painkillers, smiling at the comfort of its rattle.

As expected, the report was brief, efficient, and useless. A perimeter sweep revealed no special information. Thermal imaging analysis showed no unique, unexpected, or suspicious gatherings of people in the preceding twenty four hours. The point of origin of the blast was the south face of the building, halfway between street level and the hidden door, halfway between the fence and the plane of the door.

Something, it concluded, had floated in mid-air to the side of the building and exploded.

The explosion came from a shaped charge, aimed at the door, judging by the destruction in the hallway and the insignificant damage elsewhere. The remainder of the report speculated on types of explosives and diagrams of potential delivery vectors. Most were improbable; unless someone had known the precise location of the doorway and delivered it with perfect timing and aim, all the while avoiding detection, it was unlikely the explosion had occurred outside the building.

Yet it had.

He fought the urge to dial the four-digit code and suggest that the laboratory and analysis department reconsider its basic assumption that the attack had gone off as intended. Thirty minutes earlier he would have been a victim.

That line of thinking drew him to an unpopular idea: if the shaped charge *had* exploded in the wrong direction, with only a fragment destroying the hidden entrance, the explosion was large enough to have penetrated the hallway and destroyed the great room. Those results would have been devastating, compared to the minor damage to the two-story, flat-roofed warehouse across the street. Precautions from years ago would have kept the building standing, but the casualty numbers would have reached three digits.

The timing also worried Titian. He brushed his desk again. "I want that analysis of Barry's crash as soon as possible. Preliminaries are fine. I'll draw conclusions myself."

He walked through his meticulous list of vulnerable points as he did at the start and end of every day. The material was safe, boxed and divided and distributed. His partners were loyal. His employees were harmless if efficient, and his investments were diverse and staggeringly sufficient. No evidence linked these incidents beyond coincidence of timing and circumstance.

He flailed ineffectively at the tiny voice in his head. It danced away, still screaming "It's happening! It was always inevitable! Now it's here!"

Titian flipped the status indicator at his desk to "Do not disturb", then waddled over to an oversized chair by a fake window. The screen rippled as he walked, stabilizing into a bright blue scene from a hilltop villa overlooking an island port. He collapsed into the chair and shielded his eyes, willing his mind to push all of his calculations and worries into a background process. The sleep of the just swirled around him, but a long-forgotten memory chased it away.

He looked over an azure sea. Sea birds wheeled in the island's salty air. He smoothed his hair into place, but the wind's gentle fingers mussed it again. A handclap on his back demanded his attention.

The other man was tall and thin, regal except for a perpetual faraway stare. Titian had always wondered if their conversations would make more sense if they stood in separate rooms.

"Thank you for coming," the man said. "It's been a long time since you've been here."

"Ten years, to the day." Sadness tightened in his chest; a sigh chased it away. "Have you thought about our discussion then?"

"Perhaps my views have grown more subtle, but I haven't changed my mind. Shall I assume you have likewise remained constant?"

"As always."

The man leaned against a low railing to scan the hills. Trees valiantly grasped the rocks though whipped and twisted by fierce winter winds. Today the breeze merely carried whispers of flowers. "I admire your constancy... but I fear we can never reconcile fully."

"Our positions are not so far apart." Titian rubbed the back of his neck. The heat summoned tiny droplets of sweat. He wished for a broad-rimmed hat.

"No," admitted the other. "Perhaps our stubbornness prevents us from admitting that we have the same goals and can achieve them in the same ways."

"Have you made progress?"

"Not as you have. Truth told, that's why I invited you–not in the hope of convincing you, nor to accede, but to warn you of the danger of your path."

Titian snorted. "For a man devoted to reason, that argument smacks of a fallacy."

He shrugged off the expected baiting. "Consider the domesticated dog. Its greatest attribute is loyalty. It will lie by the side of a tyrant or a saint, as long as its master is not cruel, or has broken its spirit. Young, old, fat, beautiful, hopeful, or fearful, the dog does not care. It hews to its master's side.

"Breathe this fresh air," he continued. "Do you notice anything different?"

"The sky," Titian concluded. "The colors are brighter. The senses sharper."

"The air cleaner and the scents more pungent. The fruit of this island has tastes a thousand times more pleasing to your palate than the most exquisite banquet prepared for you in the past decade."

"Because they're wild, and nature is good, and progress inevitably ends in tragedy. I've heard populist pap before. We've both seen it end badly for everyone, more than once."

The other man shook his head. "No. These are domesticated too. I tend them and prune them and fertilize them to ensure that they will be even more lovely next year."

"What then?"

"You are out from under your own thumb here. You do not believe me now. I see it through your eyes. In your rush to domesticate your city, you've leashed yourself too. I have no wish to argue, nor the power to change the outcome of events. I was wrong. You've done well, but I fear for the future if you persist down this path."

Titian chuckled. "Is this a polite way of forestalling my offer to come back and work with us?"

"It would be impossible. I've given it all up, quite literally. One day you may have to do the same, though I hope under better circumstances."

Titian turned to leave. "Old friend, you are as oblique and confusing as ever, but other appointments beckon. It is truly good to see you. Shall I expect you for dinner sometime next week?"

The other man's eyes were sad. "Yes... I suppose you shall." He was silent for a moment, and then he called out. "Do you know why I so rarely visit, not even in secret, and then I flee?"

"Because you retired?"

"More subtly."

"You no longer believe in our work? In me? In our goals?"

A cloud passed across his face. Titian watched him breathe and count slowly until his visage cleared. "I very much believe in your work, and I hope you're the one to accomplish it. But what you're doing–it fills my mind with a haze that whispers and tempts me to abandon what I believe is important. This is no metaphor. You've spent so much time manipulating others. No matter which justification you offer to others or to yourself, you're blind to a simple truth. You've manipulated yourself more than anyone else.

"Please be careful. Please consider what I've said. It's poisonous there. I have no hope you'll remember this when you return, but I must say it. I tell you every time."

Titian paused, then smiled. "Message understood. Next Wednesday night? Bring a bottle of wine."

"Of course."

He sighed and shifted in his chair. Soon sleep chased the memory away again.

○ ○ ○

Mark David rolled down the ramp from the physical therapy office. He felt himself purse his lips into a thin, whitening line. The previous time he'd fallen, he'd been on crutches two weeks later, slow but in a walking cast. This time, six weeks later, he could barely stand on his own. He swallowed, hating the tomb of his wheelchair with every flick of his wrists on the wheels.

John-Paul was always good for a laugh. . . even when Mark David was always the smart and popular twin, witty and charming and surrounded by girls who overlooked that he sometimes walked funny and stuttered. In private, John-Paul told him to get over his gimpy self and Mark David threw a balled-up sock at him and they laughed and wrestled and fought like brothers and made up like twins and their troubles always seemed so much further away then.

John-Paul wasn't answering his phone today.

Something tiny and fast hit his arm. He looked up as another raindrop tickled his nose. He scowled and continued navigating the ramp's hairpin, half-consoled that his arms behaved, no matter how weak and disobedient were his leg muscles and nerves this week.

The van was empty as he rolled around to the passenger side. Jupiter leaned against the door, adorable even in a ridiculous oversized gray hoodie and hip-hugging jeans. Her bright blonde ponytail bounced as she saw him and grinned. Perfect teeth shone through the slight parting of her lips. "Hey, handsome! How was it?"

He snorted. "They wouldn't give me robot legs. They're afraid I might go on a rampage and destroy the city and take pretty girls captive."

She waved the door dongle. Four clicks answered. "What is it about guys and robots? I could be standing here in a cheerleader skirt screaming your name and waving pom-poms and if you'd been thinking about robots, you'd still be thinking about robots."

He shrugged. "Not sure it counts with an ex-cheerleader, unless you want to show up to intramural robot building competitions sometime."

"Imagine the riot."

He tilted his head. "Wear baggy sweats?"

She winked. "Where's the fun in that?" He didn't meet her eye, and she stuck out her tongue. "Bleh. Heh. Alright, hop in. Your mom'll think I kidnapped you if I don't get you home soon. Though if we're going to elope, you should be the one to drive."

He rolled up to the door, leaning in to flip the lift lever. They'd argued over this only once; he'd finished by warning her never to help him. After the two longest minutes of his life–her sullen silence hurt more than falling off of the barn roof as a kid–he'd apologized. She watched from the driver's seat as he augered himself into place. "Ready?" she called.

"I'm set."

"You'd better leave me a good tip this time, or you're going to lose your favorite driver."

"Pity. I left my wallet in my other pants."

Jupiter peeled out of the parking lot, throwing a fountain of gravel in a noisy parabola. "I'm sure you'll think of something." The sun peered through clouds and reflected from a black satin ribbon stretched tightly between low western hills and endless eastern plains.

Mark sniffed and made a face. "Were you smoking again?"

She turned pink. "No! It's... okay, it's really stupid. Promise you won't tell anyone?"

"And miss the chance to embarrass you a fraction of how much you embarrass me?"

"Fine." She turned on the radio. Bass and drums rattled the back speakers. Jupiter wailed along with the post-processed girl singer. She hit most of the notes until the chorus climbed out of reach, then she pounded the rhythm on the steering wheel.

"Ahh! I can't reach the controls from back here!" He waved his arms.

"What?"

"I said turn it down! Please!"

"First promise."

"Fine! I give! I promise never to tell your most embarrassing secrets, even if they torture me with bamboo under the fingernails and pull out my body hair follicle by follicle! Or if they make you sing at me."

She pushed the power button. "You have a lot of good qualities, but you're not exactly Mr. Carry a Tune."

She'd convinced him to sing a duet on the karaoke machine they rented for her 21st birthday. No one clapped harder than he did. "Irrelevant. I promised. 'fess up."

"Alrighty. Uh... you know how ratty the strings on my hoodie were?"

"Yeah. You chew on them when you're not chewing off split ends."

"Liar. I don't have split ends. New shampoo. It's a-ma-a-a-zing." She flashed him a smile in the mirror. "Anyway, I heard you can fix up the ends by setting them on fire to melt them back together."

"If it's the right fabric, you can."

"This isn't." She pulled a blackened mess out of her hoodie pocket and threw it at him.

He covered his nose and sneezed twice. "Oh, that's foul! I hope

91

you did that outside. You should bury that string, too. It's made of corpses."

She grinned. "I really will sing if you tell anyone before I get the chance. Or else I'll sneak that string under your pillow for revenge. That's a better alarm clock than coffee and bacon."

He shuddered. "You have an inordinate amount of pride in this accomplishment."

"You always tell me I can't coast on my good looks forever. What better diversification than a career amusing people with all of my stupid-Jupiter stories? Don't deny it; you're laughing on the inside."

Mark David stared out the window. They drove in silence for a mile down a two-lane road. A hard-packed dirt path crossed an irrigation ditch and became the long gravel driveway to a farmhouse nestled against a copse of trees. The three-car garage stuck out a pale square concrete tongue to lick a field of weeds and wildflowers. He sighed, remembering the wheat field as it used to be, a golden sea of summer sunlight and waves of ripening heads rippling.

Two roads intersected at a perfectly square four-way stop. Jupiter twisted to look at him. "Hey?"

"Hmm?"

"What's wrong?" She chewed the fleshy part of her thumb and looked him over.

He dropped his eyes to a fascinating discarded shoe. The pattern of wear on the right sole reminded him yet again to convince himself to pay more attention to where he put his foot, as if his twin casts weren't enough. "Nothing."

"You're a terrible liar. It's not just the therapy. I've seen you down before, but this is different." She bit on her nail, then scowled and folded both hands in her lap.

His eyes wandered to a miniature red fire extinguisher under the driver's seat. "Huh."

"Okay. Van broke down. We'll have to sit here until you tell me." She turned off the engine and set the parking brake.

"Mom'll kill you."

"Your mother's a pussycat, and she loves me, and I'll just tell her you were giving me trouble, and I'll bet you a shiny new dollar bill that she won't take your side." She unfastened her seat belt and swung her hips to sit sideways in the seat, giving him her great big active listening face.

Mark David and John-Paul spent forty-five minutes one night crafting the world's absolutely most perfect retort about the female conspiracy. He'd saved it for several months, but shelved it in favor of awkward silence.

Jupiter bounced a plastic-wrapped pack of tissues off of his head. It landed in his lap.

"Ow, hey! Nice shot, but rude."

She continued to rummage in the console. "There's some change up here too. We could compare the ballistic properties of... let's see... four nickels, a ballpoint pen—no cap, a stale granola bar, two rubber bands, an expired insurance card or... wow, is this popcorn? How old is that? Ewww. I take it back. If you tell anyone my story I'll make you clean out the van."

He sighed. "Fine. I admit it. I miss Jayp. He's having great grand adventures while I'm stuck in this stupid chair again. My life's over and his is starting. You caught me. Can we go now?"

"Oh. Oh, Mark... that's not... it's...."

He interrupted. "Yeah. It is."

"Aren't you proud of him, though?"

He squirmed and flicked his eyes to meet hers, before looking away. Suddenly the contrast between the red of the extinguisher body and its white nozzle offended him. "Well, yes."

"Aren't you moving there next semester still?"

"Not without my cyborg exoskeleton."

"Right, then. Go, team, go. Driving now." She turned back and exaggerated the motions of restarting the van, accelerating through the intersection.

The road curved along a small village. It had grown from a road-side fruit stand to include a restaurant, a curio shop, and a makeshift car dealership. His mouth watered involuntarily at the thought of fresh strawberry milkshakes, and he calculated the time until prime harvest.

"Jupiter?"

He admired the golden shine of her ponytail as she risked a glance over her shoulder. "Go ahead?"

"Why are you still here? You had the grades. You could have transferred to the big U no problem. You didn't have to stick around after you graduated. You could go anywhere, do anything. Do you not want to see the world? Are you content in our little nowhere podunk right here?"

"Leave all this?" She waved a hand at a fallow field where scraggly weeds poked through unseeded soil. "Perhaps not *that* in particular, but I love it here."

"You're not sticking around waiting for your life to start?"

"Mark, this *is* life. I'm stuck driving a hot guy around one afternoon. Oh, frustration."

He shifted in his chair, feeling the sticky warmth of sweat at his lower back. "Do you really mean that?"

"The hot guy part? Didn't your mother already give you the long, laborious lecture about exactly how to accept a heartfelt comment from a pretty girl without breaking her poor little heart all in pieces?"

"The other part."

She pondered for a moment, then spoke with slow deliberation. "The way I see it, you either wait for your life to begin or you enjoy it for what it is as it happens. Maybe you wait forever, or until you're too old to enjoy it. Maybe you bury yourself under regrets for waiting so long. It's not going to be perfect. So what? Maybe you're scared. Everyone is. When you have a good opportunity, think about it. Maybe you take it. Maybe you don't. Don't make excuses. Do something about it."

He leaned forward and rested his chin on his hand to stare again at the neighbor girl he'd known all his life. For the first time he saw again how her ponytail pulled her hair away from a long, slim neck, kissed slightly tan from the summer. He smiled at the freckles dotting her nose and cheeks, feeling his lips turn up at the memory of the mischief of her smile. The past decade of memories melted away, when she had chubby cheeks and chubby knees and pigtails and chased him around the barn with a harmless green snake.

"Jupiter?"

"Yessir."

"Thanks."

"You bet." She allowed herself a tiny smile. "I have to admit I hadda go into town anyway, so it's not like you were anything more than a pleasant diversion, Mister Grumpy Day."

"Thanks for going out to dinner with me on Friday."

She blushed at the van's sudden acceleration. "Finally figured it out. Good boy. You'd better not make your mother drive. That's not the way to impress an older woman."

Mark smiled. "I wouldn't dream of it. How else would I flirt shamelessly with a chauffeur?"

"Hmm." She cocked her head to the left and tapped her index finger against her chin. "You shouldn't make your date jealous, but you seem the easy to forgive type. You're welcome in advance."

"Um? For?"

She slowed, then pulled into the access road leading to their houses. "I might tell you someday. I have chores. Mind if I drop you off in your driveway?"

"That's fine."

She hopped out to open the side door. She leaned and gave him a ferocious hug as he reached for the lift lever. "Oof," he said.

"Oh, sorry." She took his right hand in hers, massaging it gently with both thumbs. "You're a great guy. You have a lot of good things going on."

He studied her face with a slow smile. "Thanks. I know. I really appreciate it, even if you're just buttering me up so I'll pay for lobster on Friday."

She tousled his hair. "Ick, bugs of the sea. No thanks. I'll see you soon. Meanwhile, say hi to your mother and call your brother."

"You bet."

Then her long legs ate the distance between their houses with confident strides inspiring in him equal parts jealousy and warmth. He watched the liquid gold of her hair bounce with each step until she disappeared from view at the wooden bridge overshadowed by great giant oak trees. He smiled again at nothing in particular as he wheeled himself home.

o o o

The hospital was sterile in polished white tile and steel. Whispers echoed through pristine corridors; every step and squeak and cough reverberated. Pierre winced as the clack-clack of his shoes assaulted his ears from strange angles. His hyperactive senses continually screamed, though no one followed him.

He repeated the number in his head with each step. Four four two. Clack. Four four two. Clack. It sizzled and burned into his memory, until an orderly struggling to keep his arms around a pile of overstuffed file folders joined the elevator at the second floor and asked "Floor seven, please." Pierre stared, frozen with fear that he'd forgotten the room number, then relaxed and pressed the button as his mantra returned. Four four two. Four four two.

He followed the corridor to the right, then right again, now parallel to the front of the building. Steam rose from heat exchangers on the roof of the second floor, tiny, ephemeral clouds distorting his view of a squat parking garage across the entrance road. Beyond that, the city's spine bristled with stone and metal.

The sky was a mother-of-pearl enigma, offering no insight. It simply was, and was glad to be. Cheery white clouds scudded over a sea of brilliant blue, chasing heavy gray oppression away from his mood.

Four four two. He walked on.

The room's tile floor shone with more polish than the corridor, but his shoes made no sound. The room was large enough for two patients, but the furniture now allowed only a single bed at the far end. It sprawled across the room diagonally. A tree of monitors grew from a metal pole at the far right corner; a rack of tubes and vials and baggies occupied the other.

Bandages and sheets covered the bed's occupant. A bruised left eye lay closed. A few days of stubble shaded an exposed neck. A heavy white cast affixed a right arm at an unnatural angle. Its color mirrored the brightness of the sterile walls with less personality than the room itself: a shrine to medical industrial efficiency. The figure was still. Pierre stopped moving. The only noises in the room were the gentle whoosh of recirculating air and the secret blip song of a heartbeat monitor.

A small table–empty save a small plastic cup–pivoted freely on a vertical arm. Its base was a solid mass of wheels and brakes. The room's remaining furniture was a low chair of varnished wood rectangles hugging an overstuffed red seat and suffering behind an understuffed red cushion. Pierre pulled it over to the bed; this scraping echoed. His head crested the mattress and he nearly cracked his chin on his knees as he sank into the aging cushion.

"Hey Claude," he started. "Uh... it's Pierre. I guess they're gonna get you out of here soon, maybe find someplace we can keep a better eye on you and get you some better care. Titian said he had a few places safer than HQ.

"He's really worried. Ha, you'll laugh. You can imagine. He locked himself in his office. He has his whole staff coming and going with drafts and reports. I'm surprised they haven't deposed me yet for the funeral.

"That was a big mess, big brother. Huge mess. Great fun. You'd love it, missing those old times. We woulda had some fun, just the two of us. Not the ceremony. It was dull speechifying bigwigs. Blah blah, Protector, blah blah remember when, blah blah good friend to the city. Remember those news quotes, those sound bites you hated?

The city is wonderful and they're proud, and we're the ones with dirt and blood on our hands and our faces. When did they do anything for us?

"Sorry. Anyway. That wasn't the exciting part.

"Clownie gave a great speech. Wow. She said it better than I ever could, maybe better than you ever would. I wish they'd listen now. It was after that. We walked up to Greenway Boulevard side, up the hill there. Just then, bam! Progress–the statue, you know? A replica, maybe. Progress shows up with a hundred of those troops you used to tell me about. They wanted a body, I guess, then Clownie just turns red. Kapow! She flies straight at the thing. It's seven stories tall by now, huge and fast, and it slaps her down. She goes down. We fall down the hill. You should have seen the old man, flailing just to get back on his feet. It's good to see his hands dirty.

"Anyway, Clownie's laid flat in this crater and Titian's huffing and puffing up the hill. He tells me to move it to keep the mundies safe, so I run up double-time just in time to catch the kid who's just shown up. He pulls the same move Clownie did, only *he* connects. The statue's angry now. By then I have troops on me, so I take off for the tree line, thinking I can ambush them there and Titian can clean up on whatever's left. That girl, the one who makes Clownie all jealous? She's a photographer. Maybe she's one of Fontaine's. She's there too, leading everyone else away from the fight.

"I make it to the trees with what, twenty guys after me? I pull off your trick, walking straight up a tree trunk. They're so busy thinking I'm still ahead of them that I pick off five or six from behind. They fall apart. No tactics. They have no idea I'm working my way up to the front again until I get excited and throw one of them too hard. They hear me and open fire."

He folded his hands on the mattress and bowed his head for two deep breaths. "I hated it. It feels weird to say now. I didn't feel so invulnerable then. I was worried. Seeing her swatted...seeing Barry's coffin there. He really did walk away. How close did I come to getting really hurt? Titian was terrified, as frightened as I'd ever seen him. This wasn't part of the game. This was real.

"Accidents happen, I know, but... yeah."

He chuckled and wiped his eyes. "I know. How stupid, right? Here you are, walked into a bomb. You're paralyzed maybe, or brain dead, or whatever. Nobody tells me. Here I am moaning about untrained kids playing soldier in stupid helmets and those silly pants, all lured into deep cover where I can pile them up one by one, and I'm thinking a stray shot could kill me. The worst thing for me is I scrape my arm on a tree branch when I miss a tuck and roll.

"So stupid. We're not out there risking our lives. That's been over for years, right? Even he...." His voice cracked. He sniffled and stared staring at the wall where patterns of light peeked through window blinds. "Can you remember the last time he took any damage? Heh. Remember when we used to joke about how our knuckles hurt from punching so many guys? Mine never did. But there's something different now. I don't like it. I don't like when the world changes beneath us.

"Look at us. We oughta be out there *living*, you know? You duck a little and shrapnel *bends* around you. Remember the time with Firebrand in that haunted house? He threw me through a wall and my pants caught on fire. The worst part of the day was the ribbing you all gave me for letting him get the drop on me. I loved it. That's what it should be like now, not you lying here beeping at me. Not Titian locked in his office for days or Clownie moping around or us burying... ahhhhh."

He pushed back his chair to pace. "Maybe it sounds stupid. Aw, forget that. It does. Go ahead, Pierre. Pine for the good old days of last week. Everything changes, Claude. I want normal back. Look at us. I can't lie. I can't deny it. Something happened to us all. I hate it. I'm scared.

"Come on. For me? Get up. Pull off those bandages. They're not a part of you. They're decoration. Tell me it's all a practical joke, like when you moved all of the furniture out of my dorm onto the roof, yeah? Good times...."

Pierre paused and splayed the fingers of his right hand against the window. "Look at all of them out there, however many millions.

Do you think they know? Do they have any idea? It's an endless sea of people. Here comes a new tide, dark and dangerous. They're jetsam, tossed. It's coming. You know it's coming. It's here, and it hates us. It scares me, because it's bigger and more dangerous than us. It knows that. It's already convinced me that it's gonna beat me. Maybe it's already beaten you. You were about the strongest guy I knew. Maybe you *are*. The strongest guy I ever knew is dead. That left you. Now who?"

The gentle beep skipped a beat. An endless moment passed until a staccato arrhythm arrived, then stabilized. Pierre let out the breath he hadn't realized he'd held, then reached for his brother's undamaged shoulder. "I'm sorry. I can't lay all of this on you. I'm the only normal one left, and I can't carry this alone. I didn't realize how much I'd miss him."

He squeezed Claude's shoulder. "I sound like a fool. Listen to me gush like a little girl. What I think, I say. Should I lie? Pile on sunshine and light? I can't. I'm sorry. Everything's gone to pieces. Why do you just lie there and miss out on it all? I wish you were here. You don't have it easy, listening to me whine...but I'm so sorry. Just get better, okay? I hate this all, the doubt, the darkness, but if I have to face it down and then you wake up, I will. Okay? Okay."

He paused in the doorway for one last look. "I mean it. You'd better–or else. You get it?" The room seemed smaller now. It felt warmer, as if the golden light of late afternoon had finally splashed its color on the walls. golden light. His fingers caressed the door jamb, tapping a counterpoint to the steady beeping. Then he pushed away into the long, lonely corridors. Four four two he repeated, as his shoes clack-clacked away.

o o o

John-Paul sat alone last night among hundreds of dollars worth of unopened schoolbooks scattered on the hardwood floor, rolling a single question into a dense little sphere. The geas had left him in the park, gasping for breath. He rolled over and pushed himself to his knees, brushing sticky, fine sand from purpling, achey bruises. An array of dark-suited men–identical and bland–swept him into a large black sedan before he could protest. They ignored his questions: "Where's Pandora?" and "What happened to the others?" and dropped him off, shoes still squidging wet, in front of his uncle's large and empty house.

He watched the vehicle recede. After an extravagant shower that drained the house's hot water, he wrapped himself in a huge towel and pawed through unpacked boxes for a pair of sweats. After a success, he shook water from his hair and curled up on the couch.

Early Saturday afternoon television was a wasteland in the big city, even without the strict summer rationing of tropospheric ducting. The only program worth watching was a public affairs memorial about the Protector. It began with a toothless recitation of clichés over shaky stock news footage and camera pans and zooms over still photos. The Protector had appeared during the late Reconstruction period as the city's new governing bodies had outlawed private security firms. Clashes between borough groups waned (though John-Paul wondered if the scriptwriter had confused cause and effect). The script was fuzzy on how many Protectors had existed; Reconstruction was a word grown old and moldy with time.

A commercial for fried chicken salad blared him back to full attention.

John-Paul sighed, feeling a sudden urge to floss away the sugary, syrupy residue of a puffy Boy Scout hurrah with little actual content and metaphorical speech that would seem tired even to a sports reporter. He wished Pandora or Mark David or even Jupiter were there to appreciate his clever critique.

The first interview guest was a professor of media and communications. Tiny round spectacles hid eyes set flat in a mousy face above a weak chin. . He rocked forward, punctuating speech otherwise expressionless in its monotone.

"The Protector represents an inherent dialectic in our culture.

We have suppressed and oppressed our internal violence, the internal manliness of men, from which spring problem solving skills. We've domesticated our creative urges–creative and yes, occasionally destructive–in favor of so-called civilization. With every transition we lose something important, from hunter/gatherer to farmer, then factory worker, then modern information age man.

"The Protector represents this creative urge, the wild and uncontrolled spark, a drive to accomplish great things without regard for collateral damage. He is a forceful will to power, a thirst for success, that has led us to conquer first the animals, then the ground, and now the sky and sea. Yet we can never conquer our internal struggles.

"This sets him in eternal opposition to other foes. Perhaps more accurately one may say that they set themselves in a dialectical opposition to him. They represent the urge to destroy rather than build, the urge to conquer rather than comfort. Yet that combination, that explosive spark when the two opposing urges meet, best defines our age. Will our desire to create succeed over our temptation to destroy?

"Perhaps that's why we have heroes after all, to inspire us.

"Yet will we destroy our heroes because we cannot abide the reminder of our imperfection? They may inspire us with their exploits and conquests, but how many of them conquer their demons, their inner selves? Perhaps those problems are larger than life as well. It's important to reflect, at the end of an age of a hero, that their problems are our problems as well, writ large."

A series of quick cuts between heroic action and brutal devastation formed the underlying montage. It ended on the professor's pudgy face scrunching into a piggy smile. John-Paul winced as he instead saw the flailing arm of the giant statue scrape the front of the apartment building, shearing away a brick facade to expose the hidden lives and inner sanctums of dozens of families to an uncaring world. Yet if he *hadn't* lured the creature into the bay....

The next guest was a severe woman with heavy eye makeup and a bright red jacket and skirt embroidered with thick black seams. She was an activist, a spokesperson for an alphabet soup of letters.

Sharp-edged words tumbled out, rapid and punctuated with precise, two-handed chops.

"The Protector is a solution in search of a problem. With all of his talk about law and order, it's important to ask ourselves if we're effectively safer under his regime than we were before. Look at the important issues facing us... health care, traffic accidents, obesity, trade deficits. Are a dozen so-called evildoers prancing around in jumpsuits a threat that only vigilante violence can solve?

"Would they exist without so-called heroes to encourage their antics? We reward undesirable behavior by giving it the serious attention it does not deserve. We publicize, very strongly, their private grievances. In so doing, we put our infrastructure and ourselves in greater danger, and over what? Do your children have shoes? Do you eat enough fruits and vegetables? Can we pay for social programs? Is poison rain destroying our bridges and our school buildings?

"At best, the Protector and all he represents is a distraction. At worst, his only justification is that he's somehow defeated a straw man argument that he created: without him, would society *really* degenerate into anarchy and chaos? Humanity has survived eons without him. We can do so again. For all his talk about personal responsibility and honor and the goodness of individuals who choose to do the right thing, doesn't he swoop in awfully frequently to save people who, if you believed his own rhetoric, should be able to save themselves?

"Answer me one last question. *What exactly is he saving us from?* If you look carefully, if you watch very carefully, the answer is stunning. He's saving us from himself. If he didn't exist–if he went away–so would these problems. He's a solution to the problem of himself."

John-Paul barely recognized the third speaker. Something was qualitatively different in Clownfish. She looked younger, perhaps less experienced. The hard look in her eyes was gone. In its place shone idealism... or, he decided, love. She wore a sensible outfit of muted grays. Words poured out in bursts: a sentence or two of

103

output, and then a quiet intake of air and thought. At first, she spoke fast and rehearsed. Then she relaxed and grew thoughtful. There was no montage, just the woman on a single stool on an empty stage lit with a gentle spotlight. A "file footage" warning blinked in the corner.

"You find yourself in an impossible situation, and you have to ask yourself, if you think *someone* should do *something*, why not you? That's where it starts. It's a terrible responsibility, but it's also liberating.

"You give yourself permission to try, maybe to fail, but you always fall back on that moment of clarity. You realize that you chose–*you*–to do what you thought was right. You realize that action is better than inaction. You realize that you can never take that back...but you don't have to, because it was the right choice then and it's the right choice now. It'll always be the right choice.

"No one ever asks for this kind of responsibility. Uh...I guess that's not true. You shouldn't trust anyone who ever seeks this kind of responsibility. It finds you.

"Everyone always asks, what about the copycats? What about collateral damage? Doesn't that keep you up at night, wondering if someone's going to imitate you or if you make one wrong move you're hurting innocent people? That's rough. That's difficult. I don't know if that's worse than watching someone you love or an innocent person get hurt and always wishing that you had done something.

"How many million people live here now? Thirty-five? Forty? How many incidents are there every year? Dozens? A hundred? That's pretty good. That's too many, but that's a low number. I wish it were zero, but be realistic. People are people. We're good at heart, right? How many little boys want to grow up and be him? If it weren't for him, they'd want to be detectives or firemen or other heroes, solving crimes and defeating the bad guys. Sometimes they get the girl.

"He meets a real need. People *want* something to rally around. They want someone to live up to real ideals. So what if they never get challenged on those ideals? That's okay. That's why we have people out there day after day putting their lives and their careers and their futures and yes, sometimes, our psyches in danger to make the world a little bit better.

"I don't know. Maybe the world doesn't need heroes. Maybe we're a bad idea. You tell me. I know what I've seen. The world's better off with someone standing up for the little guy. That's why I do it. That's why he does it. Maybe that's the most important thing we do, we show the world that it's possible to chase the better angels of our natures. If we each inspire even one more person to do good, well, it's all worth it. I'll take the abuse and the second guessing that comes from that, because I've found my success."

John-Paul muted the commercials again. He stretched, reveling in the hum and echo of the empty house. He'd been there for a week, living out of boxes and canned food, and hadn't seen his neighbors– no kids playing in the yards of the community, no one mowing lawns or washing cars. He drove past morning joggers on his way to the monorail station, but there was no other hum of activity in the neighborhood.

His nostrils lamented the lack of grilled meat at dinnertime; he and Mark spent their summer evenings drinking sodas by the creek, chasing fireflies at dusk, and lying on gentle grassy hills watching the sun set and talking.

The impending move made John-Paul philosophical. "Do you ever think," he asked, beneath a picture-perfect sunset of yellows and oranges, where fiery sky descended from heaven opposed by bright evening stars on the horizon, "ever get the feeling that life is an illusion, that we experience everything that we're supposed to experience, and we have no real choices?"

Mark chewed sweet grass. "No. That would make no sense."

John-Paul turned over. "What does sense have to do with it? It's a question about the nature of reality and free will. You can't prove that your senses are trustworthy. What if you're a brain in a jar with fake inputs? What if everything you experience is a lie?

What if we're just characters in some story, and when whoever reads it closes the book we cease to exist?"

Mark chuckled. "In that case, this conversation would be horribly self-referential." He threw a clump of dirt at John-Paul. "Hah, you dodged that illusion awfully fast."

"The illusion is pervasive; reflexes are part of it too."

Mark argued against the idea of historical inevitability on the grounds that the meaning of an action depended on the will of the actors and the entirety of their choices. John-Paul countered that the range of possible actions and outcomes was as much a function of the context of the decision as any self-selected expression of individuality in the same way that a rat trained that pressing the blue lever earns an electric shock while pressing a red lever will produce a treat will prefer red over blue even outside the laboratory.

Mark countered that "deterministic single-factor behaviorist studies" were poor predictors of "multi-variable complex non-repeatable phenomena" especially in "higher-order vertebrates confronted with fuzzy moral choices."

John-Paul said that he read too much and closed his eyes as the first chill of night winds prickled his skin. He never brought it up again.

The third segment explored the Protector's history. Though there was little information about his childhood or his life outside of his persona, research assistants and interns pieced together a credible chronology, based on individual statements given on and off the record.

Animated tables appeared; letters flew in from the left side to engrave themselves like hand-carved stone. They placed his age somewhere between 21 and 40, his height and weight somewhere in the top 5% of average for healthy adult males, and his cholesterol on the low side of healthy. The deadpan delivery caught John-Paul's attention.

Another montage featured recorded footage of the Protector himself, mixing formal settings with candid interviews and statements from the scenes of altercations and events.

He wore a chocolate-colored suit with a cream-colored shirt open at the collar. He crossed his legs at the ankles and leaned on the desk of a talk show host, answering around a smile, "I'm still a farmboy at heart."

He stood in costume, hand on the reporter's shoulder, speaking into an oversized microphone. "Sure, Crazy Allan's craftier than a wily old catfish who's been the legend of the lake for twenty years, but every so often someone crazier or more determined shows up. It's time for a new legend."

He dwarfed a white leather couch. "It *was* overwhelming to see the big city for the first time. I walked around staring at the buildings for the first couple of weeks. My neck was sore from all that gawking."

He held aloft a decorative golden key and leaned toward a podium. "I wish my father were here to see this. I know he's proud of me, wherever he is. This means a lot to me. Thank you. Thank you all."

He grinned at another reporter outside a courthouse. "Me and my brother used to play cops and robbers. I always caught my man. Can I say something to him? To Shock Therapy? Alright. If you're watching this, go ahead and run. Go ahead and hide. I will catch you. I will stop you. It's inevitable. Ask my brother. He'll show you a scar or two."

He wiped away sweat at the finish line of a marathon. "What's the secret? Two things. First, I have to think that right is on my side. Not in the sense of a weapon or a threat, but that people want right to succeed, even without a sense of personal involvement. My parents taught me that. Thanks, Mom and Dad! You want the law to be fair and you want the law to be just, because someday you may be on the other side, where fairness and impartiality is your only hope. That's important. Second, do what you love. There's no sense in throwing yourself into something you don't want to do, or something you're not good at. You do what you're... well, *made* to do. It's a balance. Anyone who pursues that is going to find some degree of success."

John-Paul found himself mesmerized by the simple face of the man who'd died a week later, mere feet away, a man he'd heard of only in retrospect, and a man whose secret memorial he'd attended. Even paused in mid-sentence, the man's charisma sent his pulse racing. His eyes fell to the pile of textbooks: Advanced Chemistry, Macroeconomics, Agribusiness, and Accounting, and he sighed.

The final commercial break suggested that he had no excuse for not buying a new car. "I can't even get a check for tuition," he snapped. The registrar had been very pleasant, understanding the danger of being in the wrong place at the wrong time. The matronly blue-haired woman behind the desk actually looked him in the eyes and smiled and called him hon'–apostrophe dripping honey-thick from the end of the word–and remembered when that handsome Protector once dashed past her in a crowd too. His new payment deadline was in two days.

He resolved to browse at least the tables of contents of the books of his two classes on Tuesday on the monorail, if he could find a seat during the commute hours, when students crammed themselves inside the white plastic tube, crouching over music players and phones, one great mob of individuals unwilling even to look at each other.

The final segment was short and quiet. He missed the introduction fumbling for the remote. The announcer had dropped his prepared script to address the camera directly. "... and, to my mind, that's the most important lesson to learn from the Protector. Each of us has a duty, not only to our family and friends and loved ones, but to our neighborhoods and the city as a whole, to ask ourselves, what can *we* do to make the world a better place? In the end, he's one man, but we are many. In his memory...."

The announcer was television-perfect, with immaculate hair, far too many teeth, and a tan completely independent of season and weather conditions. He oozed sincerity as a boxer might sweat: hard and fast, spraying with every juke and dodge. Patriotic music swelled. Brassy horns blared and strings swooped vertically up and down the scales. The outer layers peeled back, laying bare the manipulative effect. Yet even beyond the well-choreographed twinkle that occasionally flickered in the announcer's eye, a tiny flame of sincerity burned. He believed part of what he said. He wanted to believe and to belong and to be worthy of every noble goal and aspirations. That eyeblink second swirled around him with strength and power; he was a man of golden fire transfixed by the television's glassy eye.

"...I say, long live the Protector! He is the leader we need in times like these. We need heroes, and I'm proud to say that I believe in heroes like him. Thank you, Protector. We're with you all the way."

The music reached a tense crescendo, strings screaming in thirty-second notes to the fourth of the key and a significant pause. Then a cello whispered a low, solid note–the root of the key–and the other instruments followed in tonic resolution.

John-Paul blinked again. He shook his head; suddenly he felt powerfully sleepy, as if the room had spun a small earthquake epi-centered on his precise location. Powerful longitudinal waves re-arranged the world around him. His thumb pressed the bright red power button outside of conscious will.

He laughed, remembering.

Mark would have pointed out that that kind of delusional, solip-sistic thinking was the mark a psychopath who really would put on a costume and fly through the city destroying buildings for the so-called greater good. His patriotism had faded on waking. Building-sized figures haunted dark and violent dreams, reaching for him with cruel intents. They dared him to run. They taunted him until he spewed back curses and foul invectives. He escaped down an alley black as sin and narrow enough that his shoulders brushed mortar from both walls, finding a back room roiling with smoke and riotous laughter. Cheap fluorescent lighting cast a deathly pallor. He awoke to see the walls spinning, then rolled over and immediately fell into the same dream. The third time, he scrubbed a hand across his face, groaning at pokey stubble, and padded to the master bathroom bare-foot in flannel pants.

His eyes were bleary and his hair described complex fractals. He stuck out his tongue and tried to remember if he'd had anything to drink. He hadn't.

One shower, two pieces of toast, and a short train ride later, velvety smooth liquid melted away on his tongue, smooth and hot and hinting slightly of whipped cream and cinnamon. He savored the taste as his gaze fell on pedestrians. Office worker. Student. Tourist family. Mother shopping with toddler and preschooler. Their lives all intersected at this intersection at this hour on this day. As soon as the light turned, they'd all depart, never to meet again.

John-Paul sipped hot chocolate and eyed 111 Fifth Avenue. He felt responsibility or power or motivation swell in his breast as his eyes swiveled to the damaged building. Telltale shimmers on the building's southern face exposed a hum of work where scaffolding's telltale boxy ivy had taken over. An construction dumper shifted traffic half a lane over and heavy plastic turned the antique cannons into inappropriate packages.

"I can *do* this," he promised, and crossed with the light.

o o o

Titian waved away two assistants. They retreated to a credenza on the far wall and stacked their armsful of folders next to an enamel and brass globe. He sat in a dark leather couch in a room on the third floor. "Close the door on the way out," he suggested. "No one disturbs us except in the case of all-out war, and then only if I am the only person available to broker a suit for peace." They nodded and backed away, closing iron-reinforced doors behind them. John-Paul rested his elbows on his knees in a matching recliner angled toward the couch.

Titian sighed. "I apologize for the chaos. The past few days have been dreadful messes. None of our intelligence or surveillance suggested we were vulnerable to attack here nor at the memorial. Our intelligence failures are my utmost concern; we need to understand what went wrong to prevent similar events from happening in the future." He paused.

"You sound like a press conference."

Titian smiled. "Ah, ha ha. The appearance of practiced peda-gogy aside, our preliminary concerns *are* retrospective." He licked his lips. "I won't prevaricate; you were there. We had precious little warning."

John-Paul squirmed; the shoulder on which he'd landed devel-oped a sudden pervasive ache. "Is there a connection between the bombing and the invasion?"

Titian's internal harrumph was visible but silent. "I will per-sonally notify you of all of the pertinent information at the precise moment we have anything resembling a preliminary conclusion."

John-Paul rubbed his face. "If you invited me back to treat me like a good little media drone who'll put on his vewwy sewious face before telling the rest of the world about your grave concerns and severe internal studies to convince everyone that you're taking this with all appropriate gravitas, then you read me very, very wrong." He reached for his bag.

Titian's speed belied his bulk. Suddenly he stood next to John-Paul, closing a massive hand around his bicep. "You're right. Let me offer my most profound apologies. The events of the past week have proven difficult for everyone. Even I am not immune to stresses and strains. Offer me one more opportunity to make things right, and I will give you my most honest answers... those we have and those I am at liberty to share. His eyes were brown in this light, not the red of their first meeting.

Both men stared, frustration flashing from the younger man's eyes. John-Paul didn't blink. Titian did, reseating with a sigh. "Now then," he began. "Here's what we know. We detected no special ac-tivity in the vicinity of the explosion, nor the memorial service. We conduct routine and specific sweeps of the area around this building, with multiple layers of security and redundancy. Not even a bird can land on a ledge without us knowing where it came from and where it goes.

"None of that mattered last week. I have a question for you. Clownfish mentioned that you saw a flash of light?"

John-Paul sucked through his teeth. "A glow. Purple. More of an aura than anything. When we walked through that archway, it caught in the corner of my eye. I thought it was a security reader."

Silver rings flashed as Titian placed his fists and thumbs together. "We *do* have security readers in that doorway, but they're ultraviolet, and should be invisible to all human eyes. If you had a frequency response beyond that range, you would find direct sunlight painful, so we can rule out that possibility. Do you remember other sensory input? Perhaps a smell, an impression, a sound, or a flavor? Sometimes the most inconsequential detail is the most important."

John-Paul leaned back and willed the memory to wash over him again, ignoring a frigid splash of shock and fear. He felt himself walk up to the archway dividing the hallway from the great room. He felt the cold presence of the line of demarcation between inside and outside, perpetually knowing versus continually blissful. He counted long seconds between each watch tick. His foot rose to an arch's zenith and he fell forward to catch himself at the nadir of the arch. The process repeated.

The doors at the end of the hallway rattled as if battered by a microburst of wind. Noise rushed down the hallway. The distraction interrupted a footstep and he paused, looking for the source of his discomfort while pulling his arm away from Clownfish's determined grasp. His ear thrummed in sympathetic response, adjusting to the sonic pressure.

Somehow then he fell. No, Clownfish pulled him to the ground. He salvaged their motions into a graceless crouch. The doors exploded into sawdust falling inward. Stone particles rang off all three in tiny impacts. Rubble pelted Claude. Warm red horizontal rain spattered onto John-Paul's face.

"A popping sound," he heard himself say. "Something just outside the door displaced the air. It rattled the doors before the explosion."

Titian raised his eyebrows. "Approximate size?"

"Given the timing and velocity, fist-sized–mine, not yours. The noise could either have been the leading edge of a shock wave or a localized re-adjustment of three-dimensional space. It either travelled at the speed of sound or spontaneously displaced air molecules as it appeared."

"The purple?"

"Nothing, no–", but he yanked his arm free, dropping it to his side. Clownfish opened her mouth to protest. A flash of light burst through the hallway, ignoring doors and walls. The unworldly glow bathed all three; his lunulae luminesced while the blonde in her hair screamed electric hues. In silent eons between heartbeats, light coalesced on the other man. The unidirectional glow clumped into a focused cluster. The hallway lighting returned, as did a haze around Claude.

"Very deliberate. It, or something behind it, analyzed us all as potential targets before settling on Claude. He was closest to the entrance, after all."

Titian steepled his fingers and drank a satisfied lungful of air. "That may be very useful information. Thank you." His eyes returned to John-Paul's face. "This may seem strange to you shortly, but it's why I invited you back."

"Strange, how?"

"Permit me to answer your question with one of my own. Prior to my prying, precisely what did you remember about this event? Be specific."

John-Paul felt tension in his shoulders slacken. He nestled deeper into the chair, crossing his right leg over the other. His fingers trailed on the ground and tangled in the deep rug under the chair. "Good question. I remember the event as a single image. Images, perhaps. It feels like looking at photographs and elaborating on what happened between them."

"What was the level of detail of this memory until, shall we say, five minutes ago?"

"Blurry photographs."

"When I pressed you on the issue, you recalled many more details, even offering a plausible hypothesis with weighted analysis of the possibilities of attack vectors."

He blinked. "Why *is* that?"

The large man smiled. "You have a gift. You and I, I should say. We stand apart from the rest of the world. This gift bestows greater opportunities for good or for ill. We have the responsibility to use our gifts appropriately. You've demonstrated that several times now." He ticked off sausage-sized fingers. "One, you stood up to the city's clown prince, unprovoked. Two, you held your own against our dear colorful compatriot. Three, you found your way into our outer sanctum with the merest of help and avoided almost certain disaster on the way out. Four, you on your own defeated a large creature of indeterminate origin and goals. Five, you replayed a situation in sufficient detail to reconstruct a model of reality and expose details previously unnoticed. You have a subtle, deep gift, so rarely seen in this age. In fact, you may probably guess the name of another acquaintance so similarly blessed."

"The Protector."

"Spot on." Titian's gaze searched infinity in his visage.

John-Paul kept his face blank. "Looking for something?"

"A visible reaction, perhaps. You seem to have taken the news with uncharacteristic grace. When I reveal my impressions to people, they react with shock or, most often, denial. Yet you seem bored."

John-Paul sat up and folded his hands in his lap. "Am I supposed to negotiate? Bizarre things happen. We remember them because they are abnormal. We don't remember the overwhelming weight of ordinary events because they are so perfectly mundane. How many millions of people in this city have fallen in love? How many of them believe that their experience is strange and amazing and new? To them it may be. To the human experience, it's strange when it *doesn't* happen.

"Maybe you all laugh at me when I'm not around, or maybe this is some initiation hoax you pull on every farmboy who falls off the turnip truck from flyover country, but I saw a biography of the Protector last night. He had a similar background. His power didn't draw me in. Neither did his escapades or his fame. Do you know what it was? It was his sincerity. It was how he explained things. So what if I have a gift? If I can do something to improve the world, I will. Gift or not."

"Is that what you did?" Titian's eyes narrowed and the corners of his mouth pulled his lips flat and white.

"Something was wrong. I knew I could change it, so I did." It was John-Paul's turn to scrutinize the other man. Beads of sweat prickled out of his forehead just beneath the hairline and the last knuckle of his right hand contracted with an irregular pulse. "Did I have a choice? Not really. Would I do anything differently? Duck faster, pull them both out of the way when I saw that glow."

After a long moment of silence, Titian loosed a belly laugh that shook the room with echoes. "Ahh," he sighed. "My boy, you have the most exquisite sense of comic timing." He mopped at his face again a pale blue handkerchief. "Very well put, though, I must say. Many years ago I resolved the same for myself."

"You?"

"You might not believe it to look at me now, but Pierre and I proved quite formidable to the remainder of our interlopers after you and the large metal one departed."

"Did you send the escort after me?"

"Of course."

"Thank you. Was everyone alright?"

Titian nodded. "No one is the worse physically for our rough and tumble. Clownfish nurses an injured pride, though one might charitably say that she distracted it long enough for you to land the first blow. If anyone asks, that is my official belief. You might neglect to mention the subject to her when next you meet."

"How about the spectators? Attendees?"

"Led to safety by your lovely companion."

"Good. Your employees don't say much."

"Laconicity is a virtue."

John-Paul stood and strode to a tinted and polarized window. "I presume you invited me here for something more specific than witty small talk, comparisons to a dead man, and recollections of a bombing."

"Quite so. As you've probably already pieced together from ample evidence, we do have a nice collection of *gifted* people in tight collaboration here. You've met many of them."

"Birds of a feather commiserate together." He chuckled, then regretted it. "Sorry. It sounded funnier when I thought it."

"Quite true, in its way. What might not be entirely obvious is that we have a tidy business arrangement. Under my guidance, and with many external sources of funding, we can concentrate on the effectual exercise of our powers as a sort of, well, job."

"Was one of these other people the Protector?"

Titian smiled inwardly as the trap closed. "You catch every clue. His lamentable demise has left our organization with a very painful gap. I do realize that you have your studies to pursue, but shall I assume also that you have not yet found full-time employment?"

"Are you offering me a job as his replacement?"

"I might not use that word with such precision. How could anyone replace the city's most beloved human heroic icon? While numerically speaking, one is as good as any other one, while each person is unique in personality and in other talents. Yet yours may very well complement the rest of the team. With sufficient training and discipline, I believe you would be very effective."

"My lifelong goal has been to be, quote, effective." He scowled.

"I'm happy to share more information about your...duties, we shall say. We've already discussed compensation. I would happily give you a personal recommendation to accept it if that were not a conflict of interest." Titian summoned a plastic folder from beside the couch.

John-Paul sauntered across the room. "May I have a moment?"

"Be my guest." Titian leveraged himself to the front of the couch, then waddled to the credenza. A wall panel slid open to reveal a crystal pitcher of ice water sweating with condensation. He poured a glass and gulped it down, then another, glaring at the tottering stack of reports.

"How can you guarantee you'll work around my class schedule?"

"We can offer no guarantee that there will never be an emergency *per se*, only that we will schedule the normal course of your duties around those times when you are available. We do monitor the city and possible points of conflict, but you know first-hand that predictions of natural disasters are often unreliable."

"I suppose they'd cancel class for that anyway."

"Too right. You may also have noticed the trial period. Inasmuch as we have only interacted under limited circumstances, admittedly which ended unfortunately but revealingly, I thought it proper to allow for experimentation under more controlled circumstances. We'd very much like your assistance in our work, and we think we can work very well together, but the ultimate demonstration will be actual field work."

John-Paul closed the folder. "Field work?"

"Our next action. We'd like to include you to see how you work with a group."

"Who is this group?"

"For now, Pierre and Clownfish. We have a few other active agents, but with Claude recovering... still, a three-person team can be quite effective, especially as most of the threats we face have limited scope."

"When?"

Titian smiled. "Here's the risk. We may pay you for a year and never call you. We may shake hands and walk out of here and immediately summon you to defy death as you battle, and I assure you that this is very much picturesque language, the forces of evil. No one knows."

A long moment passed. Outside, a small construction crew continued to assemble scaffolding. Their helmets appeared at the base of the window. Beyond them, the morning fog had started to burn away. A tall ship bobbing in the bay. John-Paul flipped through the offer again.

"I'm inclined to agree to the trial, but may I take this home to consider? My grandfather was an attorney. He'd never forgive me for not reading the fine print." His skin crawled with the lie, but he promised to make up for it later.

Titian positively beamed. "Of course." He offered his hand and they shook. "Wonderful. Marvelous. You won't regret this." He tapped the communicator on his collar. "Please escort our young friend here to the equipment room." Another fungible assistant appeared and brushed John-Paul away.

Titian turned back to the credenza and idly spun the globe. Radiant beams reflected from the polished continents even as the ocean's deep azures absorbed the light. A smudge in the ocean caught his eye, and he leaned close to polish it away. Satisfied, he straightened and walked back to the couch with an armful of folders. Everything was working out nicely.

○ ○ ○

John-Paul followed the assistant down a long, straight corridor somehow illuminated by passive light glowing from the top of the ceiling and bottom of the floor. The walk was sterile and silent; the floor was a rubbery material which absorbed their footsteps and propelled them forward. They wound through a maze of walls and emerged in what could have been the same corridor, heading in the opposite direction.

"You did that just to show off." John-Paul grinned.

The other man pushed through a recessed door.

The room had a low ceiling. In contrast to Titian's dark-paneled lair, this room was white and chrome, with rounded surfaces polished to a candy-slick shine. Waist-high inset bars provided diffuse light. John-Paul fought the urge to lick a beveled table edge, fearing a sugar crash.

A rounded depression formed the room's nucleus around which high tables piled with equipment, workbenches, and three-legged wing-backed chairs described complex orbits. John-Paul followed his guide's finger to the center of the room. As he stepped into the ring, blue enveloped him from hidden ceiling and floor lights. He jerked with his first footstep; the floor glowed around his foot with an intensity varying with his weight. A pinging noise accompanied each step as the light cycled to a dusky hue.

The other man palmed the surface of an empty workbench and tapped his fingers in a well-practiced tattoo. A yellow glow appeared around his hand.

The blue light dimmed further, then pulsed in quick opposing circles, the ceiling clockwise and the floor counterclockwise. When they were at opposite ends of the circle, they doubled in intensity and draw diameters through him. A gentle breeze blew in beneath his feet, smelling of fresh straw and manure, then baking bread and newly cut sweet grass. The pace of the pulses increased to a strobe. Afterimages of the room melted away in his view until the pulsing stopped as suddenly as it had started.

His eyes watered. "What was... what just... What *was* that?"

The other man shrugged. Wall panels opened. Three identical attendants stepped to the empty work bench, opening gray metal suitcases on cue. They unpacked a man's white dress shirt, well-tailored navy slacks, a pair of brown loafers with sturdy soles, and a gold and silver watch, before retreating into the walls again. John-Paul sighed. "Not even a privacy screen?" The other man turned his back.

The clothes fit perfectly. He raised his arms well above his head and stared at the seams, but the fabric moved with him, showing no hint of strain or stress. He tried a few knee bends. "Comfortable. Now what?"

He saw the bullet leave the gun and felt himself dive out of its path. He crashed through a chair and scuttled behind a workbench.

119

The chair clattered as it landed on two of its legs, denting and bending its curved back piece. The bullet struck a heavy piece of equipment with a clunk as loud as the echo of the report.

A velvet voice whispered from behind his head. "You can come out now."

When his heart stopped pounding long enough for him to breathe, John-Paul risked a peek. "That's exactly what I'd say if I wanted to shoot me."

"It's a test of the clothes. You look nice, by the way. Leave the shirt untucked."

Clownfish's eyes sparked above a tiny amused smile. Her outfit was similar, if more feminine. "What?" she asked. "You didn't think we paraded around in capes and tights? That would give away half the fun."

He stood. The assistant made a show of ejecting the pistol's clip and checking the chamber. "I would have said, 'Hey, try this on.'"

Clownfish shrugged. "Titian has his own sense of style. He has idiosyncrasies, but his techniques work." She looked him over again, then straightened his collar. He felt her warm breath and leaned away. She pulled back her hand as if burnt.

"Sorry," he mumbled, eyes on the floor. The moment hung in the air.

"We'll contact you. There's a communicator dial on the underside of the watch. Find a private corner when it goes off and we'll tell you where and when." She stared again at his face and hair and offered a quick smile that never reached her eyes. A faint click revealed the door panel as she stepped through.

John-Paul turned toward his guide. The other man stood stoically, hands behind his back, and eyes averted. "I'm done here, right?"

At the other man's nod, he gathered his old clothes in one of the open cases and departed the building. This time, the long corridor led to the front door.

o o o

Eratosthenes paused. Weariness turned his muscles watery. He tilted his head, feeling tiny changes in the windless air on his eardrums. Satisfied, he groaned as he convinced his knees to bend for just one more step...just one more...just one more. Smooth whorls of his walking stick dug designs into the palm of his hand. He pushed forward.

Even his clothes showed the wear of his journey: fabric thinned by exposure and repetition of the final step which continued to elude him. He stumbled again and dropped to a knee, wiping a dry hand across his face, hating the bristly feel of thick stubble that he knew grew in patches, wanting nothing more than a hot shower and a soft bed.

He lowered himself further, fearing the crackling sounds of his cartilage, then lay on his back. Fire raced across the sky. Each pebble and clump of dirt underneath was an individual abomination under that brilliant display. He breathed thin air, knife-edged and cold despite the desert wasteland. He sighed out thick vapor.

A shadow darkened his vision. He snapped his eyelids open. The world reeled and jumped into focus with immediate clarity; the wealth of shapes scrambled his mind. He sat up, cringing as a muscle in his neck screamed, and looked around at the blasted landscape. "What am I *doing*?"

No one answered.

The tiny box in his pocket hummed. Its violence and volume had faded. It had shrunk since his first encounter. It was cool to his touch despite the late afternoon heat.

In the armored bowels of the basement warehouse, he walked by a pallet stacked high with identical boxes. Bronze patinas suggested age and gravity. Something drew his eyes. They slipped toward the boxes against his will, and his body jerked itself back awake after several minutes of open-mouthed gaping. His tablet had fallen to the ground and rebooted, beeping a plaintive canon for his attention and jarring him back into the present.

Theft gradually settled into his mind with the realization that it was perfectly possible, that perfect escape conditions existed and that he could rearrange the other boxes on the pallet such that no one would detect the loss until he was far, far away.

He hadn't known where nor why. The rush of eventual possession was enough, the incessant desire to have and to hold, and the certainty that it was certain. Hours or days or weeks drifted away on dream winds, always pulling inevitable actions into his mind in omnitemporal essence.

He'd slipped into an unused elevator fortunately vacated by another assistant, punching the button for the staging area while the most recent access code was still warm in the card reader's memory. His pounding heart and clenching chest forced short, quick gasps as he counted out long seconds of descent. The door shuffled open to reveal what he knew would be but still feared would not be an empty room.

A tarp covered the pallet, left haphazard in a corner. Fingerthick yellow ropes held blue in place. The warm metallic glow still drew his attention. His head whipped around and his eyes bulged; he strained to hear a sound other than the dehumidifier. He was alone.

He rushed across the room, sliding on his knees the last several yards. One hand darted under an untucked corner. The box—his box—rested second from the top. A quick yank yielded the treasure: his treasure. A dull thud reported that the other boxes had found a new equilibrium. He jerked his head around to scan for reactions.

It was warm in his hands; it pulsed with energy, seeming to bubble with pride at his success. He examined each side. The bottommost face of the cube had faint stamped numbers: 0801. Otherwise there were no markings or labels or obvious openings.

He pulled a bag from under his shirt and stuffed the box inside the dark canvas, pulling at the straining zipper. The warm kiss of the metal face still blushed on his fingers, and he sprinted to the elevator. It had remained on this floor during the shift change.

The ground floor seemed eons away. Every bump and jostle of the elevator and its gears and motor and cables startled him with taunts to expose his theft and deception. His stomach fell away as the elevator adjusted itself at the lobby; the doors again opened into marble and mirrored walls. He watched himself from inconceivable angles, passing well-tended plants until he was alone with himself again to walk out the door and down the steps and merge into rush hour's pedestrian river. The bag was heavy as duty and light as a feather.

He pulled the shades in his townhouse, blocking of tree-and-subdivision dotted hillsides, to open the bag on the living room rug. In this light, the box had an inner glow. He turned it until a rightness suggested an up and down, as well as the preferred orientation of the other sides. An electric tingle raised the hairs of his arms. He ran curious along the right and left faces.

He bit his lower lip. His devotion revealed hidden indentations to press. A satisfying click suggested heavy gears. The cover *bloomed*. Honey-covered light seeped up the room and walls, defying gravity to bathe him in its sweet perfume. He cried out for air, gasping and choking, finding only viscous light. He drank in.

Then he had a name.

The box fell away. He saw its contents in true form. He knew why it existed and understood the purpose of its countless compatriots, scattered throughout the city. He saw. They saw; they sang a slow soft song that shifted from dark beneath. The low lament resolved into words. He backed away, shoes scrabbling on the carpet, to hit his head against the far wall. He shook away the stars, then pleaded with the box still voiding its contents into the air.

"No," he whispered. "I can't. That's... No, not me!"

He walked his way up the wall, hands and feet finding few holds, and pointed a finger at the window. It dissolved into silvery ripples. "No," he cried. His spine cracked as he straightened. In jagged motions he slammed the box top closed and cradled it to his chest like a suckling child, then dove head-first through the shimmering opening.

He landed awkwardly, savoring the thin air as his lungs began to work again. He pulled himself to his knees and ran. Memory fell behind.

Now memory had returned, resuscitating his unexamined life. His forehead ached with effort; he drew his knees to his chest to shiver. An age passed.

He sat upright to stare beyond the sparse sandy ground and rugged rocks, back an unmeasurable distance to the city. The other boxes remained unliberated. They glowed and sang to each other, squirreled away against the possibility of an ugly future. He could read the signs; winter was coming.

An emptiness asserted itself in his belly and he licked lips long dry and cracked with thirst. He could not remember how long he'd run, nor where he was, but he remembered a name. He remembered his name. He cursed unpursued knowledge and wept at cowardice. Then he stood, silhouette square against an uncaring sky, to began the long, lonely walk back to civilization.

Hours later, the box pulsed to suggest an alternative.

∘ ∘ ∘

Pandora stomped out of the elevator, weaving from the unbalance of the backpack slung off of her left shoulder and the helmet in her right hand. Her phone beebled three rings again. "Just a *minute*," she hissed.

Coworkers crossed her path through the narrow maze. Those unfortunate enough to meet her gaze stepped quickly away or busied themselves, fascinated by their own worlds of papers and folders...except for Anija.

"Pandora, oh, hi! I heard this *juicy* rumor that there was a secret meeting –"

"Go *away*."

"– and they said they saw *you* there, and I wondered if it was for work or for fun or if you've finally taken my advice to be more social, a pretty girl like you, and –"

Pandora leaned back to avoid two hands waved in wild gesticulation and pushed past her, ducking into her cubicle. The walls were blank. The desk was blank, except for a small bin of paper clips with a round magnetic opening. The sides were the color of a translucent ladybug. She dumped her bag on the desk and tossed her helmet underneath before plopping into a swively chair. It sank two inches with a satisfying whoosh. "Ah," she said.

Her cubicle offered a glorious view of industrial strength copiers, printers, shredders, and other machines dedicated to glyph-based tree pulp worship—and their steady lines of devotees. On her second day, she asked for a plant to put on the shelf to block the view of the copy room in the center of the floor. A wrinkly old bat of a coworker sculpted from dried apples and smelling faintly of vinegar favored her a narrow gaze. "Some things are just not done." Interns did not appear on the waiting list for cubicle decorations. She stuffed the metal shelf full of binders, hoping they'd baffle some of the sound.

Her phone's message light blinked off, then on. She cursed its silent mockery, managing to type in her password before turning back to the phone with an eyeroll she hoped wasn't audible. Of the ten most recent calls, nine were from this morning—one, her mother, calling during breakfast to discuss the dietary habits of her hateful little dog who'd recently readopted the habit of eating items both not food and non-digestible—and the other eight unknown numbers. "Ugh," she said, flipping a mental coin. Tails won.

She stabbed the delete button and turned to her computer. The first email was urgent, anonymous, and a sentence long. "Meet me in the lobby."

She pulled a mirror out of her backpack and examined herself to find no sign of stupid. Her chuckle was her only reward; not even Anija had heard the quip. "Right," she said. "A brilliant waste of a morning." The computer screen flashed blue as another message fell into her inbox. Bright gold letters burned across the screen. "Please?"

"Hateful machines," she muttered. After another coin flip, she left her bag.

***

An man of indeterminate age and features and immaculate dress walked down the cubicle aisle from the other direction, flashing smiles of supreme confidence at everyone who met his eyes. Anija smiled and purred. "Ooh, hi!"

The word escaped like air rushing out of a long-closed tomb. "Hello." He cleared his throat. "Pardon me. Ahem. Hello. May I ask you a favor?"

She pursed her lips and looked down, toying with a necklace festooned with huge translucent plastic beads. "Anything."

"I'm looking for a Miss Pandora d'Avril. Do I have the right floor?"

She beamed. "Oh yes, I was just talking to her. I can take you to her. My name's Anija, by the way."

He ignored her hand, snapping his head in the direction her eyes had flicked. "Thank you," he offered as he departed.

She ran to keep up. "Were you with her the other day at the party? It was a party, right? She wouldn't tell me anything, but you can totally see it in her eyes when you mention it. Now that's funny, she was just here a minute ago. I'm sure she'll be right back. Anyway, like I was saying, I heard she was at a party with that handsome Protector. I've always liked him...I wonder if she'd introduce me? I bet she's shy around him. She's very pretty but so quiet sometimes...."

He paused in the doorway to soak up the scene, computer unlocked and recently started, chair still warm, helmet under the desk. Then he pushed past Anija to sprint for the elevator. She squeaked. "Hey!" Confused cubicle dwellers popped their heads above their walls at the commotion.

o o o

John-Paul stifled another yawn and sneaked a look at his watch. His margin notes had a brief calculation about how fast the classroom must move for a reliable chronometer set to measure time from a fixed point of reference but entangled somehow at the quantum level to the device at his wrist to progress so slowly. He expected this from a physics symposium, but not in a chemistry class and certainly not during a discussion of hydrocarbon chaining. He doodled a vortex around the division by zero error.

Perhaps the watch was decorative, not functional, and tapped it with his pen. A blue field exploded outward, dimming and pausing the rest of the room mid-moment.

Titian's face appeared. "Hello?"

"Oh...uh...whoa. Uh, sorry. I didn't mean to...I didn't know."

"Ah, young Mr. Harrison. I see you've outfitted yourself appropriately. Is everything to your satisfaction?" The image faded for a second, then reappeared with a sniff and a scowl. "At least you like the watch. Were the other clothes somehow inappropriate?"

"No, it's...why is everyone stopped?"

Titian laughed. "Ever curious. We did not pause time, if that is your question. That would violate causality in many unpleasant ways, not to think of the tremendous power requirements if it were even possible. This is a mere illusion. It's trickery of the most realistic form. The human mind is amazing thing. With the barest whisper of suggestion, it will paint a picture accurate to and consistent in even the smallest detail. Dreams work in the same way. I suspect," his voice lowered to a collaborator's whisper, "verisimilitude is an important principle for coping with the world as it is, not as we wish it to be."

John-Paul swallowed. "Maybe I'm in dummy mode because I'm trying to stay awake *and* take notes, but you lost me after you didn't stop time."

"Someone with a flair for the dramatic might call this a direct mental link. Barry discovered the flash of light. What was his phrase? A cool mind hack as a visual reminder? It's blue for you? That's fascinating, though I digress. We are communicating at the speed of thought."

"Oh." He paused. "I called you accidentally, I'm sorry. I didn't mean—"

"You need not beg forgiveness. How amusing a coincidence: I had prepared to do the same. We have reliable information that we will have need of your services in roughly ninety minutes. We can arrange for transport from the door of your current building as soon as class completes. Will you join us?"

John-Paul probed the field with a finger. Electricity crackled from his rising arm hairs. It certainly *felt* real. "I was planning to go to the library, but if you really need me, I guess I can."

Titian's enormous grin veered close with sufficient detail to reveal every tooth despite the wavering field. "Wonderful. We will find you. And now, back to class!"

The glow faded. The room's lights rose. The professor's last word hung in the air and he continued without pause. John-Paul rubbed his head; his brain swum with the snap between the posture he thought he had and the one he did have. He shook off encroaching nausea. His watch continued its uncertain march into the unknown—if anything, slower than before.

o o o

Clownfish skimmed the pre-mission briefing, ticking off checkboxes in her head. Pierre watched her eyes jump up and to the right with each sentence like some kind of antique brain typewriter. Then her keys tangled.

"Forty-five minutes until extraction? That's *crazy*. Titian, he might remind you of..." She closed her eyes. "He's not. Most definitely not."

Titian leaned far back in his chair, feet on the desk and fingers knit together behind his head. "We spoke before you came in. His demeanor is one of confidence."

"You didn't tell him *anything*, you toad." Impossibly long legs unfolded. She leaned over his desk. A dangerous smile curled the corners of her lips.

"I told him what he needed to know."

"Did you *see* what he did to Twist? I know. He's rogue and he's unpredictable, and that was right after the incident, and whatever other silly excuse you want to make, but Twist, he nearly killed him. This is not some patsy you paid to dress up in a costume and gassed enough to roll under a few punches. We've never been able to figure out why he can hold his own against us. And he nearly killed him. How is rushing this first assignment is a good idea?"

Titian's shrug moved only his shoulders. "He's getting as much training as we ever did. Maybe more. He has you."

She turned her back on him to lean against the desk, stretching one leg and then the other. "I hope you know what you're doing. Tell me you have some enormous, subtle plan, like always. Tell me things will only appear to fall to pieces just before you swoop in and make everything right. I'm starting not to believe that." She nodded at Claude's empty chair.

"My dear." He sat up. "If you'd like to run this operation, I will *happily* bequeath you my desk, my vaults, and the dozen-odd missions in various stages of planning, but I have difficulty believing that I could play the role of jilted lover in the press with a fraction of the style that you do."

She came across the desk at him, a miniature sonic boom rushing away from her fist. Two sausage-sized fingers stabbed the air; her hand stopped a whisker's breadth from his jawbone. They stared at each other until detente; she slumped, slinking away to pace the room.

"That's not fair, Titian. None of this is fair."

"My dear girl, when did the sweet perfume of fairness last bless our air? It wasn't fair when we watched starving neighbors freeze to death under the watchful eye of uptown security. It wasn't fair when they laughed at my pleas. It wasn't fair when they relegated you to carnival show sidekick. It wasn't fair when a stupid accident killed Steven... or Barry. It wasn't fair when the only traction and air time and attention we could get was turning him into some gawking farmboy with a simplistic aw-shucks do-gooder philosophy and big shiny muscles for the women and arm candy for the men.

"How is it fair that we bear solely this responsibility, its weight so unappreciated? We do not receive fairness. Not ever. Not now. We know that. What good is that knowledge? We never asked for this responsibility. No one gave us permission. Yet here we are. You may choose to walk out of here naked and ashamed. Go ahead. Apologize for your uniqueness. I choose instead to exploit every gift I have to accomplish every goal I had. I would make that choice in any circumstance. I never looked back. I don't have that luxury, not if we are to finish what we've started.

"I need to know now. Do you have solidarity, Sandie?"

She played through the scene. They'd arrive separately, their handlers pointing them at the threat. They would converge at a rendezvous point suitable to survey the scene. She could suggest to him how to perform the least damage if things went wrong while retaining close supervision. Titian could observe closely.

"I want his control key."

Titian raised an eyebrow.

"We can't let him get out of hand. I have to be able to stop him if something goes wrong."

"You saw him and the statue. It was beautiful. It was clean and surgical."

"Roman... I'm serious. If we're going to do this, if you want me in, give me an out." She folded her arms and motioned toward the door.

He let her touch the heavy doorknob before sighing. "Just this once. Use only in case of emergency." At his nod, an assistant disappeared through the fake wall door.

Clownfish imitated his shrug. "Trust me or don't."

"Very well then. Now you, Pierre. Do we have solidarity?"

Pierre drained his glass. "Give me a few minutes with Claude after we finish up and before the debriefing and I'm in."

"So shall it be?"

They answered in unison. "So it is."

o o o

Pandora stared at the photographs in the folder on her desk. She recognized the scrawl on the sticky note, if not WRF, the ubiquitous initials of the paper's publisher. "For your review," it suggested. She'd pushed it off her keyboard with a pencil eraser, though it continued to emit radioactive particles of attentionium.

Someone coughed nervously an aisle away. She glanced at the clock, hoping that the twenty minutes she'd been in the office so far this afternoon had magically stretched out into four hours. She'd already had one argument over the contents of her latest photography assignment and two batches of scut work reviewing rejected shots from other interns for errors in composition, lighting, contrast, and even shutter speed.

The glamour of publishing and her ability to concentrate had faded together.

The events of the past several days bore some of the blame: a snap assignment gone weird, a confrontation in her own apartment, and a funeral she struggled to remember even as the details threatened to push each other out of her mind. Concentration frightened away recall. Lights flashed. Explosions shook the ground. She yelled and gestured and at a panicking crowd. Mud spattered on her toes. A jacket hung loosely on her shoulders. She had impressions. Watery thoughts evaporated in her grasping hands.

She glanced again at the photographs, letting them blur and wash over her. A color caught her eye and memories returned, whistling and tan from extended vacations. She and John-Paul shared a limo to the funeral. She and Clownfish rode back in silence, the other woman staring sullenly out the windows. Pandora contemplated the upholstery, the scuffs on her shoes, a vague sense of unease every time the car rolled to a stop, and the way she'd left John-Paul at the funeral. He'd walked them both to the car, but Pandora stopped him there, promising that she was alright, swearing to stay safe and out of trouble, and hinting that they would, at some point in a nebulous future, speak again. She watched him from the safety of tinted windows as he stared at the car, chewing his lower lip and brushing hair back from his face.

If only she'd had the presence of mind to sprint for the tree line at the funeral, she could have documented the event for her own mind, if not the paper.

Her email blinked; peripheral vision drew her into the present. An fourth floor administrative assistant warned that the monthly refrigerator cleaning would begin in an hour, so please clean out anything you want to keep. It blinked again as she read, replies piling in, first as a request for more time and then in a flood of angry threats to stop the wide rebroadcast. Homesickness summoned the memory of quiet afternoons in her village.

The folder contained several grainy and recent photographs of Clownfish, Claude, Pierre, the Protector, and John-Paul. The technique was passable, but the photographer had obviously been in a hurry, choosing poor composition angles and a film speed which prioritized rapid-fire exposures over quality. The half-blurred final shot showed Clownfish and Pierre meeting just outside the park by the funeral. Pierre gestured with his left hand. A fuzzy blob—fog or lens debris—obscured his arm from the elbow onward.

The angle was low, looking up, as if the photographer lay on his belly in the mud.

"What am I supposed to be looking for," she wondered aloud.

"Well?"

She jumped and cracked her knee against the desk. W. Roderick Fontaine leaned against her wall, drumming swollen fingers against a blue and white checked tie laying horizontal against his belly. "You recognize this guy or not?"

She squeaked. Her mind shrugged and watched her searched her lungs for words.

"Lissen Miss Avril, I didn't want to do this, but we have two options here. Either you play dumb, or maybe we can jog your memory?" He slapped another photograph on the stack: Pandora and John-Paul riding into her garage. A greasy thumb print smeared the print. "You're too young to go senile, girl. Looks like you two are more than just casual acquaintances."

"Mr. Roderick, I –"

"No," he said. "You think really hard about what you're about to say, because if it isn't 'Mr. Roderick, I'm only a photography intern, but I know I can land you a great story about the Protector, if you only give me a chance!' then we're going to have a nice friendly discussion about what it means to work here. Very friendly."

Pandora nodded so hard her earrings rattled. "We've met."

Roderick shifted his weight. A thin beam of natural light wedged past. "Good answer. You gonna see him again? Don't answer that. You think."

He turned to leave, but held the first step's position. She imagined she could see gears turning in his massive head between his little piggy ears, then prayed he couldn't read minds. "Wait a minute, I have a better idea."

He slapped at one pant leg with a beefy fist, then shuffled to face her again. "Everybody knows the Protector doesn't work alone. He has his gal, this Clownfish lady, and at least those two screwups show up most of the time. But he's not the one in charge. There's the big guy up at the top—big guy in more ways than one, if you know what I mean."

Pandora cringed at the idea of what Fontaine considered obese.

"I give you his address and we set you up an interview, ostensibly to talk about your Protector friend but, more important, to find a real story. The real story."

"But I'm just a photographer, and an intern." Mockery demanded its time in the air, but she suppressed it.

"The perfect candidate. Didn't I say that? Connected to the Protector, young, na*iuml*ve, on a silly assignment out of her league. He'll suspect you of course, but he'll never suspect that you're exactly what he suspects." Fontaine tilted his head and closed his eyes and moved his lips, repeating the sentence. He smiled and nodded, satisfied.

She met his eyes and counted to ten. "How about a fluff piece, maybe a profile? What's your business? How have you achieved your success? What's next for your organization?" The word "organization" pealed, hollow, in her ears, but she held her breath as the publisher's eyes glazed.

Finally Fontaine nodded. "Sounds good. Call Vernon to set you up with a pass and an address and an appointment. This afternoon's good. Get on it now. I want to see your notes ... you're an intern? Tuesday."

"Yes, Mr. Fontaine."

He held her gaze for a long moment before ambling away. His heavy footfalls shook a filthy snow of dust from the leaves of her fake plant onto the low file cabinet.

Vernon answered almost before the phone rang. "Fontaine's office, Vernon speaking. Mr. Fontaine isn't here. May I redirect your call?"

"Hi, um. This is Pandora d'Avril. Mr. Fontaine just told me to call you?"

"Yes. I've put together a small information packet. Are you in the office now? If you can come up to the eighteenth floor, we can get you all set up."

"Um... yeah. I'm not really sure what I'm supposed to do here, because...."

He cut her off. "We've already taken care of it. You have a three-thirty appointment with Mr. Titian. I've included a transit pass and I've sent over your press credentials already. All you have to do is show up, be charming, and ask the questions we've prepared. Shall I assume you can read a briefing, rephrase our suggestions in your own words, and pursue any followups appropriately? Your transcripts suggest that you've already taken the relevant classes."

"Yes, of course, but I'm still not sure...."

His stage whisper thrilled her with its suggestions hidden knowledge and conspiracies. "Why you? If you promise not to tell, I'll explain."

"Okay? Okay, yes—of course."

"Mr. Fontaine is... well, perhaps the best word is *fortunate.* Perhaps perceptive. Charmed. Regardless of any description, his wild ideas often prove useful. If you asked him, he would use those words. I won't disagree. Thank whim or fortune. You are his shining star for this assignment. Perhaps it will go nowhere, or perhaps you will uncover a story. I can only give you my best advice: he wouldn't send you out like this unless he thought you were capable."

"I had no idea he had any idea who I am."

"He's familiar with the background of every employee, including interns. You have a prestigious position, Miss d'Avril. It may not seem like it now, but you're only here because we believe that you have a future with the paper."

"Um." She struggled for a response, relieved that politeness was a reflex. "Thank you. Eighteenth floor?"

"I'll have the packet waiting when you arrive."

Pandora hung up. It was the Friday afternoon before a three-day weekend. She had her first interview, ever, in a couple of hours, with one of the most powerful people in the city, at the request of another of the most powerful people in the city. She pinched herself between the thumb and index finger of the left hand. It stung.

She gathered her courage and stood, watching the elevator bank recede as she looked down the row of cubicles.

○ ○ ○

Pierre gestured at the jet-black van from cover of an alley. It turned in and he followed it, banging twice on the door. Inside, two heavyset assistants bookended John-Paul. "Nice threads, kid. Did you get your armored vest?"

John-Paul raised an eyebrow. "First I've heard of it. You're kidding, right?"

135

Pierre shook his head. One of the other men pushed John-Paul out the door. The other rummaged in the back and produced a heavy black mesh wrapped in plastic.

"I assume this goes on over the shirt?"

"We have two minutes. Tell me they gave you the belt too."

John-Paul readjusted his shirt tails and collar, ignoring an assistant holding out a small plastic disc. He threw a wad of discarded cellophane back in the van. "I didn't get the complete tour. What else? Jet pack? Sidearm? Personal invisibility field?"

Pierre mumbled something about getting everyone killed, then turned back to enunciate. "Fasten that to your belt; it'll have to do for now."

"What is it?"

Pierre hit the disc with the side of his fist. "It's on. Trust me. Clownie, you in position?"

Their wrists buzzed. "Too casual, Pierre. We'll talk later. Is John-Paul ready?"

"Give me a time machine and a month's leave." He grimaced. "No."

"We're on in forty. Get it done. Shoo the delivery team out of our way."

Pierre pointed to the end of the alley. The van's wheels spun halfway through the word "Go".

John-Paul fiddled again with his collar. "Sorry, what are we doing again? And why?"

The other man's tone stayed flat. "*You* are trying not to die or get anyone else killed. That goes double for me and Clownie. That's goal number one. Goal number two goal is to keep Titian happy, however that happens, as far as that does not conflict with goal number one. If you think he won't be happy, remember you have to answer to me first. Any other questions? Evaluate them against goal one. Get down!" The street shook. He dropped to a crouch and pushed John-Paul flat against the wall.

Screams dopplered their ears as a wave of pedestrians rushed by. A well-armored buggy screeched to a tire-smoking stop in the middle of the road where it revved its engine. Metal plates covered oversized tires and its engine compartment; bulletproof glass enclosed the passengers. Laughter spilled into the air from inside the vehicle.

A gorilla of a man in a tight black tank top and leggings jumped out of the window. "That's right! You run on home! It's time for the boys to play!" He waved a rifle and wagged his tongue at the crowds. "Big Peeeeee, where aaaaare you?" He stomped a circle around the buggy, posing every few steps to raise his hand to his ear. "Come out wherever you are, the Dirty Boys want to play!"

Clownfish's voice hissed again. "We give the normals one more minute to evacuate. Then John-Paul's on."

"On? On what?"

Electricity crackled around her sign. "You go out there and engage him."

"A citizen's arrest for bad acting? Poor costuming? Leggings this time of year?"

Pierre snickered, *sotto voce*. "You're quicker than I thought." He paused. "Don't tell Titian I said that."

The lead Dirty Boy place-kicked a fire hydrant through a jewelry store window and dodged the spray of water. "I'm making a mess out here. I'm breaking the law. Look at me, I'm anarchy and I like it! Wheeee!"

John-Paul rolled his eyes. "This is a setup. You're pranking me. There's no way that guy could have gone up against the Protector. Even that guy with the stupid belt was tougher than this."

"He's big. Remember rule one."

"Whatever. You owe me a drink." He scuttled out of the alley to a spot behind a parked car. The other man continued to pose and taunt despite the empty street. John-Paul shook his head. "I've had hangnails more threatening than this clown."

"Get *out* there," whispered Clownfish. "Go. Now."

He stepped out from behind the car. The Dirty Boy swiveled his head to follow, sonar accurate. Then the giggles struck. "Oh no... ha ha!"

The other man's eyes grew wide. His nostrils flared and red drained into his face. "What is so *funny*?"

"I'm sorry, wow. Heh. It's just... wow, ha ha, you're so ridiculous in that getup. I'm sorry. Just give me a minute." The man pushed John-Paul. His giggles disappeared. "Uh, sorry. I think there's a misunderstanding. You guys can go now." His wrist crackled again.

"I asked, 'What is so *funny*?'" Spittle flew. The afternoon sun flashed gold off of one of his teeth. He pushed harder, and the younger man stumbled.

John-Paul narrowed his eyes. "Do you have a listening problem? I told you. *You* are. Hands off."

The man turned away. "Oh. Well, then. I amuse you. I'm sorry I violate your precious little sense of personal space. Most of all...." His vicious double-handled swing came from nowhere, but John-Paul leaned back and pushed the other man's fists on their way with an open palm. The man spun and caught himself on hands and knees, immediately springing back with an uppercut. John-Paul sidestepped and kicked behind him, landing a solid blow to the kidneys. The other man skidded to a stop in front of the buggy. "Go home, Leonard. This is a waste of our time."

Silver light exploded as the car's doors swung open to reveal Leonard's two brothers. They swaggered to his side, one slapping a pipe wrench against his palm and the other wrapping a chain around his fist. They dragged Leonard to his feet with appreciative pats on the head and back. Together they advanced.

"We did the job," one called. "Give us the money and keep your smart mouth shut. Get it?"

John-Paul heard Clownfish breathe through his communicator, and he thumbed the mute button. Somewhere overhead he heard her yell, words indistinct at that distance.

Leonard slipped a hand from the small of his back and grinned as he pointed a wicked dagger at John-Paul. All three men rushed at him.

He dropped at the last possible second, sweeping a leg to trip the man with the chain and punching Leonard's wrist. The large man managed to hold the knife even as his arm went numb. The two brothers collided. The brother with the wrench swung at John-Paul's head, but he ducked at rolled to the side. "Lying on the ground," his brain admitted, "unarmed against three opponents is a poor opening gambit."

Another part of his brain flared and twinged as he willed the group to ignore tactics and rush him one at a time. They did. He ducked under a wild chain swing, throwing a one-two combination of stomach and face punches. He pushed his target into the brother with the wrench. They collapsed in a heap.

Leonard had shifted the knife to his other hand. He sliced the air with wild gestures. John-Paul faked a rush, pulling away at the last instant to land a kick on Leonard's right knee. He twisted in the air to deliver a throat punch that left the other man staggering and coughing.

The man with the pipe grabbed him from behind with a solid tackle. Momentum carried them into the alley near a whispering Pierre. "Uh?" asked John-Paul, as someone flipped him over and punched him in the face. The fireworks in his vision distracted him from his head bouncing on the pavement. The little voice stopped, then spoke slowly and clearly.

He watched the origin and trajectory and destination of the next punch as he twisted out of the way, watching the man's fist smack against the pavement. He cut short the howls of disbelief and pain by slapping the back of the man's head; he slumped to the ground with a jerk and lay still.

John-Paul stalked to the buggy, feeling the greasy chill of two pairs of hostile eyes. He slipped one hand under the front bumper and flipped over the vehicle. Metal groaned and glass shattered. "I'm through playing."

Leonard bellowed and pulled himself to his feet, clutching his arm and launching himself into a run. John-Paul caught the punch in his right hand. Leonard's run continued two steps as John-Paul sidestepped and twisted the arm behind his back. Leonard knelt, face and neck straining with inertia.

"I'm done. Are you?"

"You don't fool me. I know you're not him. I want my money, kid, and money for the buggy, and I'm gonna see you fry, you little freak. I didn't agree to this. You watch yourself when he turns off the flow and the rules don't apply. The Dirty Boys'll..."

John-Paul dropped his arm and kicked him in the back of the head as he fell, an unconscious sack of lumpy groceries.

Blue reflections flashed as Clownfish descended, angel-glorious, on a column of fire. Her eyes were as sharp as Damascus steel. A bubble engulfed both of them as time waited.

"Are you *crazy*," she yelled. "Keep your hands where I can see them. You're not going mental on me. You tell me right now what you're doing, absolutely right now, or so help me, I *will* take you down. This time I *won't* hold back." She landed lightly at her feet and crossed her arms. The blue bubble crackled and sizzled as sparks described short chords.

Adrenaline screamed through his muscles and his chest heaved. He stared back. "You told me to take care of him, and I did. Three on one. Are you rushing in here now that there's one left? You sent me in here unarmed. I made a good showing." He rubbed a bruise on the back of his head. "Pretty good. What's the problem?"

She stuck her finger in his chest. "What's the problem?" Disbelief scarred her expression. "The problem is, you've probably broken a dozen bones in this guy alone. Do you have any idea what the damage bill is on this? What are you *thinking*?"

He slapped away her hand. "I'm *defending* myself, by myself, thanks to you and Pierre. You tell me the problem." The syllables slid themselves out of his mouth in precise, discrete units as if he chewed them in reverse.

"Defending yourself? That's what you call it? Really? You called Leonard by name! You think you're in danger?" Surprise bubbled up somewhere behind her anger.

"A knife, a wrench, a chain. I'm unarmed. Yes, you're right. I'm defending myself." He pointed to an abrasion on his arm. "You think we're playacting? Didn't I have this lecture before? Should I just take it from them?"

"They're *actors*."

The word echoed in the bubble. It flitted through his skull, refusing to light anywhere for long as denotations and connotations resolved themselves. It snapped into place in an elegant gothic framework. The final piece changed the nature of the puzzle; it was no longer the sky but the sea.

"Actors?"

"Titian recruits them, juices them up for veracity, and schedules our skirmishes. It's just a show. You didn't know that? You didn't even suspect?"

John-Paul slumped and ground the palm of his hand into his face. "You're kidding me."

"Think about it. If we could predict the time and location of something like this beforehand—scheduled around your classes, of course—we could clean it up before it reached this point. Tell me you didn't realize that." Her grin twisted without humor.

"That doesn't make sense. How? Why?"

She knelt too. "Can you trust me on this, for now?"

"We're frauds? Is that it? We're just a distraction? A spectacle? What are we? If I'd let that statute keep going, would it have hurt anyone? Did I accomplish anything?"

Pain crossed her expression. She started to answer, then stopped. "The truth? That's a good question. I can't answer it. It *was* real, as far as we know."

He threw a pebble at the bubble. It sizzled and smoked and bounced back at him. "We're not completely frauds, but we *are* liars?"

"Not at all." She shrugged. "It's more like a safety valve. Sometimes you have to let off a little steam or the whole thing blows itself apart."

The world shifted again under her serious gaze, and from that angle everything made perfect sense. "I'll play along with that idea, for the sake of argument. What are the rules?"

"Exactly what you expect. Don't hurt normals, minimize damage to property, and try not to kill anyone."

"How about a gentle maiming?"

She pursed her lips. "Only if he gets on your nerves."

"This all explains that stupid macho posturing. How much of that do I have to do?"

"How much risk of me maiming you in return can you stand?"

"Good answer." He chewed his lip. "Do I need acting lessons?"

"Would they have helped Leonard? You saw him." He caught her eye and saw the joke. "Seriously, it doesn't seem to matter. People believe what they want to believe. We just help them a little bit." She stood to place a hand parallel to the bubble wall. The blue faded.

"Wait, one more thing."

She glanced back.

"If we're not one-hundred percent keeping the world safe from evildoers, what *are* we doing?"

Clownfish shrugged. "It's...complicated."

"Humor me."

"We make the world a better place." She scowled as he shook his head. "Seriously. People need something to believe in, right? If they believe they're safe, if they believe that there's a terrible swift reaction just waiting to protect the innocent and punish the guilty, well, that's why society works, isn't it?"

"Huh. Are we?"

"Are we what?"

"Are we just waiting to protect the innocent and punish the guilty?"

She shook with silent laughter. "It doesn't come up that often in an orderly society. Ha." She sighed. "You're all right, you know?" She straightened her uniform and raised a hand again. "On your guard now. Real time's coming back now."

The bubble popped. The world wrenched again as they resumed their positions. They stood back to back. Their three assailants lay on the ground unconscious. Pierre stood over the last brother, fist still arcing through the air as he continued an elaborate curse and scanned the street and air for recording devices.

Clownfish gestured him to the ad hoc fountain. He shot back a murderous look, but fished the hydrant out of the debris and jammed it in place. The flow trickled to a stop.

"Call for a cleaner team," she turned and whispered to John-Paul.

"What?"

"On your watch."

He fiddled with the dial, then mumbled "Uh, cleaner team to my position. We're done here."

Titian's face filled the air. "Wonderful job, my boy, though a little bit more aggressive than necessary at the end. Your extraction team is on its way." Clownfish tossed a rude gesture after his fading image.

John-Paul's eyes drank in the whole scene. He felt an inch taller amidst his teammates, the building, the foes, and the buggy. He smiled at Clownfish. "Not bad for a beginner, hmm?"

"Don't get cocky. You have a lot to learn."

"Where's Pierre?"

Something black and close burst in front of his eyes. His head jerked to the left; he brushed at the empty air. "I'm gone, kid. You and her have fun, okay? You tell Titian he's not going to find me. I'm done here too."

John-Paul blinked heavily, trying to clear fog from his mind. His vision resolved into Clownfish staring at him. "What?"

"You're wearing this stupid expression again."

143

"Didn't you hear him?"

"Who?"

He shushed her with a slashing hand gesture and stalked toward the alley, tilting his head and squinting. He laid his left ear against the sooty brick wall. "Knock, knock?"

Brick chips flew as his fist entered the wall. He pulled Pierre through the rubble to hold him by the collar. The other man twisted kittenlike as his feet dangled in the air.

"You, kid... you're crazy. This whole scam's over, you see? I've put up with a lot, but we're finished. It's over. Me and Claude, we have better things to do than to make ourselves targets around you. It's bad enough you're attracting vigilantes, making enemies wherever you step. It's bad enough the old man's having the time of his life sitting behind that fat desk and watching us play fight with his actors, but I'm not going to wait while you pop off and get us all killed. You're dangerous, see? You're proving it, right now."

"What are you talking about?"

"Jih-muh-neez, kid! You think you have some moral right to throw me around, just to ask me a question. Look at you. Do you think I couldn't get out of this if I wanted? If I'd put up with all of the damage it would cause? Clownie over there, you *paralyzed* her."

John-Paul turned. The woman stood statue still, mouth open in silent warning, hand outstretched.

Pierre stumbled, but kicked John-Paul's right leg out from under him. They landed in a puddle.

"Stop–hey!" Clownfish caught herself.

"Your boy's crazy, Clownie. You fix him, the old man fix him, I don't care. I'm done. We're done." Pierre pulled himself up the wall by his fingertips, brushing spare masonry out of his hair.

"You don't have to do this," she started.

"What are you–"

Pierre waved his index finger weapon-like between both of them. "Not a word. You tell the old man." He wrapped darkness around him again, then was gone.

Clownfish offered John-Paul her hand. "Way to go, *hero!*"

His eyes flashed. "Aren't you a little secretive yourself to get all high and mighty with me? How about some reasonable disclosure?"

She sighed. "No, you're right. We never should have expected you to piece it all together. It's been a bad year, alright? I'll talk to Titian, sort things out." She bit her lip, then leaned in to cradle his jaw and cheekbone with her left hand. "I promise—if you stick around."

He nodded.

She held the position to search his eyes. Whatever she found satisfied her; she nodded and grabbed his hand. "We need to make the extraction point. C'mon."

Something buzzed in his head again, but it faded as she squeezed his hand.

○ ○ ○

A man of indeterminate age in a spotless white jumpsuit opened the door. His expression of blank politeness offered his assistance even as he remained silent.

"I'm Pandora d'Avril, from the paper." She flashed her ID, covering the large "INTERN" stamp with her thumb. Hours of practice made it effortless. The man nodded and stepped aside.

Her mind's eye had prepared her for gilded marble pillars surrounded by expensive and uncomfortable furniture squatting in intimate groups of threes and fours. A grand staircase should swoop down from a beautiful balcony, framing a larger-than-life portrait of a dead rich white man hidden behind a chandelier the size of a small car.

The entryway was smaller and narrower than she expected. She stood on a landing. A doorway and a closet stood on her left and right. The carpet was thick but not extravagant; her shoes sunk into the soft padding of a syncopated pattern of ivory and black flowers fading into a dusty red background. Three steps down led into a longer hallway.

She revised her expectations downward, but the lack of cherubs frolicking naked in an oversized fountain pulled at the corner of her lips.

Pandora straightened her jacket with a yank. She resisted the urge to smooth her hair and suck any remnants of lunch from her teeth. Dark-framed mirrors peppered the walls, interspersed with sconces. Heavy doors framed in sturdy, dark wood dotted each side of the hallway. She idly wondered if she could break down one of those doors if necessary, or if pounding or shouting were audible from the other side.

They walked the length of the hall, turned to the right, and walked the same distance again. The map in her head twisted and turned until she couldn't remember the direction from which she'd entered. They stopped at an indistinguishable door; she knew she'd never pick it out of the other candidates. The man knocked softly, twice. She strained to sense any signal, but had given up when her guide pushed open the door.

The office was sparse. A massive black desk blocked floor-to-ceiling windows. A fireplace stood cold and empty to the right. Two black leather couches faced each other, capped by a double-wide chair. An immense and muted rug rested between them and two lamps held guard over each couch. Where she expected bookcases, the walls were empty and blank. A single file folder crooked on the desk indicated life in the room. Then the desk chair turned.

She recognized Titian from the funeral. He gave her guide a brief nod, then waved a massive hand. "Miss d'Avril, it's a pleasure to see you again. Please do come in and have a seat!" He rose and half stumbled toward one of the couches. She looked behind her as the door closed, then sighed and curled up on the opposite couch. He sat after she did.

Pandora fumbled in her handbag for a moment, then produced a notepad in a purple holder. He showed no surprise at recognizing her from the funeral. The implication chilled her. "I appreciate your time, Mr. Titian."

He shrugged and smiled. "Please, call me Titian. There's no need to be formal."

"Oh. Okay. As you probably know, I work for the paper. Mr. Fontaine sent me to ask you some questions." She bit her lip and pretended to skim the questions again. The words hung awkward in her memory.

Titian laughed. "Roderick is certainly a colorful fellow, isn't he? Does he still have that ridiculous mustache?"

She chuckled, surprised at the sound. "Yeah. He's curling it up at the ends now. Do you two know each other?"

Titian laughed louder. "I would have to admit that we are good-natured rivals, in a sense. Do you understand what I mean? He sees himself as a crusader for truth and justice and information he can use to sell that fish wrap he calls a newspaper—no offense, of course, as that's just a figure of speech I use to needle him. He sees our organization as, I believe the precise phrase was 'an unhealthy culture of secrecy and power aggregated in the hands of shadowy, inscrutable, and ineffable elites'."

Pandora shrugged. "Just asking. Can I ask about The Protector?"

"Of course, my dear. We have no secrets here. For all of my teasing, I greatly respect Roderick's crusade to shine the light of public attention on the great truths of our age. The truth protects us. Truth saves us. Sometimes we are unaware of the truth ourselves and need a healthy and honest external perspective to understand our place in history." He fixed her with his tiny, piggy eyes; she blinked, surprised at the intelligence shining there.

"Right. Well. I went to his funeral, yet everyone believes he's alive. Fontaine sent me here to discuss a 'so-called social event'. I think he means the funeral. What's going on?" She cringed as her thoughts blurted themselves into the room, willing her mouth to slow down to a pace which she could control. Nothing separated her from Titian; the couches faced each other in a fashion more intimate than an interview across a desk.

He stared and she blushed. His grin was slow but wide. No

laughter would follow. Where she expected elongated canines, his teeth were small and perfect. "Well," he began. "Those are very good questions. They don't sound like Roderick at all. Shall I assume that you added your own background research? I would expect no less from one of his star pupils."

Pandora began, "I was just curious... it seems –"

"Pardon my interruption, but I understand. Please, relax. As I said before, we're not well understood, but we have no secrets. Let me tell you the honest, simple fact about the Protector. It's really very simple, but I allow that it can seem complex at first."

She felt herself inch forward into the conversation.

"Suppose you have an elected official—a city councilman for the Wharf district. A man named Jones holds this position. When the city manager calls for an election, Jones decides to step down. A woman named Rosa wins the election. The people have changed, but you still refer to the Wharf Councilman as the Wharf Councilman. Has the position changed? By no means! The mere act of filling a vacancy with another person does not change the nature of the position. The actions and decisions of the person in that role may change the role over time, but that process is subtle, organic, and gradual. Yet can you say that Jones and Rosa are the same person?"

She nodded. "I understand the centrality of image in language, but are you suggesting that the Protector is a description of a position or a role more than the identity of a person?"

He spread his hands. "No analogy is perfect. We understand reality only by approximation and metaphor. Even so, if I said yes, I would have given you an accurate answer." He smiled the wide smile.

Pandora drummed her fingers on her notepad. "Why the funeral? That implies something more than a regime change, if you pardon the expression." He nodded for her to continue. "It's more *final*, if you will."

Titian shrugged. "Humanity prefers to mark its milestones with ceremony. To continue the election metaphor, think of the midnight

148

victory parades after all of the votes have been counted and the winner announced. Does that change the nature of the election? Does that change the amount or the tenor of the work? Yet from that point on we consider the current office holder impotent and . . . the past, to paint with the hues of metaphor. The victor is the future. The drama of human ceremony increases when you reelect an official. That celebration and parade and ceremony mark the rebirth of the official's position, if not his career."

"Where's the man who was the previous Protector then, and who's the new Protector?"

"Aha, you're very clever. My analogy is not without its flaws. In another sense—a very different sense—anyone in the particular role of a City Protector has taken on a unique role. Rather than being accountable to voters at whose whim he or she serves, such a volunteer is accountable only to the city as a whole. As there is no election, the need for transparency lessens. Only those for whom this action is an option need apply. Very few people are capable of protecting the city from superhuman threats, thus the position is not open to just anyone—unlike our elected positions."

She pretended to flip through her question pad. Her mind buzzed. "Are you suggesting that the Protector wasn't—or his replacement will not be—accountable to the citizens of the city for his choices?"

"By no means, my young friend! Not in the slightest. Poor choices would precipitate a lack of trust and faith. Without the good will and belief in the rightness of our cause from the fine citizens of this city, our good works would be impossible. The lack of trust is an insurmountable barrier.

"I can sense your followup question already. 'Why should we trust you?' If I may, I have debated that very question with our friend and colleague into many late nights. Sometimes trust must be demanded, though we all acknowledge the superiority of trust earned. Yet how do you earn trust? I ask you now, as I ask everyone in this city, to trust us. Consider our reputation. Consider our history. We've taken a city gripped by the cold hands of fear, distrust, revolution, restoration, and the ugly face of distrust and prejudice. Since that time, have these problems increased or lessened? Do children starve still outside the gates of rich estates? Do laborers attack the belongings of their employers? Do the streets erupt in riots? Do buildings fall? Do anxious mothers weep, waiting for any news of their kidnapped children?

"Judge us if you must. I welcome it. Yet judge us on what we have accomplished. Judge us on that which is present within the city today and that which is absent. I welcome a sober and honest appraisal of our progress."

Pandora slammed her mouth shut and scrunched her eyes closed as she tried to ignore the tiny smile dancing across Titian's face. "But there is still criminal activity. Your colleagues skirmish several times a month."

"Greed and jealousy and pride! We will never eradicate these base human emotions. A city this size will always suffer petty crimes. We can ameliorate the damage and apprehend the perpetrators for retraining and reparations. I consider us a source of benign enforcement; perhaps someday the future will reduce us to patrolling crosswalks. I welcome that world."

"You believe you can reduce all crime—murder, arson, extortion, burglary," she ticked off on her fingers, "– to jaywalking?"

Titian narrowed his eyes. Crevices appeared alongside the bridge of his nose; here was a man the depths of whose worries more than made up for their infrequency. Pandora tried not to shiver under his dissecting gaze. She forced herself to breathe deeply and stare back. "Did you not grow up in the city," he finally offered.

"Southern territories. Reedville area."

Relaxation rippled outward through his posture. "Oh, a merchant village. I've heard it's lovely there in the spring. Now you are a student, and a recent immigrant. How do you like our fair city so far?"

"It's . . . maybe vibrant is the best word." She felt her mouth racing again but managed to control it before gushing over the cutest little deli she'd found the other day, hidden away just off the main road in a tiny residential area within walking distance of her apartment. "Why do you ask?"

"In the city, the easy assumption tempts us: we are the center of the world. The simple fact of our existence is that everyone living here now came from somewhere else, or their parents did, or their parents. Even children born here now have racial memories and family imprints to a homeland somewhere else. My family, for example, were hardy farmers in subarctic climes. They braved harsh winters to endure the fleeing beauty of subtle yet determined summers... but I digress. Please allow me to characterize your perception as valid but strange. No one born or raised in the city would see things the same way that you do."

She hated the lie as soon as its stench marred the room. "Well, journalist too...."

He continued as if she hadn't spoken. "The simple truth? We've been a city of peace for over four hundred years. Flawed empires never last that long. Jealousy or scandal or greed or overextension or the desire for power always devour them inside-out. We ask no perfection. We tolerate the imperfect and the flawed—but we contain those elements which may prove, in the long run, hazardous to our long term stability."

"What might those be," she asked. "Strange men dressed in black armor? The statue of Progress crashing a funeral?"

Titian grimaced and shifted his bulk. "Merely a test. Your young friend seems to have handled himself ably, did he not?"

"John-Paul? What do you know about him?"

He shifted again. Light from the windows glinted off his eyes at an impossible angle. "Everything happens for a reason, my young friend."

"I led a few hundred people away from the fight. You still have a bruise on your forehead."

Alarm flashed on his face, and he inadvertently raised one hand, catching himself before he made contact to change the gesture into an eyebrow smoothing affectation. "Did Roderick really send you?"

151

Pandora shrugged. "More or less." Something hummed in her chest, swelling her sense of self larger than the room.

His forehead furrowed again into a long and awkward silence. She crossed her arms and watched the expressions flickering beneath his face, always punctuated by the scowl. Finally he sighed and slumped forward. "I must admit, I have no idea what that means, nor what game he is playing."

"No game. I had a few more questions, but I think I've learned everything you're going to tell me, save one."

"And what is that?"

"Where's John-Paul now, and what are you doing with him?"

Pandora blinked in the sunlight, rubbing her head. The last thing she could remember was leaning forward to hear an answer, but a pounding headache threatened to squeeze tears from her eyes. A door slammed. She turned toward the sound. She saw herself on the sidewalk in front of a nondescript building near the waterfront district.

As the monorail pulled away from the station, she opened her eyes again and wondered if she could relax enough to nap until her stop. Then she recalled the pad of questions. She tore through her purse to find her notes missing. The pen and blank paper remained, but several sheets beneath her notes were missing too.

Her phone beebled. She fumbled it out of her purse and felt a twinge of curiosity as the screen was blank. It beeped again, still blank, and she slid it open. "Hello?" Hope sent her pulse on a race as she willed the silent assistant to tell her that he had her missing materials if she could possibly return. A moment of desire chased away mortification.

Vernon's stress-pinched voice filled her mind. "Miss d'Avril?" She winced at the strain of reconciling the sound with the ambient noise of the train.

"Oh. Yes?"

"Are you on the monorail?"

"Yes, yes I am. Why?"

"We'd like you to explore a tip. Can you transfer to the inner loop at the next available stop? You're the closest person to the Reunification Square Hospital."

"Um. What would you like me to do?"

"We've found another contact in room 442; he's agreed to speak about the Protector and Titian. Can you be there in half an hour?"

She glanced at the overhead map and counted the little circles on the spiderweb of stations. "Yes, I should be." She scribbled the number on a piece of scrap paper.

"The name is Jejeux. Thank you," offered Vernon as he hung up.

She flipped her phone closed and leaned back in the hard plastic and metal seat. Other passengers stared; she shrugged and smiled back, hoping they couldn't see the mess of thoughts in her mind or her desire to lie on her couch with a tub of ice cream, a bag of potato chips, and loud, angry music.

The train slowed and dinged for the next stop. She shook cobwebs from her mind as she peeled herself out of the seat and staggered to her feet.

o o o

Clownfish punched the privacy button. Smokey glass slid between the driver and the leather seats along the side of the van. "C'mon out, Pierre. You're thinking it; you might as well say it."

A shadow coalesced out of the air into a lounging Pierre. His mouth twisted half-grimace and half grin. "Never fool you, hmm?"

Her gaze was blank as a mirror until her lower lip twitched. "Give your spiel, then get out of here. Titian won't like what he hears. You need a head start."

Pierre turned to John-Paul. "You know what irony is, kid?"

"You say one thing but really mean your mother."

"Cute." Pierre cleared his throat. "'scuse me. It's the difference between what you expect to happen, apropos of the circumstances, and what happens. You go to the Protector's funeral to see him

153

buried into comfortable rest, and he tries to kill you. Irony. Love it."

Clownfish snorted. "Bad example. Bad taste. You wrap another word around Claude's freaky conspiracy and we'll have a very short, not very friendly discussion. Don't get your crazy all over John-Paul. Let it go."

"The Protector?" John-Paul pried a pebble out of his boot sole. "He sent those soldiers?"

"Didn't say that." Pierre returned Clownfish's glare with a cold sneer. "If he had, and obviously he didn't, being both a hero and stone dead, that would be irony. It's a metaphor." He shrugged. "You still take everything so seriously, Clownie? You know what the fat man's up to?"

She looked away. "Those were good days, Pierre. Black and white were so clear. Never any questions—no doubts, just right and wrong. We were always on the side of the angels."

"'m not in the business of believing that. Tell me he didn't justify it even back then."

"What changed?" John-Paul studied her face, continually jerking his eyes back from the shuffling, flickering shadows that surrounded Pierre.

She twirled stray hair around her finger. "I don't know. Everyone. Everything. Us especially, maybe. Everyone but him." She nodded at Pierre. "How long have you known?"

"As long as you, just never wanted to believe it. Thought he could keep it together. The way you all used to talk about Steven, it was obvious. He was the heart. Barry could never meet those expectations. No one could. He's not wrong, but he's cold and alone."

The van jostled, sliding lattice patterns of light across the walls. Clownfish shielded her eyes and peered into the driver's compartment. "We're getting close. Pierre, now's your chance. I'll keep him distracted. You go now, but promise you'll consider coming back, even on your own terms."

Pierre shrugged. "Have to ask Claude about that. You two ought to take your own little vacations. Especially you, kid: make it a long weekend, visit the family, sleep in your old room for a change. Nothing like a trip out of the city to change your perspective. See you around, girl."

She shook her head, "Don't call me girl," but there was no play in it. The swirling dissipated.

"Is he always that dramatic?"

"The job gets to people in different ways."

"Storming off, like he never wants to see us again, then coming back for a philosophical discussion of right and wrong?"

"You tell me. When you're all jacked up on power, how much nuance do you have in your actions?"

John-Paul sucked air through his teeth. "Is that what you were trying to tell me earlier? Adrenaline makes us stronger but no wiser?"

She shrugged and looked away.

He savored the lingering silence. "Where's he headed?"

Clownfish pressed her eyes again to the smoky glass. "First the hospital. Then I have no idea."

"Claude's better?"

She whipped her head back and stared at him. His skin reddened and itched. "Uh, I don't mean...."

"No, of course you don't." Her face softened. "I envy you sometimes."

"Envy?"

She shifted in her seat. "It used to be so easy for us. Right and wrong. You go here, you do this, you come back in one piece. That's all. Our morality fit on an index card. We had the perfume of belief. That was enough."

"Are you always this mopey after a successful fight?" He probed the bruise on his head with reluctant fingertips, but it was less tender now.

"Tough year." She turned back to face him. Golden light slipped through the window to bounce off her eyes. He blinked at their reflection. "We'll call it an unscheduled vacation. I'll talk to Titian and get you a few days off yourself. Go home, see the family. It's a good idea. How long since you've been there?"

Time danced away as he fit oblong days and weeks into a jigsaw calendar. "Wow. A month, I guess."

"Good time to go back."

John-Paul shrugged. "As long as you're not putting me on ice after that little unpleasantness."

Clownfish leaned forward. "You did a good job today. You're still rough around the edges, but you show promise. More than that. We make a good team. Things are rough. That's not your fault. If we can trust each other, we can make it work." Her words trailed off, but she stared again and finished. "Are you with me?"

The van slowed as it approached great underground doors. "I'm with you."

o o o

Pandora brushed through revolving doors into a three-story monstrosity. She'd expected the hospital to be a study in white and off-white with disinfectant green for contrast. Instead, the combination of tans and chocolates and blues made her teeth hurt. A semi-abstract painting of Progress—twenty feet tall—adorned the far wall, overlooking a long and low information desk.

Afternoon sunlight spilled through prismatic skylights. Rainbows shimmered and shifted, sparkling off of the twin helix staircases flanking the room. Offices with glass walls overlooked the lobby.

Two paths marked by royal blue designs in the carpet led to and around the desk. As she approached, the adorned wall revealed itself an optical illusion: it divided the room. Offices, an elevator bank, and a lavish gift shop continued on the other side. She tried not to gape as she sidled toward the elevators.

Soft music assaulted her as she rounded the wall, emanating from speakers set in the bases of a series of modernist sculptures.

They depicted mankind's struggle against the classical dramatic elements, though the seventh—man versus man—showed two figures in stark relief. One struggled to rise from a fallen position and the other had apparently cast away a spear and offered an open and empty hand. "Subtle," she whispered, half-hoping someone had overheard her wit.

The fourth floor looked like a hospital should. It lacked ostentation and charm of any sort. The colors were sterile. The filtered air was heavy and stagnant. She felt right at home, remembering the small village clinic where she'd had her appendix removed as a young woman. Nurses and orderlies and aides rushed past her, soft white shoes clicking and squeaking on the well-polished floor. Dirty windows exposed an industrial scene behind the hospital, factories and warehouses reaching for the bay. The water was choppy despite the sunny afternoon, and she wondered if the winds would rattle her windows again tonight.

"Four four two," she repeated quietly. "Four four two." The first turn took her down a hallway starting from 465 and increasing. She retraced her steps the other way, turning at 451.

A pair of old men stood at the other end of the hallway. One adjusted an oversized jacket and ran his fingers through his hair. The other leaned in to whisper, jerking a finger at another room. They exchanged matching shrugs, then walked around the corner. She paused and leaned against the wall by a supply closet someone had left ajar. Her head ached again—eyes weary from straining to stay in her head—and she wanted nothing more than a cup of hot tea and a comfortable bed for napping. "You can do this," she promised herself. "Just a few minutes and you can call it an evening."

Room 442 was unlatched. She rapped her knuckles on the door. "Mr. Jejeux?" The nametag slot showed only one resident, a Charles Jejeux. The name and number matched those Vernon had given her. She knocked louder. Again no one answered.

Pandora pushed open the door. The room was sparse and clean and larger than it looked from the outside, large enough for two comfortable inhabitants. A series of rigid floor-to-ceiling dividers stood half-collapsed into the wall. The far bed was rumpled and hastily changed; a pile of dirty linens moldered in the corner.

One window hung open. A solid metal latch twisted and forced past its natural angle. The breeze threw thin curtains into action. She looked out over the rooftops below, taking in squat and boxy HVAC components and random detritus. Nothing caught her attention.

A threadbare cushion-and-wood chair lurked in the corner. She obeyed its command to sit and massaged her temples. This was the second apparent dead end, and both assignments had come from Roderick's office. Was he testing her, or had she failed at basic research such that she should give up altogether? She skimmed her paper again. The details still matched, yet there there was no trace of Vernon's call on her phone. Assuming his information had been correct, either everything was a crazy coincidence, or someone had found out about her arrival and rushed away—assuming that someone had something to hide.

She snickered at the burgeoning conspiracy and allowed herself a luxurious feline stretch. The pressure in her head began to recede and she felt a new surge of energy after discarding the maze of bizarre maybes and what-ifs. She called Vernon.

"Mr. Fontaine's office. Is this Miss d'Avril?"

"Yes... Vernon, I'm at the hospital. No one's here. Jejeux's name is still on the door, but the room's empty."

"The hospital? One moment please." The call went silent. Her heart pounded for the long seconds as she felt small and far away. Her headache returned. She forced herself to breathe. "Pandora?" Vernon's voice was reedy and weary.

"Yes?" She hoped he couldn't hear her hyperventilate through the phone, and concentrated on not gulping down great breaths of air.

"Get out, now. Please!"

His words washed through her adrenal gland, pushing her to her feet before she could think. "Wait," she gasped, foot poised to kick the window. "Why?"

"No time to talk." Vernon's voice rose in intensity and pitch. "Please go, now!"

She launched herself at the window. The pane held. The frame did not. Chunks of the room tore themselves apart; the window sagged and groaned and ripped away from the wall. She kicked again, enlarging the hole.

Pandora pawed at the discarded linens for two bed sheets. She tied them together, one end around her waist and the other knotted against the window frame. She took two steps backward, then launched herself at the hole.

The frightened little part of her mind gave up. Her headache vanished.

She burst out of the window tucked into a ball and clutching her purse. The sheets reached their length and she spun, aiming her feet at the wall to absorb the force of the swing. She dangled to catch her bearings: six feet from the roof. Her makeshift harness slipped off easily and she landed on the balls of her feet.

A mournful wind threw leaves and specks of grit. She ran toward the nearest edge. Wide sidewalks meandered below through parklike greenery around an attractive side entrance and its temporary parking area. Young ivy vines crawled up the fake brick of the building's side.

A pair of trees guarded the path. Their supple branches waved ten feet beneath her position and twenty feet away. Her mind drew unconscious arcs and parabolas and she found herself running from the middle of the roof, timing her steps to push off the ledge with her right foot.

She missed the first branch and whipped her head to her chest to avoid a nasty scratch. The second and third branches caught her, bending under her momentum. She swapped branches hand-over-hand as she dropped to the ground.

Pandora spun on her feet, breathing heavily and wiping leaves out of her hair. A parking garage hulked across a wide boulevard empty of traffic. She sprinted across the street and jumped through a low cinder block opening, crouching and cringing as the hospital exploded.

Nothing happened.

She peered over the wall. The hospital remained, untouched. She shook her head again, feeling her energy drain away. Her knees crumpled and she scrabbled at the wall to steady herself.

"Hey," said a voice. She jumped. It was the younger of the two old men. Gray flecked his hair, but his eyes were the color of rich honey. "Are you alright?" A whiff of his cologne reminded her of her grandfather's house.

Pandora straightened. "Yes...I'm...yes. I'm alright."

He stared, cataloging every detail of her face. "Well then. If you're sure." His companion pulled on his arm, and they walked away.

She rubbed her temples again, feeling a rubbery ache in her muscles. She pondered a lengthy call to Vernon to chew him out for his hazing prank but promised herself a satisfying fume on the long ride home. She cast suspicious glances at the hospital, but it failed to explode as she walked back to the monorail station.

o o o

Gravel crunched beneath John-Paul's wheels as he turned off the lonely highway to the long driveway. Someone had trimmed the poplar trees into a well-groomed if boxy archway. *Too little, too late*, whispered an inner imp, flashing a memory in the screen of his mind: overhanging tree branches pawed at the square top of an ambulance carrying his father away. "Don't take him," they rustled and whispered. He grunted and wrenched his eyes back on the road.

He parked in a weedy spot beside the unattached garage. Weeds grew around the wheels of Mark David's car, and the sheep pasture stood empty.

The sun had begun to bake the air. He left his window down and his hoodie in the driver's seat. He hefted his bag as he shuffled up the cracked sidewalk. His initials still stood where they'd spent hours racing cars and discovering new types of mundane insects every spring. The smell of apple and cherry pies tickled his nose. His stomach growled.

The screen door banged shut as he entered. "Sorry," he yelled. "No hands free."

"Baby!" His mother burst through the kitchen doorway. "John-Paul! How are you?" Flour dusted her apron. He had time to drop his bag before her hug squeezed his ribs together. Her hair seemed less blonde than it had three months ago.

"Hi, Mom." He said. "Good to see you."

She squeezed more air out of his lungs, then examined him at arm's length. "You look hungry. Are you taking care of yourself? Not eating out every night, are you? Not going out every night and partying, I hope?"

He started to chuckle, but concern in her eyes squelched it unvocalized. "No, Mom. It's hard to cook every day, but I'm really trying."

She studied his face. "I wrote out some family recipes for you. I meant to put them in a little book, but they're just loose cards. Remember your grandmother's pot pie? It's really easy. You could make it. Girls love a man who can cook. You should make it for that Pandora girl."

John-Paul tried not to blush.

"Oh," she said. "Baby, there's something there, isn't there? I want to hear more about her, but you go freshen up first. I'll get you a snack. Turkey sandwich?"

"Yes, Mom."

She nodded toward the hallway. "I kept your room like you left it, except for dusting. Don't wait too long though—I'm making a big family dinner tonight for the four of us."

"Four?"

"Jupiter's staying for dinner."

"Oh, is she out with Emdy right now?"

"They're walking the fence line. Mark wants to replace part of it."

John-Paul grabbed his bag and took a step toward his old room. "I should go help –"

His mother had the talent of producing wooden spoons out of nowhere. The eight year old troublemaker somewhere deep inside cringed, still stinging from the spanking his grandfather had given him for catching the tool shed on fire. "I need some quality mother-son time before you go running out. Five minutes, and you can talk to me while you eat. Is that so much to ask?"

He saw her differently then: worry lines on her forehead, lips pressed thin, concern shining through her eyes. She wasn't just his mother and obligated, but she *loved* him as a person too. Something inside him released, and he grabbed her again, swinging her around in a hug.

"Oof... what was that for?" She slapped him with the spoon. "Too much surprise, son!"

"Oh, nothing. It's just good to be home, Mom."

His room seemed unfamiliar, more than the open curtains and clean bedding. It seemed smaller, as if he'd had an adult growth spurt recently. Familiar patterns of light and dark in the texture of the paint on walls and ceiling—patterns he'd identified and named as constellations while waiting for sleep to take him—now seemed foreign. His old stories of the fireman and the monkey and the robot and the princess rang hollow. Other figures had replaced them, dark and strange, bearing their own savage stories.

"Scaredy cat," he told himself. The family men spent one summer replacing plaster and lathe with modern materials, rebuilding the house from its skeleton out one room at a time. He'd chosen eggplant to paint the walls, steadfast and unmoveable, but refused to sleep alone once he saw the results. Even still, two coats of eggplant couldn't hide a purple tint.

Someone had organized his closet into a neat stack of labeled boxes: JP's comics, JP's books, JP's models. The rest was storage; his parents' old clothes hung from the clothes rod.

He looked the same in the bathroom mirror, a skinny fourteen year old boy with tired eyes and hands larger than his frame should support. Even the towels were different, softer and fluffier somehow on his wet hands and face. He brushed away a stray strand of wet hair as his mother hummed and set down a plate with a fat turkey sandwich and a sliced pickle. "Milk?" she asked. John-Paul nodded.

"Oh," he said through a bite. "That's really good. I haven't had a sandwich this good in *ages*."

"Smoked turkey, cranberry, and Havarti cheese. Still your favorite?"

"Mm," he said, eyes closing as ice cold milk hit his tongue. "Tell me why I moved to the city again?"

She sat at the opposite end of the table and poured a dollop of milk into her tea. "Are you enjoying it? It's not too stressful, is it? We don't hear from you that often. Are you taking care of yourself?"

John-Paul wiped his mouth. "Yeah, I am. It's... well, it's nothing like I expected. Everything's so busy and so serious. Everyone has this, I don't know, maybe institutional knowledge of how everything works. You go along with that and pretend it all makes sense, and hope it all works out before anyone finds out you're making it all up as you go along."

Her eyes crinkled. "Welcome to adulthood."

"Seriously?" He crunched a pickle. "Is that how you and Dad felt when you had us?"

"It comes and goes. Some days I wake up and wonder if my whole so-called adult life has been a dream. Maybe I'm still fourteen and have to run off to school to take a math test. It all passes by so fast. You have no idea."

"Don't tell me you still have dreams about being late to class and forgetting to study! I was hoping those would go away soon."

This time the smile escaped. "Baby, we're all making this up as we go along. You get used to acting, you do it all day, every day. Some of us get really good. I've always tried to do the best I could with you and your brother, and we've always asked you to do your best. If you look back on the choices you make and what you've accomplished and honestly know that you gave it your all, you can be satisfied with who you are."

John-Paul pulled at a dangling corner of cheese, rolling it into a ball. "It's okay if not everything makes sense?"

"Everyone wants it, but no one gets it. Why is Mark David sick? Did I do something wrong? Did your father? Why are there droughts some years, and boom crops some other years? Why –"

The screen door crashed open. "Sorry," yelled a voice from the front room. Jupiter bounded into the kitchen. "Oh. How ya' doing, JP?"

"Hey, Jupiter. Are you staying out of trouble?"

Her grin was huge and innocent. "Funny, coming from you. Anyway, Mrs. H, I just came by to say that the fence is alright, after we patch a few spots. Can I borrow the truck to pick up some new posts?"

"Of course, dear. Where's Mark David?"

Jupiter stole a pickle from John-Paul's plate and crunched on it. "He's at the creek. It's such a pretty day out there, he couldn't resist. JP, I'm headed back. Wanna come with me?"

He looked at his mother. She smiled back. "Can you give us a few minutes, dear?"

"Sure thing. We'll be at the creek for another half hour."

John-Paul nodded. Jupiter was already at the door, pausing to pull a well-loved leather key chain off of the hook. She grinned again as she eased the screen door into place. "Always learn my lesson again the first time."

"Is she over here a lot?"

"She's such a helpful girl. She's really been good to Mark David lately. He misses you a lot, and I worried about him. He was really down. He'd have gone with you to the city if he could."

"I know." He sighed. "I know... did you know we had an arrangement? He didn't want me to, quote, put my life on hold. I didn't know what to do. I could have taken some classes at the community college and stuck around for one more semester, but would you have let me do that? Would he?"

His mother ran her thumb around the lip of her mug. For the first time he noticed a spiderweb of fine cracks under the finish, as if it had shrunk in place. "Baby, I don't know. It's difficult. You want your children to succeed, but you grow so used to taking care of them that it's bittersweet to think that they don't need you anymore."

"That's not true, Mom."

"Let me finish. I'd give anything to let Mark David run and jump and dance and sing. I would. Anything. I'd do the same for you. If the price for your happiness and success is sending you off to school far away and not seeing you and hugging you and making you breakfast every day... if you grow up strong and responsible and can then take care of other people, it's a fine price to pay. It's not an easy price, but it's a fair price." A smile tugged at the edges of her mouth, but her eyes stared somewhere sad and far.

"I always thought you and Dad had all the answers."

"No one ever does. We just get better at faking it." The oven timer dinged. "Oh, my pie!" She scooted to the oven and peered through the glass. "Just in time." The flooding scent of cinnamon and hot apples and flaky pastry washed the kitchen in memories. He felt his skin prickle as he remembered countless days of sitting right there, talking like this, mouth watering in anticipation of some fruit pie for dessert.

"Enough about me," she said, sliding the pie onto a cooling rack. "You were supposed to tell me about this Pandora girl."

○ ○ ○

John-Paul shifted, solid bark at his back and summer-baked ground beneath him. He stretched his legs, wincing at the stab of an ache along the arch of his right foot. The poplar tree at his back spun patterns of sunlight to dapple the ground and the creek.

"I was thinking."

"Hm?" Mark David sighed a waking question from underneath a wide-brimmed straw hat.

"Why is the opening in a jam jar narrower than the body? Those big plastic jars, not the jars Mom used."

"You know how to relax. Is that the biggest thought in your head?"

"I'm serious. I want to get all of the jam out, but you can't get a knife in there, and you get your fingers all sticky going after that last gob left for your toast. Why don't they make the necks bigger?"

"It's acceptable lossage. Either that, or you saw down the middle, the plastic jar anyway, and scoop out the remains."

John-Paul scratched his chin. "Inert plastic shavings on my toast. Not delicious."

"*You* might. That'd make a mess. I'd use a spatula."

They sat in silence. "Feels different from the big city." John-Paul offered his realization to the humid air.

"The lack of city is your first clue. Trees. Greenery. No tourists." Mark David toyed with a blade of grass.

"You're one set of overalls short and one pair of shoes long for the silly hat farmer stereotype."

"Crutches give me away. What's different about the city?" Mark David rolled his head.

"Sometimes I forget how beautiful here is. We have a creek and a pond. Our own creek. Our own fish. Remember when we used to ditch school at lunchtime to swim, then sneak back in time for baseball practice?"

"Everyone was wise to us. Three times out of ten you could talk us out of detention. Once you talked us out of extra chores."

"Do you ever miss those days? Seems like we're always too busy any more to sit and relax and enjoy a nice summer afternoon dangling our feet in the water and pretending that tying a bent nail on one end of a string and a stick on the other will catch us dinner."

Mark David sat up. "First of all, it's unseasonably warm and barely even spring. Second, I don't have to miss it. It's always here, anytime I want it. Any sense of loss you feel is your own problem. You moved. It didn't."

John-Paul rolled to face his brother. "Touchy! What did I do to you?"

"You left."

"That was the *plan*. We agreed. I would have stuck around a year, maybe take some classes, and wait for you to work it all out. *You* insisted I go. You argued me out of staying. Make up your mind. You know you'd be berating me right now for *not* going."

Mark David lay back down. "You've changed. I don't know. You have all of these wild adventures with your role playing group. Good for you. Really, good for you. Meanwhile I'm stuck here on the farm where nothing ever changes, waiting for my legs to work again, hoping that they'll heal this time. Maybe that day will never come. Sometimes I wake up dreaming that they didn't."

"We used to be a team. Remember that? Remember how you'd lift me up in McCleary's orchard so I could pull my way to the top of the tree where we thought the sweetest apples always grew? They were only sweet because we were a team then, John-Paul. Hard work makes the reward sweeter. Now you care more about your weekends trading punches with some guy in an equally stupid costume. How do you want me to feel about that?"

"You? How about me? Do you want me to feel guilty? I didn't ask to be born healthy. You didn't ask to be born sick. It just happens. I didn't ask to be born dumb, and you didn't ask to be born smart."

"No, JP. You're not dumb, I mean –"

"I'm not as smart as you. Fine. I can live with that. Maybe you'll get robot legs someday. An exoskeleton. Wheels. Whatever. Maybe you can't live with that. I don't know. But resenting me because of something no one can control—something that just happened—how does that work? Who's that fair to?"

"I don't *resent* it. I.... You get the fantasy life. You go out and play hero. Shouldn't that be me? Shouldn't I dream of being the big man, the one who rescues people? For goodness' sake, Jupiter and Mom carried me up the stairs a couple of weeks ago. How do you think that feels? I need rescuing. Who am I going to rescue." His eyes were big and hot and full of challenge.

John-Paul blinked. "I'm not playing, Emdy. It's no game. You want a demonstration?"

"No. I'm in no mood for games or tricks. Whatever you have there, this is the real world, Jayp. Right here, the mud on your jeans. That's real. You step in the creek, you get wet. You can't walk on water. If you get shot here, you bleed. You get an infection. You go through weeks of painful physical therapy. That's if you're lucky. Trust me." He pushed at his crutches and turned away, tucking his arms under his head.

A breeze rustled the leaves; little ripples scurried along the calm water. John-Paul concentrated, willing the water to bubble and boil. He felt the sap of the tree spread through its capillaries, carrying nutrients from root to leaf. The radiance of the sun bore down on the earth's every exposed inch.

"Come on," he said. He jumped to his feet. "I'll show you." He extended a hand to his brother. "Get up."

"No." Mark David rolled his eyes.

"I mean it. No tricks. You'll see." He snapped his fingers.

"That's really annoying."

"I won't stop until you get up."

"Fine." Mark David looked around, but John-Paul shook his head.

"No crutches. Take my hand." John-Paul snapped again.

"I'm not a dog. Stop anytime." Mark David reached out and John-Paul pulled, extending his will through his outstretched hand. He saw bones knit together, nerve sheaths reform, arteries and veins open, cells split, and DNA and RNA rewrite itself. He watched the intricate patterns of the universe span macrocosm to microcosm, directing minute adjustments toward a more pleasing arrangement.

He pulled. They tumbled backwards into the creek.

Mark David pushed himself up out of the water, coughing and spraying muddy droplets. "Are you crazy? What was that? What are you trying to do, drown me?" Rage shook his frame.

John-Paul remained seated. He stared at his hands and falling gems of clear water.

"Are you listening to me? Jayp? Hey! Have you lost your mind?" Mark David was inches from his face, voice trembling half from fear. "Talk to me! C'mon. This isn't funny. Stop kidding around. Are you nuts? What's going on? Jayp?" He reached for his brother's shoulder, but John-Paul squeezed his eyes shut, twisting and shrugging.

A second voice interrupted. "Oh no...Mark, are you alright?" Jupiter skidded beneath the tree. A plastic bag and a small jug bounced off the hard ground by the discarded crutches. "What happened?"

"He...pulled me in."

"You fell?"

"No. It was—I don't even know what it was. Now he's not talking."

"Nothing to say," mumbled John-Paul.

Jupiter pulled Mark David out of the water and eased him to a comfortable position. "I'm alright," he protested through her fussings. "Nothing's broken. Just wet."

"Your heart is *pounding*."

"My heart's fine. Never had any trouble there, at least."

Jupiter leaned out over John-Paul. "Are you going to sit there like a lump, or are you going to tell me what's going on?"

He opened his eyes. "What good would that do? You wouldn't believe me. No one does."

"Believes you about what? Is this one of your tricks? It's not funny. No one's laughing."

"It's so easy to believe things there. The fantastic is possible. You imagine, and it happens. I *knew* I could—could touch him and fix it all. No more broken legs. No more degenerating nerve sheaths. No more nightmares about falling down the stairs and drowning in a pool of blood. Just two brothers, healthy twins. I don't mind if he's smarter, but I don't want to be healthier. I...."

She snorted. "What, you wish someone different because it's inconvenient?"

Mark David interrupted. "Let it go, Jupe. It's not important. I'm okay. It's okay."

She waved him off. "Not one bit. I don't want you getting hurt. You don't want you getting hurt. No one wants you getting hurt. You've suffered enough. Why does he get to push you around? Because he *believes* he should?" Venom in her voice uncoiled and struck, whip-crack quick.

John-Paul sighed and lay back in the water, arms outstretched. He bobbed, feeling the hint of a current roll over him. His heels touched bottom.

"Are you listening, JP? You're not kids anymore. All of your stupid choices have consequences. No one cares if you run around on the weekends with your little friends and play wizards or warriors or whatever, but you drop that silly fantasy when your brother and your friends need you."

He jerked his head up. "You told her about that?"

Mark David looked sick. "Just that you've been playing some crazy game. Sounded fun. I didn't think you'd mind."

John-Paul threw himself back. His voice was low and stern. "You don't understand. I was *in* a building when it exploded. I've been threatened and hurt. I've seen things you wouldn't believe. Don't tell me they're not real. I know they're real, the same way I knew I could heal you, Emdy. Tell me I'm wrong and laugh at me. Fine. Whatever. Come with me sometime. You too, Jupe. I'll *show* you."

Jupiter turned, but stopped to look over her shoulder. "When you're done pouting, your mother asked me to bring you sandwiches and lemonade."

Mark David pulled himself to his feet with his crutches. "I'm not so hungry. I'll go with you, Jupe. C'mon, Jayp. We had a laugh. Ha ha. Good times. Let's go." He turned back and opened his hands in reconciliation.

John-Paul squinted against sunbeams which had escaped the cover of the tree and kicked himself to the middle of the stream.

○ ○ ○

Titian fumed and paced. Clownfish lounged on a leather couch, sitting on her left leg.

"Bliss," he whispered, half to himself.

"Excuse me?"

He stopped. His eyes focused. "We have no other choice."

Clownfish pursed her lips. "Is this another stupid test? First Barry, then Claude and Pierre, and now you chase me off with mind games. Who's left? The kid? He has no idea. I was an inch away from unchipping him this time. You want to dig up old ghosts?"

Titian's eyes wavered from her to the wall, and through it to a building across the street. "I can't let you go out in a pair. Tell me you want John Paul as your only backup. He's smart and he's strong, but he's naïve and green."

"Why not take a break? What's going to happen? You worry so much, coincidences spring forth from your mind into adult-born conspiracies."

He unbuttoned the cuff of his right sleeve and rolled it back to reveal a purpling pinkish wound. "I can bleed. I needed stitches. The wound opened this morning during your merry little gallivanting

171

constitutional. I may have ruined a lovely suit. Have you the mind to lecture me on caution?"

"From the funeral, or the explosion?"

"I should like to know myself." He rocked on his heels. "It may be residue from one or the other, but I find it more likely a combination. The first tested our guards. The second set the trap. Per my best guess, someone has motive and a grudge nursed strongly against us. Now we're guessing. Have you noticed any attacks on your person?"

"A delayed strike?" She shook her head.

"The likelihood of infiltration and invisibility remains low, lower even than the coincidence of my ancillary involvement in two recent actions precipitating a spontaneous hemophiliac outbreak. I conclude that someone scratched me recently. Someone bypassed my defenses to send me a message."

She slid forward. "Someone's *toying* with you?"

He turned his arm to catch better light. "Note the surgical precision. The most steady-handed surgeon could do no better job with diamond-tipped laser scalpels and a team of surveyors. This may be a test, but it's also a warning."

"About? For? Against?"

Titian straightened his shirt. "*That* is a double-question for which as yet I have no answer other than what you have already decided must not have been my answer."

"You're not bringing Bliss back."

He smiled as he buttoned his cuff. "Technically correct. I'm not bringing Bliss back. I *am* integrating the persona."

Silence swirled between as her face melted from shock to disbelief.

"You always said that was impossible. Steven himself said it was impossible."

"Always was."

"'Too dangerous,' Barry said."

"I loved him like a brother, but he had no vision."

"Steven barely had it under control at the best of times."

"How long ago were those days! How long we have labored and fought together and grown! How much we have learned in the intervening years! He would still be our best and brightest, but now even Claude can match Steven at his peak. Surely your great sadness brings great wisdom. We were rough and angry and raw and successful, but we lacked nuance and subtlety. Perhaps now only the combination of the passion of our youth and the wisdom of our experience—tempered of course by our will—can save us."

His eyes burned oxygen from the air between them; hers traced patterns in the carpet.

"Pretty words, but why am I always the one to ask who we're saving and from what?"

"You always kept our feet on the ground and our eyes to the path."

"*Bliss*, Roman? 'The Perfect Man'?" She straightened suddenly, ignoring the protest of stress-taut muscles. "He was the perfect theory, but we never knew who was in charge, if he merely humored us while waiting for an opening to start his own rebellion, or if he was a true believer. Did he ever really believe anything? Is 'he' even anthropomorphosizable?"

Titian smiled. "There was no guilt, no second-guessing. He was perfect will and perfect execution. He is an arrow loosed from the bow, shaft strong and straight and aim unfailing."

"Yet always unpredictable."

"You lack faith."

"I'm not chasing rainbows again, Roman. Count. You're down to two now, maybe one and a half. What are your weekly charades worth?"

He crossed the space between before she could draw breath. The room darkened; his bulk chased away the light. "You know exactly why we still fight, Sandie. Leave, if you want to leave. Go. Take the kid. Hide him in the farms. Barry's never coming back, not for you or anyone. Steven's never coming back. Pitch tents on Freeman Island with that old ghost. He still lives there, you know. Go on. Abandon everything they fought for because you're not strong enough or you don't believe in them anymore, or because whatever reason you think you have. You used to be stronger. You used to be fierce and brave and fearless. When did you get so small?"

He ducked under her slap and pushed her away. She came up swinging again, landing a closed fist along his right cheekbone. A rose-colored bruise purpled and he stumbled. She watched him, panting, eyes glazed in disbelief and fading rage.

Titian staggered to a chair. He withdrew a monogrammed handkerchief to dab at his lip and his cheek. "You see? Vulnerable." He threw the reddening cloth at the floor and ran for the thick door. Hinges creaked as he burst through.

Clownfish slipped off her chronometer wrist with a practiced shrug and twisted the back. One fingernail pried loose a translucent gold-hued chip. She ground it to fragments beneath her heel.

She sighed heavily, then snarled at the door where Titian had disappeared. Tiny crimson gems soaked into the rug.

o o o

Titian stormed down the hallway, reveling in the environment spreading from his mood. Heavy footfalls echoed through the stone; deep rumbles rattled vases and tilted mirrors and paintings a-kilter. Let it make a mess. Let subtle spiderwebs spread like bulletproof glass shattering, fine hairline cracks radiating outward from points of impact—damage, yes, but subtle and precise. What was a support structure but a promise to absorb the concentrated energy of fury and disperse it to areas of lesser harm?

He half expected to see the woman racing after, half ready to continue the argument and half ready to give in to the necessity of his idea. He weighed the options again: unspeakable force applied once, lever-like to force the world to a higher orbit incapable of decay, or continual minor adjustments and the inevitable, inescapable sinking feeling he'd spent his life trying to thwart. The mass of passing years pulled him into the earth with its own gravity. He'd seen too much. He knew the unstoppable passage of time, how each decision insignificant on its own invited further entropy and chaos and the grand universal disunification.

Steven had known, but he'd ignored it. Barry had never believed. Sandie had gloried in it from the start, wrapping a cloak of failure around her. "You'll see," she said. "One day," she promised. He'd considered her as the source of the threat momentarily, but she possessed neither the resources nor the will.

Even Steven's death, or disappearance, or resignation—whatever it had been—was a final act of defiance. With a hand against the cold, utter bleakness of the cosmos, he offered a challenge of will alone, even to the end. Not for the first time Titian wished that he'd pressed the issue. *Where* had the aspects come from? Were they the spontaneous expressions of human will, or extraterrestrial (extra-natural?) artifacts? Were they indeed hallucinations in some tightly-scripted fiction played out endlessly, searching for a simultaneous solution to complex equations of human behavior, love, free will, and the nature of power?

The purple monster in the corner smiled and burbled at him, setting aside a slim leather-bound volume and uncrossing smooth, luxurious legs. He waved back, coy, watching his fingers smear into doubles and triples. A little voice in his head stopped screaming long enough to titter as he mumbled an oath and fell, face-first. He watched the hand-woven carpet wrinkle underneath him and tried to align it parallel to the hallway. Painful red and black lights flashed into his vision.

○ ○ ○

The silent fall shook the floor. Clownfish stumbled. Windows rattled. She brushed plaster dust from her shoulders and her hair, scanning the ceiling for signs of damage. Wooden beams vibrated but held. She shook her head, hearing the sound of marbles shot by schoolchildren. Prismatic light sprayed the room.

She steadied herself on the desk, scrunching her eyes shut to whisper an apology to anyone or anything listening. White dust smeared her hand. The only light came from the soft glow of Titian's desk lamp and cooler hues creeping in from the hallway. A sense of repetition or familiarity pricked her skin. Cold sweat beaded between her shoulder blades; she twitched and forced her mantra through pursed lips.

The hallway was empty and tomb quiet. Even the busy chatter of pages and assistants had vanished. Oppressive silenced belayed the panicked hustle of an earthquake or bomb drill.

She sighed.

Titian lay face down inside a salon at the corner of the building, just short of an elevator bank. He looked peaceful—peaceful and awkward, left arm folded beneath him and right arm angled away from his head. She knelt and pulled against his jacket. The fabric shifted; a button popped off, but he remained unmoved. She pulled harder. His suit slipped through her fingers and she rocked back to land on the cold floor.

Clownfish bit her lip and watched heavy clouds scud past the tinted window. A flash of red reflected in the glass, and she pushed herself off of the ground with a loose fist.

"I'm not your mother, I'm not your chief of staff, and I'm not making a habit of rescuing you," she swore. "You win. We do this the hard way—but it's not my idea. Are you even listening? No. No surprise."

He had no pulse. She fumbled with his wrist, then found a sluggish, arrhythmic beat. It echoed from the edge of a vast series of undisturbed caverns. His blood sounded thick, coagulated. His lips and fingertips hinted at a sickly blue tint.

She scanned the silent hallway. Nothing moved. She reached under his collar for a handful of loose flesh, and raised Titian to his knees like a mother cat gathering a kitten. "Now you have matching bruises. I always admired your sense of color coordination." A grim smile tore at her mood. "Now comes the fun part. Don't you...." She maintained her grip to pivot around his body. "Go letting gravity...." She crouched and dropped her right shoulder under his chest. "Keep you down." She rose and grunted as his limp weight threatened to redistribute itself. "My goodness, you're heavy."

Clownfish staggered to the wall. Titian's arms and legs dangled uncontrollable and limp as she pressed the call button. "Something you ate? Overworked? Good time for a nap?"

The bell dinged. The furthest call light blinked. "Of course. You never make it easy." She stumbled through the doors before they closed again and freed a hand to wave at the blank control panel. "Eidolon storage."

Nothing happened.

She cursed again, and fumbled through Titian's dangling limbs for a bracelet, a ring, anything. "Don't make me look through your pockets. Don't tell me it's biometric. If I put you down, I'm not picking you up again. You may think the discussion's over, but you're wrong. You owe me much more than that, and now I'm dragging your sorry hide to save your life again."

Steven or Barry would have lightened her mood, the former stoic but hopeful and the latter always ready to laugh at a mere hint of play. "Look at me, stuck in an elevator with an unconscious blob of flesh, talking to myself. This was not my little girl grown up dream. I wanted a horse."

She slapped her free hand against the control panel. "Move. C'mon. Move!" The third slap splintered the glossy black perfection into carbon fibers. The fifth slap left a bloody smear to ooze down the wall as the elevator moved again. She shook away droplets of blood and broken bits of controls and counted in her head a second and a half per level. It couldn't have taken three minutes to reach him and drag him into the elevator. That left two minutes before brain damage became a real danger, in which case everyone was doomed, Bliss or no.

The doors opened into a deserted hallway in the building's oldest underbelly. A wobbly gurney taunted her from outside the elevator, and she winced in gratitude as it groaned under the sudden bulk of Titian's landing—but it held.

Beige pipes snaked overhead. Sickly mint cinder block walls loomed inward above sticky, scuffed tiles. She wheeled the gurney around a corner. A floor-to-ceiling bank vault door looked modern and new as it defied the dingy fluorescent lights and years of janitorially-neglected floor. She paused again, wiping the back of her hand across her forehead, then spun on one heel to kick the door. It groaned. Liquid honey golden light spilled from the crack, an army of dust motes skittering and dancing in its beams. She breathed deeply, eyelids fluttering, then pushed through.

The large room was empty save for thin racks of latched metal boxes and a small table at the far end. Each box had a thumb-sized depression beneath a meticulous label. Each box hummed in some dimension invisible except from the corners of her eyes. She blinked to disperse the hints of motion, but flickered suggestions pulled at her attention.

Clownfish pushed Titian toward the table. Five boxes lay there, four well-preserved and humming and the fifth covered with a thick layer of dust. She stared, then bent to blow and brush away its covering.

The center box read simply "Bliss". She caressed its sides, admiring as always the lack of visible seams, then pointed the latch at Titian and pressed. A pencil-sized iris appeared and opened. A silent explosion filled the room; the pressure of giant hands squeezed the room together. Her ears popped. She struggled to hold the box steady at arm's length, always pointed at the still figure. The room faded in a silent washout. Colors drained away to rough outlines of grays and whites, and then only whites.

Her vision returned. She saw his color return. He sucked in a huge breath, and his eyes snapped open, wide and wild.

"Don't sit up!," she hissed, but he grabbed for the box and slid off the cart. It slalomed toward one of the racks. He crashed to the floor, which dented beneath him. She reached for the cart, cringing at rumors and possibilities, but it was too far.

Then it stopped. The pressure in the room increased again, but this time the colors glowed—super-saturated—and wavered in hue.

A low chuckle dispelled the silence. She turned, slow motion, to see Titian kneeling, one finger pointed at the gurney and a tiny grin dancing in the corners of his mouth. He brought his hands together in front of his chest, then spread them apart, parallel to the floor. A strand of hair fell across his forehead; he levitated.

"I've almost forgotten how pure and undiluted this power."

"You're still poisoned. That's my best guess." Clownfish scanned his face, cataloging every wrinkle and pore in ironic phrenology.

Titian's smile was genuine. "No matter." He closed his eyes. Sweat beaded on his forehead. He sank four inches to the ground. The glow receded to a healthy tan. "Do you have a handkerchief?"

"Don't gloat. It's ugly." She handed him a wad of crumpled tissues. "They're clean."

He swabbed at his face, then tossed the damp mess into a corner. "Have someone burn that. You were right. I don't know if it's a contact poison or airborne, but that's of little consequence. Was anyone else affected?"

"Everything was deserted from the office on down. I didn't see anyone. I broke the elevator controls too."

"No matter." He reached for the box. She tried to hold back, but her muscles obeyed him instead. "Have you ever looked inside? Did Steven ever show you an empty one? No?" He fitted his thumb into the latch mechanism. Diagonal seams appeared around the box. "It twists apart. It's spherical inside but cubic outside: stacks well but contains the eidolon in its most inert configuration." The box split in halves with a soft click, and he held them out for her inspection. The inside looked soft, malleable—creamy-textured coconut milk—yet rigid.

"What *is* it?"

"It's some sort of dampening material. Steven dropped hints now and then, but the most I ever coaxed out of him was a metaphor or riddle about the mother of necessity. He found that uproarious."

She stared again at his face, eyes tracing the seems between features: eye, earlobe, chin, nose, eyebrow, cheekbone.

179

"What is it, Sandie?"

"Is that you? Is it Bliss? Who are you?"

Titian set the box on the table. "What kind of a question is that? You know how it works. It's the temporary application of a named aspect or ideal. Or perhaps you're asking who you'd be after a similar application."

She ignored the bait. "Bliss was composite. Synthetic. Steven shelved it after the Wharf Raids."

"We speak of his perfections and quirks, but never his flaws. He may have been the best of us, but he lacked will. How odd that he never discovered that one." A thought flicked across his face and he examined her reaction. "No matter. You remember his blind spots as well as you have catalogued mine."

She glanced again at the table and shifted to put the empty, closed box behind her. "The Undertow is also a low-grade synthetic composite. What did he call it? 'The background radiation of the revolution'? It was dangerous then. Can you control it now?"

He stepped closer. Black fire filled the air, eating the light. She jerked involuntarily against the table. His smile wavered, and the room returned to normal. "I may admit that, as an object lesson, that was somewhat overkill... but give me more than a minute to acclimate to not dying as well as incorporating Bliss. I consider this a success."

The dusty box teetered. They stared at each other for a moment, and, as one, turned toward the dull thud. She bit her lip as the box flew toward his hand. He scowled. "Sorrow?" he read. "Where did this come from?" His thumb caressed the release mechanism.

Clownfish pulled at his sleeve. "Probably a synthetic, a byproduct of Bliss. Bliss and Sorrow, get it? Opposite sides of a coin."

He shrugged. "Sometimes his motives tended toward the impractical. That was his greatest flaw. If anything, my flaw is the meticulousness of my plans... the weighing of every contingency. Betrayals. Counter-betrayals. Analysis and structure. Its deepest flaw is its susceptibility to simple, brash chaos. Ah, anarchy, beautiful in its self-destructive simplicity. . . ."

She removed the box from his hands and placed it on the bottom shelf of a distant rack. "I don't follow."

Titian paced, weighing his words. "The attack on the funeral, the attack on our building, the poison, they're all mindless distractions. They're feints. We could divine no reasoning or strategy because they had no strategy in and of themselves. They were merely chaos, loose ideas tied together only by the power of our self-delusion in our own analyses. Now that my mind is clear, I see that as well."

Clownfish straightened the other boxes on the shelf. "You do tend toward the concrete."

He continued, unhearing. "What we face is much subtler. I would suspect random bubbles of destruction and chaos—the inevitable fallout of our plans to reorder the world—but that does not answer one simple question. Why now?"

"Why not?"

"For all of the chaos that might appear as separate, unconnected events, there is a single strand—a narrative. Events progressed from the general to the specific. A large gathering at the funeral, with visible assailants and no particular target. A small explosion in a building, affecting far fewer but higher value targets. A poisoning, affecting one person. There is clearly an intelligence behind this. Shall we find a suitable power for you, Sandie?"

She shook her head. "I don't believe in assassinations. You were always much better at paranoia."

His chuckle sounded forced, to her mind. "The offer remains open. On another matter, I suggest we resume our patrols."

"Patrols? We haven't done that in. . . ."

Titian dismissed the thought with a wave. "Your instincts are as good as ever. Perhaps better. We need not make a show of things. Merely look around. We'll divide it into thirds when the boy returns."

"You're going out?"

He smiled again, narrowing his eyes with concentration. His hair grew long, darkening, and the bulk of his body flowed and melted until he was tall and plain, never out of place in a busy street of pedestrians. "I am not without disguises or protections. I shall return." The room folded around him, resolving itself to reveal a space he no longer occupied.

Her eyes flicked again to the rows of humming boxes, but she tore her self away to rush out of the room after him. "Fool's going to collapse, and I have to carry him all the way back here invisible," she grumbled.

o o o

Clownfish scowled and paced. Titian/Bliss was late.

John-Paul shifted on a couch. "Who's this Bliss guy?"

She shook herself back to attention. "Sorry, what? Bliss?"

"Third time I've asked. Are you alright?"

Her response was a look, frosty and sharp.

"Alright. Touchy. New question then. Is Pierre not coming back?"

"Not any time soon. He and Claude are on indefinite leave. If we're making small talk, how was your long weekend?"

He grimaced. "Raised more questions than it answered. Is there any chance I'll get some straight answers from you? Titian's *useless*. I talked to him earlier today. He said, and this is a quote, 'Everything will be revealed in due time.'"

Clownfish tapped her watch. The second hand continued to slog ahead through sticky mud. She glanced around, then also sunk onto the couch. "I can't promise I'll answer everything, and you don't tell Titian I told you anything, but I'll do what I can." Her outfit cycled from bright hues to darker, muted shades.

"Fair enough. First question. Is this all a dream? Am I unconscious somewhere, imagining everything? Am I a butterfly, dreaming I'm a man? On second thought, are *you*?" He snickered.

Lightning-quick, she leaned forward to punch his arm.

"Ow. Okay. Serious question though. Is this all an illusion?"

"Serious question?" She pointed to a luxury sedan double parked outside where a driver sipped coffee and did a newspaper crossword. "Go lift that car. Can you do it?"

"No question."

"Same answer. Belief matters. Doubt *kills*."

"I couldn't back home."

She risked a sideways glance at his face before sliding deeper into the couch. "You tried to lift a car, back on the farm? Was Timmy trapped under a tractor?"

"No, I—well, it isn't important. I believed I could do something spectacular. I did. I had a spectacular failure." Fear and memory danced in his eyes. "This is important. It's important to me to know. Can we really do amazing things? Can I? Is this all just an illusion or a dream?"

"Go lift that car. I won't stop you. Lift any car you like. Punch a hole in the Green Street Bridge, or go pound Progress flat. You've done it before. Either we've anticipated everything you're likely to do, or it's really happening. Go. Prove it to yourself."

He laced his fingers behind his head and stretched his legs until his bones ached. "Ahhh. Okay, I can believe that for the moment. I'll set aside the obvious teleological question. Next. Why couldn't I do anything when I was home?"

"Give me your hand."

"What?"

She pulled at his left wrist, then flipped the chronometer with practiced fingers. A flick of her fingernail opened a hidden compartment to reveal a tiny plastic capsule.

"What's this?"

She sighed and replaced it. "Think of it like focus. A lens maybe."

"A lens for what?"

"Will you stop interrupting?" She finished replacing the capsule and pushed his hand out of her lap. Her left leg twitched, and she shifted more weight to that side.

"Sorry." A dark rain of silence descended.

Clownfish stood and paced. "Where *is* he? There's an area of effect. Steven never figured out how to make the effects permanent without a bonding."

"The what now?"

"Close your eyes. Just do it." He did. "Imagine an iron bar. Imagine rubbing a magnet against it. Quit snickering. Adolescent! It retains some of the magnetism after you remove the source; it's realigned its internal properties."

"We're magnetic now?"

She rolled her eyes. "Metaphor, do you speak it? Imagine if you could focus some of that residual magnetism such that it's not available over the iron bar everywhere in general, but at specific points and specific times. The bar could use it for specific tasks, as it saw fit."

He chewed his lip. "A reservoir, in other words?"

"More or less."

"How does it work?"

She shrugged. "Not a scientist, just someone susceptible to the right sales pitch at the wrong time." Her pacing orbited close to the couch where he grabbed her wrist and pried off her chronometer. "Hey!"

She struggled, but he persisted. He fumbled with the secret compartment; she wriggled free as triumphed. "Aha! Oh. Hey? No capsule."

Clownfish snatched it back from his hand and replaced it on her wrist, rubbing away red marks. An angry silence gave her height and a wild, uncontrollable mien.

Realization bloomed. "Why, Clownie? What's different about me?" She sat again, folding her arms and crossing her legs. He stared. She closed her eyes. He leaned in closer. "Where does this so-called magnetism come from, anyway?"

She pushed him away. "I don't know. Not exactly. I can't answer that. Steven's the only one who really knew."

"Where is he, then?"

"Dead. Long dead."

"Oh. I'm sorry." He kicked at the ground. "Does that mean no one really knows what's going on anymore then?"

She shrugged. "Probably. Titian knows more than he lets on. I've probably forgotten a hundred times more than I remember, and it's still a fraction of what's true."

"Why, then?"

"Why what?"

"Why go through all of this?" He waved his hands at their outfits. "Why secrecy and the staged fights and weird not-quite-magnetism and . . . well, what's the difference between this and some crazy television show?"

Clownfish folded her hands in her lap and watched her thumbs circle each other. "No cameras." She winced as she said it. "You're right, I'm sorry. Flippancy's an effective inoculation against the painful truth. It sounds complicated, but it's really simple. We're better off this way. That's what we always thought at least."

"Better off lying to people? We could be out there *helping* them."

She turned on him. "How do you know we aren't? You don't. You have no idea what it was like before. You grew up in your comfortable little farm, free of overcrowding and greed and prejudice and immigration and soul-crushing poverty all day, every day, everywhere. You're stepping in it. You're bathing in it. You open your mouth and you breathe in despair. It's in your food and your water. We'd already fixed so much of it by the time you were born, you take it all for granted. Yes, we made mistakes, but you have no idea how things used to be. None. Everything seems so easy to you. *We* made it easy for you. All of it. We've held the city together for longer than you can imagine. Maybe we're falling apart now, but then again, maybe everything falls apart." Her voice broke and she cleared her throat, pushing away his hand.

"Hey, I'm sorry. Alright? I didn't mean it like that."

She walked to and leaned against the window, forehead against the glass and hands cupping her eyes. Outside the world passed. Innumerable people walked by: short and tall, fat and thin, determined and amiable. Their stories sang with potential. One couple returned from their first shopping trip together. A nervous young man rushed to a job interview. A severe woman planned to run for the vacant Council seat.

None of them had any idea what John-Paul and Clownfish were capable of, or could imagine even the barest tip of Titian's plans. Yet most of them would recognize *him* on the street, a flash of familiarity passing across their eyes. Half of them would greet him. "Protector! Hey, how's it going? Keep up the good work. Big P, you rock!"

"Belief," he whispered.

Clownfish mumbled something.

"What?"

She slapped the window. The glass rippled and bent, echoing rubbery, off-key harmonics throughout the room as it returned to a resting state. "It's all about belief. You're right. We've always abused it. We're optimists posing as cynics or cynics pretending to be optimists and we can't stop exploiting that belief. It's how we work. That's why I'm still here. No matter how much I realize what we're doing isn't helping us meet our goals, I still believe we have a chance. I still believe we can make things better. Sometimes we've even succeeded. Worse yet, all of those people out there, the ones we catalog in our heads, they all *believe*, too. Want to destroy everything good we've built? Take that belief away from them. Tell them we're not making a difference. Show them exactly what we can and cannot do. Go ahead. Destroy yourself. See if I care."

Static electricity crackled his hair; the iron in the building's bones bent toward her. She turned, and he saw the granite of her eyes. Deep hues swirled in her suit, threatening to drown him in their deluge. Her arms ascended until she stood one-legged, right foot on left knee, her horrible aura arcing outward.

"Stop it," he cried. Cold wind swept away the words.

She screamed, wordless. Probability and possibility tore at him, threatening to crumple and throw him through the back wall to skid, boneless, in the street. He fought back, leaning forward against lines of power, one hand outstretched to her bare skin.

"Please," he whispered. A whirlwind splintered the room's decorations. Shards of glass and sharp pieces of wood pierced his skin. Droplets of blood puddled and coagulated. They joined the cyclone as his skin puckered against and rejected the intrusion. He fought for progress, defying gravity and inertia to retain his position against that horrible human-shaped darkness. Each step was an agony. Each step was an eternity.

The wind broke its silence, tearing at the walls with a howl. Great swatches of paint blistered and pulled away—then chunks of stone, first in tiny clods then clumps and clusters. The building's skeleton lay bare, some long-forgotten fossil in which the children of modernity had taken residence, redecorating again and again until they'd inured themselves against all of the history required to provide them the luxury of forgetting.

"No," he whispered through gritted teeth. His muscles protested another inch. "I reject all of this."

He saw himself as through a telescope, battered and bruised and panting. The world constricted to grow distant and quieter. Every step was a distant agony. His bones ached only in sympathy. The room was bare now, stripped of everything but two figures and a whirlwind of debris grinding itself into atom-sized motes.

She... she was glorious. She was the blackness of an eclipse. She was the depth of a cave within the earth's bowels. She was the loneliness of a night without stars and the stillness of the newborn earth before any creature sucked in moist air. She was destruction and rebirth and the knowledge that all things have a beginning and all things have an ending and the beautiful futility of each generation trying to push its successors further toward some ill-defined and poorly-understood goal beyond mere survival.

She was the darkness that eats dreams and the dream that dispels darkness and the tiny jewel of a tear spilling out of her eye to slide down one beautiful, flawless cheekbone and shatter on the ground at her feet.

He stumbled and clawed at the floor's remains. He bent, still unbroken. He crawled, pulling himself by fingertip and toe. He watched himself, lending himself the will for one more pull and one more push. Just one more. Just one more. That's all it takes, just one more. The rhythm of his mantra left him breathless. He let the wind scour away everything but his creed.

He stretched fingers for her ankle, praying for his arm to extend another tremulous inch. The center of the vortex was calm. Wind whorled and danced past her body, but he willed it to pull away at her uniform and expose bare flesh under his fingers... and a tiny puff of air smelling of lavender and lilacs and licorice escaped the whirlwind. His finger touched.

A crack of thunder threw them in opposite directions.

John-Paul forced his eyes open through sticky grit. He blinked, hoping for tears. He lay crumpled in a heap along what had been the far wall of the building. Swirling dust had gouged obscene patterns in the floor and ceiling and windows.

Nothing felt broken; everything ached. He coughed up a thick wad of goo and wiped his mouth.

Clownfish knelt with one hand on the ground. She'd just vomited a thin green paste. She pulled her hair back from her face and scanned him. "Are you okay?" It was half-moan, half-groan.

"I'm all here. How about you?"

She shrugged. A cough shuddered her body. "Nothing's broken, but what *was* that?"

He scrambled and ambled to a sitting position, resting his head against a girder sanded smooth and shiny. "You seemed upset. Then all hell broke loose. I thought if I could reach you, I could snap you out of it."

She peeled her uniform back from her leg. A bruise purpled there. Smears of charcoal-black dirt splayed outward.

"I'm sorry, I guess," he offered. "I just...."

Clownfish waved it off. "No, not you. Not this time. You weren't wrong either. We *have* behaved badly. I'm not surprised things went weird. It was years in the making. I never wanted to believe it and never had the courage to say anything. I'm so tired, John-Paul. I've wasted so much time hoping things would get better, but they're as bad as they've ever been. I don't know what game Titian's playing, but we kept forcing a lid down on a boiling pot, letting out a little bit of steam now and then, hoping that the whole thing wouldn't explode under us. Some of it did, now."

He chewed his lip. "Where is he, anyway?"

"I don't know. The last time I saw him... well, this isn't the first time this has happened. It's the worst. You were there. You saw it before, that explosion. You remember the funeral. Something's coming for us, and it's bigger and more powerful than we are. It's toying with us."

John-Paul snickered, then felt his heart sink when he saw the sincerity in her eye. "What *happened*? I deserve to know."

Glass shattered and sprayed and tinkled as Titian crashed through the window backwards. He smacked and bent a post in the middle of the building. Metal whined and groaned, precipitous. The ceiling sagged but held. More dust and debris choked the air.

John-Paul stood and brushed at his pants, grimacing at futile smears. Pedestrians passed by outside, oblivious to the scene of destruction. Clownfish crawled her way his direction, and he offered her his left arm, eyes still on the broken window. She put her back to his, scanning the other direction for assailants.

Titian groaned a low sigh that broke into a sound half-cough and half-laugh. He rolled over. His bulk jiggled as he sucked in and expelled ragged, filthy air. "Ouch," he said with a low whistle. "That was the most painful experience I've ever hoped to encounter."

"Worse than the train?" Clownfish risked a glance in his direction.

"Imagine the impact of two trains, each traveling in the opposite direction, and you begin to understand the magnitude of this image." He wiggled his extremities, toes and fingers first, feeling for damage. "Fortunately I seem to have everything but my pride intact."

"What happened?" John-Paul kept his voice low and his eyes grim.

"My friend, you can stand down, however briefly. I've bought us a few minutes of time."

"From?"

Clownfish interrupted. "Whatever it is, it's attracted to strength, isn't it? The visible demonstration of power... the same way everyone outside is oblivious to it."

"Very perceptive." He lay on his back, wincing and gulping shallow breaths as he tested and moved muscles in isolation. "I've made lamentably little progress on discerning its true identity, but its mode of operation is consistent. Wherever we go, wherever we gather or consolidate our power or our plans, there it strikes."

John-Paul shrugged. "I don't get it. I tried to use my power at home. Nothing happened."

"What did you expect, young Mr. Harrison? A sobering flash of insight? Miracles, accompanied by song and fireworks? A flock of avenging angels ready to strike at your whim?"

John-Paul dropped his hands. "Sarcasm. Helpful. We were having a nice discussion before you arrived. Clownfish was explaining everything to me. Don't I deserve more explanation than you've seen fit to dole out to me so far?"

Titian sat, knees protesting. He panted for a second, then pushed himself up off the floor. "Sandie did, hmm? I suppose it couldn't be helped."

Clownfish smirked. "I told him everything you know, which is that something out there's gunning for us, and you don't know what it is or how to deal with it."

A cloud passed over the large man's face. "Did you tell him about Bliss?"

She snorted. "I hadn't realized you were serious about making yourself a target—or is this just opportunism?"

"Always the cynic, like Steven was always the optimist. I was always the realist suspended in between. Yes, Bliss lures them here. What you don't realize is that we *own* this building. It's a small price to pay to get the drop on them, so to speak."

Shock made her whisper. "It's coming here?"

"Yes, why?"

John-Paul dragged her by the hand toward the entrance. Titian called again after them. "Why? Why do you ask?"

She pulled back, but could not resist his grip. "Titian, it was waiting for us!"

The building imploded as Clownfish and John-Paul dove out through the window. Titian's voice broke off halfway through a curse. "Oh, —" he said.

They landed and scrambled for cover. Pedestrians screamed and fled as the building spewed waves of dust. A crackling noise rattled their bones; the building twisted inward and imploded. The slow-motion destruction took weeks. Floor by floor crumbled, drooping and radiating cracks from the center outward. Windows shattered. Furniture tumbled and splintered. The groaning of the ruins echoed from building to building through the city.

Clownfish scrabbled at her costume, pulling at every seam. "Is it in here? Is it there?" Crazed fear twisted her face, her eyes focusing this way and that. John-Paul pulled her behind a long black limo coated on one side in thick gray dust. "I didn't feel anything. Did you? I've seen him survive worse…or almost as bad. Did you feel that? Do you hear anything? Do you see anything?"

191

He grabbed her hands to stop her from wringing them. "Clownie. Hey. Come back to me."

An enormous grin split her face. "Couldn't fool you, could I, kid?" Her body slumped, limp and spent, as a ring of black-suited soldiers surrounded them.

Every soldier wore the same uniform, free of ornaments or visible markings. None had the mien of a leader. John-Paul lowered Clownie's body to the ground and raised his hands. He rose and stepped away. "What do you want?"

The not-her voice rose from Clownfish again. "You don't know *anything*, do you? You're no Barry. You're no Roman. You're just some hick they convinced to dress up in a stupid costume. Classy."

She'd flopped over on her side, one arm flailing out of the way. Her head lolled at a precarious angle. Her eyelids fluttered half open and half closed as her limbs jerked and twitched.

He boggled. He reached for her body again, only to hear the unmistakable click of rounds being chambered. He withdrew.

The voice sounded even less like Clownfish. "Good, you're not completely stupid. Here's what I want you to do. It's very simple. Resign."

The world swam through his mind, summoning half-realized scenes of blood and chaos and fire. He pushed them away and croaked "Resign?"

His thoughts grew clearer as the echoes of the building's collapse died down. Metal still groaned, but the debris had stabilized.

"Resign. Give up. Let it go. I'll let you leave."

"I already surrendered."

The voice's timbre carried irritation. "No. *Resign*."

John-Paul shook his head. His hands wavered. The soldiers drew the circle one step closer. "Okay, okay. I resign."

"They didn't explain *anything* to you, did they? Give it up. Dismiss it. Cast it away. Don't play dumb." A thin line of drool dripped from Clownfish's mouth and puddled, muddy on the street.

"I don't –" he began. A fresh spray of detritus exploded outward. His ears rang. He ducked to cover his head and cower behind the thin protection of the damaged car. A great shout rang out above the sound of the building's collapse.

A fresh wind smelling of the sea carried away lingering dust. The soldiers looked around, visibly confused behind their dark helmets. A familiar figure stood atop the car; its tires gasped and wheezed and burst beneath its weight. "Aha," it yelled.

John-Paul dove between two soldiers, knocking them into their neighbors. They fired, but his footing held as he zigged and zagged for cover behind another car.

Titian burned, a tiny golden sun. Bullets sprayed in his direction. He beamed; they evaporated in streams of silver steam. A mob of soldiers closed in on him. A single kick sent several of them flying, their arms describing windmills as they struggled to retain their balance. He lept to the pavement, landing in a lunge position. He punched the pavement. Great cracks radiated outward, throwing more soldiers off their feet.

"Hey kid," Titian yelled. "Catch!" With his left hand, he pulled Clownfish off the ground, then straightened and spun. He released her at John-Paul. Adrenaline and neural-wired trigonometry positioned him to absorb her momentum; he cradled her head between his shoulder and neck.

Titian yelled to run and John-Paul ran. The air was glue-thick. He ran. An enormous invisible hand pressed back, but Clownfish coughed and squirmed and wriggled and the pressure eased. Smokey black tendrils swirled around them but she pushed herself away and landed awkwardly. She swayed as she planted her fists on her hips. "NO!" she yelled.

The air wavered and shimmered, and the tendrils evaporated. "Titian," she whispered. John-Paul grabbed her arm, stopping her in place.

"He said to run."

"He can't stand up against this on his own. Not even as Bliss."

A black-suited soldier flew through the air backwards, unconscious. His arms and legs dangled. His head lolled. A spiderweb of cracks decorated his helmet. He accelerated and disappeared with a pop and a puff of air that tangled their hair.

The pressure wavered and disappeared. John-Paul's ears popped and the world was clear again. The sound of Titian grunting and striking soldiers carried. They were relentless, but he clearly had the advantage. They gathered in bundles of twos and threes, rushing from opposing angles, but he dodged and wove and struck. They staggered and flew. With every blow they rose more slowly, shaking their heads before locking onto him again.

Clownfish pulled against John-Paul's arm. He let her go, but she stood there and watched. "That's... bizarre."

"Their tactics?"

"They're not individuals. They're interchangeable parts of one large group. Look. He's not even sweating." A rosy glow surrounded Titian. He was the picture of well-exercised health. One soldier grabbed him from behind, fingertips barely touching around his enormous arms. The larger man cackled and flexed, then dropped to a knee with a forward jerk. The black-suited man careened off of a bent lamppost and crumpled.

The tide slowed. Titian sneered at ad hoc piles of soldiers. The assault persisted, ragged and disorganized.

"We should help him anyway," John-Paul offered as he ran in. The barrier offered no tingle when he passed through its previous location. He slapped the back of the nearest soldier's helmet; the figure smashed face-first to the ground.

Clownfish held back. She scanned the sky and side streets, but they were empty save high, fluffy clouds and fine gray ash.

Within moments the fight had ended. John-Paul wiped grimy sweat from his forehead, grimacing at the sticky mess on his fingers. Titian stood proud over a heap of six soldiers and patted stray hair back into place. "Sandie," he called. "All clear over there?"

The sky felt wrong. Every few steps she stole a glance over her shoulder.

"How did you get out of the building?" John-Paul panted. "I've never seen anything like that."

"I have more than a few tricks you would not believe, Mr. Harrison. I admit that our foe did surprise me, but even surprise is insufficient to defeat or delay us... certainly not now."

Clownfish stopped several feet away. "Are you feeling alright?"

"Never better, my dear. Perfect. Better than perfect. Oh, how I've missed our adventures... the perfection of human muscle and will and achievement!"

John-Paul interrupted. "What happened?"

"And what was that thing?" Clownfish tilted her head with apparent care. "It attacked me before you arrived, and it was in my head."

Titian beamed. "The last gasps of the old guard. This is the end of our revolution—the start of our golden age. Remember what we fought so long for, so long ago? This is our final victory." He knelt by an unconscious soldier. "Behold!" He unfastened the helmet and, with a flourish, removed the facepiece. "The true face of our enemy!"

An empty helmet stared out from an empty suit.

Titian scrambled through the other piles. All of the helmets were empty. All of the suits were empty. They had the weight and heft of strong, athletic men, but they were empty.

"What does it mean?" whispered John-Paul.

"I have no idea." She clutched his arm and drew closer.

The sky darkened. A whirlwind gathered the bodies with surgical precision. They spun and twirled and rode the twister into the sky. As suddenly as it had appeared, it vanished. The sky cleared. Three people stood in the street, surrounded by rubble and dirt, with no signs of melee besides their own sweat and grime.

John-Paul wheeled to look at Titian. "What kind of a game is this? Are you testing my loyalty? Am I asleep? Is this some sort of practical joke, or a power grab?" He felt his hair stand on end. Pavement bubbled under his feet, but he stood his ground. "I want answers. Now is good."

Titian turned slowly. "Bliss," he yelled. "Roman! I *win*." His arms and legs jerked in an awkward dance from invisible puppet strings; he slapped his knees and hopped from side to side. His mouth spread wide in a frozen grin, exposing far too many teeth. His eyes remained his own; horror blossomed there.

Golden beads of moisture pearled at his hairline and coalesced in great drops as they streamed down his face and dripped from his chin. Clownfish stood frozen, her fingers dug into John-Paul's arm.

"The boy, the replacement. You told him nothing. You always hid so much, Roman. The woman. She tried so hard to make sense of everything, and your planning and scheming once again led to her sorrow. Do you regret nothing? You're everything you railed against. Your glorious revolution built for you the edifices of power you fought. Did you even notice? Was it gradual, or is this your final, sudden epiphany?"

John-Paul reached out his hand as he had done earlier. Clownfish jerked at his sleeve, hissing "No...I'm working on this." He dared a glance; a swirl of watery colors snaked out from her. It darted and stretched and approached Titian from behind, diving from above to pierce his head.

Titian's smile faltered. He swung a wavering hand to point at her. She unlaced her fingers from John-Paul's arms and flinched as she flew backwards and skidded along the sidewalk. The hand pointed toward John-Paul, but he dropped flat to the ground and slapped the pavement. A wave of buckling asphalt jostled and dropped Titian. The blast chewed through several floors of the corner of a remaining building. Papers and shreds of furniture rained on the street.

"Enough talk," roared not-Titian's voice. "You wanted Bliss? I'm taking him."

Spare chunks of asphalt rose and hovered in the air. Rough air currents drew them into a whirlwind. They coalesced into an enormous hand. It flexed twice, then fell on Titian. He screamed and fought back, raising first one finger and then another. He managed to get his legs beneath him and fought it back, inch by inch. Superhuman speed drove his meaty fist into the first knuckle of the hand. It vibrated and relaxed an instant—long enough for him to slip away, brushing away pebbles and wincing at abrasions.

The hand shook itself, then formed into a fist and rushed at Titian again. He dove sideways, and the thing smashed a mailbox, shattering metal and launching paper chaff. It flipped in midair and swung again. Titian spun out of the way, but the fist opened from a punch to a slap. Its fingertips connected to send him bouncing off of a car. He rolled and landed face-down.

As the hand descended again toward the body, John-Paul focused his concentration into a single wave of thought. The rubble lost its cohesion. A rain of pebbles showered the body; larger pieces careened away. John-Paul ducked as several embedded themselves in the wall behind him. His adrenal glands squirted again and he shuddered and shivered and had to count to ten to catch his breath.

Titian's body rose from the ground, then stretched horizontally. A thin groan became a ragged scream. Darkness and light flashed in strobe, exposing the skeleton through his skin. Bones glowed white-hot, then shriveled in the heat. The large man melted and drooped and fell to the ground with a splat. "Help," he whispered.

John-Paul swatted away tendrils probing at his mind. The voice boomed again. "You're next."

Rage lent him a cool peace. "Unlikely. You're done," he countered. He touched the puddle that had been Titian. A red and orange and yellow thunderclap shockwave stole his senses as it knocked him backwards.

o o o

Pandora sighed and rubbed her forehead. Despite a restless weekend of replaying and recreating everything she could remember from Friday, her notes remained thin. Hope hung on the possibility that every misunderstanding was an internal contradiction from some bizarre hazing perpetrated by Fontaine and his assistants. She saw him as a great vain bird, preening over a shiny wad of aluminum foil woven into the twigs of its nest.

"Likely," she scowled.

A sea of people lapped at the entrance to her building, bobbing before the crawl of news tickers in the windows. The real-time display occasionally gathered a crowd, but she'd never had to force her way to the entry sensor to swipe her key, nor to surf like jetsam to the revolving doors. She skimmed the ticker, but none of the words summoned memories or images. The crowd murmured, transfixed, but did not follow.

Pandora glanced around the lobby. The click of shoes echoed in the distance, but she recognized no one. A uniformed security officer offered blank pleasantries from behind the reception desk. She returned a mirthless smile.

Vernon appeared as she turned the corner to the elevator bank. His face wore a rained-out picnic glumness.

"Oh," she said. "I didn't expect you."

He motioned her to the side of the room and leaned in to whisper. "I wanted to apologize for Friday. You didn't hear this from me. That was our fiasco. I argued against sending you, but Mr. Fontaine insisted. He said it would catalyze his long-lived plans."

A glint of light in his eye and the predatorial perfection of his teeth tickled her hindbrain's tactical retreat planning.

"Titian called Fontaine a buffoon."

"Given how we mishandled everything, do you blame him?" The accompanying shrug seemed practiced: slick charm deflecting blame. "Are these your notes?" His gesture was lazy and off-hand— not quite pointing.

"What I could recreate. I lost a few minutes in his office somehow. The next I remember, I was outside with a blank notepad, pages missing. No questions, no answers, just a headache. Then you sent me to the hospital."

Vernon began to shake his head, but caught himself and chewed his lip before the gesture became a denial. She tried to look away, but her eyes couldn't leave the slim, manicured fingers, tugging at a stray strand of hair behind his ear. "That's...unexpected. He was never that subtle before."

"Subtle?"

He blinked once, then smiled. A shiver ran down her arms, as if he'd just asked her to kneel on the ground with her fingers locked together behind her head. "Mr. Fontaine and Mr. Titian have a long and fractious history together. I'm sure you can imagine."

"Titian said as much."

"Given that the purpose of a free and independent press is to challenge existing power structures—and what could represent a greater power structure than the foundation of all freedom and security throughout the entire metropolitan area?—I'm sure you can see how our interests do not always align perfectly."

His words flowed out, well-rehearsed animal noises polished in front of a mirror, parroted in rapid bursts intended to dispel and confuse.

He reached for the folder. She slapped it against his chest. "I don't know why you needed me. I have the strong impression you don't care about what I wrote or what I think. I think you wanted to needle him. I don't know why." Something dark crossed her face and he backpedaled a step.

"It's...." He swallowed once, then closed his eyes to drink the air. His predatory smile wavered at the edges. Thin wrinkles deepened at the top of his nose. "Look." His voice dropped. "It's more complicated than you know. Titian plays a dangerous game. No one knows its extent, probably not even him. We need to find out and expose it and stop it before anyone else gets hurt. You're a good resource. You have a dog in the fight, so to speak. If we'd told you any more, he might have found out."

"Is that a threat?"

"Excuse me?"

"About John-Paul. You don't want to see him hurt." She hated the words in her head and regretted their sound in the air, but she twisted them in her mouth and gaze, copying Titian's impassive stare and metronomic breathing patterns.

Sweat beaded at his perfect hairline. "No, it's.... What are you doing?"

"I want the truth," she said. "That's why I'm here. That's why we're all here. We're the last bastion of truth in the city. We seek out stories people don't tell. We investigate. We shine the light of truth on facts and let the people of the city decide who to believe. That's the motto here, isn't it? Are those only pretty words writers sling to distract people from ugly actions?"

Each word buffeted his defenses. A buried history swirled in his eyes under the barrage. Her vision wavered—his glamour wavered. She saw him different: taller, thinner, far older, shoulders bent under the weight of the ages. His eyes had seen sadness and waste and sorrow and they dared not hope for a new dawn.

"You're right," he admitted. His eyes drank in the room and he pulled her further into a phone alcove. She jerked her arm free with a scowl and leaned against the wall.

Vernon ran his fingers through his hair and nodded for her to sit. She jammed her arms together over her rib cage. He joined her on the low bench. "Where should I start? I used to work with Titian, a long, long time ago."

Pandora rolled her eyes.

"It's true. We have a long history together."

"That makes you a better candidate to talk to him."

"There's a lot of water under that bridge. It was ... we had very different ideas about how the world should work. How much do you know about Reconciliation?"

"When they formed the city out of the five districts?"

"District's not even the right word; half of them were loose confederations of boroughs evolution forced together. Unification took a long time. Each district had its own personality and goals. Mediation would have worked, but only a few idealists believed it was anything other than the readjustment and consolidation of ever more power in the hands of fewer and fewer elites.

"Prosperity was uneven back in those days. We still have the rich and the poor, but food, housing, health care, work, those are all in the hands of anyone who wants them now. Poverty was everywhere then. Opportunity was. . . well, a mere word. I know things aren't perfect now—believe me, I know—but only a few people had money and the power. Far too many had neither.

"Before Reconciliation, Titian and I were part of an organization devoted to social justice, to improving the situation. We spent a lot of time behind the scenes fighting for the interests of the common man. We won battles, but we lost the war.

"As always, endings have their beginnings in a single personal disagreement. What are you willing to do to succeed? Titian was willing to go as far as revolution. Uproot the seats of power. Replace everything. Start over. If the ruling class wouldn't give up control voluntarily, he'd take it by force."

"I'm not so naïve as to believe that you're the white hat to his evil cackling villain."

"No. Right. I can't claim that he was *wrong*. Maybe he valued the end results so much that he was willing to pursue them single-mindedly. That's a virtue in some contexts. There's a lot to admire in that single-minded devotion to changing the world. Maybe that's the only way the world ever *does* change.

"Even so, we didn't agree. I wanted something subtler. I wanted to change minds. I lost that argument. It was clear."

She sighed. "What happened?"

"The same thing that happens to every glorious revolution. Someone stays and someone goes. We'd skirmished with private security forces. Titian was willing to drive that wedge in further. I wasn't. I left. A couple of people went with me. Most stayed. I laid low for a while. Then Mr. Fontaine offered me a position here. It was a far better fit. I have the opportunity here to shape how people think with information."

"Why the secrecy then?" Pandora relaxed her shoulders.

Vernon shrugged. "Old habits. Stress shows you who you really are. Maybe I'm the same withered old revolutionary I never wanted to be."

"What are you trying to do with Titian?"

"We know the old Protector died. We know he's grooming your friend as a replacement. We know most people don't know this. They know it superficially, but ask them if they really *believe* it. To them, there's always been the one and only Protector.

"Ask yourself this. Can the Protector die? What does that even mean?"

"It does seem unlikely."

"You're not from the city originally. You didn't grow up with a Protector. You don't know he's practically invulnerable. You know, but it's not a part of your psyche. He's the embodiment of our best hopes and dreams and aspirations. What happens when he falls?"

"That sounds unhealthy."

"Downright dangerous."

"What happens?"

Vernon unbuttoned his coat. "No one knows. We never planned for anything like this. We don't know. We can predict..." His voice droned, pleading and extricating himself from responsibility, but her mind went in a different direction.

"Wait," she interrupted. "What *is* a Protector anyway?"

His face suggested that she'd just asked him how to breathe or the purpose of food or why puppies were cute. "It's... the Protector."

"Circular."

"The Protector... protects the city." His eyes wavered with concentration. "For protection."

"Where did he come from?" Her headache returned, low and mean, a dull ache at the base of her skull. "Who is he? What does he protect the city from?"

His eyes rolled back in his head and his body shook. She slapped him. "Stop messing around. I want a straight answer now." He slumped to the floor and his eyes refocused on her. He grabbed at his face and scrabbled backwards.

"Ouch! What was that for?"

"I asked you first." Pandora stood over him, eyes ablaze with the light of the high noon. "No more games. Answer my question." She ignored the pounding of rage and pulse in her head. "I have no interest in being anyone's pawn—not yours for certain. I'm tired of being teased and I'm tired of being whispered at and about. I want a real answer." She stepped closer; something tiny crunched beneath her foot.

Vernon stared up at her. Terror widened his eyes as he pivoted his head in the same way that Titian had. She grabbed his lapels in both hands and hoisted him off the floor. "Stop that too," she hissed. "Stay out of my head. Your life can be very unpleasant very soon."

He croaked "Security!" Her mind replayed her words. She longed for a hot shower to lave away the oily and sticky feeling of her threats. He landed and bounced. She looked behind her.

The security desk was empty. Both officers on duty strained to hold the revolving door against the mob. The sky had grown ominous; it or the horizon or the earth rumbled beneath her feet. She wheeled back to ask Vernon about the specifics of his warnings, but he was gone. The carpet showed the wounds of someone dragging away a man-sized burden. The hallway showed no no other sign of their confrontation besides broken pieces of thin plastic between her feet. She bent to examine them. Wisps of golden mist evaporated. Ozone wrinkled her nose in disgust and threatened a sneeze.

"Excuse me," a voice purred in her ear. When her feet touched the ground again, she turned to see an older man with wild wisps of white hair punctuating his bald head. "Are you Miss Pandora d'Avril?" He wiped a shaky hand on a filthy duster and grabbed at hers.

She began, "Um, yes, and what is this abou–"

"There's no time to explain. You absolutely *must* come with me."

He squeezed her hand and pulled harder, but she dug her heels into the carpet. "I must? I'm going to need more explanation than that, Mister...?"

"Roberts. Please trust me."

"Again with the trust, but at least you asked. This is where I stop, and may I please have my hand back? Thank you." She wiped her hand on her jeans.

"You're stubborn. I should have expected. I suppose you know Mr. John-Paul Harrison?"

She blinked. "We've met."

"He's in danger. So are you. Everyone's in danger."

Pandora turned to go. "Right. I keep turning on the radio in the middle of this song. I'm always too late to hear the first verse, and everyone stops singing right...now. Friendly advice, take your apocalypse outside. Get some poster board and a fencepost and march up and down the street. Make up a nice pentameter rhyming couplet. You'll have plenty of followers in no time."

An elevator dinged behind them. Roberts's eyes flicked toward the hissing door. He pulled her around the corner by the arm. She tried to shake him off again, but his grip was solid.

"I don't want to do things the hard way, but you really must come with me now, or everyone's in trouble."

She resisted the urge to push him through the wall. "Security!"

Then the world went weird.

The windows blew, raining glass shards and debris parallel to the floor. A wind howled. The panicked chatter of the mob rose as the first row of people fell inside. The floor buckled and heaved.

She stumbled but he kept them both upright. The world screamed a reddish-orange tint splashed in blood and fire flickerings.

A tall blond man with thinning hair in a suit crawled around the corner to grasp at Pandora's ankle. "Come with me." He seemed familiar, somehow—even wolflike.

Pandora shook him off and straightened, catching her reflection in a large ornamental mirror. Her mouth was a slash of fury. Her eyes bore a golden glow. She cried, "Everyone just *stop!*"

Sound waves exploded from her mouth, thick and visible in the swollen air. The world paused in expanding circles. People stopped in mid-step. A pigeon hung in the air. The clouds of dust engulfing the buildings across the street slowed, then stopped, particle upon particle. Behind her a vase poised precariously on the edge of a small table, spilling jeweled droplets to the carpet.

"I'm sorry," said Roberts. "That won't work on me. I didn't want to do things this way, but ...." He tapped the wall. It rippled like the surface of a pond during spring's first thaw. He sidestepped behind her to grab her coat collar, then dove through. Then the explosion continued and debris rushed through the air and the man on the ground slumped and curled into a ball to protect himself. His screaming chased them through the portal.

○ ○ ○

Jupiter sat crosswise on Mark David's lap in his wheelchair. The sun already kissed a horizon made distant by the great plain of farmlands spilling away from their hill. Lonely clouds drifted away from the sunset, which lit them with reds and golds.

She sighed and rested her head on his shoulder. "This is nice."

"It *is*," he admitted. "Why have we never done this before?"

She tapped his nose. "Because you are a stupid, stupid man."

"If that's true, why are you here?"

"Because I'm a patient, patient, forgiving woman."

He chuckled. "Some combination. This is me not complaining, however."

She tousled his hair, trying to undo what the breeze had done. "You're getting shaggy. Are you growing it out?"

"Thinking about it."

"John-Paul looked good with longer hair. You would too." His posture stiffened beneath her. "Are you still upset?"

He shrugged. "Not really." She raised her eyebrows. "Alright, I am—a little bit. More confused than anything. I don't understand him anymore, you know? He's a different person all of a sudden."

"Change'll do that to a person."

"It's only been a couple of months. That doesn't make sense. We're twins. We're supposed to be the same person. You know the myth. We have a profound mystical connection which transcends space and time. We speak some kind of special twin language. Whichever."

"Isn't that identical twins?"

"Even so. He was my best friend, but I don't know him anymore."

She smiled. "You two were always different. Brothers, obviously, but each your own person. If you were really interchangeable, I could swap you for each other, and I'd never care about the differences."

"Would you really do that? Exchange me for someone who can walk? Someone who doesn't have bad days, who never needs his mother to wheel him around because his legs won't obey him? That's great, Jupiter. Lovely. Way to make me feel better, because it doesn't."

"Are you finished?"

He sighed. "It's been ten minutes since my last 'Alas, poor me!' speech, hasn't it? You must find self-pitying misery attractive."

"I think it's honest. You're not mad at *me*. Why should I be offended?"

His fingers closed over her hand. Despite her height, she had small hands; two of his fingers fit comfortably in her palm. "I seem to be full of complaints these days. Where's the fun for you?"

"Mark David Harrison, I *care* about you. When you hurt, I hurt. When you feel joy, I celebrate. So what if we do more of the one than the other? That's how life goes. I don't have a reservoir of sympathy you use up, cup by cup. Sometimes you're up and sometimes you're down. Right now, you're down. Soon enough you'll be back up."

"How do you know that?"

She smiled. "Like I said. I'm not as smart as you or creative as your brother, but I know a thing or two about life. So do you. We depend on life. Who understands that better than a farmer?"

"I never intended to be a farmer."

"John-Paul probably never intended to dress up in a costume and wander around play fighting on the weekends. Did you choose to be born to a farmer? Sometimes you choose your vocation. Sometimes it chooses you."

Mark David chewed his thoughts. The tree lines along meandering creeks crosscutting the valley cast unnaturally long fingers of shadow. "He seemed so sincere."

"I can't explain that either, but can you let him pursue his joy? Does it have to block your own happiness? You're watching the sunset with a pretty girl who thinks the world of you in your lap. If you can't give up the cares of the world for a few minutes now, then when?"

Mark watched his thumb rub the back of her right hand in soft circles. "He called this afternoon. We didn't talk much, but he just wanted to say hi. He was running off somewhere."

She smiled. "See? He still wants to connect with you. He has to learn balance. We all do. Maybe he's lonely too. He reached out his hand. Maybe he's waiting for you to reach back."

He shrugged. "I've had other things on my mind. We'll catch up soon."

"Good boy." She hugged him then, foreheads together.

"Jupe?"

"Yes, my heart?"

"When did you get so wise?"

"Heartbreak'll do that to you."

"Heartbreak?"

"If you let it. I don't believe in wisdom without sadness."

He shrugged. "Not everyone who's sad is wise."

"I didn't say it was easy. Just possible."

They sat in silence. Beautiful moments strung themselves together into a gorgeous evening. The evening breeze waved through great fields of golden wheat, nearly bursting with life just before the harvest. Night's clouds rolled in from the sea, hinting at salt water and tides hidden hours away over the horizon. One cloud caught their eyes: a majestic expanding tower far to the north, tickling the dome of the sky, lit from inside with fiery reds and yellows and oranges.

o o o

Screaming split the sky. Invisible energy superheated the air in wrist-thick plasma beams. The afternoon shimmered underneath a great force dome capping the city.

A thin haze rose, the color of dirty gruel. It smeared and roiled in the dome, a furious spherical Jacob's ladder, blotting out the sizzle and crackle of energy rising an the apex twice as high as the tallest skyscraper. Terror and beauty mixed below, as the trapped denizens gaped at electric fires dancing between them and distant stars. The horrible glory dimmed the city's lights; the rest of the universe shone on uncaring in unblinking splendor.

Then destruction began. Buildings crumbled from pinprick strikes. Bricks and mortar failed under the heat. Debris piled, blocking doors and windows and makeshift egresses. Panic began in small pockets.

Old prejudices returned quickly as the exercise of survival tore at the scabs of old wounds. The dome subdivided, isolating neighborhoods just as the dome itself separated the city from the rest of the world. The great translucent shell divided the city into neighborhoods, exploiting long-buried but never forgotten natural divisions lurking in the city's bones itself: the young urban creative district, warehouses, gentrification projects, bedroom communities, and even gated subdivisions peeking out behind low hills. Where boundaries and borders were once porous, now the separation was harsh and unforgiving and visible.

Human subdivision followed division, macro to micro even down to the level of individual floors in tenements and apartments. Millions of people relearned how to slink, sticking to filthy and unlit alleys when the desire for food or water or medical supplies drew too great for them to huddle together in basements and windowless rooms, waiting for terror to end, one way or another.

The city was broken. The split followed fault lines buried since Reconciliation. Neighborhood and borough pride gave way to institutional prejudice handed down as structures rebuilt themselves. The naming of streets or the layout of neighborhoods or the size and shape of buildings all gave weight to ideas and dreams of founders centuries departed. Old maps showed lines of divisions. One step either direction were the *others*, people born or living so unfortunately in the wrong place.

Outside the dome, filtered through its polarized shell, high clouds dropped cleansing rain. The mockery dribbled from the sky, suspending pure rivers and creeks and tributaries high in the air. Inside, a rain of bitter tears swept the city twice. Thin drops fell like heaven's angry arrows. It hid in the smell of smoke and it splattered dirt and mud where it landed to wash the world in dusty earth tones. Life turned filthy and gray.

Electricity powered civilization; the loss of power brought more fear. An invisible force reached out of empty air to uproot lines of transmission towers up the river to the reactor's cooling lake, overripe vegetables with steel stems and shallow roots. Lines lost their slack and grew taut and pulled on their anchors until great chunks of soil and sod and concrete popped free. Careless heaps grew to shadow the sun in the industrial district.

People huddled in cells in basements and closets. Only the most daring ventured outside in search of potable water or canned food. Their eyes never rested, skipping from shadow to shadow, as they hunched behind upturned collars and skittered across streets, backs bowed under the ever-present threat of violence raining from the sky.

They were not disappointed.

For two nights the sky waited, quiet. On the third night, two red lights appeared at the dome's northernmost end, a point directly above the waterfront park. Their slow blink gathered intensity, then began a circuit around the dome's perimeter. Two more lights followed, then another pair, and another, until they described a full circle patrol, one for every degree. Weak morning light that filtered through the smoke and dust revealed to the naked eye hulking metal monstrosities, hovering and floating, slowly progressing around the dome.

From time to time, another hulk would join the circle and one would leave, striking out across the circle to hover over a building or block. Destruction followed.

This new terror eviscerated the previous. Some neighborhoods organized sentries who hid in shadows and communicated hand signals down the flight paths of the monstrosities. Even out of the circle their movement patterns were predictable; hasty evacuations were possible.

Tedious hours of sentries and evacuations and flight drew the city into itself. In the morning everything was silent. Neither screams nor muted explosions echoed from distant terrors. People brave or unlucky enough to venture outside reported a sky crowded with flying horrors—not just the hundreds necessary for the slow patrol but thousands, perhaps hundreds of thousands.

Thunder cracked and lightning flashed at dusk. The sky lit up under the dome; sickly and weak reflections illuminated the city. Winds howled between thunderclaps, their frequency modulating upward to the banshee madness of summer fever. Silence gathered the night's cloak until a final blast rocked buildings and sent dirt swirling. An enormous bolt of lightning struck the statue of Progress in the city's central plaza. Blue electricity tickled and down its surface, seeking release. Ozone and rust filled the air. The storm broke moments later, leaving the city quiet with waiting and the dying rumbles of far thunderstorms.

Slowly, slowly, the statue groaned and shifted and fell face-first. The cement and rebar of its foundation pulled away, flailing at the sky in surrender.

No one spoke the name of the Protector. He was gone and no one cared.

○ ○ ○

Clownfish grimaced at the moldy piece of bread and scraped away the worst patches with a pocketknife. "I've been unconscious a week?"

"Three days," said the man. "You and him were both in bad shape."

John-Paul lay on a cot in the corner of the room. His face was pale and his hair had tangled with dried sweat. Slow breaths fluttered in his chest.

She pulled long at a dark metallic mug, gasping a breath to follow the water. "Has he woken up at all?"

"Not once. He had the worst of it, but nothing seems broken and there's no swelling inside."

"Is there a doctor around here somewhere?"

The man tilted his head out the doorway and across the street. "Molly's a vet and she looked at both of you. That do?"

Clownfish tried the bread again. She tried not to choke as her crunching reduced it to sharp crumbs. "I suppose it'll have to. Do you have a plan for him yet, or did you just pick us out of the street out of the goodness of your heart?"

"I know who *you* are, and he reminds me of someone. Call it an act of mercy, sentiment, whatever you want. Would you have left anyone out in the street after that mess?"

In her memory, Pierre scowled. "That's immaterial. You say there's no electricity, no communication? Who's in charge? Anyone?"

The man nodded toward the sky. "Would have thought that's an obvious answer. Whoever they are, they are."

"No list of demands? No communication, ultimatum, warning, nothing?"

"It's pretty clear they don't like buildings or people out after dark, but if you can find a pattern or message in that, you're a whole lot smarter than I am."

She set the hunk of bread on the floor and squeezed her mug as she made her way to the window. Mist and accreted dirt obscured everything but a smear of lightness where the sun might be in the cold gray of the sky. This whole block was three and four-story apartment buildings mixed with light use commercial properties, a short walk from the city's heart.

"Were there other people in the road when you rescued us? Anyone dressed in black? How about another guy, about my height, slender, ponytail, looks like he's always just heard a joke no one understood? A big guy, huge, probably covered in bruises?"

The man opened his hands wide. "Just you two. Lose some friends?"

She turned back to John-Paul. His mouth had fallen open; his breath whistled and rumbled. "Too many to count. Talk about a lack of tangible resources."

He stuck out a hand. "Name's Manston. Raymond Manston. Call me Ray."

"Sandie."

His eyes widened at the name, but he hid it behind a smile and a nod. "Want an old man's advice? I'll give you two pieces, both of them worth exactly what you paid for them. First, there's nothing much you can do. There're just too many of them. They follow no rule I've ever seen, and I've seen a few things even you might not imagine.

"Second, you have yourself, and you have your friend over there. You're standing. He's breathing. You weren't standing an hour ago. There's a progress. Hear me when I say this. You have that going for you. You have that on your side, and whoever or whatever's up there probably doesn't know you're here."

Clownfish smiled. "Graduate of the 'Go Down Fighting' school, Ray?"

"I didn't say that. You won't see me out there throwing rocks or firing guns... but I did pull two youngsters out of a street they had no business playing in."

She knelt beside John-Paul and smoothed a lock of hair away from his forehead. He didn't move. "I have a question," she offered.

"For me or him?"

She smiled again. "Tell me something, Ray. Have you ever fought a revolution?"

He chuckled. "That's a game for youth. Every day I get up and out of bed in the morning is a success."

"I used to think so too, but you're starting to convince me otherwise."

"Oh?"

She leaned over John-Paul again, feeling the cool of his body beneath the heat of hers—nervousness, anxiety, stress, fear, and excitement. She threw the think blankets on the floor and straddled him, cradling his hands. They were the cold of stone stairs at midnight, but his eyelashes fluttered and his head twitched, as if he were merely asleep and her lightest touch would rouse him.

She gathered her courage and shoved away her fear and cleared her mind of everything but pure, golden light. She leaned forward, pulling back her hair to whisper in his ear. "Wake up."

There was a silence.

His sudden movement nearly bucked her off the cot, but her hands remained on his wrists and she willed herself to stay upright. His head wobbled and his eyes swam into focus.

"Nice trick," offered Ray. "Teach me that one sometime? Better than cardiac massage."

"Ugh," John-Paul blinked. "Where am I? What's going on?"

Clownfish dropped his hands and wrapped her arms around him with one smooth motion. She aimed a whisper at his ear. "You're right where you need to be, hero."

o o o

John-Paul pushed her away. "Get off of me. I was in the middle of a perfectly horrible dream, and I'm going back to sleep to fix it." He stretched with a jaw-popping yawn and his neck cracked. He grunted as he lay down again.

Clownfish flicked his ear with a poorly manicured fingernail. He swatted at her hand and turned to face the wall. She flicked his other ear. He fumbled blindly on the floor for a blanket, pulling it over his head.

Ray snickered.

She shot a look over her shoulder and snapped. The cot's legs exploded outward. The thin mattress hit the ground with a whump, throwing moldy dust outward.

"Probably should have aired that out sometime last summer," offered Ray. "Now I have to sweep in here again... or you do."

John-Paul cursed softly and sat up. "Fine." The word sucked heat from the room. "You *win*. Let's go play hero. Hand me my tights and my cape, and I'll go beat in some heads and pose for the newspaper and the television, and everyone will believe that everything's okay, because everyone wants to believe in something. Let them. I don't care. I want to get playtime over with."

Ray snickered again. "You described him smarter'n this. Guess he's not the one who posed for that big statue used to be downtown."

Clownfish knelt and pried open John-Paul's left eye. He squirmed under her grasp. She turned his head toward the bare fluorescent bulb. "It figures. Whatever hit us cracked him on the head right as our defenses flickered. Did you check him for a concussion?"

214

John-Paul struggled and freed his head. "What are you talking about?"

Ray shrugged. "Doubtful. Molly said to let the both of you sleep. Mostly all we could do, she said. No sense in breaking into a hospital for supplies. If you'd been that bad off, nothing we could have done would help." He inclined his head toward a boarded window. "You want to go outside, go. I'll lock the door behind you."

Clownfish pulled John-Paul by the hand. He resisted, but she dragged his dead weight toward the wall. She pried away a greasy plank for a better angle. The glass had melted and bubbled, distorting the ground-floor view of an alley between two large buildings. Carbon-scorched stones speckled the pavement.

"Not such a good view there. Try the main street. It's behind the plywood there. I screwed some view holes in there, some of 'em on purpose."

John-Paul shook off Clownfish's hand. "I can walk on my own." He stretched again. Long-unused muscles complained as he walked gingerly across the room. Pencil-thin columns of dirty light pierced the darkness. He swallowed another yawn and put an eye to a pinky-sized hole.

Something had pierced the asphalt like spring's first crocus, deliberate for the sun despite a covering of dirt and leaves. Piles of thick tarry stone, dirt, mud, and broken pipes suggested a pattern his mind couldn't decipher. Burned-out husks of cars rotted here and there. Shards of glass and plaster—the facades of buildings—jutted from heaps and piles. Under his gaze the sky darkened further. Fat, oily raindrops splattered gobs of sticky mud at violent velocities.

He forced his consciousness to chase the retreating tentacles of his dark and bloody dream. He closed his eyes and leaned his head against the plywood, willing the dusty plate glass on the other side to remain intact. His effort dredged a single sensation from fading short-term memory: the smell of ozone. He pulled at that anchor and a chain of other sensations followed: a tectonic rumbling, the ground unsteady beneath his feet, and a sky darkening with tiny debris. Screaming tickled his ears. He staggered. A mountain began an arm's length in front of him, pulling him upward even as he tumbled backward. Ocean waves consumed the city's streets a mile from the bay and an hour's drive from the open sea.

Malice desired him—an empty hunger or an anger, *knowing* him but not caring who he was, merely that he had something or had done something. Its pitiless gaze scraped him.

Then all was black again.

He whirled on his heels, pretending that the wave of dizziness had started only then. "That was us, wasn't it?"

Clownfish wouldn't meet his eyes. Ray whistled tunelessly.

"Do you have something to say, old man?" John-Paul poured his concentration into a swagger, swallowing dizziness and nausea.

Ray watched him approach, then pushed himself out of the chair to stand chest-to-chest. The tip of his head crested John-Paul's shoulder. "Do I need to, kid? Think harder. You were out there, hip-deep in that mess, which is a problem not with my imagery seeing as how you were horizontal at the time. I pulled you both out of it. I helped the rest of the people on the street to safety. Go on, then. Tell me you had it all under control. I love the heartfelt, self-righteous lectures of youth. Tell me you're not the one who invited that mess right before passing out."

Clownfish interrupted. "You saw us, but you only saw two of us? You didn't see Titian?"

Ray shook his head. "Big guy? Size of a family car? He was still on his feet, last I saw him. He was wrestling an enormous dark hand. That was the last I saw of him."

Her scowl deepened and she studied his face.

He shrugged. "You asked before who I pulled off of the street, not for a census of every face in a fleeing, panicky mob. The bizarre makes it so difficult to know what's important."

"How about a big flash of light? A thunderclap? A giant sighing sound? Anything like that?"

Ray tapped John-Paul's chest and sat down again. "Like I said, in that mess, I notice one weird thing over any other. Should I write this down? Then you can call me an unreliable narrator."

Clownfish sighed. "Can you give us a moment?" At Ray's nod, she reached for John-Paul's hand, but withdrew at the look on his face. She shrugged and leaned against the wall, arms crossed.

John-Paul kept a cautious distance. "What is it?"

"How much do you remember?"

"We were waiting for someone. You were upset. Then you exploded. It made a mess. Titian showed up, excited about some ambush he'd prepared. Then the building exploded. We made it out. He didn't. Then he exploded out of the building. Soldiers appeared, he smote them, then something smashed him and that was the end of the explodeys. You passed out. I passed out. I woke up with you telling me it's a few days later after all hell broke loose outside." He paused. "Now *I'm* an unreliable narrator."

"That's as much as I remember too. Did you hear anything?"

"Besides explosions and punches and thunder? The usual. Distress, menace, wanton destruction of private property by persons unknown."

"Sarcasm. Thanks."

"I don't know what you want. I figure sincerity inures me to that by now." She didn't laugh. "I hear a lot of things. Sometimes I hear birds flap their wings. I hear the pattern of breathing as someone prepares to throw a punch at my head, and I hear the wind whistle as I dodge it. Are you listening for something specific?"

"A voice in your head, talking to you?"

His grimace dissolved into puzzlement. "I want to say no, but now that you mention it, I *think* I did. I can't remember a word it said. It was more like someone was thinking thoughts for me. The words or ideas or images weren't mine. I was some giant brain antenna. Did you spontaneously develop ESP or something? Can we do that?"

"Not to my knowledge." She uncrossed her arms and massaged her neck. "I have that same impression. Someone or something was talking to us. Maybe taunting us. Titian had a theory that whatever happened was a deliberate act of some agency that knows us and understands us and intentionally exploited our weaknesses."

"It fits. Someone had a plan. Everything Ray claims happened can't all happen by accident."

"Right. That leaves several questions. Who? Why? What's the plan? What's he trying to accomplish? Why us? The most important question is Who. If we have any chance of stopping things, we need that, but we can't answer that without more information. Maybe we figure out his goals and work backwards."

"Can we stop things?"

She jerked her thumb toward the boarded windows. "Is that the kind of world you want to live in?"

His lips compressed into thin, white lines. "That's always the question no one ever asks. That's what you tell people to hook them in. 'You can change the world!' What if I don't want to anymore? What if I'm tired of putting on a costume and playacting and pretending that what I do makes the world better? Your fat boss loves to set up cheap scare fantasy scenarios. Well done. He's outdone himself now. What do you tell the fat, dumb people lying in their comfortable beds in their cozy homes now that the men and women protecting them from evil can get caught by surprise in their own trap?"

"How do we know? He's never been exactly honest or forthcoming. Why should this time be any different?" Shadows flitted across her face.

"You could ask him yourself," Ray interrupted. Sweat beaded on his forehead. "Sorry to barge in, but I thought you might like to see this." He offered Clownie a leather-bound notebook with yellowing pages. "Looks like a diary."

She thumbed through and gasped. "No kidding. This is one of Titian's diaries. John-Paul, maybe you have your wish. Where did you find this?"

Ray shrugged. "One of those junk boxes drew me in. This used to be a Youth Corps building. He must have left it here when they packed up."

"What's it say?" John-Paul crowded in for a better look. "Can I wish for a thick steak, too?"

"Hang on," said Clownfish. She skimmed several pages. "This is more like a will than a diary. Let me start at the beginning."

○ ○ ○

Pandora's world swirled back into focus as she clenched her empty, nauseated stomach. She forced herself to her knees, hoping the half-awake fuzz in her brain a the headache departing, not arriving.

Shallow gasps revealed that Roberts was still alive on the cracked and dry ground. A bruise purpled his face; he bore the worst of the damage as they had landed, entertwined. She rolled him onto his back and probed his chest for any apparent damage. His breathing changed under her touch, but his ribs appeared unbroken.

Dark spirits of cloud wheeled and roiled in the sky, taunting the parched earth. The signs of drought were familiar from her village; her tongue stuck in sympathy to the roof of her mouth as it did from waking to sleeping. Rain was rare; rain was a blessing. Surely rain would reward the stubborn and the hardy, plants and animals alike. The village huddled in the shadows of walls and carts to pray that their great oven would break, that a breeze would stir the stagnant air, that the heavens would weep great fat life-giving tears for their plight

They were outside and alone. The horizon stretched past the point of sanity. The air crackled about them, mirage-like, whispering at their passage.

The man stirred. She rocked back on her heels, tensing her legs to run. His breathing quickened into a low, souring moan. A rough shadow passed behind his eyes. He offered her a toothy grin, charming and crooked.

219

Pandora wished for a sturdy tree branch to swing. She scowled. "This is the capper on a perfectly horrible weekend. Start by you telling me who you are, where we are, what we're doing here, and why I shouldn't slap you silly and leave you here to die of thirst."

His guffaw set her jaw at a dangerous angle. "Young lady, I have explained. My name is Roberts. I'm a friend. We're here to save the world."

Her first slap was quick and light, but he gasped as her fingertips brushed the bruise. "I don't want a story. I want truth. Tell me your real name."

"It *is* Roberts, but I suppose you want a flashy name, perhaps Clownfish or Titian. Very well. Eratosthenes." His eyes kept drawing hers back. "Does that tell you anything?"

"Not unless you're a long-forgotten painter." She squinted and imitated Vernon's and Titian's strange head-tilt. The sudden motion blurred her vision; several Roberts grimaced on the ground up at her. Then there was one and the view was as clear as a pristine mountain pool unsullied by human presence, and she knew it for truth. "No," she repeated, "but it's an honest answer. Next question. Where are we?"

"We're safe."

"On a scale of one to ten, that's incredibly vague. Try again."

"I have no idea." He shrugged and offered a strained grin as her hand twitched. "Have you long found corporal punishment an effective interrogation technique?"

Dry heaves yanked her stomach out from under itself again.

Roberts managed to sit up. "Thought so. We've been through similar experiences. You've found yourself doing unpleasant, unpredictable, and uncontrollable things." He described a shape in the air. "Was it a box about this big, lighter than it looked, whispering sweet nothings to you and then knocking you on your butt across the room when you finally managed to sneak a peak inside?"

She shook her head. "That means nothing to me." Neither duplicity of words nor intent fractured her vision. Something clicked. "You can't lie, or you're not lying. Which is it?"

His grin widened as he threw his hands in front of his face. "If I say no, will you hit me again?" Her scowl deflated his chuckles. "You know I'm kidding, right?"

"Tell me what I *know*. In the past week I've been the world's worst spy, had my memory erased, jumped out of a fourth floor window in an exploding hospital, beat up my boss's assistant, and escaped an explosion involuntarily only to debate epistemology with my kidnapper. I'm going to close my eyes and count to ten, slowly. If you're still here when I finish, we will have a pleasant, short, and concrete conversation where you explain everything. Is this clear to us both?"

He nodded.

Ten seconds later she opened her eyes to his smirk. "Alright. This is a nasty dream and I'd prefer to wake right here, but whatever. Where are we?"

"We're not in the city anymore. That's good."

"Why?"

"It's full of blood and fire and screaming. These are not my favorite things. Are they yours? Would you have stayed for that?"

"You gave me no choice. Whose choice is it to return?"

"Consider the question rhetorical."

"Why 'blood and fire and screaming'?"

"Something went wrong." Her eyes narrowed. "More to the point, something has gone wrong for a very long time but only now reached the point of wrongness where blood and fire and screaming is not only necessary but unavoidable."

"What went wrong?"

"Titian tried to control everything."

"That's what Vernon said."

"Vernon tried something similar with somewhat less catastrophic results. His failure had common elements."

She stretched and rubbed her neck. "Who does that make you?"

"Now, or then?"

"What?"

"The answer depends on the context of the question."

"I'm in no mood to guess precise and exact questions. Why should I stick around for this?"

"You can't get back there without me."

"It sounds like an awful place right now. Why would I want to go back?"

"But you do. It's your home, as much as anywhere is. You're right; you didn't choose to come here. You could ask a hundred questions about how and why and when, those thousands of little details. You may, if only to dance away from the real questions. Why are you here? Where are you going? What will you do?"

She shrugged. "I avoid blood and screaming and fire and dying as a policy. If you're finished volunteering questions, volunteer answers."

"It doesn't work that way." He scowled. "I know. It's convenient that way, but look deeper. You've adapted to the situation. You started when I brought you here. You're angry. You're upset. I don't blame you. You're strong enough to beat me if you wanted to. Maybe you should. I might have, had I been you. You didn't. You're not. You're not screaming or bargaining or threatening. You don't have to. You're capable of staggering acts of beautiful destruction, or beautiful acts of staggering destruction, and you're debating the philosophy of knowledge with the universe's least impressive clown. You know I'm right. *Feel* it. You own that power, but it's not in your nature to use it to destroy. Not now, not the last time you used it, not ever."

"Who *are* you?"

"A victim, like you refuse to be. I fell into a power struggle that began long before my birth and will continue without regard for my health, happiness, or well-being. That's everyone. Almost everyone—you've always felt different."

"Three days."

"Longer than that. You stood up against Clownfish. You went head to head with Titian. You kept your head at the funeral when even the people in charge were losing theirs. Tell me you aren't special."

She rose to pace. "How about meeting John-Paul? Everyone wants to tie it back to him. Someone manipulated me into being at the right place at the right time to see the original Protector die and meet his replacement?"

His chuckle froze her in place, facing away. "Everyone confuses the symbol for the thing itself. He's only as relevant as he makes himself. It's you we worry about." A silence passed. "Do you believe in free will?"

"What?" She looked over her shoulder. "Am I in charge of my own destiny?"

"So much more than that. Perhaps someone—perhaps *something*—arranged specific circumstances, but do you not make your own choices?"

"Says the kidnapper."

His face held no echo of the grin. "Is it kidnapping to take a sleeping child from a burning house?"

"Depends who set the fire."

Roberts sighed. "I didn't start anything. I'm just trying to help."

"Then *help*." She wheeled. Her finger accused the air. "Stop playing games. Stop making allusions. Stop being coy. Stop teasing. What did you do? Why did you do it? What next? How do we get back?"

"Don't forget 'Who are you?'"

"Who are you?"

"I told you. Who are *you*?"

She slumped and sat, hugging her knees to her chest. "I'm Pandora d'Avril. You knew that. You knew where to find me. You know too much about where I've been and what I've done. How long have you been watching me?"

"It's not like that. You know. I can't lie, remember? You told me yourself. I'm as confused as you are until you ask me the right question. You're only confused until you make the right decision. Haven't you felt that?"

"Never." She felt the lie burn beneath the skin of her face. "Not once."

"Not even when fleeing a burning building?"

"It wasn't burning. It was going to explode."

"Did it?" His eyes pierced her skull.

"No."

"But you knew you had to leave."

"And?" The word dripped venom.

He closed his eyes. "Necessity. That's what drives us, or it would if you let it. That's the difference between us. Admit it. Acknowledge it. Embrace it."

"Why should I?"

"Necessity brought you here. Necessity will take you back when necessary."

In one smooth motion she unearthed a rock from the dust and slung it at his head. He ducked, eyes still closed. "*You* brought me here."

"Perhaps I am necessity's human agency. Does my presence make necessity's intervention any less miraculous? What if another photographer had gone to the Protector's crater? What if Roderick Fontaine had sent another intern to interview Titian? Perhaps you and I, our specific selves, would not debate the events as they occurred, but someone would."

"Say fate instead and admit that by your logic I have no choice."

He beamed. "Of course you do. That's the beauty of it. You choose to turn left instead of right. Someone else meets John-Paul. Maybe there's no John-Paul. Maybe he's someone else. Maybe you're him. You reject his invitation to the funeral. Another hero leads the other mourners to safety. You stay home with a headache and another intern attempts an interview. You are the result of each of these choices, trivial to sublime. Necessity adapts to those choices to accomplish whatever must happen."

"Assuming this were true, who decides what must happen?"

"Who decides that a rock falls when you drop it? Who decides that desert winds pile sand atop sand? Who decides that flowers bud and ducklings hatch and birds sing when springtime stirs their juices? It is what it is."

She stood again and began to walk away.

"Hey," Roberts called. "Where are you going?"

"This way, until the universe wants to demonstrate that it has a voice in where I go by making me go a different direction or making this the right direction after all."

He rocked himself to his feet and stumbled after her. "Wait for me."

Her steps lengthened.

He jogged to catch up, wincing and panting. "Wow. How hard did you land on me?"

"Not hard enough, apparently." She angled away from him. He followed, jogging every other step to match her pace. After a time, he spoke again.

"Clever."

"What?"

"You're heading straight for food and water."

She stopped, fists on her hips. "I shouldn't ask. How do you know?"

He ducked away, laughing. "I put it there."

Pandora scowled until he finished gamboling. "You want to fight or it? You won't win."

"I know how to get back."

Icicles lengthened in her silence.

"I didn't know before, just so you know."

Pandora stared until he blurred and doubled. Something again snapped, and her eyes focused on his. They were clear. She sighed. "That can't be as frustrating for you as it is for me. Whatever's broken in your head, I want it to hear me. No more games. No more tests. I want the whole story."

"It's maybe ten minutes away. That's just enough time for you to tell me your story."

"*My* story?"

"How do you expect to get back if you don't know who you are?"

Her lips pursed. "That's your second warning."

"Did you know you can fly? Did you know you can force me to tell the truth, rather than telling if I'm lying? You could stop a war or start a wildfire with the right concentration. You can even make an oasis in the desert."

She turned away. They crested a small dune. A copse of trees surrounded a pond beneath them. A carpet of thick emerald ended abruptly at the parched earth beneath her feet. Even the ominous clouds seemed gentler as they scudded overhead.

Pandora jogged to the waterline and plunged her hands into the liquid. It was cool and clear, reflecting her face and arms. She scrubbed off grit and dirt, gasping at the temperature and the purity of the water.

She turned as Roberts threw himself to his knees beside her. "Did you say there's food here?"

"There should be fruit somewhere. Those trees may be in season. You should check."

She rinsed her hands again, still shivering at the water's biting coolness. "You said you hid food here," she mused.

"Did. Didn't say you didn't help."

Some of the trees bore fruit; she gathered an armful of apples and oranges and pears, as well as an exotic green and orange fruit she didn't recognize.

Roberts smiled at her treasures. She dunked an apple and pear in the water, scrubbing them between her thumbs. "Hygiene," she explained at his raised eyebrow.

"We're in the middle of nowhere. Is unwashed fruit your biggest problem?"

Her smirk mocked his. "If reality bends to support my beliefs, violating long-held—if irrational—habits would be incautious."

"You talk like a philosophy textbook."

"Journalist, not anchorwoman. Some of us can read."

"So be it."

The apple's exploded wet and bittersweet at her first bite. She devoured all but a sliver of core. The pear was even better. "You hungry," she wondered, wiping her mouth.

"In a while." He threaded fingers together behind his head and lay on the grass. Thoughtful clouds gathered to charge the opposite horizon.

Pandora scratched at the peel of the odd fruit until it came away under her fingers. She sniffed at the meat inside. It smelled sweet. A tiny bite tasted sweet, but an underlying bitterness shot through her mouth. Her stomach twisted. "Blah," she spit, throwing the rest of the fruit across the pond. She lapped at the water until the taste was a faint memory, then leaned back and examined Roberts in detail.

His height was average. So was his build. None of his features distinguished him from anyone else in a crowd. His outfit was simple: a knit shirt with a collar, tucked into light pants which brushed against matching brown shoes. He could have been anyone in the street, on the train, shopping in a store, or nodding gravely at the apartment's shared mailboxes. Only his grin, fleeting and serious, set him apart.

Something in the way his eyes flicked when he spoke concerned her. Yet always that grin flashed again, amused and curious. He chose his words carefully; certain words she spoke struck him like the arrows of old memories. His eyes would narrow, and then he'd shrug with a precise "just so", as if he'd expected the assault and had steeled himself against those exact pains.

"Heh," he mumbled. "Should have asked if you were afraid there's something even scarier in the water than on the fruit."

"Dirty water would grow algae or scum. Tainted water would smell of sulfur or other disgusting chemistry. Anything smaller, I drank already."

"How certain is your logic?"

"Sufficient, if what you said is true. If this is a vision, it can't hurt me. If it's the active embodiment of my hopes and plans and beliefs, it won't hurt me. If it's just a dream, it doesn't matter. If you have nefarious purposes, I have worse problems."

Roberts shrugged. "The rigor of logic makes me nappy. See you in fifteen minutes. I'll open a portal to take you back home after that."

She blinked. "Seriously?"

"The rest is up to you. I've done what I can."

"What now? That was it? We walk through a wasteland, argue, and that gives me enlightenment?" She kicked at his ribs, but he rolled away. "I'm not leaving without an explanation."

He yawned and stretched. "Oh, how the mighty change their tunes when they've filled their bellies."

She counted to ten. Her voice was softer. "I deserve an explanation. If you, or necessity, or the universe really have my best interests in mind, or if you think I have yours in mind, ten minutes is not too much to ask."

He shivered with the pleasure of another yawn. "Rawr. I'll tell you everything I know. Fifteen minutes. No complaining."

She left him on his side of the pond and struggled to recognize her reflection in the water on the other side. Something both foreign and familiar watched her back. It was stronger, yet softer, both more and less frightened. She decided it was her, gone back in time to meet herself as a child, to warn or to prepare herself for some fearsome, defining struggle, tasting the bittersweet truth that she might cease to exist if she succeeded.

"You," she scolded her reflection, "watch too many movies."

Roberts snored, then jerked awake. "Well," he said. "That was refreshing. Are you ready for a story now?"

"You promised an explanation."

"How about both? Once upon a time," he began.

"No," she growled. "Not like that. No games. Nothing cute or clever. What happened?"

He shrugged. "Historians have offices. I don't even have a chair."

She stood. "I should have known better. Enjoy it here. If you were telling the truth, I can make my own way back just like I made this place. If you're lying, I'm already dead and I'll deal with that on my own terms. Goodbye."

His chuckle slowed her blood. "You're waking up. Good. You're even more immune than John-Paul now."

Her stare could have stopped traffic. "Immune... to what?"

"Fear, self-doubt, panic, paralysis." Roberts ticked off his fingers. "Everyone you've met was tainted. It's a fatal flaw. Apply enough pressure and they crack—and it's additive. Take one down, you take them all down."

She leaned in despite herself. "Did you kill the Protector?"

"What? No!" His face contorted. "I...I hate this!" He threw himself to the ground and pounded his fists on the grass. "Stop it, stop it, stop it!"

When Pandora reached him, his fists were raw. Blood trickled from his nose, dripping off his chin. She threw him on his back and pinned him, marveling at her strength. "Hey, stop that."

His eyes focused and unfocused. He tilted his head sideways, tuning reality like a radio. Air coalesced around them, and then his sudden gaze stole her breath with its intensity.

"I don't have much time. It's caught me too. I was never made for this. I don't have much time, but you have to help them. You're immune. It never saw you coming. I had to spread chaos, but I saw the chance to do something good. I never meant to hurt you or confuse you. I confused it; it never realized what I was doing... but it never let me go, either. I'm sorry."

She dunked his head in the water. "One more try. What am I supposed to do?"

"Go. Find your friend. Help him. They need you more than ever. Stop it from doing to everyone else what it did to me."

"What did it do?"

His eyes grew wild again and his body thrashed. He forced the words through an uncooperative tongue. "I... I can't tell you. Let me tell you a story. You do the rest. Tell them you're there. Tell them you came to help. Let things happen normally from there. Please."

"Are you okay?"

Roberts pushed her away with a laugh. "You have bigger worries, little girl! Time to go!" He slapped the ground. The grass rippled and roiled, blades melting together into a sticky green puddle that sucked at her arms and legs. She pulled them free, then it all gave way beneath her. She fell, down, down, down, and his voice carried. "Once upon a time...."

○ ○ ○

John-Paul slipped outside, easing the door closed. He wiped sleep from his eyes and stifled a yawn. Clownfish and Ray dozed in opposite corners of the room. The sky was the color of ancient stories of witches and devils lurking to steal naughty children from their beds. The borough's hazy dome smeared starlight into an unrecognizable mess.

His skin shivered at the city's quiet. No car noise—motors, horns, tires, sires—enlivened the empty streets. No generators, lamps, lights, nor air conditioners hummed a comforting hertz. No quiet conversation, raucous laughter, nor muffled imprecations burbled and jumbled into a soothing pedestrian cacophony. No urban fauna scuttled nor tweeted nor yowled underfoot. He placed his feet lightly and cautiously, lest any misstep launch pebbles down the asphalt and alert the silent world to his presence.

Vibrations jarred his teeth as an interruption approached from behind. He whipped his head around; his eyes focused on a small, fire-gutted car half malapropos on the sidewalk. He dove past the dangling back door and peered through a warped oval window. A metal behemoth swooped overhead. He cringed to recognize a smaller version of the metal horror within arm's reach. An imaginary beam swept the road in overlapping horizontal patterns. It paused where he'd stood; its humming increased.

"Heat signature," his brain warned. He praised the cold metal of the car's exposed frame and his goosebumps.

The machine spun in slow circles for long moments before it bobbed—a shrug—to return to position in the middle of the street. It hovered on in its sweeping pattern. John-Paul quieted his breath, whispering long, tiny exhalations until the street no longer vibrated from displacement. He risked poking his head out the door and drew in a lungful of air. Grubby scraps of paper jostled in the machine's roiling wake, but otherwise the street was silent again.

He stepped out of the car and rubbed his arms until his flesh settled, then set off after the machine. The road climbed away from the water, converging with another road partway up the hill. Buildings grew smaller as he ascended. Businesses gave way to apartments and townhouses. Abandoned windows stared down at him even as he squirmed under the secret observations of frightened eyeballs disappearing behind fluttering curtains.

The squirm became a shiver. The temperature dropped ten degrees. His thin jacket was useless. Cold throbbed his joints. He flexed his fingers; they crackled. He fought the urge to roll his shoulders and stretch his spine against a lamp post.

The humming resumed as he turned a corner. It was distant, ahead and right. He flattened himself against the wall and knelt to reconnoiter. The machine had slowed again. It hovered and bobbed in front of a squat stone building. Something drew him in for a closer look. He rushed around the corner in a crouch, zigging between piles of debris that in another world had been mailboxes and small cars and facades. He stopped directly across the street, ready to escape down a nearby alley.

Fake marble pillars offered spiderwebs of cracks. Huge windows offered little illumination into the bank's large lobby. Motion within clawed his attention away from the machine: a figure mantled in shadow shuffled toward the front door, struggling around an awkward package. John-Paul pulled his own quilt of shadow over him. A wave of dizziness followed the exertion; he gritted his teeth and swallowed. The figure backed into the door handle. The door scraped in its crooked jamb, protesting the motion, even as it opened onto a broad landing three stairs up from the street.

The machine swooped into action. A siren wailed at the edge of hearing. Light flooded the landing, pulling tears from John-Paul's eyes even at the distance. The figure threw an arm across its face. The bulky package fell and careened down the stairs.

The machine darted in and out at the figure, a twisted hummingbird cutting off every escape attempt. John-Paul sighed, allowing his subconscious mind to calculate the risk of enraging the drone with the value of saving an apparent looter. He launched himself across the street.

The drone swung to meet him, but overcompensated and continued in a wild arc. His feet left the ground at the first step and he ran up the leftmost pillar, jumping and twisting in the air to land atop the machine. A mesh pad seemed the source of the noise. His fist squelched it with a satisfying crunch. He shook off slivers of broken metal and used the dent as a handhold as the machine spun and dangled him off of the ground. The lights skimmed their way up distant skyscrapers before diffusing on the dome.

The figure straightened and blinked, then dove for its dropped item. He—obviously now a masculine form—seemed familiar. John-Paul wrestled his attention back to the drone. It fought to right itself, but he kicked his legs to keep them both off balance. His left foot glanced off of an extrusion. The buzzing grew in intensity and panic, and the machine lurched again. A second kick connected. Something heavy shifted inside. They both fell.

He landed on his feet on a level surface. The drone bounced and rolled to a stop in front of the other man. "Stupid thing," he muttered. "Never even saw it behind me." A small kick sent a probe arm tinkling down the street.

John-Paul coughed dusty air out of his lungs and wiped loose, sticky spittle from his mouth. "It sent an alarm. More will come. We need to go. We should be safe this way."

The other figure shrugged and narrowed his eyes. "I can handle myself."

"We're safer together. I'm leaving. You're welcome to join me."

"I could use a hot meal."

John-Paul shook his head. The dizziness receded for a moment. "I'll do what I can. Give me a moment. That took more out of me than it should have."

"I'm half-sick around this thing, too. Can't help it for now, I suppose." He nodded toward the treasure, a metal box the size of a human head. Its sides were slippery and it had an obvious heft. Incomprehensible cataloging symbols splashed across one side. No other markings—neither seams nor an obvious opening—were visible.

"Mind if I ask," the younger man wheezed, "what's worth risking your life to steal from a bank?"

"The future."

The crooked grin stirred John-Paul's memory. "Twist," he accused.

The other man cocked his head. "Hm? Haven't been called that in a while. You don't *look* like Barry. I heard he died, if that's their polite euphemism these days. He's not the only one, given...." His words trailed off as he rolled his eyes at the ruined street.

John-Paul bit his lip. This crazy-eyed bravado felt different. A steely purpose reinforced the words. His clothes held no hint of purple and his voice had changed: his words failed to tumble out in rough misstarts and heaps, running on and stepping all over each other. "Are you...dangerous?" He willed the other man to answer truthfully, concentrating his thoughts into a simple command.

"Depends. Are you trying to stop me?"

"Are you bringing more of those machines down on us?"

"Same as you: only if they catch me."

John-Paul counted backwards from ten. "Promise you'll explain everything someplace safer. Warmer, too."

"You let me keep this, sure." Twist's eyes blazed fierce.

Shrug. "Don't point it at me, try to keep quiet, and it's a deal." He led the way back to the lair. The streets were empty of probes.

Clownfish and Ray were still asleep. John-Paul motioned to chairs on the other side of the room. "So," he began. "Um. How've you been?"

Twist grinned. "I recognize you now. You really did a number on me. Reminded me of the old days. Protty and I went a few rounds early on, before your fat friend turned everything into velvet fists and staged fights."

"You're not upset?"

"Look at me. Not a scratch. Hospital couldn't keep me. I even grew back the teeth you knocked loose. You don't beat a puppy for peeing on the rug. You whap him on the nose with a newspaper and give him a better alternative. I used to play my part. You still do. No grudge here."

"I say this a lot." John-Paul ran his fingers through his hair. Flecks of cement scraped his fingertips. "What are you talking about?"

"Your fat boss, Titian. You know he's faked almost everything lately."

"Right."

"With several important and notable exceptions."

"Starting with the death of the first Protector."

"The *previous* Protector. Let's leave it at that. You also notice that he spends a lot of time surprised by real crises for someone whose job is to manufacture and resolve fake crises."

"Starting with the death of the previous Protector."

"We come in there. Came in. Whichever." He moved the box from his lap to the floor with a paternal pat. "Our little runaround was... a misunderstanding. I wanted my own little box like this. Call it a spontaneous democratic liberation. He'd appreciate the lingo. He sent the Big P my way to stop me. Perhaps Fatty and the universe disagree in a fundamental sense about the way these meetings should turn out."

John-Paul blinked away grit and weary tears. "That's more anthropomorphism than I can handle at this hour."

"Heh." The laugh was old and humorless and full of phlegm. It became a cough, then subsided to a chuckle. "Sorry, you *did* crush my trachea. Little rings are tricky to regenerate. The process isn't as autonomous as you'd think." He eyed the younger man with skepticism. "Not for everyone, anyway. Not everyone agrees with Titian's plan, nor his execution. He may believe he's the only person capable of maintaining a position of such power, but he's not the only one who can harness a composite eidolon."

"Eidolon?"

Twist patted the box again. "You feel queasy. Headache. Joint pain, cold sweats. You're used to a smaller dose." His voice dropped to a low whisper. "Normally these are in secure locations—bank vaults, suppose—where unwashed hippie counterrevolutionaries, including yours truly, could never get their filthy hands at them. Plot those locations on a city map and you've plotted Titian's web of influence. Everywhere inside that web, you're a powerful strong boy wonder, a bishop in fat boy's grand chess game conspiracy. Walk a block too far out of range and a runaway bus will clean your clock same way it would anyone else. No one else can detect it. No one else suspects it's there. Here's the best part. It thrives on perception, feeds back on itself. As long as people are willing to believe that you're strong and powerful and effectively invincible, you are, and they believe you are, and so you are."

"But what *is* it?"

"Dunno. No one ever told me. I just woke up one day with a sense of dread and a powerful odd fashion sense. I put the pieces together myself."

John-Paul scowled. "You're not giving me confidence."

"You pay attention. You hear things. You see things. It costs time and energy and attention, and sometimes the big guy smashes you up, but eventually everything comes together. You go to zoning meetings and wonder why Titian cares so much about the locations of new banks and safe houses. You draw maps. You ask yourself why your head swims every time you turn down *this* corner and why it goes away when you turn away.

"Did you know there's a little bead in the underside of your wrist gadget? It presses against your wrist. It focuses the emissions. It's an antenna. That's one reason you're so susceptible to this one."

John-Paul fiddled with his watch. Through the milky film of the plastic bubble, he could see tiny electronic components of bright colors. After several deep breaths the nausea and nervous headache faded. "That's crazy. I wondered why I still had this on. My uniform must have been an unholy mess."

Twist nodded. "I know what it's for, but I can't tell you why or what it is."

"Then why are you, what, liberating them?"

"You want this much power in the hands of one person?"

John-Paul smiled. "You're kidding, right? There's Titian, me, Clownfish, Claude, Pierre, apparently you...."

"Six people. Seven. Eight? Under ten. How many people live in the city? Ten is a fraction of a percent of statistical noise of the entire population. All of this energy goes to charging up a double-handful of people for a show, all of this power concentrated in the hands of a few. Nominally it protects the city from danger and disaster and criminal mayhem and catastrophe. How well did that work? Look around. Titian was unprepared, but not unaware. Pity the rest of the city who had no warning. You're the puppy, by the way."

"Why should I believe you?"

"Because he's right." Clownfish yawned and stepped out from behind a pillar. "Titian was overconfident. He often is."

Twist's reaction was swift; he stood, knocking his chair backwards to straddle the box in a fighter's crouch. "I'm not giving it back. You can't make me. I'll go through you."

She waved a hand. "Don't worry. I don't care. If I'd had the courage to say something a long time ago, I'd have done the same thing you did. Maybe. If I'd known what Roman was doing." His eyes remained tense at her approach. She crossed behind him to right his chair. "Go ahead. You know I'm still powered, same as you. If I'd wanted a fight, I could have ended it ten minutes ago."

He sat.

John-Paul leaned back in his chair. "Let me recap. We're smack dab in the middle of a conspiracy to gain and hold, well, political or social power, based on hoarding these boxes? These boxes juice up a handful of people? This has been Titian's grand goal for *years*?"

Clownfish crossed her arms. "Conspiracy is a dirty word. I wanted to make the world a better place. Still do. We all did. I'm sure Titian still does. I won't judge his intent. I can't judge my own. I have to live with my choices. I don't regret them. Most of them, anyway. We did the best we could. Now we see the consequences and live with the results."

Twist snorted. "That may be the faintest praise I could ever offer."

"Says the man best known for failed bank robberies in a purple jumpsuit." Her mockery hissed through a feral and feline smile.

"I have a question about that." John-Paul lobbed the sentence into the room. "You seem a lot more lucid than last time we talked."

"Dying'll do that."

"You gave it up?" Clownfish leaned in despite herself. "How did you do that?"

"Nothing that easy. Your boy here beat it out of me, something your other toy could never do, probably not even to his own self."

"But you're powered, still!"

Twist shrugged. "Maybe less, maybe more subtly, maybe it's under control. You tell me: was everything administered to the Youth Corps a composite, or was some of it pure?"

She rolled her eyes toward the ceiling in recall. "Good question. I don't know. I never thought of that."

"I preceded Barry. He replaced me."

"Were you in the second wave of experiments?"

"Titian never told. I can only guess."

Ray's voice cut through the discussion. "The Youth Corps experiments, there were two main waves. Three, if you count the preliminary experiment, but it went so wrong no one ever talked about it. I assume you were in the first group. He never reported that one to the others." He offered Twist his hand. "Ray Manston. Used to be a volunteer myself. Dragged these two to safety here when things went weird outside."

Twist gave him a strange look. "How'd you know about the experiments?"

"Found a set of diaries in some boxes while scrounging around for light and heat. That phrase caught my eye. It's ominous. I didn't read much, but what was there sounded relevant."

John-Paul rubbed his forehead. "*You*'ve heard of eidolons and powers too? Is there anyone in town who doesn't know the secret?"

Ray laughed. "There were always rumors. Every group has its own lore, fraternity, fraternity, secret society, or battalion. Maybe it's a metaphor for something greater than ourselves, the sum of our experience and respect and camaraderie. We're greater together. People do funny and amazing things when they feel they belong somewhere, when they believe other people are counting on them. Maybe that explains why I risked my skin for you two."

"Convenient."

Clownfish smirked. "Steven used to say that there's no logical reason to question why something occurred. It's always cause and effect. Ray was here because he was walking down the street, getting a muffin or visiting a friend or enjoying sunshine and fresh air. There are no coincidences. Would you ask the odds of an event not happening? It's only notable that he was there because he's here for you to ask what would have happened if he weren't there."

"The anthropic principle." Twist stifled a yawn. "The pretty way to tell people not to ask silly questions."

"You never wonder about things like that?" John-Paul turned to Ray. "Do you still have those diaries?"

"Sure, if you think they're interesting. No reason to go out again tonight. Read them if you want." He jerked a thumb toward a dusty box.

Clownfish stood and stretched. "I'll read them. I love reading out loud. I used to be a librarian." She frowned as she walked away. "What? A librarian has to be able to defend herself too, you know." She dug out a slim, faded notebook. "Looks like Titian's handwriting. Anyone interested? Gather round, children."

Twist scoffed. "Yes, mother." He folded his arms, but his eyes kept wandering back in her direction.

"Ray?" She smoothed her clothes and sat again, straight-backed, in her chair. The leg wobbled.

"Go ahead. I have other things to do. There's an old landline phone switch in the corner. I may be able to dial out. John-Paul, are you interested in talking to your family?"

He jerked. "What? Oh...oh yeah, I'd love to. Do you need any help?"

"I'm good. Only room for one person in the closet anyway. I don't care about this story as much as you do. I'll be back in a few minutes. You rest for a bit."

Clownfish flipped past several pages. "Lots of uninteresting notes, but here's a long entry way back from when this all started. Everyone ready?"

○ ○ ○

Once upon a time, two princes supped in their kingdom. One ruled by law. He loved justice. His advisors and ministers and lieutenants upheld the law. The other ruled by reason. He loved ideas. His advisors and judges and counselors debated and argued.

Both believed they had a mandate from the people. Both were loved and respected.

The princes ruled the same city-state. Half followed justice. The other reason. The land was peaceful and the people prospered, yet always the princes wrestled with their philosophies.

"The rule of law is universal," one suggested.

"We must judge each situation on its peculiar facts," the other countered.

One day, they agreed to parlay on neutral ground. The outcome would forever settle their disagreement; their compromise would forever heal the rifts dormant in their people. Why should the disputes of princes worry their subjects?

Their courts made their way to the shore, where the princes removed their fineries and bade goodbye to advisers and courtiers and lieutenants and judges. They took turns rowing a small craft until their kingdom was a blur beyond the horizon. They landed on a small island and watched the golden ball of the sun set over the water.

The night was warm and the sea breeze fresh. Stars jeweled a clear sky. Sleep came upon them, a deep sleep of mercy—and dreams.

A figure appeared to each of them, promising wealth and power and wisdom and fame in exchange for release from its entrapment on the island. "You must not tell the other," it pleaded.

Under the morning sun, they agreed that their shared dream was a temptation. "There is no logic to burdening myself alone," said one prince.

"The people approve of our partnership," agreed the other.

The second night was more beautiful than the first. The breeze brought scents of honey and exotic flowers and unknown fruits. The incessant, insistent surf lulled them to sleep.

Another figure appeared in their dreams. It spoke of darkness and death and destruction. It urged them to prepare for times of trouble—yet in secret.

The morning air was crisp and cool. They agreed that the dream was a warning, and that difficulty and trouble was the natural course of life. "We prepare for tragedy with the knowledge and consensus of our people," said one prince.

"Good times and trouble follow each other in an endless cycle," agreed the other.

A storm chilled and frightened them the third night, despite the gentle shower of warm tropical rains. No birds sang. Clouds covered the sky. The sea pounded against the sand. The princes slept fitfully.

One prince dreamed himself in a lush garden. Fruit burst off the trees into his hands. He tasted and knew them for virtues of mankind: truth, nobility, honor, sacrifice. Words roiled in his mind, their true names, unspoken by human tongue, but they slipped away before they could cross his lips. He wept, knowing that this was not his task.

The other prince dreamed himself in a dark, stinking fortress. Behind him slaves shook off their chains and stood on shaky feet. They blinked, barely daring to imagine their freedom, and he smiled though the raid had cost him dearly. He wept, knowing that they'd traded one master for another. Ahead, daylight pooled like molten gold.

The final morning was cold. The sea lay silent and brooding. The princes did not speak of their dreams. They shook hands over a meager breakfast, promising to maintain their peace, to temper reason with justice and justice with reason.

They agreed to retreat to the island again in ten years.

o o o

"You won't believe me now. I don't. After a modest, average, and ordinary life, I have become one of the most powerful men in history.

"I say this neither to brag nor to bias future biographers; merely to explain what happened and why. One day you may find yourself pushed forward by a movement you never began and cannot control. Then you will understand.

"My story starts on the eve of the last war. The city was a sprawl of neighborhoods and boroughs, not yet unified under the polite fiction we now know of as Reconstruction. Freeman Island was an ugly, abandoned lump of rock in the bay. I left my village to seek fame and fortune and opportunity in our squat metropolis. I was one—faceless, nameless—of millions.

"My youth was fat dreams and shallow beliefs untested. I sold shoes: sturdy soles for men, gaudy heels for women, cheap canvas sneakers for children. It was humble work. It was honest work. I knelt at the feet of the workers. Daily I gazed into their soles."

Clownfish rolled her eyes.

"I lived in a brownstone apartment. It was cheap, but it was clean and warm. A young couple lived across the hallway. I smiled at her from the hallway every morning and evening. She grew round with their first child. We shared few words; we shared no language.

"A tall man lived in the apartment beneath me. He was a self-described inventor and artist, part businessman, part creator—and, I suspect, part shyster. He introduced himself one lazy summer evening as I lounged with a beer on the building's steps. He was younger. He seemed older, perhaps wiser or more worldly. We drank all six bottles as dusk washed the block in tans and blues.

"The next morning I stared at myself in the mirror and realized where I knew him from: a newspaper photo, modeling the hat and malaria net he'd invented. He was a teenager then; I was not much older. It saved lives in our village. It saved lives everywhere.

"No one else questioned him. No one else remembered him. It was a poor neighborhood, but warm and safe. Consider now my guilt over my youthful naïveté. My building was full of inventors, models, shoe salesmen, struggling writers, telephone repairmen, and, yes, a student of conchology. I have forgotten more about molluscs than any layman should know.

"Perhaps I felt that neighborhood was too small for my ambition. Perhaps I went unsatisfied as a seller of shoes. Those years are long gone; I do not remember. I recognize now that something drew us together more than cheap rent for four walls and a ceiling. A deeper purpose stirred within us.

"When the weather cooperated, I walked home. It wasn't far. The side roads were safe and quiet. There's a pleasure in walking. Even if the bus had stopped directly in front of my building, I always felt more productive in motion than sitting and waiting. Perhaps that's a flaw in my character: the need for perpetual action.

"Spring began to reclaim winter's harsh wet air. One fine evening I saw for the first time that justice was dead.

"Many artists lived and loved and worked in our neighborhood, clumped together in unsuccessful defiance in tiny, drafty lofts. Their great, blank-eyed windows looked out over our borough. Few sold anything. Fewer still ever saw a commission.

"The doors of our neighborhood revolved under a steady stream of incoming idealists and bitter, escaping realists. A monster lived there, feeding on dreams. Yet there was a gallery, a bulwark against the darkness. The stars reached down and blessed a tiny white-washed building. Its great glass eyes smiled at us from the ground floor. Light spilled out in pools, drawing us to swirls of color and imagination.

"Somehow that night, this gallery attracted all of the right people. The city's rich and powerful stood behind velvet ropes on deep red carpets rolled out in our neighborhood like rivers of blood. I smile as I write; irony twists my grin. Tuxedoes and gowns swaggered and tittered, flashing rings and necklaces and brooches, sending clouds of perfume and aftershave upward into the dark night. If that's all there were, perhaps nothing would have happened. Perhaps the fault lines were already there. Perhaps the same pressure before or after would have sent similar shocks throughout the city.

"The oldest son of a wealthy family turned of age. They would give him the sun and the moon. Instead, he chose our gallery—in our neighborhood—to shame his parents. See the rich and powerful step through diseased slime. See them wipe their hands after they brush against our walls. See the cruel glint in the eye of the feted son as he wallows in their humiliation. They must live for a few short hours as we unfortunate live our lives.

"They could laugh about their escape later. How distasteful! We must merely survive it.

"We weren't on display, not really. I hear the exhibit was a fine example of the gritty realities of our lives. In those days, we called them photographs. There was no weight of social contempt or desire for revolution. They were photographs. There was no particular message of hope or struggle or poverty. This was only our neighborhood, seen through the eye of an artist.

"I had forgotten the men's shelter in the same building. We may have been poor, but we were proud. Many good people had trouble finding steady work. We were fortunate for what we had.

"That night, they closed the shelter. Not by intent, of course. They blocked the streets for their limousines. They turned away hungry, tired, poor men with their bodyguards, their so-called private security forces. They turned away men with nowhere else to go.

"We are all victims of our circumstances, happy and otherwise. Any of us could have been hungry or tired or homeless. Some were born poor. Others were born rich. Some were healthy. Others were sick. Some had made bad life choices, as the current cliché suggests. Others suffered misfortunes no one could rationally describe as the punishments of justice.

"That night, the rich and the powerful amused themselves, lowering themselves to our shabby neighborhood, and thus denied the basic comforts of a warm bed and a hot meal to hard-working people who never complained that their lives were unfair—not by design, but by mere accident.

"Even then, I grumbled. I grumbled as I saw the PSFs cordon off the streets. I grumbled at my inconvenience as I climbed the stairs to my tiny apartment with dreams of hot water, clean sheets, and a homemade meal.

"I wonder how many grumbled that night as a blizzard took fingers and toes and, yes, lives.

"I promised myself then that the world would be a very different place if I were rich or powerful. Steven tugged at my shirtsleeve as I descended the stairs the next morning. He pulled me inside his apartment, even as I protested.

"'Roman', he said, 'There is a way.'

"I nodded, unblinking, expecting that his genius came from an empty bottle and no sleep.

"'Never underestimate the power of a small group of people with the desire to change the world. Nothing else ever will.' He grinned. I saw no madness in his eyes. What I saw frightened me more. Hope.

"Countless years later I recall those days. I cringe, and it cannot conceal my shame. I was 23. Answers were cheap and simple and easy. One rich family—one fool of a child even younger than I—could stain crimson in my eyes every moneyed family. One corrupt politician could tumble the whole governing structure of as irreversibly irredeemable. Perhaps you judge me less harshly when I reveal my youth—our youths. Perhaps you do not. I cannot decide, myself.

"Steven gathered several of us in the lobby and handed out cameras. We were to document power inequities within our neighborhood. 'They want art,' he said. 'We give instead truth.' I later learned that his childhood friend was an editor at a borough newspaper, perpetually searching for *something* to fill the gaps between classified advertisements.

"I took photographs for two days. I had considered that neighborhood my home. It was my own backyard. I believed myself a worldly man, the salt of the earth, bearing the street's wisdom tempered with common sense. Then I saw the world through a lens much more tiny and much more powerful. Honesty removed my filters. Honesty changed me.

"I saw hunger. I saw poverty. I saw violence and the abuse of every vice and virtue. My stomach clenched with nausea with every guillotine-snap of the shutter. The shadows hid the dirty and the sick and the ugly. The city stacked its refuse harmlessly out of the way. Now I sought it.

"This was the real crime: not that it affected my neighborhood, but that it affected people.

"I adopted a feral orange kitten with half an ear and matted fur patchy from half-healed wounds. I named him Dusty and fed him from an eye-dropper. He grew into a loyal, lean terrorizer of birds. Yet I could not adopt and heal other human beings. Who could?

"Steven's plan worked, to a degree. He and a shy young woman from upstairs took to the cameras as politicians to fund-raisers. Their near-anonymous photos gravitated from the depths of the ads through the middle of the neighborhood sections to the front pages. Soon letters to the editor debated their verisimilitude. A reporter investigated our neighborhood after a series of images of an immigrant family crammed fourteen to a room. She wrote a week's worth of stories to call into question the zoning board, health inspectors, child services, the department of immigration, and the construction board for allowing and perpetuating the situation.

"Please don't misunderstand. Our neighborhood was no seething cauldron of resentment or rage. By and large we were happy and content, even as we missed an ineffable *something*. Everyone misses that ineffable something. I see now great pockets of inequity, comparing what we had to what others had. We were an afterthought to the decision makers—the ruling classes, if you will. By no means were we the only neighborhood so afflicted, nor the *worst* afflicted. Yet as I look back, I recognize the layers of neglect that pressed down on us.

"We all shared the belief that someday our hard work would take effect. Maybe we'd never be rich or famous or powerful, but we'd get ahead. The rules were fair. Luck may play a factor, but there is a system of well-understood rules. Now that we had an advocate, we rejoiced!

"Someone from the city council called the newspaper and had her fired.

"Then I could see only injustice. Construction and gentrification gradually pushed young families, working families, old men and women, children, out of the only homes they'd ever known, the only homes they could afford, further from the rich, the clean, the nice, the safe neighborhoods, further into darkness, further away from the sight of those who controlled zoning and taxes and policing. Times were tough then, but those who sacrifice the least often continue to sacrifice the least. It was obvious.

"The greasy haze and stench of that slow rot hung over the city through the summer. I asked questions. Whispers spread rumors about corruption and bribery and kickbacks. Somehow there was always money to reimburse the rich who'd lost their vacation homes but not enough money to rebuild tenements and family businesses.

"Two men died the night of the party. Two men died! Steven had photographs. Their bodies had frozen in a huddle of heat and companionship on the step of the shelter just inside the velvet ropes. I spent years wondering why Steven hid those photos for so long. Now I know. His gift was timing. He needed people he could trust, people who saw the world from the perspective detached from short term gains in favor of the long view. He needed people not lost in the rubble of their own desolation and humiliation, but ankle-deep and rising above it.

"He also needed a way to capture an idea and to absorb its power.

"At first I thought an aging elderly female relative had left him the contents of her pantry. Rows of stubby glass jars lined the back of his shelves. Their contents were miniature golden half moons."

Clownfish paused. "What is it?" hissed John-Paul.

"I never heard this part before." She skimmed ahead before resuming.

"History will judge me harshly. Our mistakes form a peculiar

247

gravity which pulls at and distorts our surroundings. Yet my apology remains: we did that which we believed to be right.

"Still Steven waited. Our photographs appeared with decreasing frequency, yet the city hummed around us, awaiting something. You may not understand this, not after the war and Reconstruction, but fear greased our nerve. Who did not wonder, in passing, if the uneasy truces between tribes and neighborhoods would devolve into fiefdoms and petty jealousies over ideas as simple as economic reconstruction zones? Our mortal gods shuffled and stirred and pitched battle fierce over zoning laws and tax holidays and industrial stimulus subsidies. Mighty debates and conflicts and clashes trickled down to distrustful glances on the rough borders between city states reluctantly smashed together by centuries of accretion.

"I walked those edges sometimes. The fastidious men of St. Joan bore prideful callouses. Bohemian artists and the young and upcoming merchant class brandished fad after fad in the broad streets of Gemmen Corners. The rough and rugged shipyards and factories of the South Bank spilled forth rowdy brawlers, as ready to drink and fight as to work. That left the rich and the farming families—occasionally indistinguishable—in the Green Mountain Borough. My people, immigrants all, crowded into the seams carved out of what would become the Central City.

"I write seams, but I read fault lines. Rumors and fears and irrational old hatreds built up pressure beneath earth's crust. It pressed and probed for weak spots. Where those neighborhoods intersected—our borders and boundaries of self—it burst forth. The riots began.

"The word sadness is a dessicated shell. We have a poverty of understanding the depth and texture of loss in all of its splendor. Even as I abandoned my pleas to justice and my faith in the rightness of action of the mortals we considered swooping gods, a sharp copper bitterness filled my mouth. My bones shriveled. *That* is the sight and smell and sense of loss I knew the night of the first skirmish of our last great war.

"As apostate as I believed myself then, I still believed. Someone, somewhere, had our best interests in heart. Someone, somewhere, worked for our unity. Someone watched over us.

"I burst into Steven's apartment that evening. His blue eyes stay unfocused in my memory even as his sly smile sneaked onto his face. Nothing ever surprised him. 'I know,' he told me. 'It was inevitable.'

"A thousand people lay wounded and dying, piled in the corners around the coliseum. Private security forces patrolled the area. Mobs and gangs prowled by torchlight, blunt weapons at hand. They swept in from shadowed edges into the light, hurling rocks and bricks and bottles. They advanced in waves. They retreated as individuals, running ragged, bleeding, and thinned.

"We never heard what triggered that bloody night. 'Inevitable', Steven called it. Yet some mornings I awaken early with an unspoken word hanging in the air above my bed. This word can deploy armed guards with the order to protect and to defend. The word fades into indifferent air.

"We sat around Steven's table that night. Shock made our stares long and distant. He passed a bottle of wine. No one drank. He excused himself to rummage in his kitchen, returning with a golden moon jar.

"'Peaches?' I asked. He smiled at the comparison.

"'Protection of the weak,' he answered. He twisted the lid. Golden rays of light danced around the room. We all fell back. Then the eidolon came upon me and I tore open the balcony door and leaped several stories to the ground."

John-Paul shifted. "That's an eidolon?"

"Steven always called them eidolons. The name stuck. Whatever they were, or are, it was like pulling an idea out of your head and holding it in your hand. Put a name to an idea, like justice or mercy or compassion, then make it tangible. How does it smell? What does it weigh? Is it prickly? Is it warm? Angular? Soft? Then look at it. Concentrate. Breathe it in. How does it feel? You do that, you attune yourself to it, and then it sort of, I don't know, surrounds you, like perfume from an atomizer."

"Then you're the embodiment of justice, or shame, or hunger, whatever?"

She chewed her lip. "It's more than that. Maybe less. Remember how you felt at the funeral, like you didn't have a choice not to fight that statue and you didn't have a choice not to win?"

"There was no thought or feeling, just action."

Twist snickered. "So introspective."

Clownfish giggled. "He'll make some woman lucky someday." John-Paul scowled; she offered a shrug of reconciliation. "Sorry. Inappropriate. Maybe it's different for everyone, but for me it was always like I was doing the right thing. Maybe the *necessary* thing."

"How does that work with putting on a cape and prancing around play-fighting actors?" His eyes were intense then, piercing. She remained silent. "Well?"

"It's...complicated. They locked away the boxes for safe keeping a long time ago."

Twist leaned forward, into the conversation. "And I'm here now." The challenge hung like feather-light gold dust in stagnant air.

Clownfish sighed. "Maybe there's more here. Most of what he's written I only heard by reference."

John-Paul drew his feet under him. "Might as well continue. I'm not going anywhere."

"Beats a kick in the head," Twist offered.

"They still had the trains running that night, despite the riot. How hollow this promise sounds now, but if I'd been in charge, I would have blockaded roads and bridges and footpaths. No one goes in. No one goes out. Secure the perimeter. Contain the rioters, one block at a time. They're unruly. They're scared. They're unpredictable.

"They're all in one place.

"You keep them safe, there. You keep them safe. You watch them. You contain that fear and anger where you can watch it. They yell. They cry. They rage. Maybe they throw rocks. Maybe bottles. They don't go home. They don't get shotguns and knives.

They stand there in the cold and the dark, waiting for the sun to rise. Morning sunlight washes it all away. They're tired. They're hungry. They wake up from a dream and suddenly they're normal people again who want nothing more than a shave, a shower, and a sick day.

"That's not what happened.

"Don't let yourself get surrounded. Don't fight just to keep your position. You'll fall back to the most defensible position. You think you're keeping your forces in one place, avoiding division and flanking, but there's no rationality to a riot. You can't plan it. It's anger and the smell of blood and gunsmoke. You don't think clearly. Seconds crawl. Hours flash.

"The coliseum was a few miles away. My shoes left scorch marks on the pavement. I was there in minutes. I woke hoarse the next morning; I must have bellowed the whole way.

"I wove in and out of the terrible tapestry. I disarmed guards. I pulled projectiles from the air. I created a DMZ between rioters and rented law and order.

"Then the conflict had a third side.

"A low helicopter emptied its belly over the crowd. Tear gas. They stumbled in blind panic. Drop saltwater on an anthill. They scattered: any direction to escape choking, gagging air. Any direction was right.

"I paused. Thick, humid midnight held the haze. My breath burned cold in my chest. Weariness pulled my limbs toward the earth. I blinked away the golden tint to see myself standing alone. Rioters stumbled. Rioters crawled. Some lay unconscious. Some lay worse. Guards retreated, guns drawn and trained. I may have broken arms. I don't remember.

"Then a different scream tugged at my attention. 'Alizea! Where are you?!'

"You may ask what kind of a parent brings her daughter to a riot. It's a fair question. Some days when I feel less grace, I ask it myself. Remember that trouble falls on the righteous and the unrighteous.

Remember that justice requires that we protect the helpless even as we punish the guilty. Perhaps more. We so rarely exercise our souls, it's a wonder we ever feel them.

"A driverless train cut wild through the street south of the coliseum. Even now the faces of the passengers scream silently, pressed against the windows. Their mouths form perfect letters O. White rings their pupils. Their fists pound. I could draw this scene to each eyelash.

"The tracks curve and follow the land, rising from the river. A driver might lean on the brakes then, for stability. Driverless, this train hurtled onward.

"Even in the dissipating miasma, no adult would linger near a train track in the middle of the night. A child might.

"I remember small details—the flash of light, the scent of old perfume sweet in the stagnant air, the blood rushing to my face. Sweat beaded and rode my spine. I stood an arm's distance from the rest of the world. It was a short step. It was a simple step. I stepped.

"It came upon me again.

"The train reached the curve. Its wheels skittered in and then out of deep grooves. Sparks lit the air as steel wheels failed to find purchase on pavement. Metal buckled and screeched.

"I knew we'd find few survivors when the train came to rest upside down in the bay.

"My legs pumped and my lungs drew air. Sunlight spread around me as I leaped for the child. I spun in the air to pull her close and protect her with my body. Torn metal slid a gnat's whisker away. I tucked and rolled, aiming my shoulder for the street. I felt the child stiffen under sudden velocity.

"I rolled and bruised, my parcel untouched. Her eyes grew wide as she slipped out of my arms. She began to wail.

"'My baby!' yelled a parent. 'Alizea!'

"I brushed away flecks of dirt and my vision expanded as if I were entering my body again.

"The mother tore her child away, then turned as if to offer thanks. I've forgotten the look she gave, but not its implications. Something red flashed in her eyes. She limped away, leaving me alone, surrounded by the unconscious on all sides—and on and neither side.

"The walk back to my apartment was long and lonely and I minded not at all."

"Midnight Riots," John-Paul asked.

Clownfish nodded. "The details fit. This predated the monorail. It was one of the reasons for the monorail."

"The same riots that preceded Reconstruction?"

She nodded again.

"Impossible. No one lives that long."

Twist grinned. "Everyone's an unreliable narrator in his own diary, kid."

Clownfish cleared her throat. "There's more.

"Steven beamed, as if everything had been his plan. He leaned far out of the window to wave me up to his apartment. 'Hey, Roman! We're breaking out the champagne in your honor.' I waved back, rudely.

"He cornered me in the hallway when I emerged, two days later. A fierce hunger drove me to replenish my empty fridge. 'Told you it'd work!' he grinned. I tried to brush past, but he pinned me to the wall with one finger. 'Hey. We're in.'

"'What did you do?' I spat, more an exclamation than a question. 'What happened?'

"He grinned harder. 'We're protecting the innocent, like you always wanted. Like we always talked about. That's all. A little trick to focus all of that nervous energy of yours into something more productive.'

"'Productive? Dodging bullets, trading punches, getting tear gassed, and almost becoming the hood ornament for a seventy-ton locomotive?'

"Steven shrugged. 'Two days of sleep and the only mark on you is a bruised ego. Think of all the people you saved.'

"'How many died in the train, and how many cops have the building staked out now?'

"His answer shocked me. Maybe I should have listened. Maybe I should have thought more. Maybe he was right about my ego."

John-Paul snorted. "Pompous windbag. He's trying to convince himself more than he's trying to convince us."

Clownfish pursed her lips. "Maybe he was right about my ego.

"Have you ever had an epiphany connect so hard it sounds like a piano string snapping? E flat below middle C. Great spot for a minor third, I know now. He leaned in so close that I could his misshaven stubble. 'No one knows. No one remembers. They don't have to. That's the beauty of it.'

"I knew his plan then. I saw the flaw then. Maybe that was my flaw. Maybe he was right all along, but when that epiphany snapped, I knew.

"I pushed away his finger and spun him around. 'What good is that,' I grinned, 'when we can make waves.'

"His pupils drifted up and left. Thoughts wheeled in his mind.

"'Simple,' I nodded. 'Instead of uniting to fight a common enemy, this time we unite behind a productive cause. Our cause.'

"Maybe he was the purest of us all. Maybe his overriding motivation was the desire to accomplish *something*—anything. I believed so long he was naïve to serve as the mouthpiece in public but to defer to me in private.

"Now I wonder. He'd never succeeded before. Idealism alone had guided his actions. Maybe I overthought it all. Maybe he wanted to be part of something greater. Maybe he had a plan far subtler than I imagined. Maybe I saw it all flash across his eyes in that brief moment. He stuck out his hand. 'Toward a long and glorious partnership!'"

Clownfish flicked her eyes toward John-Paul. "It continues like that for a while, but nothing relevant."

Twist unfolded. "The prior was relevant?"

She sighed. "There's so much he never told us. He and Steven had it all worked out, I always knew, but the eidolons... well like you, I thought we were special."

John-Paul twisted his face. "We *are* special, Clownie. The kind of special that destroys the world, or lets it get destroyed, or makes convenient targets, or whatever. No one cares. Why should they?"

"Special as in this is all intrinsic power. At some point we started believing our own propaganda. Way back, years ago, all I ever signed up for was the chance to do some good, make a difference. Somewhere along the way that changed. The first time was when Titian—though this was before we had names, you understand—the first time was when he said he thought I could fly."

John-Paul looked up. "You can *fly*?"

"Used to, back in the day. It came in handy once or twice, but less often than you'd expect. Like I said, only in times of great need."

He snorted. "Great need, like when I punched him—", he jerked his head at Twist, "– into a coma? 'I remember only small details' of that too, right? Convenient. When did you start defending the city from made-up enemies? Was that right at first, or did you run out of real problems before you felt relevant enough?"

"Aren't you several hundred years too young to be such a cynic?"

Twist spat back. "Haven't you manipulated yourself several hundred years too long not to be?"

Clownfish scrubbed her fingers through her hair and stood. She tossed the book on the chair. He watched her with a half-amused sardonic smile. "We really believed we were doing the right thing."

"Yeah, and you were following orders. Look around. Your fat man started a war. Here's the result of your glorious little revolution. Several million people are on the wrong side of the plastic in the world's biggest hamster habitat, and your merry little band of do-gooders can't do anything. Have you noticed?"

Ray's footsteps interrupted. The old man's eyes lit on the book. "I found a second volume."

Clownfish stood. "More useful than the first?"

"Mostly inventory of somethings or other."

"Eidolons?" John-Paul raised his head. "Storage boxes?"

"Didn't say."

"Did it give locations?"

"I remember a couple. One's down the street."

Twist snorted. "Already *knew* that. There's no bank in the city worth the name without at least one of his boxes hidden away in a vault. That's how you get the right to put a bank here."

"Wait," John-Paul wondered. "How long have you known what's in them?"

"Long time. Years. Things get fuzzy the further back I go. I don't have the luxury you have of being hand-selected guinea pigs. Love that description, by the way. Irony piles on irony. One day, best I can recall, I woke up and I was special. Maybe me and Titian, we had more in common than I ever thought."

"You weren't in the Youth Corps?" Clownfish's eyes narrowed. "Not even a volunteer?"

"Pretty sure it was shut down by the time I made it to the city. I grew up in the mountain country, moved here a while back."

She looked at John-Paul. "You're from the farms back east, aren't you? Ray, did you grow up here?"

"Born and bred."

"Me too. Interesting. Just on the outskirts of the northern kingdom, but well within the city limits now."

"What are you getting at?" Twist sat up straight. "Your boy here, he's accidental like me?"

"We didn't recruit him specifically. We did, but not before he exhibited abilities."

Twist rubbed his jaw. "And how."

"I don't follow either." John-Paul glanced at Ray, who shook his head. "What's the difference?"

"Steven speculated once that there might be a difference between a first exposure to an eidolon in a moment of stress and a prolonged background exposure. If you'd grown up here, would you have manifested abilities so suddenly?"

"Anyone in the bank that day would have done the same thing, if they hadn't grown up here?"

Clownfish shrugged. "It was idle speculation. There were complicating factors, if I recall. The most important may have been if you'd bound to a specific eidolon."

"How would I know that?"

"You're asking the wrong person. Titian may have had some idea, but Steven was the real expert, and . . . ." She lowered her eyes. "That was a long time ago. We lost a lot of good people."

Ray flipped through the book. "Most of this is empty, but the last entry sounds interesting, like a will or an apologia." He held the book open for Clownfish to read.

"That's strange. He was always fastidious. It looks like he wrote it in a hurry." She lifted her head to the group. "Anyone want to hear the rest?"

Ray shook his head. "No need. I came to say that I should be able to make the electricity more stable—there are some backup batteries, old but functional—and then I may be able to get the phone system working. It won't last very long, and we'll have to bounce any calls off of a satellite, but it's a possibility."

John-Paul started. "I'd love to use the phone if you can get it, but I wouldn't know how to help."

"I almost have it anyway."

Twist closed his eyes. "What are the chances you'll let me out of here to do my own thing? Minimal? Go ahead, entertain me. Maybe your fat man'll say something to impress me, but why ruin his perfect record now?"

○ ○ ○

I've failed.

257

I sit on a gilded throne, comfortably ensconced in the luxurious lap of my little empire. The world we labored to build crumbles. Wrack and ruin and rust gnaw at the edges—and the edges eat themselves inward, toward the center. Barbarians lean drunkenly on our gates. I languish in my stupor, heady from mere vapors of my senses of self-importance and self-righteousness. I can no longer recognize the signs of the imminent destruction of our plans and our history and our future.

Someone, somewhere wants me to believe that. Somewhere, someone wants me to admit that.

I close my eyes and open my ears to the sound of my breathing. The world behind my eyelids is comfortable in its blackness. Thoughts leap into my mind faster than I can deflect them. They spring. They wait for my thoughts to sink deep into that tractable, blissful unawareness. They pounce. They distract me. They interrupt my sleep. They permeate my waking. They sow discord in my steps and poison the air. Others notice.

This voice is not my own.

We chose virtue and righteousness. We had unquestionable intentions. We were young and brilliant and motivated. We poured time and energy and youth and lives into a beautiful, shared dream.

Precious few remain: myself and Sandie. A few came later. They came. They went: Barry, Pierre, Claude. Strange to say I miss even Steven's quirks and arguments. Our disagreements came from the passion of small details rather than a grand philosophical divide.

I *am* lonely. I *am* alone. No one else can carry this burden. Even my most loyal partner has her own griefs to bear.

What is the weight of the burden of strength? How does your back bear up under decisions which touch millions of lives? How do you stand, knowing that your most intimate, nauseating, and sleepless decisions remain forever hidden? How do you meet the eyes of countless anonymous lives who see you and look away, unrecognizing and silent? This is your success.

My failures, I fear, are visible and obvious.

Have I sabotaged myself? These attacks have subtlety and precision; they press my slightest weaknesses to their advantage. They leave little trace, little evidence of revenge or lunacy. They strike, then vanish. Yet they have also drunk deeply our most painful shames. My worst fears, escaping my nightmares and draping themselves with flesh, frighten me no less.

Steven would never hear of doubt, but his cold and dispassionate dismissals ever assured me of the importance of our work. His frigid reason may have ever refused to proffer unrefutable conclusions, but his theories never failed to fit the facts. He was no epistemologist; somehow his mind brushed away the questions that haunted this revolutionary as a match dispels cobwebs.

What would he say now? Do we reach the limits of our power? Do we depend too much on the credulity of a willing populace? Are we dreamers in the universe's cruel morality play, doomed examples of hubris and overreach? I am blind to my own flaws. I have little desire to see myself projected large enough for my fellow citizens to rend me back into man-sized pieces.

That cycle repeats, but I believed our intentions granted us immunity.

Perhaps young Mr. Harrison represents our best hope for a stable future. He's unreasonable and untrained and unyielding—and malleable. He believes that which he sees. Few questions or doubts plague him, even as I dance away from his questions. Unlike the remainder of the city, he may possess the strength of character to see our revolution through to the next generation.

Some days my age weighs on me far more than it should. Perhaps I bear the weight of the ages. Perhaps I am the focal point of the city, borne down by my self-imposed geas.

Bliss calls to me again. Sandie accused me of considering this lightly. If only she knew. My place has never been on the front lines, hand-to-hand with our adversaries. I tried. I succeeded by force of will and fortune.

My strengths are thought and strategy. The Youth Corps was a failure. We could not sustain our ranks. A precious few joined us. They've all abandoned us. Why do I remember that minor footnote? Perhaps the seeds of our current destruction fell unheeded from that doomed bloom.

Is belief sufficient? Anyone will pledge our cause. Everyone praises justice. Everyone desires mercy. Everyone seeks love and peace and security... until they see the horrible beauty of the results. They count costs. Compromise taints their vision; they cannot take those final steps.

Not even the unconscious approval and support of several million contemporaries can overcome self-doubt.

I still heed Steven's warning. The purer the aspect, the more dangerous. Justice almost killed me once—and I was young then. My joints ache now on cold mornings. Bliss is seductive. Steven excised all passion from his life to survive his sole encounter. Even as a composite it aged Barry. Have I the strength to dismiss it when I no longer need it? Will it overcome and subsume me, until I remain only a blob of tissue, a host for the most pure expression of human desire and potential the world has ever seen?

Can I choose my own good over the hope of a future?

If our enemy truly is self-doubt, if we've sabotaged ourselves through secrecy and conspiracy and compromise, I know of no other way to restore our souls. We have not yet won. Enemies harangue us within and without. We cannot rely on the will of the people to rally them into action for a fight of which they retain blissful ignorance. We've cut them away from our glorious revolution with the precision of surgeons and scalpels fighting to buy a dying patient another half-year of life.

Perhaps that sounds futile. Perhaps futility whispers softly of the darkness that has fallen on my mind.

The youth is unpredictable. Ages past I might have removed him as an option for that characteristic alone. Yet is that his strength? Perhaps for too long we've looked inward for leadership. Perhaps the Reconciliation begun so long ago must finally spread to the outer territories.

I do not know the game the other powers of the city are playing. I felt Barry's eyes at his funeral. I shared his memory in the explosion. Should that be a sign? Is that his calling card, forcing me to see the world from his point of view? Perhaps he has no accusations. Perhaps he merely tired of our self-inflicted endless struggle against entropy and amnesia. I do not know. Could he voluntarily give up his power? I cannot.

Pierre and Claude I mention only for completeness. They are content to drift on history's breeze as long as they have each other. I admire the nobility, but do they feel no connection to the greater family of mankind? I dismiss them for their shortsightedness.

Sandie has been my rock even as oceans of grief and sorrow attempt to erode her. She may disagree, though never as stridently nor carefully as Steven, but she is above reproach and worthy of my complete trust.

Perhaps there is another player? This nagging sense of self-doubt may be the betrayal of my own mind. How ironic that would be! Brutal honesty requires me to admit that the buffoon Fontaine managed to rattle me. Sending that child to "interview" me... where is the sense in that? Was her connection to Mr. Harrison simply to remind me that Fontaine believes he can control opinion, that he also has eyes and ears in the city?

Her behavior bears consideration. Unless his game is more subtle by far, she was under prepared and still managed to stand up under assaults that have puddled kings and prime ministers in compliance. Perhaps he merely desired to demonstrate that he believes I am not invulnerable.

Even still, I dismiss him as the architect of our attacks. It was imprecise and unsubtle and sowed mere confusion.

How unfortunate that that realization leaves only two unpleasant conclusions. Either self-doubt and my double-mindedness tend the crops of our own destruction, or there is another player present, with access to aspects identical in identity or power to our own.

I cannot say which option I prefer. Years sloughed away the rough edges of our beliefs. We honed the cold, crystalline perfection of our mission. Yet the power of an idea may slay bloodlessly even the most impervious foe—even ourselves.

Perhaps if future generations read this, they will understand why I have no choice but to authorize the release of Bliss. There is a danger in this action, but the danger is greater if we fail to act. The safety of our future depends on swift action. I cannot stand idle to watch our edifices crumble. Now is the final opportunity to cement our revolution in the hearts and minds of our beneficiaries. We fight for them. Let us save them now.

Let us save ourselves now.

○ ○ ○

Clownfish scowled. "That can't be true. I was there. He took Bliss before that point. Something attacked him in his office. Bliss saved his life."

John-Paul shook his head. "I beat this guy to a pulp the other day and he's here in front of us, if less crazy than usual."

"Clean living," offered Twist.

"It's not that." Clownfish sighed. "Whatever Titian found or thought he found or doesn't want us to know about what he found, it found his weakness. It knew exactly where and how to strike."

"What's Bliss?"

"An early experiment to build the perfect man. Mixed aspects are powerful, but they're not nearly as powerful as the pure ones. They're easier to manipulate and control."

Twist smirked. "Two things Titian never refused, offered or not."

"It's not that either." Nostalgia softened her scowl. "The pure ones are very, very hard to get rid of. Once you've taken on that aspect, it sticks with you. That's what we always thought."

Ray spoke. "Sorry to interrupt this little reminiscence over history rewriting and villain mongering, but I have the phone working temporarily. If you want to use it, you need to use it now, kid."

"Oh. Yes. Excuse me." John-Paul followed Ray to the bowels of the building. A series of smaller offices and closets clustered around an L-shaped hallway. a big room took up two thirds of the floor. The older man opened a door into a supply closet. Another doorway stood to the right at an odd angle. It held a rusted metal ladder with flaking paint and the smell of musty water.

"Down here." The ladder dropped ten feet to a simple concrete and cinder block room. Its lowest two rungs had rusted away. The building's nerves converged in a boxy metal ganglion: heavy monitoring equipment bristled with gauges and dials hulked against one wall. Utilitarian rolling chairs had turned hard and brittle with age, their foam cushions losing a battle with rot decades earlier.

"Must have been impressive in its day."

"Glorious," Ray beamed. "Two people could run the entire building from here. The Youth Corps always had the best equipment."

"How long were you part of it?"

"Years... long enough that the youth part of the name no longer applied. Those were good years, but everything ends. Everything changes. Live with it or don't, you don't get to decide if it changes. More's the pity."

John-Paul's laugh echoed between the walls hollow and bitter. "I know this song. Next up, make the most of the time you have. Have you *looked* outside lately? If we get out of this, how can we be anything but grateful?"

"You'd be surprised." He flipped switches on a dusty control panel until a green-on-green display hummed. The air grew sickly from illumination. "Pick a phone number."

John-Paul punched the numbers into an ancient keypad. A speaker squawked and squealed, then vomited several clicks as the older man tapped gauges and dials. "Too many of these are stuck. You might have five minutes. We're bouncing off a satellite, and it'll be out of range. The land lines are all down. We're lucky to get this much." He handed John-Paul an analog headset cracked by age and dusted with disuse. "It's not a lot, but it's something."

"Thanks...."

The line buzzed with ominous bursts of white noise, but resolved through heart-stopping silences to a soft ring. John-Paul let out the breath he hadn't realized he'd held. "Answer," he willed it. "Please answer."

"Hello?" His brother sounded far away. Metallic echoes swam in his ears. Dust and memory squeezed his tear ducts; he remembered how they used to yell back and forth through the terrifying two-story enclosed slide at the school playground.

"Emdy? It's Jayp."

"John-Paul? Where *are* you? Are you okay? What's happened? We've heard lots of crazy rumors. What's going on?"

"I'm okay. It's bad. I won't lie. The city's basically... well, I don't know how to explain it. It's barely even a city anymore. It's chaos and anarchy, completely out of control. No one knows what to do."

"What about you? Don't do anything crazy."

The chuckle escaped his dark mood. "Since when have you known me to do that, brother? Hello?"

"I'm here. It's just... we hadn't heard from you since it all went crazy. What were we supposed to think?"

"I'm okay. I'm seriously okay. We're all going to be okay."

"Did you do this? Was this the crisis you were training for?" The panic wore away, leaving Mark David's voice wary and tired.

"It's been building for a long time. I was in the wrong place at the right time. Emdy, I miss you and Mom. I miss Jupe too, strange as it seems. I'll be home as soon as I can, but they need me here for now, just for a little while."

"I didn't believe you, you know. I'm sor–"

"I wouldn't have either," he interrupted. "Don't worry about it. Right now I'm trying to be the right person in the right place at the right time. I'm okay. Seriously. Better than okay. I know what I need to do. I know why I'm here. I know who I am, and you're a big part of that. I haven't been good about that lately. I owe you the apology, big brother."

Mark David's breaths sounded distant and small. "I miss you."

"I miss you too. I promise I'll be back soon." Ray made a hurry up motion. "Listen, the line here's about to die. I have to go. See you soon. I promise, okay?"

"Bye Jayp. We'll hold you to it."

The line crackled and faded. Clownfish put her hand on John-Paul's shoulder. He jumped. "Oh! I didn't hear you come up. How long have you been here?"

"Long enough. Must be tough."

"What?"

"Lying to your family."

"It wasn't a lie."

"You know who you are and what you have to do?"

"Oh." He chewed his lip. "I *meant* that. Maybe I don't have all the details worked out, but what other option do we have than to undo what we did and make it better?"

"It wasn't your fault."

"I'm in it now, like it or not. We can debate that later. I realized something, talking to Mark-David just now. We don't often get to choose our circumstances. We make the best of them, or we don't. I'm not happy with everything, but I'm willing to save that debate and blame for later, if I get to see my family again."

She nodded.

They rejoined the group in silence. Something hung in the air. Iron bands encircled his chest, and he fought for air. The terrible pressure caught in his throat. He coughed.

"They're okay," he began. "My family, I mean. I should be grateful, I suppose, but what about all of the other families, here in the city? We're a handful of strangers thrown together. How about everyone else? Are there children trapped under rubble? Families split by distance? Who's starving? Who has food and water?

"We're strong. We know that. What good has that done? We used it to play. We showed off. If Titian's right, we brought this tragedy on ourselves, on the city, for misusing... for hoarding that power. No one else should have to make things right for those of us who are left.

"I didn't start the problems, but I'm going to solve them. I can help." He looked around the room. "Ideas?"

Twist snickered. "You know what I want already."

Ray nodded. "We're outnumbered and severely outgunned. You take down one of those things, and they send a thousand more. You tear it into little pieces, it puts them back together. You're treating the symptom. The disease is somewhere... something else."

Clownfish shrugged. "It's suicide, and I have nothing better. Even with Titian and Barry and Pierre and Claude, this'd be crazy. Assume Titian's right. We're all infected." She turned to twist. "Even if you can open one of those boxes, you'll taint it. Won't that make the problem worse?"

A heavy silence descended. "We still have to try, don't we?" John-Paul glanced around the room. Ray and Clownfish refused to meet his eyes. "We could, anyway. Right? There's a chance?"

"I'm an old man." Ray sat down heavily. "I don't know what good I'll be. Lookout, maybe. No way I can open one of those things." He reached toward the container, but Twist blocked his hands.

"Don't break it. We believe you."

Clownfish shook her head. "It's your funeral, John-Paul. I'm tired of burying friends and colleagues, but I learned a long time ago that I can't stop determined people from doing stupid things. Sometimes it's even for the right reasons."

He pulled her in a tight hug. "Hey. It's okay. We're still alive. Maybe there's a better way out of this. We don't have to do anything tonight. Maybe we'll have a better idea in the morning. No rush. Right?"

She pushed him away. "I've heard that too often. Just wait.

Things'll get better. It'll all be fine when this happens or that happens. It wasn't true. Never was. Now is all we have. I'm tired of waiting for now to be perfect. It never was. That now is gone now."

The building shook. Lights flickered and swung in erratic ellipses that sent nauseating shadows askew. Silt rained down from seams in the ceiling. John-Paul dove under a table, gasping as he scraped his elbow.

Something outside crashed again. The lights went out and the floor buckled. John-Paul heard everyone else scramble for cover amidst muffled curses and exclamations. He shook away a spell of dizziness. "Ugh," he began. The plate glass window and plywood covering imploded, showering the room with splinters and shards. An angry wind sucked at the raw opening, but pulled only debris. He heard Ray yelling "Seal the hole!" He stumbled toward the side of the building to help the old man wrestle an extra plank into place. "You hold it here," Ray shouted. "I left my hammer over there."

The wind wrestled him for the board, but he wedged himself against the remnants of the blockade and willed himself to stay put. Grit caked his hair and eyelashes again. He blinked furiously, wishing for his earlier tears.

Twist appeared next to him, leaning on the board. "Quick reflexes. I'm impressed. Your friend Ray is fast on his feet too."

One last time something banged against the wall. Their feet slipped and their muscles ached, but they held. Three times it struck, then Ray drove in four nails with quick, sure strikes. The pitch of the wind rose in frustration, then vanished in an uncertain silence of echoes and tinnitus.

John-Paul turned to see two crumpled bodies. Clownfish knelt over one. The other was a soldier in uniform.

"Don't bother," she said. "Empty, but look at the markings on the helmet."

A familiar pattern of cracks decorated the helmet.

"Is this the one?"

"Yep. Titian punched him so hard he landed three days in the future. Something has a lousy sense of humor."

Twist worked off the face mask. There was no body inside. "Creepy. I'll take my chances outside with those flying things instead of invisible soldiers."

A familiar voice pulled John-Paul back to the present. "Ouch." Pandora sat up. "Landed harder than I expected."

John-Paul sat down. "Oof." He tried to work his mouth, but nothing comprehensible came out. His brain surrendered and his vision went black.

○ ○ ○

"Ahh," Pandora said. "Tense." She rubbed her neck.

Clownfish stood over her. "Sorry. We're not exactly in luxury's lap right now. I assume you saw outside?"

"One moment I was standing peacefully in a beautiful oasis, and the next I fell through your window here. Oh, John-Paul's awake. Hey. How are you feeling?"

He rubbed his eyes. "Now I *know* things have gone weird. Where did you come from?"

"Try when. It's still Tuesday in my mind. I never figured out Tuesdays."

"Let me start at the beginning. Gah, silty." Pandora made a face and set down her mug. "I'd gone to interview Titian, about you actually. It didn't go well. Mr. Fontaine and Vernon sent me personally. I don't know why. I assume they had some goal in mind, but they gave me no guidance. He had nothing to say, no surprise there. I think they wanted me to rattle his cage."

"Can't imagine that," John-Paul said.

Clownfish shook her head. "He was well rattled before. He'd been on edge before, even before the attacks. Paranoia is a way of life."

Twist looked up from Titian's diary with a snort.

Even in the dingy light, Pandora's smile shone. "It wasn't my favorite assignment. They sent me to a hospital after that, chasing another interview. No one was there. The room was empty. Two jobs, two failures."

Ray tensed and turned around. "Which hospital? Do you have a name?"

"Reunification Square. Juney or something like that. Why?"

He flushed, then returned to examining the makeshift blockade. "No reason."

She shrugged. "Tuesday morning, there was a huge crowd around the building, watching the news ticker. Is that when things started to go weird around here? When were you here?"

"We were close," John-Paul said. "We're a few blocks from your building now."

She smiled again. "I had a disturbing chat with Vernon in the lobby. He was nervous about something."

"Vernon?" Ray stepped back.

"Mr. Fontaine's assistant."

"Medium build, indeterminate age, good dresser? Enunciates his words funny?"

"Yes, that's him. Do you know him?"

Ray scowled. "I know the type. He probably runs things for Fontaine."

"I get that impression."

Clownfish jumped in. "You were just getting to the good part."

"Right. Sorry. We heard explosions outside. Vernon went crazy and disappeared. Someone calling himself Roberts started to pull me aside." She glanced at Ray. "Roberts. He tried to explain something, then pulled me through a wall and then we were in a desert and now I'm here. What's the plan?"

John-Paul chewed his lip. "That's ... convenient. Who is this Roberts?"

Ray shrugged away their glances. "No idea. Never heard of him."

"He obviously has some kind of attunement," mused Clownfish. "Portals are difficult."

"Why you?" John-Paul met Pandora's eyes. "I mean, not that I'm complaining. It's great to have you here, aside from the circumstances and the surroundings. I'm not helping, am I? I'll shut up now."

Clownfish rested a hand on his shoulder. "You have a point. Why are you two always in the right places at the right times?"

"Do you mean wrong and wronger?" Twist grinned. "You attract unwilling volunteers."

"That's a good question. I could never get a straight answer out of Titian or Vernon, but Roberts said something curious. He called it purity of heart. He said I was different, or I could be different."

Ray slapped his forehead. "Fontaine? That idiot! You blundered right into it."

Pandora chewed her lip. "What do you mean?"

Ray grabbed the box from under Twist's feet, over the other man's protest. "Open it," he offered. "Give it a shot."

Pandora reached for the box. Colors swirled around her hands and illuminated her face. "Smells like roses," she marveled. She turned it over in her lap, looking for seams or latches. "How does it open?"

"That's enough." Clownfish interrupted. "No need to push any further. Good enough for you, Ray? None of the rest of us could get a reaction, even currently powered."

"I get dizzy looking at it." John-Paul swallowed. "Like it's only halfway real."

The colors melted as Pandora set down the box. "What was that all about?"

Ray smiled. "I think Fontaine's given us the solution to our problem after all." A stray beam of light gleamed golden in his eye.

"I'm not complaining, but why her?" Twist shook his head. "I spent a lot of time getting my hands on one of these, and for what? Your pretty little friend here drops out of the sky and you can't wait to hand her several?"

"You couldn't open it either," said Clownfish. "Are you going to argue with results? Aren't you getting what you want?"

"That kind of thinking, my dear, is what your brought down your proud and fat leader."

"Fill me in here?" Pandora stretched her back. "If this isn't another hallucination, can I get some clarification?"

John-Paul stood and paced. "We found Titian's diary. Long story short, you know how sometimes I'm a little beyond average? Something in that box, in several thousands of those boxes hidden around the city, is responsible. It magnifies our good qualities, like the desire for justice or compassion." He glanced at Clownfish, who nodded. "Titian was starting to wonder if it magnified our not-so-good qualities. Maybe that nightmare outside is our collective self-destructive nature."

"Roberts seemed to agree. If that's true, do you want to let it loose?" Pandora scowled.

John-Paul reached for her hand. "Love is an act of will. Maybe it's the only thing that can heal the world."

"Shared burden," Twist said. "Stop letting it poison our hearts."

Pandora smirked and pulled away. "Never had any of you pegged for new agey wishy washy thinkers."

"I'm bad at sarcasm, but I beat up a giant walking statue. That's a concrete argument."

"If I assume this is all true, where do I come in?"

Clownfish sat in the newly-vacant chair. "Just this. We get you in the proximity of some of these boxes, you open them up, we let sunlight disinfect them, so to speak."

Pandora nodded. "Simple enough."

"Any objections?"

Twist shook his head. "Tell me you can't feel your brain rewiring itself not to object. Something wants us to go along with this plan. The questions are who and what and to what end?"

"I agree." Ray sighed. "Whatever's plucking people out of time and putting them back in clearly has an agenda. We follow that at our own risk and avoid it at our own risk. We need what's in these boxes."

"It may work," Clownfish offered. "It may not... but we're out of options. It powers us up more, we have a chance. It has no effect, we're in trouble. It makes things worse, we're still in trouble. Other thoughts?" Her eyes lit on each of them around the circle. All but Pandora nodded.

"I'm still not clear. What if it doesn't work? What if things go worse?"

John-Paul paced again. "It picks us off one by one. It drives us apart. I've seen the paranoia and fear. I felt it try to tear me inside out. No more secrecy. No more hiding. We undo the damage we know's already done and take whatever we get from that."

Pandora smiled. "You're wiser than I thought at first. I'm in."

"Sometimes wisdom's the best you can expect from sorrow and pain." A wistful smile danced in Clownfish's eyes. "It's unanimous then. We find another box, open it, and go on from there."

Pandora yawned. "How about in the morning? If it's my last day on earth, I want a good rest and a nice steak dinner. I'll settle for the sleep though."

"Agreed."

As they shuffled the furniture to accommodate one more cot, no one noticed Clownfish sneak off carrying an empty notebook.

o o o

Amber-hued ambition ran honey-thick from my lips and fingertips. I must have left a sweet, sticky trail as I calculated and plotted and cajoled my way through our negotiations and experiments. Perhaps when some future historian catalogs the scars on my lifeless body they will realize what it cost me and what I gained.

Many people believe that epiphanies stagger you with their sudden flashes of insight. Reality is never that clean. A tsunami invaded my thoughts to sweep aside rough and hasty edifices. In seconds it rearranged my continents. The painful work of sorting through muddy debris continues.

In those days, Roman and Steven were still willing collaborators. The world laid its secrets bare before us. We had unlimited potential. We had limitless power. We brooked no concept of boundaries. The bright adolescence of our rebellion shone forever ahead.

Now I know the fear and the pain of barely concealed aggression. I remember the chill of their cold war of wills, with piercing glances shot at backs retreating down long hallways. Is this always the price we pay for ambition?

Steven spent his days and most nights in careful stepwise experimentation and refinement, emerging unshaven to blink at unexpected sunlight or darkness and wax about the wonders and glories that were certain to follow. Though we had the fourth floor of the old Monarch Trust bank building to ourselves, we usually met around card tables and folding chairs in a cramped break room. It was cozy. It was dusty. Wrinkled apples and expired sodas waited unchosen in unpowered vending machines as we laughed and joked and planned grand dreams.

Roman's new project was his Youth Corps, devoted in part to a careful recruiting effort for new officers and—perhaps someday—partners. You may remember them from Reconstruction. He operated secretly before then, guarding our public actions almost as carefully as his ambitions.

The rest of us found odd jobs as they appeared, when emergencies did not dictate the precise and quiet application of power. Roman's initial foray into the practice of Justice and his subsequent, if voluntary, imprisonment had left us the rest of us cautious about our efforts and our actions. "What good is power that we can't use," he preached one Sunday afternoon.

Steven's usual faraway look disappeared. "Power for its own sake is useless. *Applied* power interests me. The flick of a switch or the perfect word in a listening ear. A lever. A pulley. It's finesse. It's results. It's efficacy, Roman. The *they* you always talk about, Roman, they have power. See where it leads. We must direct it and focus it toward our precise ends."

Roman drummed his fingers. "What good is finesse without power? I've been powerless. We all have. A starving man will eat anything. A rich man can afford fresh vegetables, well-cultivated meats, natural foods. Power gives a surfeit of choice; it provides options."

Steven leaned back in his chair with fingers twined behind his head. Miranda coughed. I returned to my magazine. The debate always ended here.

Roman slammed his hand on the table. I jumped. Triumph shone from his predator's smile. "You were right." He threw a hand toward Steven as if introducing a headline act. "Finesse, not just in the application of power but the *choice* of power."

Steven's chair legs bumped the ground. He leaned forward, fascinated. "Where are you going with this?"

"This latest research of yours; it's a combination of forces?"

"They seem to combine appropriately. There are affinities and catalysts, but I haven't devised a fundamental chemistry yet. I'm confident...."

"The details...."

"...that I...."

"...don't really...."

"...will, but.... What?"

"...matter. You've identified stable combinations. Stable over a period of at least several hours?"

"Weeks. Years, maybe." Steven rubbed his eyes with the fleshy parts of his palms. "What are you thinking?"

"Can you dispense them in controlled amounts? Justice nearly tore me apart."

Miranda snickered and batted her eyelashes at him. "Tha' why you crash so hard too. Like drugs."

Roman waved her away.

Steven mumbled, lost in thought, then looked up. His piercing gaze again bore into Roman. "If we had the proper containment, something more than a simple valve, perhaps. I assumed that either a component is present or it isn't, with no gradients. I haven't been able to measure discrete quanta, but *if* that were possible... perhaps...." He closed his eyes.

I nodded to Roman. "Temper justice with mercy?"

He grinned back. "I had in mind a holy warrior, equal parts pride, honor, and justice."

"Always justice with us, isn't it?"

"What else is worth fighting for?"

Only now do I recognize that the storm which stirred tidal waves in my psyche started with a single word: a word I voiced. It was a simple, honest, everyday word spoken by countless people uncountable times in immeasurable contexts. The word by itself has nothing to recommend it. It's a mere collection of letters forming syllables when breathed over the tongue, through teeth, and past lips. I can say the same of every other word in all other human languages spoken and forgotten. The word is simple. At any other moment it would have faded into memory with the hearing of subsequent words.

"Glory," I said. "Patriotism. Money. Love."

"Cynic," he chuckled. "You believe in justice as much as the rest of us."

Steven's chair buckled underneath him as he leaped to his feet. "One hour," he hissed, picking himself up. "I know how to do this. Roman, you are, as always, an unwitting genius. Sandie, Miranda, thank you too." He vanished. Two upended chair legs pawed the air. In my memory, they wave with infinite sadness.

The thought had left my conscious mind as soon as I said it, but somewhere else, ambitions stirred. Somewhere, somehow, the perfect plan developed. Perhaps it was destiny. Perhaps the gods or karma punish hubris. Perhaps universal laws of nature require obeisance and balance. Perhaps the purpose of my life is to demonstrate the proper use of irony. I do not know.

Steven's plan worked.

Two hours later we huddled together in the ice-cold basement. The vents he'd had drilled into the vault for airflow were silent; instead he ran great fans year-round. I amused myself by seeing how far my breath would mist before dissipating. Miranda kept herself warm by glowering. "Hungry people come by soon enough. You best hurry, 'less I go do so'thing real, hear?"

Roman crouched, face pressed tight against the glass of an airtight observation box. Something as substantial as the mist of a breath swirled inside on unseen air currents. His eyes danced between particles moving by their own devices.

Later Steven explained Brownian motion and the underlying apparent randomness of unbalanced small forces too small to see. I drank another cup of tea and nodded politely.

In those days, he'd shown little flair for the dramatic. Roman's antics may have influenced him, but I trace his subsequent personality changes to that moment. Perhaps Roman's suggestion had also triggered a subtler suggestion, one by which he could finally win their argument. I don't know. I'd always found it more academic than practical; that seemed to bother Roman the most. Where he bled for the cause, Steven happily puttered away with his research.

Maybe Roman had given him the key to its practical application. He'd never appreciate the irony of that hint also giving Steven the final say in all subsequent decisions.

"It works," he mumbled around a sandwich. He wiped crumbs from his mouth with his sleeve and fumbled in a pocket. "Mercy, justice, compassion. It's a blend. It's not all or nothing. They *want* to combine. Naturally. They seek their own stable configurations on their own. In small amounts, they're stabler together than apart."

He produced an atomizer and sprayed it in Miranda's face.

"Hey!" she bellowed. Her eyes widened and she reached her

right hand toward him. "Hey," she repeated. "You have a ring o' fire around ya'. Rainbows. Clouds. Ver' pretty."

"How do you feel?" His hand darted into his other pocket.

She closed her eyes. A shiver passed through her body. "Stronger, but I'm no' leapin' out any windows, hear me Roman?"

He lashed at her belly with a scalpel. Neither Roman nor I had time to reach out before he was on the ground, face first, arm held between two of her fingers. The scalpel dangled impotently. Her eyes were still closed.

Steven said a single word. Her eyes opened; she gasped and stepped backwards, dropping his arm. He pulled himself to his feet and brushed imaginary specks from his lab coat. "A slight numbness in my right shoulder, but otherwise untouched. I don't even have a mark on my cheek, do I?" His eyes studied my face.

Blood drained from Miranda's face. "What di' you do?"

"Do I?" He nodded toward me.

I shrugged. "Crumb." I brushed my cheek. He wiped his mouth again.

"I was a threat, but a minor threat at best. You reacted with the minimum necessary force to end the threat. I won't even have a bruise tomorrow."

"I don' need this. You're a crazy man." Miranda stormed out.

Roman straightened. "What if she *hadn't* gone easy on you?"

Steven produced another scalpel and stabbed at his own chest. The metal whined as it bent a hair's breadth from his coat. Roman grinned. "You took some too?"

"A much larger dose."

I rolled my eyes. "How do we know it's a real scalpel?"

He drove the dull end several inches into the table. Splinters few. "Okay," I admitted. "Dumb question. You answered my next one too."

Roman turned back toward the observation tank. "She didn't

know. That's interesting. I assume the intensity of the response increases as the threat makes itself more apparent?"

Steven nodded. "So far."

"That's good. That's very good. Justice was difficult to control. I felt like I was too small for my skin, like some grand god were trying to burst out of my chest and lay waste to ... well, evildoers I suppose. What an awkward metaphor."

"I feel faster, more agile, and mostly indestructible. Watch this." Steven took a deep breath, then sighed heavily. To my eyes, the room grew, or he shrank, or came into sharper focus. Words fail my memory. Somehow he was *different*, yet still the same. He slapped his cheek. The hand print reddened. "It's all gone now. You can give it up any time you want. Why you'd want to, I don't know, but you can."

Roman beamed. "Would have been handy after stopping that train...I was this close to dragging it half a mile to the river, just to get it out of the way. That's the problem with being an unstoppable force. You can't stop being an unstoppable force." His hearty backslap sent Steven staggering.

"Now what," I wondered. I hadn't realized I'd spoken until they both stared at me. Their smiles faded. The room's temporary warmth bled away again.

"Can you reproduce it?" Roman jerked his thumb at the box. "Exact measurements and everything?"

Steven frowned. "Mechanically. It's equal parts—"

Roman cut him off. "We'll need its duration, its effectiveness, and possibly how to detect it. Appropriate dosages, side effects—remember how Justice left me with cold sweats for a week of Sundays?"

"Was that why you turned yourself in?" Steven's smile was harsh. This was a sore point between them.

Doom never feels inexorable until you pass the point of no return. This was my second step down that dark path. "And a name." They stopped staring each other down and wheeled to look at me.

"None of the others were usable until we'd named them. Remember? The first thing anyone ever does is to describe how it feels, and only then does it start to work reliably."

Steven brandished the atomizer. "You do it then." I ducked to avoid most of the cloud, but then I caught a whiff of oatmeal cookies, freshly cut grass, and my father's aftershave.

"Parenthood," I blurted. It came upon me then, a desire to protect and the sad knowledge that punishment was difficult to administer fairly. I felt invincible and fragile, caught between twin needs to promise safety and teach responsibility.

I shook my head and willed it to leave.

"Make yourself useful," Roman said as he stomped out. He was only half joking.

The season passed that way. Steven emerged from his lab several times a week, bleary eyed and yawning. He recorded my observations in tight script in an engineer's notebook. He typed his notes every night, saving backups on thick tapes stored in a community bank down the street. The other vault slowly grew racks and racks of storage boxes, each with a black-on-white label explaining a simple word. Peacemaking. Fairplay. Nurturing.

Then came Bliss.

Roman recovered from the loss of face far more quickly than I expected. He was always versatile, but he'd found some hidden reserve of determination. Perhaps the demonstration with Miranda had given him the final piece to unlocking the puzzle that was Steven. The trick was to appeal to intellectual curiosity. His experiments were play. What would happen? What could happen? We were a grand sandbox in which he could test the limits of his mind.

Roman's strength was subtlety. I do believe Steven had ideals. Justice and equality and universal brotherhood—Roman threw these in his face, but noble Roman won the war when he realized that he could manipulate Steven by telling him it was impossible.

Once, Miranda called me the heart of our operation, between Roman's relentless pursuit of deeply-held ideas and Steven's cold, calculating desire to measure the universe with test tubes and centrifuges. "What does that make you," I asked her. "Practicality?" She blushed.

Roman trusted my designations; everyone did. Somehow I could detect nuance where others threw up their hands. Only after I had named them could anyone else distinguish between them.

Field trials began in secret. Roman had convinced Steven to use composite microdoses on Youth Corps leaders during patrols where he expected skirmishes with police or private security forces. His intentions were noble and his words lofty: to protect their safety and minimize damage. No matter how I paint Steven to make my point, he was a man of compassion besides his ravenous curiosity. We all believed in our mission. We failed not because we lacked a shared vision but because we could never agree *how* to achieve that vision.

Roman made special badges to identify his lieutenants. He told us they provided tiny, experimental composite exposures. composite doses. Even though the Youth Corps had gone through whip-crack training (only one in ten made it to any leadership position), the results showed 50% improvements—and more—with fractional applications of mundane eidolons. He pored over mission logs for any sign of impending danger. He hated the thought of casualties, believing himself more than lucky to have escaped Justice unscathed.

Sometimes I wonder if his self-imposed incarceration gave him penitence as a weapon.

Our fourth-floor discussions repeated with a short period; he argued Steven in circles, begging for improvements, for more power, for less detectable influences.

Steven had almost convinced himself it was impossible. Every blend he'd made had strong allusions to its components, but its substantially decreased power. A sub-second exposure to Justice was orders of magnitude stronger than a full exposure to Parenthood, for example. His experiments grew less stable the more components he added or the smaller amounts he blended. Their half lives plummeted.

One week later—suffering no progress and incessant needling—

Steven brought several old jam jars upstairs in one of the battered cardboard boxes he kept for sentiment, I suppose. He slammed them down on the table in front of Roman. "Here," he dared. "Here's what's left. You figure it out."

Miranda and I boggled. This was as close as he'd come to showing a temper.

Roman stood slowly. Chair legs scraped the tile floor. He palmed a jar, examining it from all angles, then hurled the whole box against the wall. Shards flew. Lids ricocheted. He whirled to meet Steven's eyes. For the first time I noticed how much taller Steven would have been if he'd stood straight. Roman started in a whisper. "This is useless." He shouted the last syllable. The echo reverberated with power.

I stood and pinned him to the wall with a thought. He squirmed and blinked, and a flash of lightning knocked me off my feet. Miranda's energy shield surrounded her and Steven.

A fireball tickled the palm of my hand, and I hurled it at Roman. A gust of wind peeled away tiny flames; a pea-sized pebble bounced harmlessly off of his head. I rolled away as a sonic boom split the table beside me. A snowfall of chromatic confetti swirled.

"Stop!" cried Miranda. Her piercing voice drilled into my skull and rattled my brain. I couldn't concentrate. I slumped to the floor. A thud from the other side of the room revealed that Roman had done the same.

Steven snapped. A whirlwind gathered and reassemble the glass shards, pulling one from my bare foot with a spray of blood. A moment later, one jar—larger than the others in the box—hung in the air before him. Golden light sparkled.

I shook off the incipient migraine and rolled onto my back. Roman rubbed his neck and coughed a small cloud of black smoke.

"Amazing," wondered Steven aloud.

"What *was* that?" Miranda poked a thick finger at the jar.

"You tricked us." Roman dragged himself to his feet, pulling himself up the wall. "If you wanted a trial run for something more dangerous, you should have asked. I can get you volunteers."

Steven's eyes shone. "You don't understand. These were inert. They were unstable compounds that fell apart. They've been dormant for days or weeks. Now they're... Sandie, what do you call that?"

I rubbed my eyes. "Aggression. That was new. I've never encountered anything like that."

"No subtexts?"

"Just aggression."

Roman sighed. "Don't tell me. Now you have more to catalog. You've discovered a new prime. Now you mix it in precise doses with everything else you've made and it's weeks before we're back to where we were last month."

"You don't understand. This one's *new*. It didn't exist before. We discovered, maybe *created*, a new prime. Those failures weren't inert. They weren't unstable. They needed to reach a new point of stability before they could combine into something new."

"Keep this one lock' up," Miranda suggested. "'s dangerous." She glanced around the room. Roman met her eyes, then flinched and nodded. Consensus felt awkward but natural, like visiting home after twenty years in a foreign land.

His change was gradual, but obvious on reflection. Naked aggression was never his style. Even then his favorite technique was subtlety. Perhaps he realized that, given the right motivation or instigation, any of us were willing to stand up to him. Perhaps seeing the destruction he also carried in his bosom frightened and sobered him.

I've always known I was willing to protect people I cared about. Perhaps it's the fabled nurturing instinct. Sometimes you hear about mothers capable of fighting off attackers or lifting heavy objects to protect their children. Love grants strange and wonderful powers.

Steven threw himself into his work anew. Miranda mothered him, delivering food outside his lab door, covering him with blankets as he sprawled on his desk asleep, and encouraging him to stare blankly at a sunrise or sunset on occasion.Roman made himself scarce, though once in a while I'd catch his face in a photograph or in the corner of a town hall meeting or hearing on the television. Politics suited him more than direct confrontation.

I researched. I documented. I categorized. Every few days Steven asked me to name a new unique compound, but most deadend, shallow copies of aspects we'd already cataloged. Nothing fazed him. He spoke of the knife-edge of a world-changing breakthrough.

Time has changed my perspective; he was always the optimist. A new understanding was always right around the corner. One more realization, or experiment, or one more hour of research, and he'd unlock the next mystery. Perhaps he put up with us only because we provided the raw material of humanity to feed his ravenous curiosities.

Both Miranda and I tried to get him to open up even as he withdrew. On slow afternoons, I'd lounge in the bright orange half-moon chair in the makeshift lobby area of his lab and ask him to explain, yet again, his theories of aspects and their effects. Miranda was more direct, always prying to their origin and his initial discoveries. Where he'd drone on in answer to my questions, so endlessly patient to the repetition that I suspected his mind was always elsewhere, his head snapped to focus on her as he answered every time "I can't tell you. Not yet." That daily dance satisfied her. I tried to draw him out with rephrasings and clarifications, but his mood never shifted with me.

His greatest moment of discovery was undramatic. One day he was waist deep in piles of papers and chemical implements, asking me to confirm a delivery of containment boxes while muttering about third and fourth derivatives. The next day, I found a note on the door that he'd fled his lab for a quiet moment in his apartment.

I followed his directions. Steven had left a blank label and felt pen on the table. A scrubbed container pulsed with the golden aura we'd come to associate with high-performing aspects. I ran my hands over the thick plastic and glass enclosure, trying to absorb any information about its contents. None came. I sighed, and released the valve.

Wisps of willful color wafted around my head. I closed my eyes. No sense of empowerment came over me, instead a clear focus and presence of mind.

It was intoxicating, but I retained full facility of all of my senses and thoughts and desires. More than that, I had extended facility. I could use my entire self—mind, body, and spirit—to full potential. I could walk through the wall and make it close behind me. I watched dust motes form pseudo-random patterns in the air, marveling at the unseen currents and molecular rhythms behind their dance. If I'd wanted, I could have touched each speck to send it twirling after my own desires: perhaps spelling my name or building a castle in the air.

I wrenched myself back to the present and closed the pipet. The room sighed as color and clarity drained from every sense. The word "perfection" tickled my cerebellum, but I persisted. I wrote the single word that made the most sense: Bliss.

My fingers found their way to the box again, resting on the controls. I tried to resist, but they threw open the nozzle... and nothing happened. Golden light still swirled and whorled, but I felt nothing. I slapped the box. I kicked it. I destroyed it ten times over, but it did not budge. It remained, despite protestations and efforts, unmoved and unscratched.

I closed the nozzle and sobbed.

Hours later—perhaps minutes, but even now time stretches—I raised my head from forearms moistened by tears to see a pile of empty boxes stacked recklessly in a corner. The top box glowed a sickly pale light.

Steven had left no label. There was little indication he'd even noticed this aspect, save the closed nozzle. I thumbed it open full-bore. The scent of perfume filled my nose: a hint of musk, the sweetness of a flower, a spray of citrus. There was no flash of lightning nor sense of power and control underneath my skin, just a pleasant dose of memory. The feeling was the sweetness of dark chocolate—a touch of bitter made palatable by decadent luxury.

Everyone who saw me loved me. Everyone who knew me feared me—not with terror but respect. My words resonated, etched on statues and printed as epigraphs in books of history and philosophy and poetry. I mattered, no some ragtag revolutionary in a broken down neighborhood in a forgotten borough of a city still alloying itself from warring tribes, but as me and myself, intrinsic and powerful in personality and presence. I was everything I had ever wanted to be—everything I'd never admitted even to myself, lying in bed in the dark at the hour of deepest honesty.

I was *glorious*.

The box had contained only a wisp. In the moment it took me to catalog my thoughts, it was empty.

I scribbled the first word that came to mind—Sorrow—on a card, and shoved the empty box in an empty spot on a shelf in our library of identified composites, then crammed Bliss in front. In the furor over the Bliss discovery, Steven never brought up the other box. To my knowledge, he never knew. No one did.

○ ○ ○

Morning struck. Filtered sunbeams meandered through cracks in the planks and plywood covering the shelter windows. The air was heavy with possibility, yet quiet as the moment before creation itself.

Pandora stretched and opened her eyes. Three other bodies still slept, peaceful and quiet. Her mind swum until she placed herself in time and space again. The smell of coffee had awakened her. An ancient percolator burbled in the corner of the room. She padded across the floor, sock-footed, to turn down the heat.

As she turned back, mug in hand, Clownfish appeared. "Ahh!"

"Sorry. Didn't mean to startle you."

"S'okay. Coffee?"

"If you can call it that."

Pandora made a face. "True, but it's hot and caffeinated." She offered an empty mug.

Clownfish accepted. "Your story." She sipped. "Roberts? Vernon? Fontaine? Titian? You've had a strange life lately."

Pandora shrugged. "I can imagine a lot of people out there have it worse. Maybe Titian and Vernon deserve blame for starting a little war, but Fontaine and Roberts seemed like innocent people caught in a mess."

"Most people are. Maybe it won't mean anything, but you deserve an apology from me too. I can't apologize for everyone, but I can apologize for myself." She searched the younger woman's eyes and posture.

"Yeah. Apology accepted." The second pause was longer. "You have it worse, don't you? You always have. You, me, them, even Titian and Vernon. My father used to tell me to get used to life spinning out of control, because that's what life does. Hang on and enjoy the ride. When it lets you get your feet on the ground, push off in the direction you want to go and see where you end up."

"Wise man."

"He also said that wisdom always comes with sadness, but not always the other way around—but you already know that, don't you?"

Clownfish shrugged.

"Maybe they can't see it, looking at you—but I can. I recognize it now. You have a broken heart, and not only because you were in love with the Protector.

"They all broke your heart, didn't they? Every one of them, Steven, Barry, Roman, whomever. There's the ironic part. You were the heart. If anything, you deserved the title. Without you, the whole thing would have fallen apart ages ago."

"I don't know about that."

"I was jealous for a while. I don't even know if I even *like* the guy, but now I realize that change is as hard for you as for anyone.

Maybe worse. You have the power to make things happen, but you can't move the human heart."

Clownfish shrugged again.

"It's okay. I admire you. If this works, it's because you really are the heart. That's all I wanted to say. Someone should have said that a long time ago."

They sipped their coffees in silence, watching dust motes dance in thick, golden sunlight.

Twist groaned as he rolled out of bed. "Any food?"

"Some canned stuff, powdered eggs, old biscuits, if you believe the labels." Clownfish kicked a dusty crate toward him.

He grabbed two containers and tore open a freeze-dried omelet package. "If there's an argument for restoring the city to rightfulness, the lack of a decent breakfast tops the list. Where's Ray?"

The box was gone too.

They woke John-Paul. He rubbed sleep from his eyes and narrowed his eyes at Twist.

"He left during the night," offered Clownfish.

"What does he want?"

"The box," Pandora mused. "Did you see the way he eyed it when I grabbed it?"

Clownfish grimaced. "He won't get far. It's a last gasp."

"There are four of us and one of him. We have the advantage of numbers, unless he was holding out on us." Twist brushed away crumbs. "You coming?"

John-Paul shook his head. "You're all in on this plan?" Their faces gave assent. "Alright," he sighed. "Here goes nothing."

He and Twist pulled back the planks from the door. The streets were empty. The sky was clear. Only the dome lurking overhead suggested any menace.

○ ○ ○

Pandora took John-Paul's hand. Her skin felt cool, cooler even than the morning air. Somewhere outside the dome, the sun rose. An unearthly glow of orange and red light diffused across its transparency. "Looks like the forge of creation," he whispered.

She glanced at him. "Never knew you to be poetic."

"There's a lot you don't know about me."

Clownfish scouted ahead. Her face was grim, but her movements were lithe and graceful and determined. Her posture had relaxed. "She seems... softer, somehow."

Pandora nodded. "Mama bear, protecting her cubs."

"I'm not her cub."

"Not you in specific. Not us. Merely everyone."

Twist walked alone in the middle, humming a tune that slid between melodies and keys and never resolved to a tonic.

"He's chipper too." Pandora smiled. "It really is a lovely day, isn't it?"

"Guy's nuts. Probably always was, but I did hit him pretty hard."

She slapped John-Paul's shoulder. "You should stop doing that. I hear violence isn't the answer."

"I knew that a long time ago. It's a difficult lesson to keep re-learning."

"Grownups overcomplicate things. Look at Titian. Don't be so hard on yourself."

Clownfish paused mid-step, then pressed herself against the side of a building. She peered around the corner, throwing quick gestures to the rest of the company. Two, above, coming this way quickly.

John-Paul pushed in front of Pandora, hissing at Twist to cover the other side. The other man shrugged and sauntered back, hands in his pockets. "Could you be more casual?" John-Paul's whisper evoked silent thunderclaps. "For someone facing the end of the world you're awfully carefree."

"End of the world, beginning of the world. Same thing. Don't you see? We're here. We're alive. We're outside... such as it is.

How could none of you enjoy a beautiful moment without planning and scheming and jostling for control?"

Pandora chuckled. "He has a point, John-Paul."

"Neither of you were infected with Self Loathing." He pushed against the smile raising the corners of his mouth, but he smelled spring's first roses and freshly baked bread and just-cut hay and wanted to sing and spin and splash in the icy water of the creek. Their laughter joined his.

Clownfish scowled and motioned again. Get down.

Two drones rounded the corner. Angry angles and threatening protrusions decorated their midnight cases. Clownfish dove behind a pile of brick and concrete. They swiveled to track her movement even as they dove toward the other three.

"Get down," repeated John-Paul, angling to stay between Pandora and the drones. He felt her cringe behind him, still giggling, and failed to stifle his own laughter. Twist took three dancer-quick steps sideways as a a beam of light blinded John-Paul. He ducked and blinked at blurry after images.

Twist motioned one hand. Metal tore away. The grinding sound wrenched at him, but he brought up his other hand. Their outer shells spiraled out into hot debris, exposing their cores. He drew his hands apart to pull wires and cogs and intricate steel clockwork into long, sticky metal taffy. The devices plummeted, meteors too attracted by gravity to retain their orbits.

The impact rocked the street. John-Paul opened his eyes to see metal piles vibrating at his feet. Twist had an odd look of concentration. He dropped his hands and mopped his forehead with his sleeve. "Disassembly's more work than I thought." He shook his head hard and blew out a sigh. "That should be the last of it."

Clownfish bent over to shake metal shavings from her hair. "Did you have to splatter them my way?"

"Argue with the laws of physics. Irony too. I didn't tell you to sit there."

She rolled her eyes and looked around the corner again. "All clear, but something probably heard us."

Pandora squeezed John-Paul's hand. He looked into her eyes. "You ready?"

She smiled back. "I was born for these times."

Twist kicked at a cooling puddle of steel. "Next bank's not too far."

Ray was waiting for them outside the vault. He held the first box in his skinny hands. His sheepish expression suggested that he'd been there for a while, and that he'd made no progress on the vault or the first eidolon.

"Huh," said John-Paul. "I didn't expect to see you again."

Ray shrugged. "I figured a head start wouldn't hurt anything. Maybe I owed everybody one last shot to put things right on my own." He returned Clownie's stare. "Or maybe I'm stubborn 'til the end."

Twist grinned. "Don't you wish you were powerful like me?"

"I wouldn't want the responsibility." He stepped away from the vault, still clutching the box.

"Let me," said John-Paul. Twist stepped aside with a flourish, and the younger man spun the heavy wheel. The door stayed closed. He growled and spun again. Still nothing happened.

"It's not really *that* volatile," offered Twist. "The last one only caused hallucinations, paranoia, delusions of grandeur, and nausea for a few hours. Death and dismemberment, those are the dangerous ones."

"How could you tell?" John-Paul grunted and strained once more.

Clownfish ran her fingers against the seam. "It's solid here too. No leakage. It can't hurt much."

"I'd rather he stand outside and watch. Nothing's more effective against those flying things than someone who can take them apart with a gesture."

Twist chuckled. "Two at once, that's no trick. You want to lay odds on a full-out attack from several thousand?"

Pandora laid a hand on his arm. "Not everyone appreciates gallows humor, I'm afraid."

"Nuts to this." John-Paul punched a hole in the wall beside the vault. "Concrete and steel cladding. Easy enough. Any objections to pulling off the wall? No? Good." He motioned Clownfish to one side and Twist to the other. "Get the wheel, Pandora?"

They concentrated. Tiny cracks appeared. Concrete flaked. Steel peeled away. A rumble shook the room. The door popped. Air pressure within and without equalized with a hiss. John-Paul waved away dust from fresh ceiling cracks and pulled at the door. "Pandora, will you do the honors?"

"Here." Ray offered the other box. "Might as well do two at once, if you can do any. It's a little thing, but the more we free before the sky falls on us, the better."

Their hands grazed as John-Paul took the box away, and for the first time he really *saw* the older man: more wrinkles here, fewer pounds there, but still the same combination of intensity and weariness in the eyes. The scheming was gone, and the twinkle of vivacity remained only in muted flashes, but he knew this man. "Titian," he whispered.

Ray shook his head. "No longer."

"Is this. . . ?"

"No. This isn't my world any longer. It's still my fight, yes, but I've seen the consequences. I'm sorry to leave this burden to you, but. . . perhaps it's the curse of wisdom to realize what a sorry mess we pass on to the next generation."

John-Paul clapped him on the back. "Mark David would say that alternate presents and alternate futures are completely unknowable. I'm not going to judge you for what happened. You're here now, and we're going to right what's wrong as far as we can."

"Speaking of which," Ray turned to Clownfish. "Once this is

over, we could go looking for Barry and the others. If they want to be found, that is."

Her jaw clenched. "Are you sure they're alive?"

He nodded. "I managed to resign before it was too late. It wouldn't surprise me to hear they did the same. I'm sure I took the worst of it."

She smiled. "It'll be like old times. Way back when."

"I hate to put the screws to touchy-feely-huggy time," Twist called from the doorway. "You were right about the sky hammer coming down on us hard. Several hundred of those things are on their way. I can delay, but whatever you're going to do, the sooner is very much the better."

John-Paul handed Pandora the first box and pulled at the door again. They both stepped through. The second box was easy to locate; its drawer hummed with power.

Pandora knelt on the floor, both boxes in front of her. They pulsed with urgency. Greens and golds played over her face. "I'm not sure exactly how to do this," she called.

Twist's muffled curses wafted in, joined shortly by Clownfish's shouts of triumph. Ray peeked through the door. "It should be an act of will, if you can attune to them."

John-Paul knelt beside her. "You look beautiful."

She smiled. "You flirt too much, but when we get out of here, how about a nice long drive in the country?"

"I think you'll like my family."

"Too soon, but I'll forgive it as sudden boldness at the end of the world." She rested one hand on each box and closed her eyes. A smile crept over her face. Colors swirled. The scent of exotic spices rose with the the sound of the sea on a clear day. The neighborhood awoke from its long slumber, stretching and greeting the promise of a new sunrise.

Then the sights and smells and senses were gone, diffused throughout the air, leaving the brush of a kiss on their lips and two very empty boxes on the floor.

"Did it work?" Pandora's eyes fluttered.

"I don't know." John-Paul took her hand. "Something happened."

"That's two out of several thousand. We have a long way to go." Ray glanced at the doorway where the shouting continued. "It might not get any easier."

"I'm ready." Pandora smoothed a stray hair back into place. She stood. They walked hand-in-hand outside, through an arch of falling debris, under a dome ringed gold by sunrise.

After

"It didn't work."

He held their attention in his hands like a hatchling—fragile, delicate, but full of potential. He let the words rattle through their minds, raising clouds of questions and implications to swirl as thoughts and impressions. Then Pandora kicked him under the table.

"Not entirely. It didn't work as they thought it should. Nothing ever does. You make a grand plan and measure every piece and place every pawn. Then you make your first move and the universe gets another idea. In a flash, all of your plans are useless, and you're back to the first step again.

"Except—this time, you know something more. You've stared an imperfect world in the eye and you didn't back down. Maybe that's the source of all change in the world. Maybe it's you, yourself. Maybe that's the only plan that really matters. Are you the person you want to be, now more than ever?

"If so, you really did win. As for the rest of them...well, time will tell."

He winked at Pandora. She smiled back and nodded at the other side of the room, where Jupiter idly kneaded Mark David's shoulder. His scowl of concentration broke into an eyebrow-waggling grin when he caught his brother's eye.

A child's hand shot up, three rows back. "Yes?" John-Paul pointed.

"Um. I want...I want to know. Um. What happened to the Clown lady? She sounded funny!"

"Funny. That's not the first word I would use to describe her." Pandora rolled her eyes. "She helped during the first few months of reconstruction, but she wanted to see the world. The last I heard from her, she was sailing between tropical islands."

He kept the postcard in the top drawer of his desk. "I've found him!," it read. "If he wants to be found, I should see him in a few days."

"Always chasing something," Pandora grinned when she read it. "I almost wish I'd met him."

The child continued. "And Tishun?"

"He's building houses now. Sometimes we help him. He's good with a hammer."

"Twist was a crazy man."

Everyone laughed. "I won't ever call him crazy again. He was saner than the rest of us in some ways. I like to think he's out there somewhere, watching carefully. That idea keeps me honest."

"I have a question." The librarian unfolded her arms and straightened in her chair. "Why didn't the council work?"

"Hm, that's a good question."

Pandora turned around. "Same reason Titian's organization didn't work: too much power concentrated in the hands of even the most well-meaning people. It was a painful lesson, but when they realized that they were heading down the same road of secrecy and conspiracy...well, we've all seen how that ends, haven't we?" The class nodded.

Mark David interrupted. "The only way to heal a wound like that is to take action yourself. It's forgiveness. It's never easy. You have every right to feel upset and wronged and to want revenge or vengeance or justice, whatever you call it—but only ever leads to the same cycle of hurt and pain. You have to accept that pain, then let it go. It's the hardest thing I've ever done, but it's the only way to make things right."

John-Paul nodded. "If there's one lesson I've learned, it's that. You can't *make* people do the right thing. You can't take away their power to make good choices. It always backfires. You can't ever predict what'll happen, and you can't prepare for the consequences.

"The best you can do is be honest and straightforward and do what you know is right. It's not easy. Sometimes it's the most difficult thing you'll ever do. But I don't know of anything better."

He sighed, enjoying a twinge of sadness. The beauty of the moment broke his heart: two dozen childish faces drinking in his bitter experience. Perhaps someday they'd avoid those mistakes. "That's all. Thank you all for being such good listeners."

He wished he had something more positive to say. He knew that story hour would soon end, and the children would scamper out of the library into sunlight marred with the skeletons of buildings still under reconstruction. There were shadows, to be sure, though from clean, pure sunlight filtered through high, thin clouds stretching across a pale blue spring sky. Maybe they'd believe him. Maybe they'd remember his story. Maybe some of them would pretend that they could climb a building or throw a car or defeat a giant walking statue... but he hoped none of them would ever have to face and ignore death and destruction in favor of rebuilding a world.

They rushed out in a cacophony of footfalls and chatter. The librarian called after them to watch their voices. Pandora lifted him off the ground in a hug. "Oof, I didn't know you could still do that."

"I hear it'll wear off over time... or it won't. Supposedly there's another map of still more boxes."

Mark David clapped him on the back. "That was a good story. You're getting better at telling it."

Jupiter nodded. "Seriously, you're a good storyteller. If we can get you into a costume, you could be on television. They're doing amazing things with computers these days. You could pretend to fly."

"Ha ha, very funny. I just hope they believed me."

"Why worry about them?" Pandora grinned. "It's more important that *you* believe you."

He shrugged. "Some days I even do."

"Meet you back at your place?" Mark David helped Jupiter with her wrap. "We'll bring lunch."

"Sounds great."

John-Paul walked over to the window.

"Even the bay looks more peaceful." Pandora scratched a speck of dirt from the glass with her thumbnail. "What a difference five years makes."

"I don't know if it'll ever be enough," he admitted. "It's so easy to forget."

"Maybe so," she said. "But in the meantime, can't we enjoy what we have?"

Birds wheeled in the air. Cranes lifted beams. Countless people bustled as they stepped through their lives in the toylike criss-cross of streets below. To the north and east, he saw the invisible lines between boroughs and neighborhoods overgrown with trees and traffic and new construction. The city still had scars, just like its people, but new life grew as it always did.

"Maybe so," he admitted. "That sounds very nice."

Pandora pulled him away from the window. "Come on, hero. If you hurry, we can get a cake and some ice cream on the way back."

He smiled, and they walked out into the afternoon.

About the Author

S. Christopher has worked in a recording studio, built houses, taught preschool, driven an ambulance, written software, unpacked dry ice from a truck, written training materials for a box-making factory, and gone on the road as a traveling actor. Compared to that, writing novels is maddeningly sane, even when his cats sleep on his arms while he attempts to type.

His first novel, **Gravitas**, is available from Onyx Neon Press. This is his second. For information on these and upcoming works, see:

http://identi.ca/scthewriter
http://twitter.com/scthewriter

He lives in the lovely Pacific Northwest.